O9-AID-386

The
Apostate's
Tale

The Apostate's Tale

MARGARET FRAZER

BERKLEY PRIME CRIME, NEW YORK

THE BERKLEY PUBLISHING GROUP
Published by the Penguin Group
Penguin Group (USA) Inc.
375 Hudson Street, New York, New York 10014, USA
Penguin Group (Canada), 90 Eglinton Avenue East, Suite 700, Toronto, Ontario M4P 2Y3, Canada
(a division of Pearson Penguin Canada Inc.)
Penguin Books Ltd., 80 Strand, London WC2R 0RL, England
Penguin Group Ireland, 25 St. Stephen's Green, Dublin 2, Ireland (a division of Penguin Books Ltd.)
Penguin Group (Australia), 250 Camberwell Road, Camberwell, Victoria 3124, Australia
(a division of Pearson Australia Group Pty. Ltd.)
Penguin Books India Pvt. Ltd., 11 Community Centre, Panchsheel Park, New Delhi—110 017, India
Penguin Group (NZ), 67 Apollo Drive, Rosedale, North Shore 0632, New Zealand
(a division of Pearson New Zealand Ltd.)
Penguin Books (South Africa) (Pty.) Ltd., 24 Sturdee Avenue, Rosebank, Johannesburg 2196,
South Africa

Penguin Books Ltd., Registered Offices: 80 Strand, London WC2R 0RL, England

This book is an original publication of The Berkley Publishing Group.

First edition: January 2008

Library of Congress Cataloging-in-Publication Data

Frazer, Margaret.
     The apostate's tale / Margaret Frazer.—1st ed.
         p.   cm.
     ISBN 978-0-425-21924-9
     1. Frevisse, Sister (Fictitious character)—Fiction.   2. Great Britain—History—Lancaster and York, 1399–1485—Fiction.   3. Great Britain—History—Henry VI, 1422–1461—Fiction.   4. Women detectives—England—Fiction.   5. Nuns—Fiction.   I. Title.
     PS3556.R3586A87   2008
     813'.54—dc22   2007034566

PRINTED IN THE UNITED STATES OF AMERICA

10   9   8   7   6   5   4   3   2   1

For Cindy,
with love, admiration, and gratitude

. . . for ye han falle in freletee,
And knowen wel ynough the olde daunce,
And han forsaken fully swich meschaunce
For everemo . . .

—GEOFFREY CHAUCER
The Physician's Tale

Chapter 1

As they rode under the gateway's broad arch, the horses' hoofs were suddenly loud on the cobbles and the rain briefly ceased to batter at Cecely's cloaked shoulders and head. Her dearest wish had been never to see this place any more, never to be here ever again, but now no matter that the rain-grayed walls under the dismal, drizzling sky looked even more a grim prison's than she remembered them, she was as thankful to be finally here as she had ever been for anything.

Ahead of her, Dame Perpetua said at the backs of the two men leading them, "We'll ride straight on to the cloister door, not to the guesthall at all," and one of the men answered, "Yes, my lady."

Cecely felt as if she had been "riding on" since forever,

and if the cloister door was the only way out of this cursed rain and to a chance of dry clothing, a fire, and a warm drink, then she was ready to be even there, despite of everything and no matter what.

Tented under her cloak in front of her in the saddle, Neddie stirred, making a small sound of weariness and probably complaint. Cecely said down at him, "Almost there, little love. Almost done. Don't start whimpering now. You're not a puppy," and prodded him a little to be sure he heard her.

The horses plodded out of the gateway's far side and into the rain again and the nunnery's guesthall yard with its close surround of buildings and the church looming over all, its tall front blurred beyond the rain but not blurred enough. Cecely could feel what lay waiting for her beyond that front, and her shudder had nothing to do with the day's rain-chill. But there was no going back now. The men had already drawn rein at the cloister door on the yard's far side and were quickly dismounting, one of them going to knock loudly at the cloister door, the other coming to help Dame Perpetua from her horse, while their fellow, who had been bringing up the rear, dismounted, too, and went past Cecely to help the other nun, the one who had not been here in Cecely's time.

Cecely waited. Of course, being the nuns' servants, the men would see to both of them first, and then probably to the other woman, the older one who anyone could see was not well, but the nuns might have—should have—ordered them to see to Neddie first, he was just a little boy. Then she could have got down, too. Why wasn't someone answering the door?

As if to her thought, the cloister door opened, and now both nuns, awkward in their long skirts and rain-heavy cloaks, were on either side of the older woman, helping her toward the door, while two of the men were gathering the horses' reins to lead them away, and only finally was the third man coming toward her. Impatiently, pulling her cloak away from Neddie, she said, "Here we go, lamb. We'll be inside in just a moment. Let the man lift you down."

Neddie, poor little thing, leaned sideways into the man's hands and let himself be dragged from the saddle. Cecely expected the man to set him down and turn to help her then, but instead he carried Neddie away toward the cloister door, leaving her, stiff with cold and riding though she was—surely just as cold and stiff as the other women had been, if not worse—to get herself to the ground.

Thinking bitterly that everything here was just as stupid as it had ever been, she dragged her rain-soaked skirts, sodden cloak, and weary legs clear of the saddle and eased herself to the ground. One of the men made to take her horse's reins but she snapped, "At least give me my saddle bags. Do that much for me."

As grudging to help her as everyone else was, he untied the bags without a word, lifted them off, and handed them to her. She did not bother to thank him, just stood clutching her bags, and when he had taken her horse and followed the other men and horses away, she went on standing there, suddenly unwilling to go where she had to go next. Behind her, everything her life had been was gone. Ahead of her the black emptiness of the open cloister doorway waited for her. The women and even Neddie were already disappeared into that darkness. Now she had to go, too. There was nowhere else. There was there, through that doorway—or there was here, standing in the rain. Those were her only bitter, bitter choices, and slowly she went forward. Because what else could she do? What else and where else were there for her?

SPRING of this year of God's grace 1452 had been fretful, with days of cold sunshine broken by days of cold rain. When Dame Perpetua and Dame Margrett would return had been as uncertain as the weather, with the first expectation being they would be back by Palm Sunday; but that had passed without them and so every day in Holy Week thus far they had been expected, because surely they would be here before Maundy Thursday, surely before the Easter Triduum, and now, on Wednesday, here they were, and drawn by Dame Amicia's glad cry of, "They've come!" St. Frideswide priory's other nuns were hurrying from wherever they had been at work around the cloister to where Dame Perpetua and Dame Margrett stood in the cloister walk, dripping onto the paving stones at the end of the passage from the outer door.

Dame Perpetua was trying to greet everyone at once, but Dame Margrett was saying past everyone to Dame Claire, "Please. My mother. If she could be put to bed as soon as might be . . ."

Mistress Petham, huddled shivering and shriveled in the curve of her daughter's arm, did indeed look more in need of care than greetings, Dame Frevisse thought, and Dame Claire, the priory's infirmarian, must have thought the same because she went instantly to put an arm around Mistress Petham's waist, taking her from Dame Margrett while saying, "I'll see to her. You finish your greetings and see to getting yourself dry. You can come to her afterward. Dame Frevisse?"

"Everything is ready," Frevisse said, coming to Mistress Petham's other side. "The fire was laid and lighted a while ago, on the chance they'd come today."

Presently St. Frideswide's hosteler, Frevisse's duty was the care of guests, but care for Mistress Petham went beyond plain duty. In these ten years since Dame Margrett had taken her vows in St. Frideswide's, her family had been good to the priory, both with money and gifts of food. St. Frideswide's was neither large nor rich. The widow who had founded it over a hundred years ago had died before fully endowing it, leaving it to lean times. It was presently, for one reason and another, doing well enough that Lent's fasting had been a willing choice rather than the dire necessity of some years not very long past. Still, gifts were always gratefully welcomed and repaid with prayers, those being the only thing the nuns had in abundance, and when word had come a few weeks back that Mistress Petham had been ailing through the winter and wanted her daughter's company on a Lenten pilgrimage to St. Alban's shrine in Hertfordshire, Domina Elisabeth had ruled that Dame Margrett could go, and because no nun should go out of the cloister unaccompanied by another nun, the prioress had added, "And Dame Perpetua will go with her."

Dame Juliana, being presently sacristan and precentor, with the church and the Offices of prayer her duty and worry, had protested, "But the Offices! There'll be only seven of us! With Easter coming!"

"We're eight with Sister Helen," Domina Elisabeth had answered. And added flatly in the way that meant talk about a matter was finished, "Besides that, it's our prayers, not our numbers, that matter."

"But *Easter*!" Dame Amicia had wailed, probably not least because Sister Helen, presently St. Frideswide's only novice, while lovely of voice, was still uncertain at the Offices, and those for Holy Week and Easter and Easter Week were demanding beyond even the ordinary.

But Domina Elisabeth had said back at her, "Mistress Petham has asked she be permitted to spend Easter among us. Dame Perpetua and Dame Margrett will be here when they're most wanted," firmly quelling any more protest.

And here they indeed were, with Mistress Petham openly in need of every care and comfort the priory could give her; and Frevisse and Dame Claire between them helped her along the cloister walk and up the stairs and into the chamber there, where—just as Frevisse had said—everything was ready, even to a nun's undergown hung, warming, over the chair's back near the hearth and the bedcovers turned down to air.

Mistress Petham laughed, began to cough, laughed despite it, and said as she caught her breath, "You meant it when you said everything was ready."

"Of course," Frevisse said, pleased she was pleased but more concerned to have her into the dry, warm gown.

So was Dame Claire, and they made short work of it, helping Mistress Petham take off her headkerchief and wimple, then quickly having her cloak, gown, and undergown off of her and the warmed one onto her. She was a little woman, much Dame Claire's height and maybe close to Dame Claire's age, but Dame Claire wore her years with a determined vigor, while Mistress Petham's years were telling on her, along with whatever was ailing her. She had once been a plump little woman. Now she was tired flesh on bones, and when she sat down on the edge of the bed, it cost Frevisse no effort worth the mention to lift her legs and swing them up and around for her so she could lie back.

Mistress Petham settled against the pillows with a long sigh, closing her eyes and saying while Dame Claire pulled the covers over her, "Even a warm stone at the bedfoot. Bless you, my ladies." She opened her eyes and smiled at them. "Now, is it warmed, spiced wine I get next, or some brew of yours, Dame Claire?"

Mistress Petham had stayed at the nunnery more than once since her youngest daughter became a nun there; she knew something of Dame Claire's medicinal brews. This time, though, Dame Claire said, "Just now I think warmed, spiced wine *is* the brew best for you, to counter the cold humour of the day. My bidding is that you're to drink it down as soon as it's fetched to you."

Mistress Petham closed her eyes again with another satisfied sigh and said, smiling, "Whatever you bid, my lady."

That sent Frevisse and Dame Claire from the chamber with smiles of their own that lasted to the foot of the stairs, but they came out into the cloister walk again to find the other nuns still gathered there, clotted together in an odd, stiff silence, a few of the cloister servants around the edges, and all of them facing a woman standing as if at bay just where the passage from the outer door came into the cloister walk, her hand tight on the shoulder of a small boy clutching a pair of saddlebags to his chest with both arms.

Frevisse's first thought was to wonder why the woman and boy were there instead of sent to the guesthall across the yard. She was just starting to wonder why everyone was standing there staring at each other like dumb-struck statues, when Dame Claire said, sounding half in disbelief, "Sister Cecely?"

And then Frevisse knew her, too.

Sister Cecely.

Gone these past nine years from the nunnery. Gone and never found. Fled, all her vows to Christ forsworn.

And now—God and his saints help them all—she was come back. With a child.

"Has anyone told Domina Elisabeth?" Dame Claire demanded.

The nuns scattered confused looks at each other, but Dame Claire could see as plainly as Frevisse did that they were all there and she ordered, "Dame Juliana, best you go."

With a flurry of black skirts and veil, looking glad of reason to be away, Sister Juliana hurried past Sister Cecely and disappeared up the stairs to the prioress' rooms while Dame Claire said sharply at Dame Perpetua, "Did she come with you? Where did you find her?"

"We came on her yesterday," Dame Perpetua said in a tired rush. "At the monastery where we stopped for the night. I might not have known her but she knew me, came to me after supper." As if crumpling under the weight of remembering that, Dame Perpetua sat down on the low wall between the walk and the cloister garth, still under the roof that kept the walk a dry place in wet weather, although the stone surely made cold sitting. "She said she wanted to come back here. I didn't know what else to do with her. I simply . . ." She made a helpless gesture with one hand. ". . . didn't know."

Frevisse would not have known either, was thankful the trouble of decision had not been hers, and was more than willing to leave it now to Dame Claire who said, "Before anything, you and Dame Margrett need to be out of your wet clothes. Does someone have your bags? Go to your cells to change, then to the kitchen to warm yourselves right through. Shouldn't the rest of you be at your work? You, Sister Cecely, and your . . ." For the first time, Dame Claire faltered, looking at the little boy, who had not moved at all and now only blinked, his face otherwise dead-still as Dame Claire's gaze fell on him. A little more gently she said, "The two of you can wait in the guest parlor until Domina Elisabeth will see you." She turned to Frevisse, starting, "Dame Frevisse . . ."

Sister Cecely broke in, "We need food and to change and be warm, too. Neddie does," she amended as Dame Claire's look came sharply back to her.

Sharp to match her look, Dame Claire said, "Dame Frevisse will see to whatever is needful."

Which was only right, Frevisse supposed, since she was hosteler and the boy at least was in some measure a guest. So as the other nuns and the cloister servants, reminded they had other duties, began to draw away to them, Dame Margrett helped Dame Perpetua to her feet and away toward the stairs to the dorter on the far side of the cloister walk, Dame Perpetua at a slow, stiff shuffle, Dame Margrett keeping a hand under her elbow as if to steady her. Dame Claire looked after them with a worried frown that Frevisse would have matched except she was left looking at Sister Cecely and the boy, both of them looking back at her.

The guest parlor, where nuns could talk with any visitors permitted them, was there, beside the passageway to the outer door and the stairs to the prioress' rooms, and Frevisse said more to the boy than Sister Cecely because even looking at her was difficult, "If you please to go in." Gesturing for him—for them—to go ahead of her. "The wait shouldn't be long." Then she called to Sister Helen, nearest among the departing nuns, "Sister, have someone bring bread and warm milk for the child, please."

Sister Helen bobbed her head, put up a quick hand to the white veil that marked her for a novice among the nuns, her final vows not yet taken, stooped quickly to pick up from the stone paving the pin that had fallen out, and hurried her leaving.

Her hand still held out toward the parlor door, Frevisse said, this time at Sister Cecely, "Go in," no please about it.

Chapter 2

mong everything Cecely had willingly forgotten about St. Frideswide's was Dame
Frevisse. Always one of the older nuns, the
woman had a way of never showing on her face what she was
thinking. Even when the irksome rule against talking in the
cloister had begun to ease while Cecely was a novice, Dame
Frevisse had mostly kept to a forbidding silence that always
made Cecely certain that, whatever the woman was thinking, it was unkindly.

Yet now, having seen her and Neddie into the guest parlor as if Cecely were a stranger who had never been there before, she looked down at Neddie and asked, as if it mattered
to her, "Is he chilled? Should he go to the kitchen to be
dried and warmed?"

Cecely instantly put out an arm, drew Neddie to her, and said, "He was under my cloak. He stayed dry, didn't you, Neddie? And he isn't cold either, are you, Neddie?" Neddie had been goodness itself these last difficult days, doing what he was told to do and making no more trouble than he could help. Now, never mind that Cecely could feel him a little shivering against her—but that was probably more from fear than anything—he obediently shook his head that, no, he was not cold. Cecely had told him over and over these past days that he had to be a brave boy for her. Now, as Dame Frevisse reached out and laid a hand on his shoulder, he proved his bravery by not flinching away from her touch.

For her part, Cecely glared at the woman, defying her to say his cloak was damp and that he was shivering, but before Dame Frevisse could or could not, Dame Claire said from the doorway, "Dame Juliana says Domina Elisabeth will see them. We're to bring them up. Both of us," she added in answer to a swift look from Dame Frevisse.

Cecely remembered where the prioress' parlor was. Seeing no reason to wait to be taken, she pulled Neddie away from Dame Frevisse's hand and started out of the chamber. Dame Claire, as if afraid the touch of Cecely's skirts might taint her, stepped well aside. Pleased at that, Cecely turned toward the prioress' stairs. Dame Juliana was standing on the lowest one, but to be out of the way she scurried back up them, nimble for so old a woman, Cecely thought, following her with firm hold on Neddie's hand. He stumbled a little on the steepness, and she jerked to keep him on his feet. At the stairs' top the door to the prioress' parlor stood open. Dame Juliana was just saying, "She's come, my lady," when Cecely swept past her into the room. Or would have swept if Neddie had not stumbled yet again, this time on the threshold, so that she had to pause to pull him firmly upright again.

That done, she took in the room with a single quick look, judging both it and Domina Elisabeth standing beside the table in the room's middle. Seeing it still all the same both reassured and sickened her. St. Frideswide's prioress lived better than her nuns. They made do with no more than a narrow sleeping cell for each of them in the dorter and a shared, rarely lighted fireplace in the warming room. The prioress had this parlor, its fireplace, and a bedchamber all to herself, and because sometimes she had to receive visitors who were maybe important to the nunnery's good, the parlor was better furnished than anywhere else in the cloister, with two chairs where otherwise everyone had only stools, a woven Spanish carpet over the table, and embroidered cushions on the bench below the wide, glassed window overlooking the guesthall yard.

When Cecely's aunt had been prioress, there had been other comforts in the room, and a bright sense of life happening. Those and that were all gone. Everything still here simply looked older and faded and over-used. Including Domina Elisabeth, Cecely thought savagely. Her ten years as prioress had aged the woman. In the white surround of her wimple, her face was far more lined than Cecely remembered, and she looked tired.

Would that help or hinder? Cecely wondered. Had she softened or hardened with years?

It was too soon to tell, and Cecely did as she had planned, ended her swift forward movement halfway between the doorway and the prioress by pushing Neddie to his knees by a hand on his shoulder and following him down, falling to her own knees, her hands lifted prayerfully as she entreated, "My lady, I beg forgiveness! I've sinned and been sinned against, and I beg shelter and sanctuary for my poor child and for me the penance and punishment that are my due. In Christ's name and in Christ's mercy, I beg it of you!"

Tired though Domina Elisabeth might be, her voice was

crisp enough as she ordered, "We kneel on both knees only to God and Christ."

Cecely immediately struggled with her wet skirts until she was only on one knee, then clasped her hands together again, ready to renew her plea, but Domina Elisabeth demanded, "Who is the child?"

Cecely immediately put her arm around Neddie's shoulders and drew him to her, to make plain how precious he was while saying, "The son of my shame. His father was the man I fled with. It was with his father I've been all of this time. If not in mercy to me, then in pity for him, I pray you . . ."

Behind her, Dame Frevisse said, "He's wet and he's shivering and he should be beside the fire."

"He is and he should be," Domina Elizabeth agreed. "What's his name?" she asked Cecely with no particular kindness.

"Neddie," Cecely returned in kind, then forced herself to say more humbly, "Edward, if it please you, my lady."

Kindly to him at least, Domina Elisabeth said, "Edward, take off your cloak and go stand near the fire while we talk."

Taking her arm from him, Cecely said, "Do as my lady says," as he looked questioningly at her.

Moving as if he were sore or stiff, he stood up and went to the red-glowing coal fire on the hearth. Cecely would not have minded being there with him but Domina Elisabeth was asking sharply, not interested in her comfort, "Where is his father now?"

"He's dead." Cecely did not try to stop her voice's tremble. "He died at sea two months ago. Now his cousins have taken everything and cast us out."

Beside the fire, Neddie was fumbling with his cloak's clasp, unable to loose it one-handed while still holding the saddlebags. Cecely was about to tell him to set them down, when Dame Claire crossed the room to take them from him, laid them on the floor, and was undoing the clasp for him as Domina Elisabeth went on coldly, "So you've come back to us not in repentance for your sins and your broken vow to Christ, but because you have nowhere else to go."

Cecely knew she would have done best to bow her head to that, but she could not, could only answer steadily, "I've known my sin all this time, but while he lived, I wasn't free to return."

"He held you prisoner all these nine years?" Domina Elisabeth asked, more with scorn than honest question.

"There's more than one kind of binding." Cecely jerked her head toward Neddie standing close to the fire with his hands held out to its warmth while Dame Claire carefully spread his cloak over the back of the prioress' chair to begin drying. Bitter that no one offered her like comfort, Cecely went on, "There were other babies besides Neddie. Three others. But they died. All my babies but Neddie have died. For my sins," she added, her voice threatening to break. She struggled to hold it now, wanting to be believed on this next part. "So I want to give Neddie to the Church. He's all I have left. I want him safe. I want him to live. While I suffer the penance that I've earned by my sins."

Only after a long moment and somewhat more gently, Domina Elisabeth said, "You would have done best to go to your bishop with that wish and your repentance."

Cecely shook her head hard against that. "Here is where I betrayed Christ. Here is where I needed to come. Your brother is an abbot. He can speak better than I can pray to the bishop for Neddie's sake. He would even take Neddie into his abbey, wouldn't he? If you prayed it of him?"

Whatever Domina Elisabeth was thinking she kept behind her stiff face, only finally saying, after a long pause, her level voice giving away no more than her face did, "All that is to be thought on. There are other questions for you to answer, but not now. For now, you will begin your penance on your knees in the church before the altar, begging for the forgiveness you so deeply need, while we arrange matters for your keeping and your son's. Dame Frevisse, see her to the church. Set someone to watch her and come back to me. Dame Claire and Dame Juliana, I'd have you stay here."

Chapter 3

he boy made to follow his mother as she moved to leave, but she said quickly, "Stay warm there beside the fire, dear-heart. If Domina Elisabeth allows?"

With a short jerk of her head, Domina Elisabeth allowed, and Frevisse turned away to lead the way down the stairs. Behind her Sister Cecely said tenderly, "All will be well, dear-heart. You'll see," then followed her. At the stairfoot, Malde, one of the cloister servantwomen, was just coming with a cloth-covered tray that had to be the bread-in-warm-milk that Dame Claire had ordered, and she paused, looking uncertain what to do, meeting them there.

"Take it to my lady's parlor. It's for the boy," Frevisse said. Malde slightly curtsied and stood aside for them to pass. Frevisse thought she heard a small sigh of longing from Sister Cecely behind her, passing by the food, but ignored it. Sister Cecely would be going without more than warm milk in the days to come. Day-old bread and cold well-water were the best she would likely have for most of the time, with just enough of other food sometimes to keep her in health. Frevisse could only guess how long a penance a bishop would give to an apostate nun after nine years of sinning in the world, but penitential fasting would be part of it. Still, for a woman to have sworn herself to Christ for life and then to have abandoned him for an earthly passion, for bodily lust . . . What penance could ever be enough?

But then outward penance in itself was never going to be enough, Frevisse thought as she led Sister Cecely around the cloister walk to the church. The true cleansing of a soul had to come from within—from the grieving, broken heart and the last crumbling of the mind's pride into a full and final surrender of its failure. Only then could true healing come and Frevisse suspected that for Sister Cecely the way between here and there would be both hard and long, with much prayer not only by her but by all of them *for* her.

Frevisse silently admitted her hope that Abbot Gilberd would see fit to take Sister Cecely elsewhere, because Frevisse could see nothing but trouble coming from her being here. Abbot Gilberd had seen to his sister becoming prioress of St. Frideswide's and, because of that, had shown the priory favor over the years. Surely at Domina Elisabeth's asking he would take an apostate nun off their hands.

But that could only come later. For now, Sister Cecely was here, and that was very probably far harder for her than for any of them. Or if it was not, it should be, Frevisse thought tartly. How much from the heart had been Sister Cecely's plea to Domina Elisabeth of her shame and her need for penance? To Frevisse, it had seemed planned and practiced, but as they came to the wide wooden door from the cloister walk into the church, Frevisse made herself ashamed of that thought. Sister Cecely *should* have been thinking on her shame and need for penance long before now, and so she could well have had those words burned into her and ready.

With a small prayer for forgiveness at her uncharity toward a penitent, Frevisse opened the door into the chill, shadowed silence of the church. There was nothing like Lent for bringing on much praying over every thought and feeling, and here was the place best to pray. Here, in the church, was the nunnery's heart. All else in the priory existed so that the nuns might come to pray, in the way the Rule required of them each day, the Offices of psalms and prayers that wove through Benedictine life in an ever-changing, ever-returning pattern. For Frevisse those Offices were her life's core and joy. Or usually they were. Sometimes—there was no point to pretending otherwise—the effort to drag her mind through an Office was as much dull work as scrubbing dishes in the nunnery's kitchen could be.

In truth, there had been times when she had preferred the scrubbing of dishes, and in her young days in the nunnery she had worried when those times came on her and taken her worry to her then-prioress, Domina Edith, who had been so old when Frevisse first came to St. Frideswide's that she hardly seemed to grow older through the years that followed. Then with seeming suddenness—but her nuns should have seen it coming long before they did—she had faded away and died, and Frevisse had felt the loss of her ever since.

But long before then there had been the day she had knelt in front of Domina Edith and told of her plight with the Offices, and Domina Edith had laid a hand on the veil of her bent head and said far more kindly than Frevisse had expected, "It comes to all of us, those times when prayer seems a useless thing and our souls a dry place in a comfortless world."

Because it had seemed impossible it could ever be that

way for Domina Edith, Frevisse had echoed doubtfully, "To all of us?"

"To all of us," Domina Edith had assured her, kindly. "The thing to remember in the midst of that desolation is that, true as it is while it is, its opposite—the joy you've had in prayer—is also true. Because you are not in joy does not mean joy does not exist, only that you are not in it. But since joy is a true thing, you can find your way back to it. And you will, and will be the stronger for having gone through the darkness. But remember that you have to go *through* the darkness, not sit down in it and wail about being there."

Despite all the years since then, Frevisse could still hear the gentleness of laughter there had been behind Domina Edith's words. The laughter of someone who had faced that bitter inward battle and won and knew how good the victory is, even while knowing more battles would almost surely come.

Although perhaps, for Domina Edith, they had not. Frevisse was finding her own times of darkness were fewer as the years went by. When they did come, they were as dark as ever, but at least they did not come as often, and she knew now that on the far side of each one of them she would find she was changed to the better, more than she would have been without she had had to find her way through the darkness into light again.

She would have to pray, she supposed, that it would be the same for Sister Cecely.

No, she did not "suppose." She *knew* she would have to pray it would be the same.

Still, while she held the door open for Sister Cecely to come past her into the church, she had a brief hope of seeing something of Sister Cecely's feelings on her face as she returned at last to the place she had so wrongfully abandoned, but Sister Cecely's head was bowed too low and, unsatisfied, Frevisse closed the door, shutting them into the church.

The priory's church was a long, narrow, unpillared space under a bare-raftered roof. A carved wooden rood screen separated the choir—the nuns' part of the church—from the nave where everyone else might worship, and there in the choir was the only place in the nunnery, besides her sleeping cell, that a nun might think of as particularly her own. In the two rows of high-backed seats facing each other longwise up the choir, each nun had her own place all her years in St. Frideswide's. Only death or becoming prioress would take her from it.

Or flight out of the priory altogether.

Sister Cecely's place had been kept empty, partly for shameful remembrance of her apostasy, partly because St. Frideswide's had had only two novices come to it in the years since she had gone and there was no dearth of other seats for them, the priory never having grown as its founding widow had hoped it would. So Sister Cecely would still have her place. Not that she would have need of it immediately, Frevisse supposed. For the time being she would probably not be sitting in the choir but kneeling at the altar, and for more hours than simply those of the Offices.

At least she would not be often alone in her kneeling the next few days. Through these last days before Easter, the nuns set aside as many usual duties as they could, instead making a great cleaning of the nunnery in a glad readying for Christ's resurrection. Everything that could be swept, scrubbed, polished, or laundered, was. At this end of Lent, with hunger everyone's constant companion, the work was especially hard and therefore especially a gift to God, with the reward that as each task was ended, a nun was free to go to church and pray until she had to begin another. That made Holy Week a more-than-usual weaving of the work and prayer that St. Benedict had intended in his Rule, and presently there were two nuns kneeling at the altar, heads bowed, hands prayerfully clasped. Sister Helen was easily known by her novice's white veil, and Frevisse did not need to see the other's face to know she was Dame Thomasine. Even from the back and despite all the nuns, save Sister Helen, were in matching black gowns and veils, there was no mistaking Dame Thomasine's thin-boned body nor the way she knelt, not settled back on her heels but staff-straight up from her knees, as if the longing for God and heaven pulled more strongly on her than on anyone else. Perhaps it did. From her first days in St. Frideswide's—more than twenty years ago now, which Frevisse found startling to think on— she had always been in prayer in the church at almost every chance, not merely at Eastertide.

Frevisse stopped a few yards behind the two of them, looked at Sister Cecely who had finally raised her head, and pointed at the floor. Sister Cecely opened her mouth toward saying something, then must have understood that Frevisse was keeping silence here and so should she, because she closed her mouth and knelt where Frevisse had pointed. Frevisse watched while she settled back on her heels, grasped her hands together, and stiffly bowed her head over them. It was all the outward seeming of prayer, and all Frevisse could presently do was hope it went deeper than seeming.

They had not even let her dry her cloak, Cecely thought bitterly. They could at least have let her dry her cloak and warm herself before putting her here. Was Domina Elisabeth hoping she would die of cold and lung sickness? If *that* was what the woman wanted, she would have to go on wanting it, because Cecely did not intend to oblige her.

But, lord, try though she had through the years to forget this place, everything about it was just and too much the way she remembered it, and with its familiarity her old sick outrage at it all was come back on her. She had not known how terrible it would be to come into the cloister again, to pass through that doorway into that low, dark passage, knowing what was at its end—the church and cloister buildings closed in their tight square around the square cloister walk around the square cloister garth that was the only place there was to see the sky in here, except for narrow glimpses through little slits of windows high in walls in one cold, bare room or another. Yes, there were the garden and the orchard where the nuns could sometimes walk, but only with permission, and no nun ever supposed to go beyond them, so nowhere to go from them but back into the cloister. How did these women endure it year after year, their lives withering away?

How was *she* going to endure it?

Heaven was said to be changeless, but why would anyone want to live their *lives* that way, the way these women did? Oh, certainly she knew how it was supposed to be: better to live in Hell on Earth so you could live for Eternity in Heaven. But the priests insisted that repentance and the last rites washed the soul clean at the moment of death, so what was the point of all this misery while alive?

Certain Dame Frevisse had truly gone, was not spying on her from behind, Cecely unclasped her hands and, moving carefully so the nuns in front of her would not know what she was doing, made a pad of her cloak's long hem under her knees that were already beginning to ache on the unforgiving stone floor. She had to ease them, even at risk of "disturbing" the nun and the novice so they tattled to Domina Elisabeth. She remembered how she and Johane had been good at tattling on other nuns. Until lately it had been years since she had thought of Johane. The two of them had been sent to become nuns here because their aunt had then been prioress, and while their aunt was prioress they had made the best they could of the bad business. Only when Domina Elisabeth took her place had everything become past bearing.

Then Guy had come.

Dame Perpetua had been teaching her the hosteler's duties that summer. Tedious though the lessons had been, they had at least taken her out of the cloister every day, and that was how she met him. Guy Rowcliffe. Tall and well-featured. Carrying himself like a young prince among the general dross of travelers that sometimes claimed Benedictine hospitality for a night or two.

Because his horse had picked up a stone in its hoof and lamed itself a little, he had stayed three nights, and that had made all the difference in what had happened then. Afterward, she knew that he had caught her heart from the first moment she saw him, but at the time all she had wanted was more chance to look at him and so she had found reasons to go to the guesthall without Dame Perpetua. Then seeing him had not been enough. She had needed to talk with him. Just to talk—that was all she had meant to do. Have him look at her, see her—see *her* instead of a blank nothing in nun's clothing.

So she had watched for her chance and it had come on his second morning there, when she had come on him sitting idly in the sunlight on the guesthall steps, watching the doves strut and flutter around the well across the yard. It had been bold of her to speak to him when no one else was there, but she had found he was as willing to talk as she was. More than that, they had talked again later in the day, when she made another reason to be out of the cloister. That had been when they planned for a true time alone together, and when the hour came for recreation, between supper and Compline, she had told the other nuns she would spend the time in the church. She had not said "in prayer" but of course that had been what they thought, making her laugh to herself while she refused Johane's offer to come with her. They were cousins, but she had not been about to trust Johane with her secret. It was only a little secret. She had meant to keep it all to herself for the little while she would have it.

That God was not against her having this little pleasure was assured when even dreary Sister Thomasine had gone to the garden with the others. With the church to themselves, she and Guy had talked in a shadowed corner, worried every moment that someone would come in, would see them, and truly she had meant only to talk. She would give oath even today that that was all she had meant to do. But somehow talk had become not enough. She had wanted to touch Guy and she had. Had laid her hand on his arm. Very lightly. That was all. Then he had touched her. Had just laid his warm fingers against her cheek. That was all. But it was the first time a man had touched her since she had taken her nun-vows, and fire like she had never known had blazed up hot and fierce in her, and she had wanted more than his touch on her cheek and had found the same blaze of desire was in him, too, and when he rode away from St. Frideswide's the next morning, she had gone with him.

Not openly, of course, but quietly, between Tierce and Sext. Had gone by the back path along the garden and into the orchard instead of to the kitchen to cut vegetables for the nuns' midday dinner, and in the orchard she had bundled her skirts to her knees and gone over the earthen bank around the orchard. After that had been the most perilous part, because anyone seeing her would have known she should not be where she was. But Guy had been waiting, and no one saw them. He had put his cloak around her to hide her nun's habit and lifted her up behind his saddle and ridden away with her.

They had ridden a long way that day, avoiding anywhere they might be seen and remembered if there was hunt for her afterward. Only that night, blessed miles away from cloister walls, on the grass in the shelter of a hedge, had they finally, fully made love for the first time, and the joy of giving way to her desire and his had been everything and more than she had ever dreamed of. It was as if all the dross of her nunnery days fell away from her like a dirty gown that she had never meant to put on again.

Yet here she was, and despite she had thought she was braced and ready for the sudden shrinking of the world into this little place where everything was walls, she was finding more and more by every moment that she was not ready after all. Was not ready at all.

Chapter 4

The rule of silence that had held when Frevisse first came to St. Frideswide's had slipped from use over the years. The quiet she had so valued was now only sometimes part of nunnery life, but should have been most especially part of this week, when Lent's solemnity and silence should be deepening toward the darkness of Good Friday and Holy Saturday, the better to be ready for Easter Sunday's joy.

Instead, in these few hours that Sister Cecely had been here, the cloister was a-seethe with talk among the nuns and the servants, too, and if Frevisse had been so simple as to think the news of an apostate nun's return might not spread beyond the cloister walls, she would have lost that thought when she went to the guesthall in the afternoon. Every

Benedictine house was required by the Rule to receive and care for anyone who asked for shelter. Since Frevisse was presently hosteler, the guesthall was her duty, taking her in mornings and late afternoons out of the cloister and across the courtyard, this afternoon to make sure all was well for such guests as were already there and whatever travelers might still come before the day's early, rainy dark set in.

Because the office of hosteler went turnabout among the nuns, in many ways it was old Ela, a guesthall servant longer than Frevisse had been in St. Frideswide's, who knew best how things were there. Over the years she had risen to be head of the guesthall servants until, in her increasing age, she had been allowed to let go her duties and settle into ease, expected by everyone to live out her days in the nunnery's care there in the guesthall. For now, though, the guesthall was hers again while the woman who had taken her place was healing at a daughter's house in the village from a broken leg got in a fall on an icy step in mid-Lent, and because it was not old Ela's wits but her body—bent-backed and shuffling—that was worn out, Frevisse was ready for Ela's sharp question at her, "It's true then, is it? Sister Cecely's come back after all this while and brought a child with her?"

"It's true," Frevisse granted. "How far has the talk gone, do you know?"

"If it's not gone to the village already, it'll be there with such as go home to supper." The village of Prior Byfield being only a quarter mile away, there were nunnery servants who went daily back and forth rather than nighting at the nunnery. They also went visiting relatives in neighboring villages and some went to the weekly market in Banbury. Scandal being scandal no matter how old it was, Frevisse supposed word of Sister Cecely's return would spread until it thinned away among folk who knew neither St. Frideswide's nor anyone here. Or until a better scandal overtook it.

Her back so bent, she had to cock her head sideways to look up at Frevisse, Ela said, "Master Naylor," the nunnery's steward, "has told Peter to ready himself to ride to Abbot Gilberd with whatever message Domina Elisabeth sends. Not today surely? There's no point in risking him and a horse this late in a bad day, I'd say."

"I doubt she'll send before morning," Frevisse said. "Weather and roads are all so bad, it will likely be a three-day ride to Northampton no matter when he leaves."

"He'll be glad to hear it's not today, anyway."

"I'm not saying that's how it will be," Frevisse said quickly. "I'm only guessing."

"You're good at guessing," Ela said. "She's not gone all fretful and foolish at this then? Domina Elisabeth?"

"Of course she hasn't," Frevisse said. Domina Elisabeth was—had always been—a steady woman. Why would Ela think she would not be now?

But Ela nodded as if pleased over something that had been worrying her and said, "That's to the good. Best there be a few calm heads when the henhouse goes into a flutter."

Quellingly, Frevisse said, "Ela."

"I'm only saying." She slipped back to business. "Mistress Turnbull and Mistress Wise came in an hour ago."

They were two widows from near Oxford, who had taken to coming twice a year to St. Frideswide's—at Eastertide in the spring and at All Hallows in the autumn—to make their devotions, with dispensation to make their Lent's-end confessions to Father Henry, the priory's priest and Mistress Wise's nephew. They were kindly ladies who never made trouble for either the nuns or guesthall servants and always brought a ham in the spring and two fat Michaelmas geese in the autumn as guest-gifts to the nunnery, and Frevisse was pleased to hear they were safely here.

"There's Mistress Lawsell come, too," Ela went on. "With her daughter. She sent word ahead, remember."

"The one who hopes her daughter will be a nun," Frevisse said.

"That's the one, aye."

The woman's letter had come last week, along with a gift of pickled salmon that had made a feast of Palm Sunday's meal. It had been perhaps too fine a food for Lent, but Domina Elisabeth had ruled it would have been ungrateful to both God and Mistress Lawsell to dishonor such a gift, the more so since Mistress Lawsell was bringing her daughter to St. Frideswide's for Easter's high holy days in the hope of stirring the girl's devotion, and God knew that the priory could do with another novice. Since Dame Emma's death at Shrovetide, they were a house of only nine now, and that was counting Sister Helen who had not yet taken her vows.

Their need, though, did not mean they would take whoever came, and Frevisse asked, "Have you seen enough of the girl to think anything about her?"

Ela sniffed a little. "All I can tell of her so far is she looks healthy enough, nor she wasn't making moan over the weather and hard riding."

That was something, anyway, Frevisse thought. Larger, better-endowed nunneries might be able to take on the burden of nuns unfit to bear a full share of nunnery duties, but St. Frideswide's was too small, was too constantly near the edge of poverty to be taking on off-casts whose families could find no other use for them.

"Not that there's much would count against her if her family offered enough to make Domina Elisabeth think it worth the while of having her," Ela said glumly, her own thoughts clearly going somewhat the same way as Frevisse's but not so favorably.

Because in a small, disquieting corner of her own mind she too fully understood Ela's doubt, Frevisse asked briskly, as if she had not heard her, "What of little Powlyn? How does he?"

Ela brightened. "Better than when he came, that's certain. His parents have begun to smile sometimes."

They were a young couple who had come five days ago from Banbury, carrying their only child who had been sick most of the winter, they said, with a harsh cough that was not easing though spring was come. Unable to afford a long pilgrimage, even so far as St. Frideswide's great shrine and church in Oxford, they had brought their child and their prayers to here, into Dame Claire's and Dame Johane's care. To the good, it now seemed.

"Dame Claire has told them they must stay through Easter," Ela said, and added with a look at Frevisse as if it were her fault, "That means we've seven people to see to and feed tonight and for at least these four days to come. Let be what others may come that the weather has held up. Or are just slow." Years of seeing to guests had not given Ela a high opinion of mankind.

All mischievous piety, knowing what Ela would answer, Frevisse said, "We'll simply have to pray that God will provide. Remember the loaves and fishes."

"Which is more than we'll have left by Monday if God *doesn't* provide," Ela returned.

It was an old half-jest between them, but only half a jest, since it cut too near a constant truth. The odd thing—or not so odd a thing—was that God always did provide, if not bountifully, at least enough that as yet no guests had ever been turned away unfed or the nuns starved.

Had gone somewhat hungry sometimes, but never starved.

Someone began to ring the bell in the cloister's garth, calling to Vespers, a summoning that enjoined immediate silence as well as immediate obedience. Willing to both, Frevisse nodded her farewell to Ela and left the guesthall. The rain had stopped but the clouds still lowered. Dark would come early this evening, she thought as she crossed the cobbled yard, making her way between puddles. Coming

almost dry-footed to the cloister door, she let herself in, shut
the door firmly between her and the world until tomorrow,
and followed the dark passageway into the lesser shadows of
the cloister walk. Dame Claire was just passing hurriedly
toward the church, a faint, trailing odor of mint telling she
had been at work with her herbs. Frevisse followed her, finding herself last into the church. Curtsying to the altar before
slipping into her own place in the choir stalls, she saw Sister
Cecely had after all been allowed to shift into what had
been—and was now again—her stall. Kneeling there after
all these years, did she feel relief, even gratitude, that the
circle of her life had brought her back here? Frevisse wondered, then let go thought of her as Domina Elisabeth began the Office.

The waning afternoon's gloom was enough that the candles had been lighted along the choir stalls, making a softly
golden glow along the two lines of heads bent over their
breviaries open on the slanted ledges in front of them. The
varied voices—Domina Elisabeth's firmly leading, Dame
Perpetua's light and confident, Dame Juliana's lately beginning to waver with age, Dame Claire's deep and determined, Dame Thomasine's thin but completely given over
to the pleasure of prayer, Dame Amicia's wandering in search
of her note and rarely finding it, Dame Johane's steady as a
watchman's tread, Sister Margrett's richly weaving through
the words.

What her own voice was and how it seemed to others,
Frevisse did not know. For humility's sake, she reminded
herself of that now and again, because in her early years in
St. Frideswide's she had been too often distracted from the
Offices by annoyance at others' ways and voices, had known
it for a fault and struggled to overcome it, sometimes
strangling it down but never being rid of it, until finally in
her third or maybe fourth year of nunhood she had found
herself so angry during Prime that she lost her own place in

the second psalm of the Office and, in her confusion, broke the pattern of the prayer. For that, at the Office's end, while everyone else remained seated, she had had to rise from her place, go and kneel before the altar, and kiss the hem of the altar cloth in sign that she humbly admitted her fault.

Truly humbled, she had asked leave later that morning to speak alone with Domina Edith, and kneeling in front of her in her parlor, had confessed her trouble—had even been able to bring herself to name it a fault without being prompted—and asked for help. Domina Edith had laid a thickly veined old hand on her shoulder and said, kindly, "You are not the only one to whom Dame Emma is a trial."

Frevisse had startled at that. She had named no names, but Dame Emma, with a busy mind that did not run deeply, had a way, when she was not thinking about something else during an Office, of throwing herself at the psalms with a vast eagerness that had no heed for what the words meant, only for saying them as vigorously as she could, and while she was not the only nun with ways that irked Frevisse, she had indeed been Frevisse's undoing this morning. Domina Edith had leaned a little toward her and said, as if imparting a deep secret, "She wears worse than anyone else on me, too."

Frevisse was so relieved not to be alone in her fault that she had burst out, "If only she prayed as if she understood what she was saying!"

With a hint of laughter in her voice, Domina Edith had answered, "We're commanded to sing joyfully in the Lord's name. The psalm says nothing about being a delight to the ears of others while we do it." While Frevisse paused with surprise at that way of seeing it, Domina Edith had sat back in her chair and added, "Now, there is your fault to be mended."

Frevisse had stirred restlessly at that. No matter what her

intent, she had still found it hard to think of her irk at dis-
cordant prayer as a fault.

Probably easily reading that thought, Domina Edith had
said, "There is, of course, the matter of penance for your
anger and for losing your place in the prayers, but I suspect
that learning a quiet-hearted acceptance of others 'flaws'
will serve best as both your penance and your cure together." She had smiled. "I would tell you, as our Lord told
the adulteress, to go and do no more sin, as if that would
settle your trouble, but I know, as surely our Lord knew,
that it isn't as simple as that."

Unable to keep her dismay to herself, Frevisse had exclaimed, "No, it isn't!" She had wanted Domina Edith to
somehow make things better, not lay a task on her that she
had instantly and deeply doubted she could do.

But very quietly Domina Edith had said, "Child, it's not
in having our own way in everything that we come to God.
It's in giving up ourselves that we free our souls to grow."

"I've never understood . . ." Frevisse had started but
found herself already discouraged enough that she had been
unable even to finish the sentence.

Gently, Domina Edith had said, "It's among the hardest
of things to understand. We're too wrapped and led by our
bodies and our thoughts to understand easily the freedom
there is in going free of both our body's and our mind's
demands. Nor is it an effort you will succeed at once and be
done with." She had smiled. "Not unless you become a
saint. Although I gather holiness doesn't always sit easily on
even a saint. No, child, you will not find this quest an easy
one, unless by God's mercy you are particularly blessed."

Frevisse had not been particularly blessed. With more
failures than a few in her long struggle toward quiet-hearted
acceptance, there were times when she did not feel blessed
at all; but in those times what helped the most was the last

thing Domina Edith had said that day. After bidding her to rise and making a small, dismissing movement of one hand, she had said while Frevisse curtsied to her, "Remember, too, when next your impatience rises, that you don't know how well or ill your own voice accords among your sisters. You may be as much a trial to someone of them as Dame Emma is to you."

These years later, Frevisse could laugh at how that thought had startled her young self, but then it had discomforted her enough to let her begin the long work of learning that Domina Edith had set her. And a long learning it was, nor yet completed, she feared. One thing she had come to understand, though, was that holiness need not include outward loveliness at prayer. For an instance, Dame Thomasine was more removed from the world and probably closer to God than anyone Frevisse had ever known; it had not made difference to her thin and reedy voice in the Offices. But with her wider understanding, Frevisse had come to accept—which was a step further than merely knowing—that all the nuns' voices were part of the pattern of prayer that was the heart of the priory's reason to be at all, and it had been with an unexpected ache this Lent that Frevisse found she missed the part that had been Dame Emma's, now that Dame Emma was no longer with them but buried in a quiet grave in the nunnery's orchard.

Domina Edith had been right—she was larger souled for being less wedded to demanding how the world should be for her.

At least she hoped she was larger souled.

But if nothing else, she was able now, most of the time, to give herself up fully to the Offices' prayers and psalms, to the heart-easing, mind-lifting pleasure of letting go the world's weight and going into mindfulness of all there was beyond the passing matters of every day. As she and the others were now saying, "*Domine, non superbit cor meum . . . Immo composui et pacavi animam meam. Sicut parvulus in gremio matris suae; ita in me est anima mea."* Lord, my heart is not prideful . . . Rather I have settled and quieted my soul. As a little child on the lap of his mother, so in me is my soul.

Here was the reason for all else. All the duties and rules and limits of her life were for this—these times of prayer when she could reach beyond life's limits toward God and joy and the soul's freedom.

But Vespers came to its end, trailing into quietness, and for once Domina Elisabeth did not immediately rise but stayed seated, her head bowed in thought or further prayer for a long moment more. Beyond the rood screen, such folk as had come to the Office from the guesthall and among the servants rustled and shuffled into movement, away to their suppers and, for the servants, what evening duties they might have. The nuns, perforce, waited for their prioress.

Such a wait was unusual. Domina Elisabeth brought to the Offices the sense that they were owed to God much like a business debt, a repeated daily payment for his blessings. Seeing it that way, she always saw to it that her nuns made their payments on time and well, and when the payment had been made, she always promptly moved herself and them on to their next duties. That was why there was now a moment of poised waiting and then, when she did not stir, a slight head-turning among her nuns, enough to look past the edge of their veils, first toward Domina Elisabeth, then at each other.

Frevisse, finding herself doing it, stopped and set her gaze firmly on her hands folded together on her closed breviary. Of all weeks, this one before Easter, with the wonder of Christ's sacrifice of his earthly life for the sake of mankind's eternal souls and then his resurrection in promise of mankind's resurrection into God's forgiveness and love, was the one most likely to draw extra prayer from even the least prayerful, and Domina Elisabeth was far from being that. Still, whatever prayer—or thought—holding Domina Elisabeth now was brief. Only Dame Amicia had actually begun to shift restlessly in her place before Domina Elisabeth lifted her head, put out the candle beside her, came briskly to her feet, and stepped from her place to lead them from the choir and to their supper.

Chapter 5

hile the nuns filed out, Cecely stayed on her knees in the choir stall but dropped her hands from the slanted ledge and breviary in front of her to hide how tightly they were clenched together. Of all the weeks to come back here, this one had to be the worst. Not that she had had much choice in the matter. This was how things had played out and here she was, but she had forgotten how long the Offices were in Holy Week. Long enough on ordinary days, they were hideously longer now. Add that to the hours Domina Elisabeth looked likely to keep her kneeling penitent in front of the altar and she was likely to die of the tediousness, if not of her knees' pain and her back's ache, before this was over.

Now the church was empty, dark except for the small

glow of the lamp above the altar and what slight gray light came through the small, high windows. Everyone else was gone. That meant she was freed to go, too. Domina Elisabeth's order had been plain: when the nuns were gone to supper, then she could go, too. Her stomach growled at her as she climbed to her feet. She stepped from the stall, made a low curtsy to the altar, and left the choir, going out into the cloister walk where, as she expected, a nun was waiting for her. Dame Juliana, she thought. Older than Cecely remembered her and grown more grim with her years in this place, the way they all seemed to have done. She did not even nod to Cecely, just turned and walked away, expecting Cecely to follow her, as if Cecely could not find her own way to the refectory. St. Frideswide's was too small a place for anyone to forget where anywhere in it was, no matter how long they had been gone, but after all Dame Juliana was her guard, not her guide, and Cecely followed her silently through the deepening gray twilight, around the cloister walk to where the refectory door stood open to a yellow glow of candlelight.

Dame Juliana paused to wash her hands in the waiting bowl of water on the stand beside the door and dry them on the towel there, then stood aside while Cecely did the same. The water must have been hot when it was first set here. It was barely tepid now, chilling quickly in the evening air. It chilled her already cool hands, too, so that she barely dried them in her haste to tuck them under her arms and against her body to warm them. Dame Juliana's look at her reminded her that was unacceptable, and Cecely grimly folded them together humbly in front of her and bowed her head. Satisfied, Dame Juliana led her finally into the refectory.

Did nothing ever change in this place? This room, too, was the same as it had been nine years ago. Open-raftered to the roof and with plain-plastered walls, it was hardly different from a well-made barn except for the nuns' long table stretched down the room's middle with benches along both sides and a stool at one end for the prioress to over-watch what were laughably called meals. Single candlestubs burned at either end of the table, casting a deceptive sheen over the tabletop's scrubbed boards, while in a far corner a taller candle was set at an upper edge of a long-legged, slant-topped desk where a nun stood alone, waiting to read aloud while the other nuns ate. The rest of the nuns were standing with bowed heads at their places along the table. No one looked around at Cecely as she followed Dame Juliana into the room, though Cecely thought there was here and there the glint of an eye shifted toward her, curious.

They *should* be curious, she thought. They had never dared anything but being here. *She* had dared to go out into the world, had loved, been loved, and even if she was back here now, she had all that to hold to and remember, while all they had was a bare-roomed, comfortless nunnery, each other's dull company, and their prioress' heavy hand over them.

Dame Juliana led her to a dark corner at the far end of the room from anyone and with a small gesture silently bade her stand and stay. Discomfited that she was not going to be allowed to sit and knowing she would not be allowed to lean against the wall either, Cecely tried to keep her irk hidden as Dame Juliana joined the other nuns along the table. Not that anyone was looking at her now. They were all thinking too hard toward their supper as Domina Elisabeth gave thanks for what they would receive.

It was excessive thanks for not much, Cecely thought. This being Lent and food scant, every meal was desperately looked forward to. Not that there were that many meals, or what could be called meals. Something to silence the stomach in the morning, one true meal at midday, then a slight something for supper. Her own stomach was growling again. She could only hope she wasn't going to be made to watch them all eat before she was given food, too.

Domina Elisabeth finished thanks, the nuns sat down, and two servantwomen came in with laden trays, to set a cup of something and a portion of dark, unbuttered bread before each nun, with Domina Elisabeth's no larger than anyone else's, Cecely noted. What was the point of being prioress if you couldn't have more or better than your nuns? But very likely she would have something else in her room, with no one to know it, Cecely thought resentfully.

Her stomach roiled more, and she had the frightened thought that maybe she was going to have no supper at all but be made to fast until tomorrow; but when everyone else had been served, had begun to eat and the reader to read, one of the servantwomen came back silent-footed from the kitchen, bringing to Cecely a thick-cut piece of heavy, dark bread and a wooden cup. Cecely took them eagerly, but the servant kept hold, so that Cecely looked at her and found her looking back with both worry and question. More than that, Cecely knew her and said on a breath that was barely a whisper, "Alson!" She held back from a smile only because someone might be watching but knew what Alson was silently asking and shook her head in a small "no." Alson, with her back to the room, dared a small smile at her before ducking her head and hurrying out, leaving Cecely not quite so barren with loneliness as she had been. She after all wasn't without a friend in this place. That was more than she had dared to hope for.

What Alson had given her to eat, however, was miserable. The bread was dry and stiff. It had to be yesterday's, and she would swear it was more chaff than flour, while the cup held ale so thin it might as well have been water. Penance was one thing. Starvation was another. How long did Domina Elisabeth mean to keep her this little fed? She hoped Neddie was better seen to than this, poor little mite. The church had been so shadowy that, with the rood screen in the way, she hadn't been able to see if he had been

brought to suffer through Vespers, and she could not guess
when she'd be allowed to see him again. Domina Elisabeth
might decide that to be separated from him should be part
of her punishment.

But no. No matter what the nuns did to her, Cecely
didn't think they would be that cruel to a small child. Let
him cry for his mother, or even ask for her piteously enough,
and they would be merciful. She had told him that and was
certain she could depend on him to do that much.

If nothing else, Alson would surely help her. Cecely said
a quick and general little prayer of thanks for her good fortune in finding Alson still here.

That did not help her to choke down the miserable
bread, though, nor did she dare take time to soak it much in
the ale. When the nuns finished eating, she would be expected to be done, too, she supposed, so she chewed at it
and, to take her mind from it, listened to the nun reading
aloud at the room's other end, only after a while realizing
that what she was hearing was the same sermon for Tenebrae, the dark days before Easter, that had been read at them
all this same way in her last Lent here. Dear saints above,
did nothing *ever* change in this place?

She was washing down the last of the bread with the last
of the poor ale when Domina Elisabeth rose from her place
to show the meal was done. All of her nuns rose like shadows with her, and grace was said again—little though there
was to be thankful for, Cecely thought. Maybe they were
giving thanks there hadn't been less.

Now came the one hour of recreation they were allowed
each day. Given the cold and wet, they would probably go
straight to the warming room, Cecely supposed, and supposed, too, that she should simply stay where she was until
told to do otherwise. The nuns left, save for Dame Juliana.
Cecely looked at her, and she pointed at the table for Cecely
to put the cup there. When Cecely had, Dame Juliana signed

for her to follow her, and they went from the refectory and around a corner of the cloister walk to, as Cecily had expected, the warming room.

With its fireplace it was one of the more comfortable places in the cloister, but not very. A fire was usually allowed there only from October's end until April's, and it was as plain a room as the refectory but far smaller, the nuns' retreat in poor weather and where they sat through the daily chapter meetings where nunnery business was dealt with, confessions made of common faults, and penances given for them. Cecely had expected she would be dealt with in the morrow's meeting, but found that the nuns, rather than at ease and in talk and at the various light pastimes allowed in this while of recreation, were seated on their joint stools in a partial circle facing the prioress' chair, and as she followed Dame Juliana into the room every one of them looked toward the doorway. Toward her.

Her heart sinking a little, Cecely stopped on the threshold, looking back at them. Not in the morning, then. Now. Tonight. While she was still tired with travel, still chilled from the rain and the church. Still hungry.

She straightened her shoulders and lifted her head. So be it, she thought defiantly.

Then she remembered she was supposed to be humbly contrite in her disgrace, and bowed her head and let her shoulders slump. Not soon enough, it seemed, as Domina Elisabeth, standing at her chair, said sternly, "Come forward to me and kneel here, facing your sisters."

Head down, Cecely went. Behind her, Dame Juliana shut the door and went quiet-footed to sit in the place left for her among the other nuns. Cecely had had enough of a cold floor under her knees when she was in the church, but she knelt where Domina Elisabeth had pointed beside her chair, keeping her head down but feeling all their stares. Let them stare. They had little else in their lives, so let them enjoy her infamy, her shame. Their staring would never give them as much pleasure as *she* had had.

That thought briefly warmed her, might almost have brought her to silent laughter if the next thought had not come swiftly, bitterly—that her Guy was gone and all the pleasure and love there had been between them would never be again. Resentful tears rose so suddenly in her eyes that she could not stop them swelling and spilling over. Well, let them spill, she thought, making no move to wipe them away. These women would think they were tears of contrition, acknowledgement of her shame.

They would likely think, too, that tearful contrition was only the beginning of what she deserved if the unalloyed coldness in Domina Elisabeth's voice was anything to judge by, saying at the others, "By now you know from talk among yourselves all that need presently be known about our Sister Cecely's return. Nine years ago she fled with a man. He is now dead and she has returned to us, bringing her child. More than that you do not need to know about her apostasy, and it will be to everyone's good if talk about her among you ceases hereafter, at least until Easter is done." Downward, at Cecely now, she went on, "You have come at a goodly time for your own soul, not at so good a time for us."

Cecely bowed her head lower to show she heard and was suitably sorry for it.

"From now through Easter," Domina Elisabeth said, "our duty of prayer is heavier than ordinary. These are high holy days. You will not be allowed to distract us from them. You will be more fully seen to after Easter, the more so because no word can come from our abbot until then, surely. In the meanwhile, you are the least among us. Even Sister Helen, young to the cloister though she is, is above you in all things. You will remember this and, remembering it, you will behave with deep humility at every moment of every day, thanking God for the mercy of your return. For your better governance, you will each day have a nun to oversee and direct you. From now until Vespers tomorrow, it will still be Dame Juliana. You will obey her, and the others after her, while you're in their charge. You will be given a nun's gown to wear, but in open token of your shame you will go without wimple and veil."

Cecely almost raised her head in protest at that. Would they force the unseemliness of going bare-headed on her? Surely there were limits even to shame.

But Domina Elisabeth went on. "You will be allowed your coif but only your coif, and you are to mind it covers your hair well. The cutting off of your hair we will leave for now. The abbot may want a public shearing as part of your penance."

At least she was spared it for now, Cecely thought and, despite herself, shuddered with a silent sigh of relief that she hoped Domina Elisabeth took merely for outward sign of inward grief.

Whether the prioress did or not, her voice stayed flat as she continued, "You will have your place in the choir as you had it at Vespers today. You will sleep in the dorter. You will dine in the refectory, standing as you did tonight apart from your sisters. You will keep silence at all times unless there is absolute need to speak. All of this is for our sake as much as yours, that you trouble us as little as may be through these high holy days. When they are over, we will take other counsel concerning you. Do you understand?"

Was she supposed to be stupid? The woman had made it plain enough. Lips tightly together and head still low, Cecely nodded.

"If you have any question, you have our permission to ask it now," Domina Elisabeth said.

"My son?" Cecely said.

"He is being cared for here in the cloister. You will be allowed time with him once a day. For his well-being, not yours."

"Will I be able to speak to him?"

"You will. Briefly. Again, for his sake, not yours, lest he grieve more than need be."

"Thank you," Cecely whispered, trying to sound sufficiently grateful for that "mercy."

"Now Dame Juliana will see you to your place in the dorter. You will change into the gown waiting for you there, and she will bring away your other clothing. You are to stay there, praying on your knees until your sisters come to bed. Then you may also lie down to your rest. Go now."

Cecely stood up and curtsied to her, letting herself waver on her tired legs.

Unsoftened by that, Domina Elisabeth ordered, "And to your sisters."

Teeth set, Cecely did. Despite they were all looking at her, not one head bowed even slightly back at her. That was to show to her how undeserving she was of even their smallest courtesy, but she did not care. It was what she had expected. What they did not know was that she did not in the least care what any of them thought or did or did not do. She had had what she had had, while they had nothing except this place and this death-in-life. Let them have their bitter disapproval. It was probably the closest thing to inward warmth they still had in them. She had been dreading the narrow, thin-mattressed bed that would be hers in the cold dorter, but even the cold dorter would be better than their eyes upon her, and she willingly followed Dame Juliana out of the room into the darkened cloister walk.

She had had and dared in her life what every one of them was afraid to have or do. Whatever their scorn, whatever Domina Elisabeth chose to give her by way of punishment, she would endure it until this was done.

If I don't first run out of here screaming, she thought.

Not that these women meant to give her any chance at running.

In the darkness, with Dame Juliana's back to her and no one else to see her, Cecely gave way to a small, taut smile at that thought, because what she was given and what she chose to take could be two very different things.

Chapter 6

There was silence in the warming room after Dame Juliana and Sister Cecely left. Domina Elisabeth sat down, head bowed. The rest went on sitting, some with prayer-bowed heads, others looking for something to say.

It was Dame Amicia who found words first, turning to Dame Johane to ask, "There then. What do you think of it? Of seeing your cousin again and all?"

In the white circle of her wimple, Dame Johane's face turned a deep red that was probably distress rather than anger as she answered miserably, "I don't know. I didn't think I'd ever see her again. I didn't *want* to see her again. Then to see her this way. See her . . ." She groped for the words she wanted.

"Penitent?" Dame Perpetua said, not as if that was the word *she* wanted to use.

"Yes?" Dame Johane agreed uncertainly. She looked to Domina Elisabeth. "*Is* she penitent? Or . . . or . . ." Dame Johane made a helpless gesture, as if to lay hold on the words she wanted.

Domina Elisabeth stood up. "We can only pray she's truly penitent. We'll pray for her, keep watch over her lest she waver, and await Abbot Gilberd's answer. Now I suggest you use what time remains before Compline for other than Sister Cecely."

She made plain that she was done with the matter by leaving, letting in yet another draught of chill evening air as she went out. Almost as one, her nuns left their stools to cluster to the fire's warmth, only Sister Thomasine remaining where she was, probably drawn too far into whatever prayer-filled place she lived to take heed of whether she was cold or not, Frevisse supposed. Dame Juliana hurried in, bringing another draught, slammed the door shut on it, and hurried to join the others beside the hearth. Frevisse moved back to make place for her, shifting to stand beside Dame Claire and taking the chance to ask how Mistress Petham did. Dame Claire paused before saying, "I'm not certain. I somewhat think that, rather than ill, she's simply worn out in body and mind. That what she needs more than medicine is rest."

"Has her life been that hard?" Frevisse asked, not quite keeping a slight mockery out of the question. A well-off merchant's wife did not have to deal as rawly with life and its rigors as many women did, and she surely had servants to come between her and the heaviest work.

But Dame Claire said, "I gather two of her daughters had babies this past year and were both unwell for a time afterward, so she was tending to them as well as seeing the babies were well-cared for. And a son and his family have come back from Gascony."

"Oh," Frevisse said, understanding. The year before last, the French had finished retaking Normandy from English hands. Then they had turned and retaken Gascony with almost the same ease, sending a new flood of fleeing English into England with everything lost behind them.

"They've been living with her and her husband while they settle what they'll do here," Dame Claire was going on. "The son and his wife and their three children all suddenly on her hands at once, while she had two ill daughters to worry over, too."

Frevisse had no trouble seeing how, yes, a woman could be worn thin in body and mind by all of that coming at once.

"Besides that," Dame Claire went on, "we tire more easily as the years go by, and she's no longer so young a woman."

Since Frevisse thought Mistress Petham was much about her own age, she slipped past any comment on that and said, "Is she in need of bleeding, do you think?"

"I think rest and the end of Lent's fasting will do her the most good at present. She could have dispensation from the fasting but she's refused. As soon as there's other meat than fish to be had, I'll see to her having strong broths."

"There will be the ham Father Henry's ladies brought."

"That will be a start," Dame Claire said. "Bless Father Henry's ladies."

Yet again the door opened, this time to let in Alson carrying a tray with wooden cups and a towel-covered pottery pitcher. While Sister Helen hurried to close the door behind her, she said cheerily, coming to set the tray on one of the stools, "Spiced hot cider, my ladies. Domina Elisabeth said you're to have it."

With pleased exclaims, they gathered around her as she took the cloth off the pitcher, letting out a plume of cinnamon-scented steam that was answered with sighs of delight all around. Lent's long fasting was wearing badly on everyone. With meat, eggs, milk, and anything made from milk forbidden in the weeks between Ash Wednesday and Easter Sunday, the one full meal allowed most days came mostly down to bread, vegetable pottages, and dried or salted fish cooked various ways. That fasting was part piety, part necessity; through the latter weeks of winter into spring, food was too often scarce for most folk. Lent helped stretch what there was until the time when cows and sheep came into milk and chickens began their laying again— making a virtue of necessity, as Frevisse's uncle had been wont to say dryly.

With a cup now clasped warmly between her hands, Frevisse sipped at the cider and smiled at the thought of her well-loved uncle, dead these seventeen years now. She paused on that thought. Could it be that long? It hardly seemed so, he was sometimes so immediate to her. Hard as it was sometimes to believe that it was forty years since her father's death, thirty-eight since her mother's.

That was among Lent's purposes—to bring the mind to pause from its usual forward course into remembrance, and by way of deprivation make awareness of what blessings there were in life and thereby grow the gratitude for them that was too often otherwise lost under life's daily busyness. Then at the weary end of Lent came Holy Week and finally Easter with its bounty of hope, with souls meant to be as refreshed by their Lenten journey as bodies were refreshed by the end of Lent's fasting, and the fields and pastures with spring's new life.

Meanwhile, mercifully, Sundays in Lent were not fast days, but while through the rest of a week each midday's dinner might be sufficient to quiet stomachs for a while, suppers were never enough, and when time came in the darkest hour of the night to leave bed and go to the church for Matins, Frevisse too often found her hunger threatening to come between her and her prayers. She mostly tried to offer up her hunger as her sacrifice in humble return for Christ's sacrifice of himself and sometimes she succeeded, but all too often it was a close-run thing and sometimes she failed completely, her body's need too much for any intent she tried to have. They were all suffering that way, she knew, and Domina Elisabeth, mindful that they were going to cold beds, often allowed a final warm drink before Compline, the day's last Office. Tonight especially the warm, spiced cider was a needed mercy because at Matins, Tenebrae began, the shadowed last days of Holy Week, when the dark passions of sacrifice and death were sorrowed through all over again before the joys of Easter morning. Through these coming three days the Offices were longer, their prayers and psalms more densely woven, asking much of fast-wearied bodies and minds. Mindful that the hours given to sleep before Matins were always too few, the nuns did not linger over their cider, partly because it would go cold if they did, partly to be done with it before time for Compline, when everything but prayers had to cease for the day.

Yet Tenebrae was one of her favorite times of the year, Frevisse thought a few hours later in the church, as she shifted from her knees to slide backward into her choir seat and resisted the urge to hold her cold-stiffened fingers out to the warmth of the candle burning in its holder between her place and Dame Amicia's. She tried thinking downward at her stomach, hoping to soothe it to quiet while she joined her voice to the others in, *"Nam zelus domus tuae comedit me, et opprobria exprobrantium tibi ceciderunt super me."*—For zeal for your house consumes me, and the taunts of reproach at you fall on me.

It was a bracing beginning and much needed this middle of the night. Matins could sometimes be the hardest Office, even at the best of times, with the nuns dragged from sleep and their beds for it, but it had an especial beauty with its weave of words and candlelight in a world otherwise silent and in darkness. Beyond their island of light and prayers there were only the night and its silences. No other duties hovered interrupted and waiting beyond the choirstalls. At this hour there was only prayer.

And a sneeze from Dame Perpetua at the end of the antiphon.

And a long, straining yawn from Dame Amicia.

And Dame Margrett jerking her head up from a deep nod toward sleep at the beginning of the first psalm.

And a shuffle of her own feet as Frevisse found she was thinking more of her cold toes than anything she should have been and brought herself sharply back to, "*Laudabo nomen Dei cum cantico*"—I will praise the name of God with song.

Perfection, alas, was never of this world.

But the first psalm ended and the wonder began.

Because this was Tenebrae, the days of Shadow and Darkness, a tall triangular stand with fifteen burning candles stood in front of the black-covered altar, between it and the nuns, throwing out a halo of warm light across the altar and the choir stalls. Now, at the first psalm's end, Father Henry, who had been kneeling on the altar steps since before the nuns came into the church, rose to his feet. He had been so deeply still that Frevisse had ceased to heed his unusual presence at the Office, until now, surely stiff with his long stillness, he turned to the fifteen Tenebrae candles and with great care put one of them out.

The darkness beyond the altar, under the roof, behind the choir stalls crept a little closer, and the shiver down Frevisse's spine was not from cold this time.

Father Henry returned to his knees, facing the altar again, and the Office went on, until at the end of the next psalm, he rose and put out another candle and the darkness crept nearer.

And on it went through Matins and into Lauds. One by

one the candles went out and the darkness closed around the altar and the nuns in their stalls; and Frevisse, whether she would or not, was aware on one side of her mind of Sister Cecely kneeling, rising, sitting along with them all but silent, forbidden by the Rule, in her disgrace, to say any Office with them until she was purged and cleansed of her fault and sins. Yesterday Sister Cecely's presence had irritated and irked, and surely it would again, but in this while, just now, Frevisse felt only pity for her, cut off as she was from sharing aloud in the wonder.

Now only one of the Tenebrae candles and the candles on the altar were still a-light. And in the Benedictus, his voice now joining them, Father Henry with great care put out the candles on the altar one by one until as the nuns chanted softly, "... *ut illuminer eos, qui in tenebris et in umbra mortis sedent, ut dirigat pedes nostros in viam pacis.*"— ... to light those, who sit in darkness and in the shadow of death, to guide our feet in the way of peace—he put out the last altar candle. Only the one Tenebrae candle on its stand and the ones lighting the nuns' prayerbooks still burned and the darkness seemed very near.

But not as near as it would be.

Having said the antiphon that closed the Benedictus, the nuns almost as one leaned to blow out their own candles and slipped forward onto their knees, finishing Lauds while Father Henry took the last Tenebrae candle and set it with great care on the altar, to show that one Light still burned in all the Darkness. Then, while the nuns said the last prayer of Lauds in silence, each to herself, he took that last candle and hid it, still a-light, behind the altar.

Only a faint glow in the darkness showed it still burned for a hope and promise that light would come again beyond the darkness of Christ's dying. All else was lost in shadow.

Returning to the front of the altar again, Father Henry made the sign of blessing over them, and still in silence and with bowed heads they rose to their feet and made their way from their stalls and the choir, out of the church into the cloister walk and night.

In the normal way of things, they would have returned to their beds now, but after the long effort of Matins and Lauds, there was hardly time enough before Prime to make that worth their while, and instead of toward the dorter, they hurried in a whispering of skirts and soft-shoed feet around the cold cloister walk to the kitchen where two sleepy servants had the fire built up on the cooking hearth and cups set out on the broad, scrubbed worktable. Allowed no talk among themselves, the nuns crowded around the table, each taking a cup and holding it out for one of the women to fill with warm cider, then taking it to the hearth, crowding in haste to the warmth there.

Sister Cecely was still with them. Humbly coming last from the table, she made to stand beside Dame Johane at one end of the hearth. Dame Johane drew aside more than was needed to make place for her, as if Sister Cecely were someone too unclean to be too near, unpurged of her sin as she yet was. Frevisse averted her eyes, knowing she would not want to be looked at if she were in like case. Besides, she would rather give all her heed to the pleasure of warmth and drink while she had them, knowing the respite would be brief.

It was, and she found it hard, when Domina Elisabeth made sign they were done here, to move away from the hearth's warmth. Nor was she the last to give up and leave the kitchen for the cloister walk's chill dark. Shivering as she went, she thought wryly of how strongly the body fought to prevail over the mind's soul-longing. Whatever her mind's intent, her body did not want the cold church and more prayer; it wanted the warm kitchen and more sleep, wanted them very badly, and there was no comfort in knowing it must be the same for everyone. Only for a saint, she supposed, would the desire for God be so great they could not only forgo but even forget the body's desires.

She also thought, equally wryly, that if that were the way of it, she was assuredly very far from sainthood.

The day went its particular way. With the Offices lasting longer, there was less time for the nuns' other duties, which were therefore done with haste and sometimes, by such of the nuns as did poorly on too-little sleep, with ill grace. Frevisse was able, through practiced effort, to avoid at least the ill grace. Her downfall came during the morning time given over, during Lent, to reading. At Lent's beginning, each nun was given one of the nunnery's books that she was to read at that set time each day. This year Frevisse's turn had come around again to Dame Julian of Norwich's *Showings*, and that had pleased her. She had brought the book to St. Frideswide's herself, given to her by her uncle to be part of her dowry. She had read it some several times over the years since taking her vows, and so knew the work and valued it, but maybe knew it too well because this morning she found herself nodding over it, more asleep than awake and not helped by the fact that not only had the rain stopped but the sun was come out. Thinly, yes, and somewhat watery, but sun nonetheless and just warm enough to lull her toward sleep where she sat on the low wall between the cloister walk and the square garth where spring showed in the young green of herbs and someday-flowers. More than once her head falling forward into sleep jerked her awake, nor was hers the only head nodding over books elsewhere around the wall and she doubted she was the only one relieved when the cloister's quiet was broken by Domina Elisabeth at the foot of the stairs to her rooms slapping the wooden halves of the clapper together, the sharp clack-clack-clack-clack-clack making more than one of the almost-dozing nuns jump.

Frevisse, who had seen her in time not to be taken by surprise, cast a longing look at the bell under its pentice in the middle of the garth. Through these days of Tenebrae it would not be rung to call them to the Offices. Until Easter, it was joined in the mourning. Only with the Resurrection would it ring out clear and sweet again and be all the more welcome for the while they had gone without it.

For longer than anyone remembered, St. Frideswide's had made do with an ill-made, dull-throated bell, one that clanged rather than rang. Then, something like a year and a half ago, Frevisse had given help to her cousin in a dark time and afterward parted from her in anger. No word had passed between them since, but last summer this bell had come as her cousin's gift to the priory.

That had been well-witted on her cousin's part, knowing as she must have that Frevisse would have refused any gift to herself. This way, Frevisse's thanks had been included perforce in the general thanks the nunnery had sent, but she had somewhat sharply refused Domina Elisabeth's offered permission to write to her cousin with message of her own. The sharpness of her refusal had warned her that her anger was gone too deep, that she needed to do more than simply wait for it to fade, and through this past autumn and winter she had fought to quell and cure it, had failed, and at Shrovetide had finally confessed both her anger and her failure to Father Henry, the nunnery's priest.

Whether it was that Father Henry had grown in the years he had been in St. Frideswide's or that she had become better able to see his virtues, the time was long past when she thought him too slight a man in spiritual matters to be of much use. He had heard her out with kindness, had not been able to give her absolution for a sin she was still in but had set her prayers meant to help her grow free of it. She had labored at those prayers all through Lent, and labor was precisely what it had been until, just a week ago, she had found with surprise that she was come out on the far side of her anger—that it was worn away and left behind her and she was able to look back at it as one looked back on an illness, feeling—as one did after illness—the lighter for being done with it. Lighter, and whole again, and glad to be cleansed of the ugly burden that her anger—like an illness—had been.

Father Henry had warned her, though, when first setting her the task, that her penance, when she was done, would be to ask Domina Elisabeth for permission to write to her cousin and then to write not only with thanks for the bell but to ask her cousin's forgiveness.

"You might as well have any anger at that out of the way along with the rest and be done with it," he had said. "Then you won't have to do penance for that in its turn."

That had been well-forethought on his part, because it *was* going to be hard to ask Alice's forgiveness. Not as hard as if she had tried to do it while still lost in her anger, but hard enough.

That was what made it penance.

Closing *Showings* and rising to her feet, Frevisse smiled to herself. What made the penance of true value was accepting it with a glad heart. Able to do that now, she found that the freedom it gave her was worth every hour of the struggle it had been.

The struggle to get through the rest of the day was another matter, but she made it and at her end-of-day visit to the guesthall learned from Ela that three more guests had come—one Master Breredon and his two servants.

"He means to stay through Easter," Ela told her, sounding happier about it than Frevisse would have expected. "His servants, they're a married couple. Seems the wife is poorly, and so this Master Breredon has brought her for her to pray for healing and so on. Her husband's already had word with Father Henry. I thought you could say something to Dame Claire."

"Or Dame Johane," Frevisse said. "Yes. Not tonight but tomorrow surely."

She briefly wondered why Master Breredon had chosen here instead of a shrine known for its healing. Surely his circumstances were better than little Powlyn's parents if he had two servants.

Ela went on, "He's given dried fruit, some flour, and a large ham for guest-gift." Which explained why she was not unhappy at him being here. "I hope you'll leave it all to us and not need it in the cloister," she added pointedly.

Frevisse assured her that the guesthall could keep it all, relieved but keeping to herself the unworthy fear she had had that the nuns might have to give up some of their Easter feast to their guests. If it had come to that, she and the others would have given thanks that they had something to give, but being thankful to have enough to give and being glad at having to give it were not necessarily the same, and shameful though it was to admit it, Frevisse would not care to say how little glad she would have been. Lent had gone on a very long time.

She was privately laughing at herself for her weakness until Ela asked, her words more polite than the scorn in her voice, "How's that run-back Sister Cecely doing, if there's no trouble in my asking?"

"She's doing well enough," Frevisse said quellingly. Even if there was no way to stop talk of Sister Cecely, neither was there need to encourage it by saying much.

"Early days yet," Ela said. "Even when she was here before, pretending to be a nun, she was never anything but trouble. That her own boy she brought with her?"

Starting to leave, Frevisse answered even more quellingly, "Yes."

Behind her, Ela sniffed.

That, at least, Frevisse could let go unanswered and did, but she took Ela's "pretending to be a nun" away with her.

She had been trying to put off thinking more than need be about Sister Cecely until Easter was done, but some thoughts would not stay away, and Ela's words were a prod to them. Sister Cecely could never have been deeply rooted in her nunhood or she would not have fled from it. That being true, Frevisse could not help wondering how truly ready was she now to take on the full burden of penance for her apostasy.

But why else would she have returned if she was unready for that penance?

Why else indeed?

Because if it was not for penance she was come back . . . then for what?

Chapter 7

Every memory Cecely had willingly put away from her over the years had been returning on her like heavy vengeance ever since she had walked through the cloister door. She had begun to choke on them even before she knelt again in front of the altar or put on the heavy dreariness of the black gown. Now she was finding that among the worst of the things she had forgotten was time's terrible tediousness here, and there were no days more tedious than these at Lent's end, when the prayers went on forever—hours of praying every day and for what seemed more than half of every night.

How did these women keep from going mad?

Or had they already all gone mad, and that was how they could bear it?

And how long would it take for *her* to go mad, trapped in this narrow world among these narrow women all horribly alike in their Benedictine black gowns and Benedictine black veils, their faces tightly surrounded by their white wimples as if they needed one more thing to bind them from the world. How did they bear being tied and bound and in-held against everything their womanhood should demand was theirs? How could they bring themselves to forget so much of what it was like to be alive?

Even Johane, her own cousin, in those first moments in the cloister walk had stood staring at her as if she was a ghost or, at best, a stranger never seen before. But then Cecely had hardly known her either, she was so changed—not just older but looking as if she had gone flat, gone stale, with nothing left of her except the part that could be called "nun." Cecily had more than half-hoped to find Johane an ally, but the little fool was keeping even more widely away from her than the others did. They all acted as if she had a disease and they might take it from her; all of them too stupid to see *they* were the diseased ones, with Johane as diseased as the rest and no use to her at all.

Still, and despite her own old sickness at this death-in-life that was worse with every hour she was here, she thought she was doing well enough. Maundy Thursday was past, anyway, and she had not broken into laughter when she had been sat down with the others along the cloister garth's wall, and Domina Elisabeth had knelt in front of them, one by one, and washed their feet as Christ had washed the Apostles' feet. She had even washed Cecely's feet and that had been when Cecely had had to fight to hold in laughter, wanting to dabble her bare toes in the basin and flick water at the woman who had surely been hating every moment of that humiliation.

She had had altogether another urge when Father Henry—saints in heaven, even the same dull-witted priest was still here—had told her he would not give her Communion. She should have foreseen that, but she had not. This was the one time in the year when someone besides the priests were given Christ's Body and Blood—the *one time*—and she was refused it because Father Henry was unwilling, he said, to "take on the burden" of her confession and penance. He said they were too much, that it was for Abbot Gilberd, not him, to deal with, her sin was so great.

The size of her resentment at his refusal had surprised Cecely. She could only hope her disappointment had masked her fury at him. She had wanted to shout into his face, "I was in love! You don't even know what love is! You and all these withered women! I *loved* Guy!" Instead, she had bowed her head very low, whispered acceptance of his stricture, and kept her head bowed, hiding her face while he signed a cross over her and went away.

Still, she had got something a little her own way, she thought as she followed Dame Claire up the stairs to Mistress Petham's chamber where poor Neddie was being kept, the sickly woman apparently willing for him to share her chamber. Yesterday Cecely had had to spend her time with him there and been able to drag only a few words out of him. It seemed he was being fed and that Mistress Petham was being kind to him, but the poor little mite had hardly talked except to answer what she asked him. He had just kept his head down and shook or nodded it for answer when he could, while across the chamber Dame Juliana fussed over the sick woman.

Two old women with one foot in their graves and their heads in the charnel house, Guy would have said, and he and Cecely would have laughed together, the way they had at his old aunts more than once.

No. Don't think of Guy. Not now.

Think instead how she had got her own way about Neddie, making certain Dame Juliana saw how poor Neddie had hardly talked to her there in Mistress Petham's chamber, so that afterward she had been able to ask humbly, with deeply bowed head, if he might be allowed alone with her in their time together. "In the church, perhaps?" she had asked softly. "Outside the rood screen, where we'd trouble no one. It might help him, too, when . . . when . . . he's gone away to be a monk?" she had wavered. Dame Juliana had made a great matter of having to ask Domina Elisabeth about it. Then Domina Elisabeth, granting leave for it, made plain that Cecely should understand it was a great favor she was being given, for the child's sake, not hers, and that she should be hugely grateful for it.

Hiding her bitterness, Cecely had humbly thanked her, but it was with hidden triumph she now followed Dame Claire into Mistress Petham's chamber again. Neddie must have heard them coming. He was standing ready with his cloak. Cecely held out her hand to him, and he came to take it as Dame Claire, her guard today, said, going toward the bed, "I want to see briefly how Mistress Petham does. Go on to the church. I'll soon be there."

Cecely murmured, "Yes, my lady," and with a flare of hot triumph at gaining even those few moments of "freedom," she grasped Neddie's hand and pulled him out the door.

Then came her next piece of good fortune.

Alson was coming up the stairs, carrying a covered cup of something meant for Mistress Petham.

There were so few moments to be alone and unwatched in this place. To meet Alson in one of them was almost unhoped for luck.

Except it was not luck, Cecely realized, as Alson said hastily, looking past her, up the stairs, "I had hope she'd linger with the old woman. They're keeping close hold on you, aren't they?"

Cecely let go of Neddie, caught hold of Alson's free hand with both her own, and whispered gladly, "Alson! You have the only friendly face in this whole place. They never found out you helped me, then?"

Alson let go her worried uncertainty and whispered back as gladly, "They found out I'd taken your place in the kitchen, that's all. You never saw such a to-doing as there was when you were found gone and well away. It's been well with you, then? Worth it and all?"

Gladness drained out of Cecely. Bleakly she said, "Until now. Now everything is . . ." Without she meant it to, her voice broke.

Alson squeezed her hand and said, "I know. We've all heard. Poor lady, to have lost him. He was such a goodly man to look on."

Cecely nodded, momentarily wordless with her grief.

Alson looked up the stairs again. "We can't be caught talking. But maybe later?"

"Today," Cecely said, not about to waste this chance she had hoped for since she first saw Alson was still here. "At recreation time. In the necessarium." *There* was somewhere the nuns let her go alone.

Alson's eyes and mouth went "Oh," with surprise, but she gave a ready little nod, and they went their separate ways.

Only at the foot of the stairs did Cecely pause to lean close over Neddie and say in his ear, "*Never* tell anyone that Alson and I spoke together," giving a jerk on his hand to be sure he understood.

Chapter 8

hile the Offices of these holy days were longer, daylight was not. The dark rigors of Good Friday were nearly done, but only because their supper had been so slight did the nuns have time at all for what should have been their hour of recreation before Compline and bed. Still, Frevisse welcomed even that little while and was come out with those nuns who were free to it into the fading twilight to walk the graveled paths of the cloister's high-walled garden.

It was a needed respite for those who had it. Ahead were tonight's prayers, then the long mourning of Holy Saturday, and finally the night of vigil and prayers that would bring them at last to Easter. This pause in the effort of Holy Week's prayers, this time of simply walking in the garden, gave minds and bodies chance to rest and ready themselves for the more that was to come. But Domina Elisabeth and Dame Claire were not there. From now until Easter two nuns would be constantly at vigil in the church, turn and turn about. This was their time.

Dame Margrett was absent, too, allowed to spend this time with her mother, but Dame Thomasine was there, standing alone beside the pear tree, her face lifted to the pale sunset sky as if she were watching the last soft yellow drain away, so thin in her black nun's gown and so still that she might have been another tree rooted there beside the path. Dame Juliana was, as usual, bent over the very young plants in one of the beds she so lovingly tended, while Dame Amicia and Dame Johane were walking together, their talk keeping pace with their brisk steps although their voices were too low for words to carry. Sister Helen usually walked with them when she did not walk with Dame Margrett, but this evening she was walking alone, her hands tucked into the opposite sleeves of her novice's gown, her head bowed in thought or prayer.

For her part, Frevisse was standing just outside the gate, not free to go into the garden yet. Her turn at watching Sister Cecely had begun, and as the nuns had come along the slype—the narrow passageway from the cloister walk to the garden—Sister Cecely had said suddenly and somewhat desperately, "I must go," and turned aside to the stairs up to the necessarium. Frevisse had let her go. The only two ways to the necessarium were this one and a door to the nuns' dorter. Not believing Sister Cecely was going to flee from the necessarium to the dorter and from the dorter down its stairs to the cloister walk and away, Frevisse had felt no need to follow her, was simply lingering in sight of the door, waiting for her and watching the others.

Or, now, was watching Sister Helen in particular, who was come to a stop not far from Dame Thomasine and was standing watching her watch the sky. This was Sister Helen's first Eastertide in the nunnery, and Frevisse suspected that, as was usual with novices, she was seeking to match the high holiness of the days by working over-hard at her prayers and penances. Only experience and maybe the careful guidance of others would teach her that zeal was best balanced by consideration of the body's need for reasonable rest from the rigors of prayer, lest both prayer and body suffer and fail together. Silently, Frevisse hoped that Domina Elisabeth was having quiet words with the girl on the side, guiding her. Or, if nothing else, was warning her that Dame Thomasine's holiness was beyond the ordinary and not for a novice to copy but only to grow toward, the way that Dame Thomasine had grown toward and into it. As Dame Margrett not long after taking her final vows had told Frevisse, a little sadly, "Domina Elisabeth told me we can't seize holiness out of God's hand by force. She said we have to grow to where we can receive it from him. Is that what you've found?"

Keeping to herself both her surprise at such wise advice from Domina Elisabeth and the wry thought that she did not know since she was not holy yet, Frevisse had answered, "Having seen Dame Thomasine over the years, I would say, yes, holiness is a thing we grow into, not simply get. Although in another way"— She had paused, trying for outward words for what she inwardly felt—"what's needed is a lessening of our selves, because if we're too bound up with worry over this, desire for that, pleasure in things too apart from God so that we can't see him for looking at them, then there's no place in us for holiness to come. It's as if our hands were too full of earthen tableware to take a golden platter someone is holding out to us. He can't give us what we aren't able to take."

"He gave it to St. Paul on the road to Damascus," Dame Margrett had ventured uncertainly.

"He did, and at a time when it was probably the last thing St. Paul thought he wanted. So we know it can happen that way to a soul already great enough. But," Frevisse had said dryly, "first, I know quite surely I'm far from being that great a soul, and secondly, I'm not sure I want to be blasted into holiness."

That had made Dame Margrett laugh, which was to the good. The Rule was firmly against unseemly laughter but Frevisse had found that laughter rightly made could clear thickened thought and let it flow again.

She wondered if her congested feelings about Sister Cecely would clear if she could find something about her at which to laugh. But she could see nothing even slightly worth laughter where Sister Cecely was concerned. Moreover, as Dame Claire had said on an aggravated sigh this afternoon, "If she stayed away this long, why couldn't she have stayed away until after Easter?"

Why not indeed?

But here she was again, coming down from the necessarium. She had been there over-long for someone who gave no sign of being ill, and Frevisse suspected she had used it for an excuse to be away from them all for a while, which Frevisse did not mind, being all too willing to be likewise away from Sister Cecely, but as Sister Cecely joined her at the garden's gate, the clacker made its sharp summons to Compline, ending recreation and turning them both back toward the cloister.

Cecely had been enduring everything these women forced on her, but having that hard-faced Dame Frevisse keep watch on her was nearly too much. Along with all else, it meant that when, just after Lauds, Dame Frevisse took her turn at keeping vigil in the church, Cecely had to keep it with her, and that meant no going to the kitchen for warmth and something to drink. Instead, here she was, kneeling in the pitch-black church behind Dame Frevisse and Dame Amicia, cold and hungry and with nothing to do but think. Of course she was supposed to be praying and she kept her head bent to that seeming, although how anyone would know in the darkness whether she did even that much, she didn't know. How did these women find so much to say to God? She remembered that her own prayers in Holy Week had been mostly, simply, for Lent to be over. The weeks of fasting, hard enough in the usual way of things, had been almost impossible to bear in the nunnery. Why did women with so few chances to sin think they had to be more penitent than anyone else?

Now, besides the discomfort of it all, she hated having the time to think. All thinking brought was chance to hurt with missing Guy. He had been everything she ever wanted. He and their life together. Now everything was gone except Neddie, and she was hungry and cold and could not stop the fear that she might fail at what she meant to do, nor hold back the tears that brimmed over and slid down her cheeks there in the darkened church. A sob came with them, and she let it. If she could not help crying, there was no use in wasting it. Dame Frevisse and Dame Amicia would likely take her sob for an outward sign of penitence, a sign that her broken heart was seeking to mend itself in Christ.

Let them think whatever they wanted.

Lord of mercy, she hated it here.

Still, the night finally ended, Prime and Tierce were endured, her time with Neddie came, and with it came reward for all her "humility" since coming here. This was the hour when the nuns were either nodding over their Lenten reading in the cloister walk or else kneeling at the altar, intent on being as pious as possible these last hours before Easter. Yesterday Dame Claire had felt no need to keep absolute watch on her while she was with Neddie, had instead been satisfied to join the nuns kneeling in yet more prayer at the altar. Today, Dame Frevisse saw fit to do the same, leaving her and Neddie to go alone into the nave.

Or as alone as they could hope to be.

Yesterday, to the sorrowful chanting of the nuns, Father Henry had carefully removed the Host in its silver and crystal pyx from the altar and put it in the Easter sepulchre, set into the church's wall and closed with a pair of wooden doors carved with the crown of thorns and whip and nails of Christ's suffering. There the Host would stay until Easter, shut away as Christ had been shut away in the tomb. In token of mourning, all lights in the church were out, the altar cloth was black, the church altogether gloom-laden, making it a place Cecely would have avoided if she'd had any choice, but besides the nuns kneeling at the altar beyond the rood screen, there were common people kneeling here and there about the nave. Not many but some. Here to share in the holiness of the day, Cecely supposed. And God bless you all, she thought, so long as you stay away from me. For one thing, since they were gathered closer to the rood screen than not, they gave her reason to take Neddie farther down the nave, closer to the west door, and aside to the stone bench that ran along the nave's wall for such folk as were too aged or ill to stand through an Office or the Mass.

The nuns, of course, sat in their stalls beyond the rood screen, where "lesser folk" were not allowed. As if nuns, by being nuns, had made themselves better than other folk, Cecely thought. She knew for a truth they were just women without the courage to be women, and she sat herself and Neddie down on the cold stone and pulled him tightly against her with an arm around his shoulders. He was her proof that she had dared *not* to waste her life away inside nunnery walls, and she lightly kissed his smooth hair and said, "Talk to me, Neddie. Tell me what you've been doing."

He was clinging to her free hand with both his own, his head burrowed against her, his face hidden and his answer muffled so that she had to bend closer over him and ask, "What, dearling? I didn't hear you. You've been doing what?"

With his face still hidden against her, he said, a little louder, "Nothing."

"You've been doing nothing? Surely you've been doing something."

He held quiet a moment, then said, still muffled, "Reading."

"Reading?" She freed her hand from his, slipped a finger under his chin, and pried his head up so she could see his face. "What have you been reading, dearling?"

"A book. To Mistress Petham."

"You've been reading to Mistress Petham?" Jealousy stabbed at Cecely. She had never thought of having Neddie read to her. How dare the woman make such use of her son?

But, no, it was maybe just as well. It meant the nuns weren't watching him, were leaving him to Mistress Petham, who had yet to leave her chamber. And very comfortable *that* must be—to come to a nunnery and never have to go to prayers, just lie about and be waited on.

Cecely kept that sharp thought tucked under her tongue, instead kissed Neddie on the forehead and said, "That's lovely. What a good boy you are."

But thank the saints for Alson. Cecely had supposed she would have to use Neddie, but with Alson here there was no need yet for that. With a servant's usual sharp ways, she had slipped away from whatever duty she should have had last evening and been waiting in the necessarium when Cecely came. Not to waste any of the little time they probably had, Cecely had caught tight hold on her hands and said, "I may need your help. Will you help me?"

Alson's eyes had widened. "To do what?"

"I can't stay here."

"But you came back."

"Not to stay."

Alson's eyes had widened farther and her mouth opened in silent "Oh." Much about Cecely's age, she seemed never to have married: she had no ring, still wore only a plain headkerchief of the sort suited to a servant but not to a wife. With what pale prettiness she had once all faded from her, she was unlikely ever to marry now, poor thing, Cecely thought. But the merriment that Cecely remembered was still in her and with her surprise turning to mischievousness, she had asked, "What are you going to do?"

Cecely had squeezed her hands in thanks. "Can you take a message to someone in the guesthall without anyone suspicious of you?"

"To who?"

"Can you?" Cecely insisted.

"My brother is still there. I go to see him sometimes."

Cecely had forgotten Alson had a brother, he had not figured in anything she had needed all those years ago. He would be useful now, though, and she had thrown her arms around Alson in a quick hug, then told her what she needed, making Alson's eyes go wide again.

"Can you do that?" Cecely had demanded.

Stifling a laugh with a hand over her mouth, Alson had nodded that she could. Cecely had given her another quick embrace and said, "I can't linger. That dragon Dame Frevisse is waiting for me."

"Oh, *her*." Alson had shrugged. "Stiff as a stick, that one."

Cecely entirely agreed, but this morning she would forgive Dame Frevisse that and much else, just so long as she stayed there at the altar with her back to the nave.

The nave's west door, used by anyone not of the cloister, opened, letting in a slant of sunlight across the nave's stone

floor and then a man. The sunlight slid away as he closed
the door behind him, before Cecely had seen his face, but
she had never lost her keen eye regarding men. She had met
Master Breredon only a few times, but with the urgency of
waiting she was certain of him and stood up, pulling Neddie with her. The next moment she thought better of that
and sat again, pulling Neddie down and drawing him
firmly to her side with an arm around his shoulders. Both
she and Master Breredon should make this seem an unexpected meeting, and she bent her head over Neddie, mur-
muring to him about nothing in particular while watching
Master Breredon come up the nave.

In the "holy gloom" she still did not clearly see his face,
but this had to be him. The stocky body, not particularly
tall but carried well. The steady, centered tread. It was him.
Except he did not come to her. No. He went past her, to the
rood screen where he bowed toward the altar in the shadows
beyond it, then knelt and bowed his head.

After her first flare of disappointment, Cecely realized
that was good. The less there was for anyone to note about
him, the better.

Even so, she could not help her impatience as she waited
for him to finish the show he was putting on. Neddie moved
his head restlessly away from her hand. She realized she was
stroking his hair back from his forehead somewhat too hard
and stopped, bent to quickly kiss the top of his head, and
said, still watching Master Breredon, "There's a good boy.
Just be quiet." Then, "Here's someone I want you to meet,"
as Master Breredon stood up with the ease of a man with
no aches in his bones, bowed again toward the altar, backed
away several paces and bowed once more before turning
away, looking as if he would leave the church now. After a
few steps, though, he turned aside as if on a chance-come
thought and came toward her.

Good, thought Cecely. If anyone was watching, it would not look her fault he stopped to talk with her.

Better yet, no one bustled forward to interfere, so chance was they were as unnoted as she hoped. She stood up, drawing Neddie up with her, and curtsied. Master Breredon gave her somewhat of a bow in return, and said quietly, to suit where they were, "Mistress Rowcliffe."

"Sir." She pulled Neddie from where he was half hidden behind her skirts, still clinging to one of her hands with both of his. He had always been such a bold little boy that she did not know what to make of all this hiding and clinging, but she wasn't having it from him just now. Just now she needed him to be as presentable as possible, and she turned him by his shoulders to face forward, saying bracingly, "Neddie, this is Master Breredon. You remember Master Breredon, don't you?"

Stupidly, Neddie shook his head that he did not, but at least he kept his head up, looking Master Breredon in the face; and Master Breredon all unexpectedly sat down on his heels, bringing him more to Neddie's height, and said, "It's unlikely that he would. There's been too much happening to remember everything, hasn't there . . . Neddie?"

Neddie nodded, then whispered, "Edward."

"Edward? That's your name?" Master Breredon asked. "That's what you want to be called?"

Neddie nodded again.

"Edward it is then," Master Breredon said, as solemnly as if they were making a pact between them. He stood up, lightly touched one of Neddie's shoulders, and said to Cecely, "You still hold to your purpose?"

"If you hold to yours," Cecely said. Master Breredon's dark green surcoat over a deeply brown tunic was trimmed around collar and arm-slits with beaver fur. She had always admired his furs and now had to resist the urge to reach out and stroke these, their rich softness so contrasted to all the nunnery's stale harshness. He had wealth and used it well. That was one reason she had chosen to deal with him, and keeping to business, she said, "I'm too closely watched to-day for anything, but tomorrow . . ."

"Tomorrow is Easter," Master Breredon said quickly.

"So the nuns will be over busy with prayers and things. Tomorrow is when they're most likely to forget me." She wondered how he could be slow to see the good chance that gave them.

"But it's Easter," he insisted. "That's not a day for doing this manner of thing."

Cecely was held speechless for a moment. St. William! She had not counted on him being that narrow! But too much depended on his willingness, and she swallowed down her anger that he could be so stupid—she had chosen him because she thought him well-witted—and said, smiling in a way meant to warm him to her, "Monday then, yes?"

"Monday," he agreed. "Your man will bring me word of when and how, the way he did this?"

"Yes," Cecely said, wondering, What man? He must mean Alson's brother. Why had Alson told *him*? Damnation and the devil! The more people who knew, the more chance someone would say something they should not! But she and Master Breredon were out of their time. A nun was moving beyond the rood screen, easily able to see them if she looked this way, and Cecely said quickly, "He'll bring word, yes. I must go."

She made him a quick curtsy, and before Master Breredon had finished his return bow, was pulling Neddie away with her, back toward the choir, seeing now that the nun was that unblessed Dame Frevisse and she was surely looking their way. Distrustful, prying woman. Why wasn't she still at her praying?

There was only time to snap in a sideways whisper at Neddie, "Tell her nothing," squeezing his hand hard to be sure he understood, before they were to the rood screen where Cecely gained a little time by pausing to curtsy toward the altar before going aside to where Dame Frevisse stood, her face hard with suspicion, devils take her.

Chapter 9

revisse did not know why she had left off her praying and turned to see what Sister Cecely was doing. Holy Week's little sleep and Lent's last fasting had her light-headed with weariness and hunger; it was maybe simple restlessness rather than suspicion that paused her praying, rather than the wave of unease that seemed to flow around even mere thought of Sister Cecely. Sister Cecely had been a trouble to St. Frideswide's from her first coming here—trouble enough that, in truth, St. Frideswide's had been the better, in some ways, for her being gone. She and her cousin had been there only because their aunt, prioress for a time and ambitious for the priory, had persuaded her family to send the girls to be novices. By force of her will and unwise indulgences, she had seen the two of them through to taking the final vows that made them fully nuns, but when Domina Elisabeth succeeded her as prioress, the full measure of Sister Cecely's ill-suitedness had begun to show itself. Always careless of the Offices, she had become resentful of all her duties and skilled at drawing not only her cousin Sister Johane into her slackness but several of the lighter nuns.

And then one spring day she had disappeared.

Fear that some manner of mischance had come to her had vanished when Domina Elisabeth's stern questioning had brought the servant-girl Alson to tearfully admit she had taken Sister Cecely's place in the kitchen so that Sister Cecely could meet someone in the orchard. No, Alson did not know who. Well, maybe a man. Yes, all right. A man. She was going to meet a man. No, Alson did not know what man. No, truly she didn't. And no, no, and *no*, she didn't think Sister Cecely was gone off with him. Sister Cecely had said she would be back before anyone but Alson knew anything about it!

Suspicion had of course turned on the well-featured young man who had left the priory the same day she had, but since it was not the guesthall servants' business nor the hosteler's, then, to deeply question those who stayed there, there had been uncertainty about even his name—Ratcliffe, maybe?—and no thought about where he had come from or where he was bound. He had not had much talk to any nunnery folk, and while he might have spoken more to his fellow guests, the few there had been were as gone on their ways as he was. There had been search made for him and her of course, at first nearby and then with questions farther afield with help from Abbot Gilberd when he was appealed to. One report of a woman who might be Sister Cecely was had from a village miles east of St. Frideswide's, along with word that she had been riding pillion behind a man, looking glad to be there. If that was her, it had been the last that was known. Not much beyond there, she and this man would have reached Watling Street, the great north-south road that could have taken them to London in one direction, to almost the border of Wales in the other, and in the great flow of travelers along it no report of them had been found, and that was the end of that.

What had not ended then had been the close scrutiny both Abbot Gilberd and Bishop Lumley turned on the priory. The scandal and the retributions attendant on it that had brought Domina Elisabeth to be their prioress had already scoured the nuns to their souls. Both their faith and the priory's accounts had been investigated in length and breadth and depth, and although Sister Cecely's flight had not brought the accounts into question again, the nuns had once more had to undergo strong questioning, with Sister Johane, as the apostate's cousin, taking the brunt of it. It had been an angry, unhappy time, and yet Frevisse thought that Sister Johane, in having to defend herself, had only then found out how much she truly wanted to be a nun, and surely in the years since then she had grown and deepened in her place here, become Dame Johane and nearly as skilled at healing as Dame Claire was.

As for the servant Alson, Domina Elisabeth, believing her plea that she had not known Sister Cecely meant to flee and seeing no point in dismissing a heretofore good servant from the cloister, had forgiven her for her foolishness and let her stay.

So all the rending caused by Sister Cecely had eventually healed over and been smoothed away by time, and in many ways it was a pity she was here again, not least because of the uneasiness she was making between Frevisse and her prayers, and it was impatiently that Frevisse finally amened, crossed herself, rose, and turned to see what Cecely was doing.

Afterward Frevisse had to wonder if her flare of anger when she saw Sister Cecely in talk with the man was righteous and allowable or a sin in itself. Best might have been a firm regret for Sister Cecely's sinful weakness, mixed with prayerful hope for her amendment, but at the moment all that Frevisse felt was plain anger that Sister Cecely could not be trusted even so far as the church, not even in her son's company. Knowing her anger was compounded with irk at having to deal with the woman at all, she did try to curb it, or at least hide it, but knew she failed at both.

Sister Cecely, seeing her, broke off her talk and came away from the man, bringing her son with her. Frevisse waited at the rood screen for them, stopped with a gesture whatever Sister Cecely was opening her mouth to say, and led her and the boy out of the church, into the cloister walk and around to the narrow slype. There they could talk with least disturbance of anyone, and Frevisse turned on Sister Cecely, who was clinging to her son's hand, her head very humbly bowed in appearance of deep shame, but Frevisse knew for herself and all too well how much a bowed head could hide and she did not soften her demand of, "Well?"

Head still bowed, Sister Cecely said, "It wasn't my doing. We were simply sitting there just as we did yesterday." She stroked her son's hair with her free hand, as if to make clear she had not been alone in the church. "The man was praying there. He started to leave. Then he came aside and spoke to us. As soon as he did, I went away from him. And you came."

That had not been quite how it looked to Frevisse, but she might be wrong. She might be wrong, too, that there seemed more resentment than penitence under Sister Cecely's words. Or it might simply be Sister Cecely's shame making her sound more resentful than contrite or humble. If that was it, Sister Cecely needed to work on her shame; there was still too much of pride about it.

Unfortunately, Frevisse could not help her own too much anger as she answered, "I'll nonetheless have to tell Domina

Elisabeth what I saw. For now, for the while you have left with your son, we'll return to the church, but now I'll sit near you."

"As you will," Sister Cecely said with stiff mildness, head still bowed.

The boy was looking at the wall beside him, away from Frevisse and his mother both, and he went on looking away as they returned to the nave. There Frevisse pointed Sister Cecely to sit on the stone bench along the wall again, then sat herself a distance away, wishing she had her Lenten book to read but having to settle for folded hands and her thoughts. It surely was not wrong for her to pray and hope so hard that Abbot Gilberd would see fit to send Sister Cecely away to another nunnery. For Sister Cecely's sake as much as St. Frideswide's, Frevisse tried to tell herself, but was not fooled. What she wanted was Sister Cecely not here. Where Abbot Gilberd sent her or why made no difference, just so long as she was not left in St. Frideswide's.

That did not stop Frevisse being sorry for the child, sitting there with his head hanging while Sister Cecely bent over him in whispered talk. He was unfortunate in his mother, Frevisse thought. She could not speak from motherhood herself, of course, but she had been a child and did not think she would have cared to be fawned at, the way Sister Cecely seemed to fawn at him.

Sitting there in the nave's quiet, she found herself moving from simply irk at Sister Cecely to wondering how much she had been changed by her life and living outside the nunnery. She surely must have been changed. First there had been the giving of herself up to a man despite all the vows she had taken otherwise. Then there had been the pretence of being his wife for all those years. If they had been together all this time, it must have been under the seeming of marriage, to hide she was a nun, because an apostate nun and anyone sheltering her were liable to civil law as well as to the Church. Living in such a lie had to have had some corrosive effect on the soul. And then there were the deaths of her children. Sin-begotten though they were, they had been hers. She had held them, loved them, seen them die, and had to bury them. Frevisse could only imagine what pain there was in that—pain almost beyond bearing, surely. And then her paramour had died, and except for her one last child, everything she had gained by her sinning had been lost to her.

Had it been that that had finally brought her to humility and contrition enough to bring her back here to make good the wrong she had done when she fled from St. Frideswide's?

Frevisse prayed so, but found that—prayer or no—she doubted it.

More than that, she found she doubted everything else about Sister Cecely, from her claim of contrition to her grief to her . . . no, not to her love for her son. That was surely true.

And none of it is my business, Frevisse reminded herself. Her duty was to pray for Sister Cecely's good amendment and to tell Domina Elisabeth that she had seen Sister Cecely in talk with a man in the church. Everything else was Father Henry's and Domina Elisabeth's business, thank all the saints.

Later in the day she was likewise thankful when she was able to leave Sister Cecely at work in the kitchen under Dame Amicia's eye while she made her own end-of-afternoon visit to the guesthall. There she found that no more guests had come and that Ela, as expected, had everything well in hand. That gave Frevisse chance to move among the present guests, speaking briefly to each, both for courtesy's sake and to be sure all was well with them. She said nothing to Master Breredon about having seen him in talk with Sister Cecely, only asked how his ill servant did, remembered to thank him for his food gifts, and found him a courteous, quiet-spoken man.

She spoke to his servants, too. The woman, who indeed did not look well, claimed she was comfortable, and her husband said he was grateful that Dame Claire had already been to see her.

The parents of the small child glowed with pleasure when she asked how little Powlyn did. With him so much better, they were having a happier Easter than they had dared hope for, they said, and they thanked St. Frideswide for it.

It crossed Frevisse's mind that the child's bettering had as much to do with Dame Claire's and Dame Johane's skills as saintly care, but her next thought was to wonder who was to say that Dame Claire's and Dame Johane's skills were not the saint's gift? The older she became, the more she found that faith and life's mysteries twined together, with often neither faith nor life at all understandable.

But then, faith was not something to be "understood." It was something to be lived.

But—come to it—that seemed to be true of life, too.

The two widows were making merry over a game of tables and dice when she came to them. One of them jestingly offered to let Frevisse take her place at the board for a while, and Frevisse as jestingly answered that, "If you're losing so badly you want me to play, I assuredly will not take your place," making both women laugh.

Frevisse had meant to make particular effort to talk with Mistress Lawsell and her daughter today, too, having done barely more than nod in passing to them since they came. Her intent was only increased by Ela telling her, on the quiet, that they had been to every Office since they came, even to Matins and Lauds. "And then up again for Prime," Ela said. She did not sound approving, but Ela's approval or disapproval aside, Frevisse was curious whether that devotion was only Mistress Lawsell's, with her hope her daughter would become a nun, or whether the girl shared it. Ela could not tell her, was only able to offer, "She's a quiet thing, the girl. Keeps her head down and her words to herself. It's the mother does the talking."

That was warning as much as report, and Frevisse found it to be true enough. Asked by Frevisse how they were, Mistress Lawsell said readily and at length that both she and her daughter were in great good and comfort of both soul and body, that their stay here was all she had hoped for, that they had nothing for which to ask. The daughter only nodded unsmiling agreement to that, not saying a word, her gaze steadily downcast until—at the last moment, when Frevisse was parting from them—she looked suddenly up, such taut misery showing in her eyes that Frevisse almost asked her outright what was the matter. But Mistress Lawsell was saying how much they looked forward to the rest of the Offices today, and Frevisse decided that some other time, without Mistress Lawsell present, would be better to talk with the girl. She realized, though, that she did not even know her name, her mother merely saying, more than once, "My daughter"; and Frevisse cut across Mistress Lawsell's flow of words to ask the girl, "Please, what's your name?"

Both mother and daughter looked startled, Mistress Lawsell even breaking off whatever she had been saying, making a pause into which the girl said shyly, "Elianor, if it please you, my lady."

Frevisse bent her head in a single nod of thanks and left before Mistress Lawsell could begin again, taking with her a doubt that Elianor had any desire whatsoever to be a nun. The best she might have was desire to please her mother, and that was not enough. But Mistress Lawsell meant to stay on into Easter Week. That gave Frevisse time to find chance to talk with Elianor alone, or else suggest to Domina Elisabeth that she should do so.

Vespers came, and then supper. Domina Elisabeth, mindful of the long night of Offices ahead of her nuns, saw to their supper portions being somewhat more than they had been of late and then that they had their full hour of recreation before Compline.

The early evening was warm under a clear sky, the hope of a clear Easter looking likely to be fulfilled after the days of fitful weather. Only Dame Claire and Dame Perpetua, taking their turn in vigil at the altar, and Sister Cecely at her penance with them, did not come out into the garden for the while. In their place, as it were, was Mistress Petham, come slowly, at Dame Claire's urging and with Domina Elisabeth's permission, leaning on Sister Margrett's arm, her other hand resting on the shoulder of Sister Cecely's son as if to steady herself. She sat on the bench nearest to the gate, openly grateful that she need go no farther, but her smile was full of pleasure as she looked around the garden and at the sky, like a prisoner newly freed.

The boy sat down beside her, but she patted his back and said, "You don't have to sit with me. Domina Elisabeth will likely give you leave to walk here."

"Better yet," said Domina Elisabeth, "Dame Amicia and Sister Helen can take him to the orchard. He can run there if he wants. Or climb the trees." She smiled at the boy. He stared solemnly back. "Would you like that? Would you like to go to the orchard with Dame Amicia and Sister Helen?"

"If it please you, my lady, yes," he said. He looked at Mistress Petham. "If I may?"

"If Domina Elisabeth says you may, you may," Mistress Petham assured him. "She's lady here."

His face lighted with the first smile Frevisse had seen on it. "Thank you, my lady," he said.

Dame Amicia was already going toward the garden's gate, smiling, too. She held out a hand toward him, and they went out of the garden hand in hand, Sister Helen following them, and not immediately but soon and now and again through the while left until Compline, Frevisse heard him laughing from among the apple trees beyond the garden wall and found herself smiling at it. It was good to know he could be a happy child despite everything. Nor did Mistress Petham look the worse for having his company, so likely he was well-mannered, too. Frevisse supposed there was good chance that before all this came on him he had had a good life, had been well-cared for and well-loved. She hoped so. However wrong his birth had been, God forbid that either blame or punishment for it should fall on him, the one innocent in it all.

The hour ended with the clacking summons, and Frevisse turned her mind toward Compline's prayers with pleasure. This was the final readying toward tomorrow's joy, the triumphant glory of Easter with, *"Surrexit Dominus vere!"*—The Lord is truly risen!—and through Matins and Lauds the glad, oft-repeated, *"Alleluia, alleluia, alleluia!"* All the deprivations and contemplations and prayers of Lent would come to their fruition then, and Frevisse found she was smiling with forward-looking pleasure, because *Multi sunt qui de me dicunt: "Non est salus ei in Deo."*—Many they are who say of me, "Safety for him is not in God." But, *Tu autem, Domine, clipeus meus es, gloria mea* . . . —But you, Lord are my shield, my glory . . . And Easter was the glory that crowned all.

Chapter 10

n Frevisse's years in the nunnery there had been
sometimes an Easter made difficult by illness
among the nuns, or by bitter weather, or by worldly
worries that could not be kept at bay. This Easter, for a
blessing and despite Sister Cecely, went as beautifully as the
best had ever done. During Prime, as they were saying, *"Hic
est dies quem fecit Dominus; exsultemus et laetemur de eo"*—This
is the day that the Lord made; we are joyful and glad in it—
the rising sun struck through the choir's eastward window,
flooding light—multi-hued scarlet and azure and golden—
the choir's length, over the altar shiningly covered with its
white altar cloth now Christ had risen, over the polished
wood of the stalls, across the black and white clad nuns in
their ordered rows. More than one of them lifted her head

and turned her face toward the light, the psalm not faltering, instead taking on new strength, as if fed by the light and all the promises of hope and life that came with it.

Later even Father Henry's familiar Easter homily—of how, just as each dawn the sky colored with the promise of the coming sun, so they must color their lives with holiness for the Coming of the Son who has been and ever will be— seemed somehow fresh.

Besides that, because the nunnery's hens had begun to lay again when winter was done, and because Lent's fast was over, there was a boiled egg for each nun at breakfast, causing many small sounds and sighs of delight along the refectory table.

Just thus, Frevisse thought with an inward smile at her own savoring of her egg, were the soul's need and the body's mixed together, inseparable until death.

The one pity of the day was, of course, Sister Cecely. Frevisse had feared her presence would taint everything, but set against the day's glories, Sister Cecely was such a small thing that she barely mattered. It helped, of course, that Domina Elisabeth took on herself the duty of watching her, sparing Dame Amicia her turn for today at least and thereby removing Sister Cecely as much as might be from their midst.

Domina Elisabeth also took on herself the care of Dame Thomasine, who was gone so far into prayer, was so glorying in the day's glory, that it seemed her body hardly had existence for her. Except that Domina Elisabeth took her by the arm and led her to meals, she would probably not have left the church at all.

Seeing to both women meant that Domina Elisabeth, rather than being able to give herself up to the pleasure of the day, spent it dealing with the two outermost ways of nunhood—Sister Cecely and Dame Thomasine—and that was a pity, because surely their prioress was as ready as all the rest of them for the end of Lent. Certainly Frevisse found

during the late morning Office that her Lenten-fasted stomach was answering the wafting smells from the kitchen on
the far side of the cloister with an ache stronger than her
heed of the psalms, but for once she did not care, and the
meal, when they at last sat down to it, was everything that
could be hoped for. Besides the lamb roasted in a sauce of
garlic, rosemary, pepper, eggs, and its own drippings, there
were a cheese tart thick with eggs and heavy cream, small,
soft rolls of the last of the year's fine white flour, with butter
to go on them, and a fig pudding rich with almonds, raisins,
honey, and ginger.

After that it was just as well the afternoon was given over
to ease until Vespers, with leave for the nuns to spend the
time as they would in the cloister walk and the garden and
the orchard. Even Sister Cecely, having been allowed to sit
at the far end of the refectory table during dinner and given
half-portions of everything, was let off her penance in the
church, to spend the time with Domina Elisabeth in the
prioress' parlor. Frevisse thought that probably made the afternoon more a penance than a pleasure for Domina Elisabeth. Then she willingly forgot Sister Cecely altogether,
went to walk for a time in the orchard, and afterward—
giving way to the satisfaction of a full stomach and her
tiredness—sat and drowsed in the garden's warm sunshine
for a while.

She awoke from an unremembered dream to find herself
with what seemed a quite unreasonable urge to return to the
church. Surely she had spent enough hours there of late that
she did not need more just now, she thought, and stayed
where she was until—more fully awake and finding the urge
did not leave her—she looked at it and found it was not
duty moving her to it but joy. She was so suffused with happiness that she needed to be closer to the heart of it, and she
rose from the bench, a little stiff with having sat still so
long, and obeyed her desire.

At this hour of so sun-filled a day, the now-shadowed church seemed almost of another world, and Frevisse paused just inside the door from the cloister, to let her mind and body take in the quiet waiting there, to give it chance to reach into the deep places of her self, balm and blessing together. Candles still burned at the altar. After the blackness of the past few days, their brightness and the glowingly white altar cloth made plain how light and life could come out of darkness. As expected, Dame Thomasine was there before her, kneeling at the altar as straightly upright as one of the candles and probably burning, Frevisse supposed, with an inward flame as strong as their outward ones. Dame Thomasine lived in a state of prayer and grace that Frevisse could deeply respect and wonder at while nonetheless admitting—if only to herself—how much she was frightened by the thought of so much losing herself. That fear was a weakness she had prayed against without yet fully overcoming it, and yet sometimes, in her deepest praying, she brushed close to how it must be for Dame Thomasine and for a brief breath of time felt the wonder and freedom, the unbounded joy there was there, beyond the bounds of all the world's seeming. And whatever her fears, afterward she always hungered to be there again.

Only as Frevisse moved forward, away from the door, did she see Elianor Lawsell in the nave, kneeling just beyond the rood screen. Or not so much kneeling as crouching. There seemed little that was prayerful about the way she was huddled down, one hand spread over her face, hiding it, the other stretched out and pressed against the screen. Another pace, silent-footed in her soft-soled shoes, brought Frevisse near enough to see the girl's shoulders were unevenly shaking, surely with crying.

Frevisse sighed. However unwilling she was to the duty, she went around the rood screen, now deliberately not quiet-footed. The girl grabbed her hand back from the screen and began wiping at her face, her head still bowed, but when Frevisse lightly touched her shoulder and she looked up, tears were still coursing freely down her cheeks, nor did she seem ashamed of them, wiping at them more defiantly than as if hopelessly trying to hide them as Frevisse asked, "Is it as bad as that? You want so little to be a nun?"

The girl gasped. "No!" Still on her knees, she grasped at Frevisse's skirts with one hand while wiping away yet more tears with the other. "Please. No. Don't think that! I'm crying because I'm so glad. To be here. I'm praying I never have to leave!"

Frevisse leaned over, took her by the elbows, brought her to her feet. "You want to be here?"

The girl clasped her hands together. "I want it so much!"

Frevisse let her go, took a step back, tucked her own hands into her opposite sleeves, and said with what she hoped was a balance between sternness and sympathy, "Your mother brought you here in hope of this, but . . ."

"No," Elianor interrupted fiercely. "She brought me here in hope I'd see how drearsome and over-burdened a nun's life is. But it isn't!"

"It can be," Frevisse said quellingly. "It often is."

"Everyone's is," Elianor returned. "You can't tell me they aren't."

"I won't. But this is not what your mother wrote to our prioress."

"It wouldn't be, would it?" Elianor returned scornfully. "No. What she wants is for me to give up my hope and settle for whatever husband she'll choose for me."

"She's a widow?"

"My father finds it easier to let her do as she will," Elianor said bitterly. "He says the matter is between us. Between my mother and me."

"And if, after this while here, you still don't agree with her, what will she do?"

"I don't know."

"Punish you? Force you?"

Elianor lightened into sudden, silent laughter. "When our quarrel started, she threatened to beat me, even to lock me up until I 'behaved.' I went to our priest. He laid order on her that I'm not to be forced in any way. I'm to be 'persuaded' or else allowed my choice. She was very angry about that."

Frevisse could well imagine she would be.

"It's not as if I were depriving her of all hope of marrying a daughter well," Elianor said. "My sister can hardly bear the wait for a husband and household of her own. She'll do everything Mother asks of her, once I'm out of her way."

There were a number of questions Frevisse wanted to ask, but it was not her place to do so. This matter was for Domina Elisabeth. But there was no need to disturb her peace today, and Frevisse settled for saying, "Tomorrow ask Father Henry for leave to speak alone with Domina Elisabeth. Your mother will have to allow that at his word, and he'll give it. That will put the matter between you and our prioress." Who would not be pleased at having been misled by Mistress Lawsell.

Hope, relief, and gratitude bloomed in Elianor's face. She looked as if she would have kissed Frevisse's hand in thankfulness, but Frevisse kept her hands firmly up her sleeves, gave a short nod, and gladly escaped to the other side of the rood screen, going, as she had first intended, to kneel down at the altar and give herself into prayer.

Chapter 11

ecily fell asleep in anger and awoke the same, both when Matins dragged her from bed and again when she had to rise for Prime and truly begin the day. After all the Easter praying yesterday what harm would there have been in taking some manner of ease from the Offices now? She valued Easter as much as anyone should, but she had always thought the *hours* spent at it here in the nunnery were beyond reason, and this morning, kneeling at the altar yet again in this farce of "penance," she thought it more than ever.

She could only hope that Master Breredon was satisfied he had done his duty to God and be willing to have her and Neddie away as soon as might be. He had after all been right about Easter not being the best of days to make her escape;

she had not counted on Domina Elisabeth's attending to her all the day, and what a misery that had been. But Master Breredon had not known that would be the way of it and he had better not refuse the next chance that came. Tomorrow Sister, no, *Dame* Thomasine would have a turn at keeping watch on her. There was a woman so unbrained with holiness she probably could not keep watch on a wart on her thumb. All Cecely need do was get word to Master Breredon of when and get her hands on Neddie at the necessary time, and this miserable place would be behind her again. Tomorrow for a certainty, before she ran mad, she thought grimly.

It was a pity she needed Master Breredon's help at all, and a pity that her need had brought her back here. Still, the place had served its purpose. She had not known how long she would have to wait for him to come. She had needed somewhere safe for her and Neddie, where Master Breredon would be surely able to find her, as well as somewhere no one would think to look for her. St. Frideswide's had served all those purposes well. Now soon, soon, soon she would escape from here as readily as she had done before and never be dragged from bed in the middle of the night for prayers or see any of these dreary women again. Mercy of the Lord! They didn't even have sense enough after Lent's lacks and Easter's rigors to make merry the way most people did!

Kneeling on her aching knees, her hands clasped so hard her fingers hurt, Cecely had sudden, sharp memory of her Easter Monday last year when the three of them had ridden out together to watch the games and merriment in the village, Neddie on Guy's saddlebow, safe between Guy's arms, her riding pillion behind them, an arm around Guy's warm waist. His summer doublet when she rested her cheek against it had smelled of the southernwood and rosemary it had been stored with through the winter, and one of the village women had given her a garland of spring flowers to wear around her neck. When old John Jankin's feet went out from under him in the tug-rugget and he'd pitched backward, knocking down the whole line of men along the rope behind him, she had laughed herself near to falling off the horse, had had to grab hold of Guy's belt to save herself.

They had been so happy together. Not just then but so many times. It was unfair, it was *wrong* that he was dead. Wrong that she had to endure this place again. Wrong that she and Neddie had to be here. Wrong that she had to deal with Master Breredon. Wrong and wrong and wrong! The only grief there had been between her and Guy in their years together had been their lost babies. Now he was gone from her forever. How was she supposed to love God when he'd taken away from her what she loved most in the world? How was she supposed to love God when he was so cruel?

Cecely found tears of anger and grief were washing warm down her chill cheeks, and she raised her head, lifted her gaze to the altar. There was no point in wasting those tears. Dame Amicia, her keeper today, was in chapter meeting with the other nuns, but there was a servant standing somewhere behind her, keeping watch. Let whoever it was report she had cried. Domina Elisabeth would probably think it was in contrition and sorrow for her sin and be glad of it.

But what had been between her and Guy had *not* been sin, Cecely thought angrily. They had been so *happy*. How could their happiness have been sin?

Someone laid an uncertain hand on her shoulder. She looked around and up, startled. It was Alson. Alson! Sent to watch her just when Cecely needed her most!

Eagerly Cecely grabbed her hand and pulled her down beside her.

FREVISSE, when the morning's chapter meeting was done, went to see how things were in the guesthall and was in time to see Father Henry waving farewell to his aunt and her friend as they rode out of the yard with laughter and promises to be back come Michaelmas. Frevisse joined him in a final wave as they disappeared through the gateway and said to him as he turned around, "You're fortunate in your kin, Father."

He was smiling. "I am indeed."

"As they are fortunate in you."

Father Henry looked at her in open surprise. "Are they?"

"They are. As St. Frideswide's is in having you for our priest."

She was as surprised to hear herself say that aloud as Father Henry seemed to be at hearing it, and she left him standing there, still startled, as she went on to the guesthall.

Happily, the two widows were not the only guests leaving today. As Frevisse came into the hall, little Powlyn and his parents were almost readied to go, taking with them Dame Claire's assurance their child was fully on the mend. On Dame Claire's behalf, Frevisse took their thanks and a thank-offering for the priory, promised the nuns' prayers for them and their child, and saw them away.

After that she spoke briefly with Mistress Lawsell and Elianor, saying nothing about yesterday.

Like the Lawsells, Master Breredon preposed to stay on a few days more. Indeed, Ela said that with the widows gone, he had already made bold to ask to move into the guesthall's best chamber with his two servants. As he had been so generous with his Easter gifts to the nunnery, Frevisse made no pause over agreeing to that and made a point of going to thank him again for his gifts and to ask how his servant did.

"Much better," Master Breredon assured her. "Ida is a favorite with my wife, so I'm as grateful to your infirmarian on my wife's behalf as Ida's husband is on his."

Frevisse accepted his thanks on the nunnery's behalf and said it was pity he had had to spend Easter away from his home. He agreed but said some things could not be helped.

Sext took her back to the cloister before she was finished in the guesthall, and it was afternoon before she was free to return and take council with Ela in the guesthall kitchen not only on how food was lasting for the present guests but—more worryingly—how they would fare if other guests came.

"We're that low on flour, there'll have to be more grain ground if there's to be bread after tomorrow," Ela said. "A bit of meat wouldn't come amiss. What's left of the ham won't last long. Some lamb or mutton, maybe?"

"Send to ask Hamo." The nunnery's shepherd. "If there's sheep to spare, I suppose it will have to come to here. We can go on with fish in the cloister a while longer." Frevisse held back a sigh at the thought of more fish after all the fish there had been through Lent. Besides that, the priory's fish-ponds were somewhat over-fished just now, so the nuns would likely have to make do with the last of the dried stockfish from the bottom of the last of the barrels laid in last autumn. Spring was always a difficult time for food.

"Still," she said hopefully, "the cows are in good milk. If nothing else, we can oat-pottage everyone in cloister and guesthall alike when all else fails."

"We're nearly out of oats," said Ela.

They settled on deciding that Frevisse would bring the matter up in tomorrow's chapter meeting, to be talked over and decisions made there. Ela made no secret of being glad she would have no part in that. Frevisse held back from admitting she wished she could avoid it, too. Instead, she thanked Ela for her good, steady handling of the guesthall's guests and servants.

"Oh, aye," Ela answered, making a grumble of it but her pleasure at the thanks showing through. "Well, there you are. It's less trouble in the long jog to handle things and people well from the start."

Frevisse left the kitchen, going up its outer stairs into

the yard. The morning was become softly warm, the sky strongly blue between light streamers of scrubbed-white clouds, and she paused a moment, her face turned up, eyes closed, to the gentle sunlight, pleasuring in the brightness and warmth. But only briefly. At the sound of soft-soled, running footsteps she opened her eyes and saw Sister Helen running through the gateway from the outer yard where no nun had any business being and most especially not alone.

All her momentary ease falling away, Frevisse started toward the girl, not sure whether to be angry or—now that she saw the girl's frightened face more clearly—alarmed. Certainly Sister Helen looked glad rather than guilty to see her, running to her so headlong that Frevisse caught her by the arms to stop and steady her. Sister Helen grabbed her arms in return, gasping to catch her breath, giving Frevisse time to demand, "What were you doing out there and alone? What's the matter?"

"Dame Johane," Sister Helen gasped. "I was with her. Someone from the village was hurt. He was bleeding. His friends brought him. They sent someone ahead and we went out to meet them. We did. In the outer yard." She paused her rush of words to draw a few quick breaths, starting to steady but her grip on Frevisse's arms bruising as she made to pull Frevisse toward the cloister door, saying more urgently, "But there's men come. Riding in. Dame Johane said I should come to warn everyone. We have to . . ."

"Yes," Frevisse said. She could hear the horses now, coming at a hard trot, and she began to move toward the cloister door without Sister Helen's pull. Before she and Sister Helen were to the door, six men rode through the gateway. They had the dusty look of hard travel on them, were plainly in haste about something. They had no bared weapons in hand, though, which was to the good, and it being too late to reach the cloister door, Frevisse stopped herself and Sister Helen with a tight, steadying grip on Sister Helen's arm and ordered under the clatter of shod hooves on cobbles, "Stand calm. Just stand calm," then let go of Sister Helen and tucked her hands up her opposite sleeves while lifting her head and setting her face to a quietness that did not match the hard beating of her heart.

Beside her, Sister Helen drew a gasping breath and fumbled her own hands into her sleeves. Whether she was able to feign an outward calm to go with it, Frevisse could not see because her gaze was fixed on the lead rider now drawing his horse to a stamping halt a few yards in front of them. He was a firm-built man of late middle years, in plain doublet and high boots for riding, with his clothing and horse all of good quality. He was not wearing a sword, only a man's usual dagger, and some of Frevisse's alarm at his harsh coming eased a little. The men had come in haste but not ready for violence, it seemed.

With her black veil and Sister Helen's white one, he knew which of them was senior and demanded at Frevisse, "A woman and a small boy. Are they here? Have they been here? Come within the past few days? Do you still have her here?"

"God's blessing on you," Frevisse said firmly, hiding her mind's immediate and angry turn toward Sister Cecely. She looked a little sideways to Sister Helen. "Sister, please, if you would, tell Domina Elisabeth we have new guests."

Blessedly quick-witted enough not to question or hesitate, Sister Helen made a quick half-curtsy to her and retreated to the cloister door. The man made no effort to stop her but said sharply at Frevisse, "If they're here, I'll find out. You can't keep them hidden forever."

Purposefully misunderstanding him and hearing the cloister door shut behind Sister Helen, she answered, "We keep no one here against their will, sir. Sir—?"

"Master Rowcliffe. John Rowcliffe," he answered impatiently. "A woman called Cecely. I don't know what else she might call herself. It better not be Rowcliffe. And a boy. She used to be a nun here. So it's said."

Before Frevisse could form an answer that would win Domina Elisabeth a little more time to ready to face this man, he gave way to his impatience, swung down from his horse, threw his reins to a younger man on a horse beside him, and went past Frevisse to the cloister door. She did not try to get in his way. There was only so much she was willing to do to guard Sister Cecely, and getting in his way was not part of it.

He had a leather-gloved fist raised to pound on the door's thick wood when the man who had caught his thrown reins said, "Ease down, John. Give the woman chance to answer you."

Master Rowcliffe spun from the door. "Well?" he demanded at her. "Is she here?"

"Sister Cecely has returned to us, yes," Frevisse answered evenly.

"What of the boy? Is he here, too?"

"There's a child with her that she says is her son."

The second man laughed. "'Says is her son.' She knows Cecely."

"Then she's here!" Master Rowcliffe made that an accusation.

Frevisse could not see where accusation came into it, and before she could answer, a third man, much younger than the other two, sitting his own horse the other side of Master Rowcliffe's, said to him calmingly, "So we don't have to carry on like madmen. We've overtaken her. She won't slip away again."

"By Saint William's bones she won't!" Master Rowcliffe snarled.

Having had time to look at them all, Frevisse judged the three men were likely related. They resembled each other in face and garb and good horses. The three other riders, hanging a length or more to the rear, looked by their clothing and lesser horses to be servants, probably ready to give aid if needed but equally willing to leave the shouting and all the rest to their betters—and *very* willing to be distracted by the guesthall's two servants, Tom and Luce, just come up the steps from the guesthall kitchen and starting across the yard toward them, carrying trays laden with wooden cups.

Frevisse sent a quick prayer of blessing toward Ela for the distraction. Men with a welcoming cup of ale in hand were less likely to be reaching for weapons, and she reached for a cup from the tray of the servant coming to the two men nearest her, saying with forced outward calm, "Thank you, Tom."

Tom ducked his head in answer. He was trying to keep his face servant-straight but she could see the unnerved fright in his eyes and she gave him the slightest of smiles, hoping to reassure him. The nunnery did not need its servants going useless with fear.

Holding that smile, she turned back to Master Rowcliffe who had now taken a step back from the door and was glaring at it, probably adding its offence at staying closed to all his other angers.

"Master Rowcliffe?" she said courteously, holding the cup out to him. "If you would do us the honor?"

He swung around. "What?" He glared past her at his companions, all of whom already held or were reaching for cups of their own. He hesitated, but courtesy won over ire for the moment and he took the cup from her, mixing muttered thanks with, "This makes no difference."

"Still," Frevisse said quietly, "if you're not pounding on the door, someone may be the more likely to open it to you."

Small snorts of laughter from his two companions earned them Master Rowcliffe's glare before, unwillingly, a smile tugged at his own mouth. He drowned it with a long gulp of ale, then held the cup out for Tom, still standing nearby, to take and said, "Right then, Symond, and yes, Jack. She won't get away again and there's no need for me to carry on like a madman." He switched his look to Frevisse and demanded, "I want to see her. And the boy. Is he well?"

"He's well," Frevisse said. She moved past him to the cloister door, adding, "For the rest, you would do best to speak to our prioress about it."

Before he could answer that, she knocked lightly at the door and to her relief it immediately opened. Master Rowcliffe started to stalk forward, and the younger of his two companions began to dismount as if to follow. Before Frevisse could say that allowing Master Rowcliffe into the cloister was as far as she was ready to go, the other man put out a hand to him, bidding, "Stay, Jack. Leave it to your father for now."

Master Rowcliffe looked over his shoulder and nodded agreement with the man who must be Symond, and Frevisse, thinking that explained something of who the men variously were, went into the cloister, letting go the smile she had been keeping on her face. Sister Margrett, standing with her hand on the door's latch, whispered as she went past, "Should I bar it?"

Not knowing if Master Rowcliffe heard that but having to suppose he did, Frevisse said, clear-voiced, "No need. They've come on reasonable business and mean no harm." Except perhaps to Sister Cecely, and Frevisse had to admit, if only to herself, that just at this moment she would not mind harming Sister Cecely herself for having brought this on them. Whatever this was.

Frevisse could not help the sharp suspicion that, whatever it was, right was more probably on Master Rowcliffe's side than Sister Cecely's, and trying to curb the anger simmering under that thought, she led Master Rowcliffe into the cloister walk, where she came to a startled stop, confronted by St. Frideswide's nuns gathered in two groups, one to either side of her, standing at the near corners of the cloister walk, barring any further way into the nunnery without they were dealt with first.

There were not many of them, admittedly, even when Sister Margrett slipped past to join those on the right, but grouped in the walk's shadows, garbed alike in black and white and standing all together, with Domina Elisabeth one pace ahead of those to the right and all their heed and hers fixed and stern toward Frevisse and Master Rowcliffe, their offered challenge was enough to pause anyone.

Frevisse felt Master Rowcliffe come to a full and startled halt behind her. She turned back to him, to see him holding up his empty hands in token of surrender even while his gaze searched among them for Sister Cecely. Frevisse had looked for her as quickly as he had, but she was not there, and he brought his heed back to Domina Elisabeth and said with the care of someone meaning to stop a quarrel, "My lady, I mean no harm here. I swear it. I've only come seeking someone who's done me wrong."

"If so," Domina Elisabeth said sternly, "then you should have come with less show of anger, frightening us all."

Frightened was not what they looked. Defiant, yes, and ready to be openly angry if pushed to it. But frightened? No. Domina Elisabeth had made good use of the time that Frevisse had gained her, and Master Rowcliffe bent his head to her and said as if he meant it, though choking a little on the words, "For that I apologize. I was in the wrong."

Domina Elisabeth accepted the apology with a gracious single nod of her head. "Let us talk peaceably then," she said. "If you'll come with me." She moved forward, toward the stairs up to her parlor, adding, "Dame Frevisse, come with us. The rest of you thank God that all is well and return to your tasks."

Since no nun should be shut away alone with a man,

someone had to go with Domina Elisabeth as she led Master Rowcliffe up the stairs to her parlor, the chinging of his spurs on the stone steps a harsh, strange sound in the cloister. Frevisse followed them willingly, sorely wanting to hear all of what Master Rowcliffe had to say, not whatever shortened version might come to chapter meeting tomorrow.

In the parlor there was evidence of the flurry Master Rowcliffe's arrival had brought on, but he probably took no particular note as Domina Elisabeth said with a nod toward the desk standing where the light from the window fell well, "If you would, my lady." While Domina Elisabeth crossed to the tall-backed, carven chair that had been every prioress' since St. Frideswide's was founded, Frevisse went to the desk to stopper the inkpot there and wipe clean the pen that Domina Elisabeth had dropped in her haste. A black spatter of ink from the cast-down pen marred the clean surface of the page she had just begun to write on but Frevisse thought a little careful scraping would make that right.

Meanwhile, Domina Elisabeth sat, said, "Now, sir, what do you claim is your quarrel with us? And your name, if you please," making a gracious gesture that gave him leave to sit in the room's other, lesser, chair, facing her from the other side of the fireless hearth.

Her manner and that she had sat and begun to question him before giving him leave to sit were all meant to make clear who held authority here. Maybe not sure how he had been put so completely wrong-footed in the matter, he sat, then answered, respectfully enough, "I'm Master John Rowcliffe. I come from near Wymondham in Norfolk. I've no quarrel with you, my lady." He scowled. "Not unless you mean to protect her."

"Protect whom?" Domina Elisabeth asked evenly, making him work for it.

"My late nephew's whore."

Domina Elisabeth's eyebrows rose and Master Rowcliffe said defensively, "Well, that's what she was. Now he's dead. Drowned two months ago, along with another nephew of mine. I'm left their executor, and she's run off with what isn't hers to take and my nephew's son. You're welcome to her. Sure as sinning, I don't want her back. But I want back what isn't hers to have!" He went sullen, having to know that outburst put him in the wrong again. He cast an angry look, as if it were her fault, at Frevisse where she now sat on the bench below the window, her hands folded on her lap. Then back at Domina Elisabeth, he said, "This is where she came from. She's come back here, hasn't she? From what this woman says, she has. I want to see her."

"Where she came from?" Domina Elisabeth asked, dangerously quiet.

Seemingly not hearing the danger, Master Rowcliffe lost hold on his patience again and burst out, "Saints' breath, woman! She was a nun! Now she's run back to the hole she bolted from!"

"You knew she was an apostate nun?" Domina Elisabeth said coldly. Because a nun or monk who forsook their vows was supposed to be thereafter an utter outcast, neither sheltered nor protected by anyone but given over immediately to the law, for the law to give back to the Church for discipline and penance. To have known his nephew had a nun for his paramour and done nothing about it . . .

"Of course we didn't know! Guy sang us some song about her being a poor orphan of good family but no fortune about to be forced into a brothel, and how he had rescued her."

"You believed that?" Domina Elisabeth asked, echoing Frevisse's own doubt.

"Why not?" Master Rowcliffe returned. "It was the kind of idiot thing Guy would do, given the chance. Besides, he was of age, with income of his own. Who he married was his business, not ours. They were clearly besotted with each other and we left them to it."

"When did you find out the truth about her?" Domina Elisabeth asked.

"A week ago, if that much. After she ran off. I'd have let her go and good riddance, but she took Edward with her."

"He *is* her son, isn't he?" Frevisse put in.

"He is, poor whelp."

"How did you find out about her past?" Domina Elisabeth asked. "She surely didn't tell you."

Master Rowcliffe gave an angry snort. "Last year, when my fool nephew had had just about enough of her, he told—" He seemed to think better of saying who had known Cecely was apostate and yet done nothing about it until now. "He told someone, who told us after she disappeared. We didn't have anywhere else to look. Or we had too many ways to look, but thought we'd try this one first. So here we are. Now, where is she?"

Domina Elisabeth answered coldly, "You cannot take her from here. Our abbot has been told . . ."

"Saint Apollonia's teeth! I don't want her! You're welcome to her. What I want are the deeds she stole. And Edward. What's she going to do with him, kept in here? I want my nephew's son, and I want those deeds. After that, she's all yours. I wish you joy of her."

"Word of her has been sent to our abbot," Domina Elisabeth said, yet more coldly. "We're awaiting answer from him. You are welcome to wait with us. This is plainly something not to be settled on your word or mine alone."

She stood up. Perforce, so did Master Rowcliffe and Frevisse.

"In the meantime"—Domina Elisabeth started toward the door—"you surely wish to speak with her. I'll take you to her now."

Openly off-balanced by her suddenness, Master Rowcliffe followed her from the room and down the stairs, and Frevisse again followed them both. Only in the cloister walk, going toward the church, did Master Rowcliffe recover enough to say at Domina Elisabeth's back, "I'm not here to make trouble. I don't want anything from her but what's rightfully mine. That's all I'm here for. You understand that?"

Without looking back at him, Domina Elisabeth said, "I understand I have heard something of Sister Cecely's side of the matter and something of your side. Beyond that, I look forward to hearing what you have to say to each other."

So did Frevisse.

Chapter 12

omina Elisabeth had sent the nuns back to their tasks, true enough, but following her and Master Rowcliffe into the church, Frevisse saw that somehow those tasks all seemed to be there. Sister Margrett and Sister Helen were sweeping the nave's stone paving. Dame Juliana and Dame Perpetua were working dust cloths through the fretted wood of the rood screen despite it had just been dusted for Easter. Even Dame Claire had forsaken her usual work among her herbs in the infirmary and was with Dame Amicia along the choir stalls, polishing the brass candleholders as if they, too, had not been well-seen to last week. Other than Dame Johane who was likely still with the injured village man, only Dame Thomasine was where she might best be expected to be—just standing up from where she had been kneeling on the lower of the two steps up to the altar.

Sister Cecily was at the altar, too, but had not been kneeling, instead was standing with her back to it, stiffly straight, head up, hands clenched together at her breast.

Master Rowcliffe started toward her with a triumphant, "Hah!" but Domina Elisabeth put out an arm, barring his way, then pointed into the nave beyond the rood screen and said, "There. You can talk to her from there."

"From there?" he protested. "But she's . . ."

"She will come forward. You will stand on that side of the rood screen. She will stand on this. We will all talk," Domina Elisabeth said.

"I won't!" Sister Cecily cried.

"You will," Domina Elisabeth corrected coldly. She gave a nod to Dame Claire and Dame Amicia. Needing no better order, they instantly dropped their polishing cloths and went to Sister Cecily. Each taking her by an arm, they shoved her forward. Master Rowcliffe, apparently satisfied, went around the rood screen into the nave and turned, hands on hips, to confront Sister Cecily as they brought her to the end of the choir stalls, still several yards from him and still firmly held by them both.

None of the nuns were pretending to any work now, were all openly staring, save for Dame Thomasine who had turned away to kneel again.

If Sister Cecily was frightened, her defiance and anger were hiding it as she twisted her arms free from Dame Claire and Dame Amicia and challenged at Domina Elisabeth as much as at Master Rowcliffe, "You can't force me out of here! I claim sanctuary! For Neddie, too!" She pointed at Master Rowcliffe. "You want Neddie dead. I claim sanctuary for us both!"

Before Domina Elisabeth could answer that, Master Rowcliffe said impatiently, "Oh, give over, you dawe-brained woman. I don't want you out of here, and he's safer with me than with you any day of the year. These women and your abbot and all are welcome to you. What I want are Edward and the deeds you stole." He looked around. "Are you sure you haven't lost him? You're that careless it wouldn't surprise me."

"Of course I haven't lost him!"

Domina Elisabeth said quietly. "He's safely here. You can see him later, if you like."

"So long as he's well," Master Rowcliffe answered.

"You can't have him!" Sister Cecely exclaimed. "I claim sanctuary for him, too!"

"You give me those deeds and we'll talk about Edward."

"I don't have them. I don't know what you're talking about."

"You have them. I want them. They're not yours."

"I don't have them!"

"What deeds?" Domina Elisabeth asked.

"To two of our best manors," Master Rowcliffe answered. "I knew as soon as I knew she'd gone that she would have taken more than just the boy. That's how she's paid back Guy's putting up with her all these years. By stealing from us."

"They're Neddie's manors!" Sister Cecely exclaimed hotly. "They should have come to Guy when George died, so they're Neddie's now!"

Master Rowcliffe heaved a huge sigh of impatient anger and said aside to Domina Elisabeth standing like a judge between them, "George was my elder brother's son. Guy was my younger brother's boy. They were both of them my nephews, and they drowned in the same shipwreck, both without heirs of the body, and so all the family lands they held come back to me. That's how the inheritance was set up two generations back."

"Guy has an heir!" Sister Cecely said furiously. "He has Neddie!"

"Your Neddie is a bastard. You and Guy were never married. Couldn't be, could you? Not when here is where you belonged all along. Neddie has no claim on anything except the manor Guy bought and willed to him."

"You'd take even that from him if I didn't protect him!"

"I would not. What's his is his," Master Rowcliffe replied with the harsh patience of someone who has had to say that several times too often. "What I want—what we all want— is to protect him from you."

"I'm his mother!"

"You're a whore and a fool," Master Rowcliffe threw back at her.

Someone among the nuns gasped at that bluntness. Sister Cecely was already too colored with anger to color further with shame—supposing she felt any—and before she could make any answer, Master Rowcliffe added, "Nor it's not as if you were left with nothing, woman. All you had to do was bide where you were and behave yourself."

"And wear black all my days and live on whatever nothing I was allowed and do as I was told and be expected to be grateful for it," Sister Cecely scorned.

Master Rowcliffe raked her with his gaze. "You're wearing black now, seems to me. And what's this 'nothing' you're on about? Guy left you a good widow's dower out of Edward's manor. You'd not have lived poor."

"Until Neddie came of age!"

"That's ten years and more away!"

"And then what happens to me?"

"You could always have come back to your nunnery," Master Rowcliffe said with hot mockery.

"God damn you!" Sister Cecely screamed.

Domina Elisabeth stepped forward, saying in a voice flat

with authority and the intention of being obeyed, "Enough. Enough from both of you."

"I haven't . . ." Master Rowcliffe began as Sister Cecely started, "I won't . . ."

Openly not caring what they did not have or would not do, Domina Elisabeth said, "Dame Frevisse, please see Master Rowcliffe to the guesthall since it seems he'll be here at least the night."

"I'll be here a good while longer than that if I don't get those deeds. I'm going nowhere until I have them. And Edward," Master Rowcliffe said.

"I don't have the deeds!" Sister Cecely cried at him.

"While I see to Sister Cecely," Domina Elisabeth went on, cutting ruthlessly across their quarrel. "I promise you, Master Rowcliffe, she'll be here for you to talk with further. Dame Claire. Dame Amicia. Bring her, please."

They unhesitatingly took hold on Sister Cecely's arms again, tightly enough that she winced, and not gently forced her, writhing against their hold, after Domina Elisabeth. Frevisse caught glimpse of several servants scattering from where they had been listening outside the open door to the cloister, but her own charge was Master Rowcliffe who had been left flat-footed and a little gaping by Domina Elisabeth's suddenness, and she said, matching her prioress' authority, "If you'd come this way, please you, sir," going not toward the cloister but into the nave and toward the church's west door. She moved and spoke as if there were no question of him coming with her, and he did, at first slowly and then more quickly. He even passed her as they reached the door, so that he was able to open it for her, standing aside for her to go ahead of him into the sunlight.

The other men were still there, some of them still mounted, but the man called Symond was at the well at the near end of the yard. He had drawn up a bucket, was drinking from the cup that came with it, but seeing Master Rowcliffe, he set down the cup and called, "We heard the shout-ing. How went it?"

Closing the church's door, Master Rowcliffe answered, "She's denying everything about the deeds. We're staying here until it's settled."

"What of Edward?" asked young Jack from where he stood beside his horse, still with one of the cups of guesthall ale in his hand.

"I didn't see him," his father said and looked at Frevisse to ask with what sounded like true concern, "How is he? He was still hurting badly with his father's death when I last saw him."

"He's surely still grieving," Frevisse said with careful mildness. "But he's well and being kept in the care of some-one other than his mother."

"Good!" Master Rowcliffe was fierce about that. "No one should be in her care. She's a dire fool."

"We were feared for him and for how badly she might try to taint him against us," said Symond, leaving the well.

Both seemed reasonable worries, but Frevisse had no answer to either and merely said, starting toward the guesthall, "If your men will take your horses to the outer yard and stable, I'll see you settled here."

Master Rowcliffe gave order for that to his men, adding, "Bring our saddlebags when you come back," while his son swung from his saddle and handed his reins to one of the men. As their servants rode off, Master Rowcliffe and his son and Symond—whoever he was in this mess of things—followed Frevisse the rest of the way across the yard, up the short stairs, and into the open-raftered guesthall where Ela was overseeing Tom and Luce setting up the long trestle tables for supper. Later, with the tables taken down and set against the wall, there would be bed-ding laid out on the floor for such of the guests as did not have their own bedchamber. Those chambers were few and mostly small, giving privacy but not much else. Only the one the widows had shared was larger and with some comforts, and Frevisse might have offered it to the Rowcliffes if it had not already been given to Master Breredon. As it was, she was starting to say something about which small chambers they might share but broke off as a whole new anger darkened Master Rowcliffe's face. Not at her, because he was looking past her. In the next moment he burst out, "Breredon! What are you doing here, damn you?" and Frevisse whipped her gaze to where Master Breredon was standing in the doorway to his room, his manservant not far behind him.

To Frevisse they looked to have been purposefully waiting to be seen, and that was possible because surely the Rowcliffes' arrival had been no secret and there were windows enough in the guesthall for Master Breredon to have seen them in the yard. Nor did Master Rowcliffe's instant anger at him seem any surprise to him. Instead, he held where he was as Master Rowcliffe started toward him. Neither man had drawn their actual daggers, but in every other sense it was daggers-out between them, and Symond said quellingly, "John," while Frevisse made a sharp gesture at both him and young Jack to stay where they were as she went after Master Rowcliffe.

Ela, Tom, and Luce were standing frozen in surprise and probably alarm at the sudden angers in their midst. On the far side of the hall so were Mistress Lawsell and Elianor. Frevisse, with anger for that added to her other angers, said at Rowcliffe and Breredon both, "Gentlemen!" as sharply as if calling dogs to heel, sufficiently startling them that their heed broke from each other to her long enough she was able to come between them the way Domina Elisabeth had come between Master Rowcliffe and Sister Cecely in the church. Keeping more curb on her anger than she wanted to, she demanded, "What is this you're at? And *stop it*, whatever it is!"

Master Breredon bowed his head as if in obedience to that demand, a little smiling, but Master Rowcliffe said with unabated anger, pointing at him, "Our first thought was that she might have run to him, but all his folk swore they'd none of them seen her."

"Nor had they," Master Breredon said.

"And when you didn't leave your place until days after she'd run, we had to think there was nothing in it. But there was, wasn't there?" Master Rowcliffe demanded. "Because here she is and here you are!"

Master Breredon shrugged easily, said lightly, "She swore no one would think to look for her here."

"She's a fool," Master Rowcliffe snapped.

That was plainly his refrain where Sister Cecely was concerned, but despite how much Frevisse agreed with it, it solved nothing, and she said impatiently, "You're frighting the other guests in a place that's supposed to be at peace. What is this all about?"

"Your damned nun," Master Rowcliffe snarled.

Symond and young Jack had come forward to join him, one on either side. They were neither of them so rawly angry as he was, and it was Symond who answered her evenly and without heat, "She's run off with some deeds to lands that aren't hers. We want them back rather than waiting to find out what trouble she means to make with them."

Missing deeds had been some of Master Rowcliffe's theme in the church but, "What's Master Breredon's part in it?" Frevisse asked, trying for calm despite her angers.

"He wants the lands those deeds give," Rowcliffe snapped. "By foul means, since fair haven't served him."

"I know nothing about stolen deeds," Breredon said calmly. "I'm here for Edward and nothing else. She's offered me him and his manor in ward and the right to his marriage."

"In return for helping her escape," Frevisse said.

Breredon favored her with an approving smile. "You have

it. I was to pay her well for Edward and help her away from here. With money in hand, she could do whatever she chose to do next."

"Leaving you with control of his manor until he comes of age!" Rowcliffe accused, "*And* likely marry him to one of your daughters."

"You know how well that manor of his suits with my other property there," Breredon answered. "I'd have bought it outright three years ago except Guy was ahead of me."

"So having failed to have it by fair means, you meant to have it by foul," Rowcliffe snarled.

"Someone will have it until Edward comes of age. Why not me?" Breredon asked.

"Because Edward is ours!" Rowcliffe exclaimed.

Still keeping in check her own anger at both of them, Frevisse said, "Didn't Edward's father give keeping of him and this manor to someone in his will?"

"To his 'dear wife' the will says," Rowcliffe said sullenly. "Since they weren't truly married, that means nothing. Guy could be an idiot sometimes."

"And the land isn't held of some lord or else of the king?" Frevisse persisted. "Someone with some say over it?"

"Guy bought it from some guild in Norwich that didn't want the bother of out-lying land anymore," Symond said. "It's clear of any overlord. There's no one."

That was a pity, because Frevise would have been more than glad to tell them to ease back their angers until someone with better authority could rule on the matter. If there was not anyone, then it would come to lawyers, she supposed. In the meantime, though, the quarrel was here, where it had no business being, and she said, "Then there's nothing to be done but clear yourselves back to your homes and sort it out as best you may there."

"If I can take Edward with me," Breredon said.

"Edward comes with us!" Rowcliffe snarled.

"Edward goes nowhere," Frevisse said sharply. "His mother and he are both staying here until . . ."

"You're welcome to her," Rowcliffe said. "She's yours. But the boy isn't. He's ours!"

Frevisse turned to fully face him, near to matching him in height and even nearer to matching him in anger. It was an anger coldly in her control, though, and coldly she said, each word distinct, "Edward is under this priory's protection. Our protection and the protection of the Church. No one lays hand on him without our prioress' leave or that of Abbot Gilberd of Northampton. Our abbot has been sent word of Sister Cecely's return. Whoever he sends in answer to that can deal in your matter, too. But until he comes and as things are now, Edward is going *nowhere*."

She put all the force of Domina Elisabeth's authority behind that final word, everything about her daring Rowcliffe or anyone else to say otherwise.

No one did. She could see Rowcliffe struggling not to burst out at her and could guess what he was probably thinking: that she was a woman and therefore—to his mind, he being that sort of man, she suspected—to be overborne. But she had invoked both the power of the Church and of an abbot against him, and while the Church might be distant and sometimes slow in its workings, an abbot could be very near and his hand immediately very heavy. Still, abbots could be brought around if need be . . .

"Abbot Gilberd," she said, "is our prioress' brother."

Like a final weight added to a scale, the shift that gave to Rowcliffe's decision showed so plainly on his face that Frevisse almost could have laughed. She certainly hoped he did not hear Breredon's muffled snort behind her, and she said, turning to include Breredon, "This leaves you both with the choice of leaving here, to have news sometime of how things are decided . . ."

"We're staying right here," Rowcliffe snapped.

The other men nodded sharp agreement with that, and Breredon, too. It was very probably the only willing agreement they would ever have, and Frevisse said, still coldly, "Then you'll do it peaceably. You're here as the guests of God and you'll do well to remember it at every moment. Remember, too, that there are others here, come for better reasons than either of you. If they are troubled by your troubles for even one moment beyond this present one, the priory will no longer be bound to honor your guest-right. Do you understand that?"

The men all nodded again, grudgingly this time and eyeing each other as if to see who would break the peace first.

"Unfortunately," Frevisse went grimly on, "we have but the one best guestroom and Master Breredon is already there. Therefore, Master Rowcliffe, you and your people will have to do with either the hall itself or one of our lesser chambers, as you choose." She did not wait for his answer to that. She did not care what his response was. Instead she pointed at Ela and went on, "There is Ela who is my voice here in the guesthall in my absence, which must be now because Vespers will be soon. You might all do well to attend the Office. I shall see you again in the morning."

Without waiting for any response from them and somewhat more vehemently than was maybe proper, she turned from them and crossed the hall, going first to the Lawsells, to reassure them that there would be no more trouble now, silently praying she was right. Leaving them, she went to Ela, Tom, and Luce to say for only them to hear, "The ale was well-thought, Ela. And thank you, Tom, thank you, Luce, for bringing it. It came timely."

Ela sniffed. "Seemed a good thing. I'll see to them having plenty tonight, too."

"Not so much as makes them quarrelsome," Frevisse cautioned.

"Enough to make them sleep both soon and late, the lot

of them," Ela said. "If they take it otherwise, there's Tom to see to them."

"And you're welcome to," Frevisse told him. Tom's weak chest was one reason he was a guesthall servant, rather than at fieldwork, but he both looked and was strong-armed enough to give someone pause if he stepped forward and told them to stop whatever they were doing. Frevisse glanced back and saw that Breredon had withdrawn into his room and shut the door, while the three Rowcliffes—whoever Symond was, he was plainly some manner of family with them—were gathered head to head in talk.

"Serving Master Breredon and his people their supper in their room tonight might be best," Frevisse said. "I doubt he'll object, and the Rowcliffes will likely stay more quiet if he isn't in sight."

"They'll stay quiet," Ela promised.

Frevisse had a sudden vision of the little, bent-backed woman standing toe-to-toe with Rowcliffe, shaking a finger at his nose and telling him to behave himself.

"Invoke Abbot Gilberd if you have to," Frevisse said and left. She was almost to the outer door when a question she wanted to ask Breredon came to her and she almost turned back, but the bell began to ring for Vespers, enjoining silence and obedience on her, and she went on, more than ready for the peace of her choir stall and prayers.

Chapter 13

nhappily, there was little peace to be had either during Vespers or afterward. During the Office, questions beyond those already asked kept coming into Frevisse's mind, pulling her away from where she wanted to be, and although at supper Domina Elisabeth's stern eye from the table's head kept them all in proper silence, those nuns who could barely wait for the recreation hour ate with unseemly haste, then had to sit restlessly while the others—Frevisse, Dame Claire, Dame Thomasine, and Domina Elisabeth—finished more deliberately, giving the blessing of food the honor it deserved. Only finally did Domina Elisabeth say grace and nod that they were free to go. "Slowly," she added and more sternly, "*Seemly*," at particularly Dame Amicia.

That got them from the refectory and into the cloister walk with no one tripping over anyone else, but from there, with Domina Elisabeth momentarily out of sight, there was a scurrying of the younger nuns away to the slype on their way to the garden, their voices rising in talk as they went. Dame Perpetua and Dame Juliana followed almost as quickly, only a little more aware of dignity, leaving Frevisse, Dame Claire, and Dame Thomasine behind with their prioress, who said as they all moved toward the refectory door together, "Dame Frevisse, would you keep watch on them, please, and as much ward as you can on their tongues? Dame Claire . . ."

"My lady," Frevisse said, "there's something else you have to know."

Domina Elisabeth looked at her. "Please, not more trouble."

"I fear so, yes," Frevisse said and told what had passed between Rowcliffe and Breredon in the guesthall.

Domina Elisabeth heard her out in increasingly stern, strained silence and at the end said, "Then she never meant anything except to use us."

"It seems so, my lady," Frevisse agreed.

Domina Elisabeth stood considering that, weariness etched on her face, then said, "Dame Claire, I'd have you come with me. Dame Thomasine—"

Dame Thomasine lifted her head, her face pale and quiet in the white surround of her wimple. She did not speak, only looked at her prioress from whatever place she lived in, aside from them all.

"Dame Thomasine," Domina Elisabeth said as quietly as Dame Thomasine's look, "I'd have you pray for all of us, if you would."

Dame Thomasine bowed her head in a small accepting nod and without raising her head again went quiet-footed away toward the church.

Domina Elisabeth watched her for a moment, then said, "Dame Claire, if you would," and would have started away except Frevisse said, "By your leave, what's been done with her?"

There was no question which "her" was meant. Domina Elisabeth gave a sharp glance away across the cloister garth. "She's in the guest parlor. It's where she can be kept and guarded with least trouble in the cloister. I've set Malde to guard the door for now, but we'll all have to take turns at it until Abbot Gilberd says what else is to be done with her."

She spoke crisply, with open anger that it had come to this, then walked away. Dame Claire followed her and, alone, Frevisse went slowly out to the garden.

The clear weather that had blessed Easter Day and most of the day was gone under a thickening overcast, but there was no rain yet and certainly the lowering sky had not lowered the nuns' readiness to talk. They were all standing in an eager cluster just inside the garden, words whipping among them, and Dame Perpetua shifted to let Frevisse join them, with immediately more than one of them asking what had passed with Master Rowcliffe in the prioress' parlor and then in the guesthall.

Frevisse told them something of it all, and an appalled silence fell among them briefly, before Sister Margrett said, almost whispering, "Then she's lied to us."

"In everything she's done and almost everything she's said, she's been lying to us, yes," Frevisse agreed.

Dame Perpetua said with horrified wonder, "It makes me feel so . . . unclean, just having been near her."

Some heads nodded at that, but Frevisse did not feel unclean, only angry. Angry at Sister Cecely for her deceits. Angry at Breredon for his. Angry at the Rowcliffes for less reason but just as surely. Wanting to keep her anger from the other nuns, needing time to work through her own clutter of thoughts and feelings and questions, knowing there would be no keeping curb on their tongues, no matter what Domina Elisabeth had charged her to do, she walked away. With all the new fodder for talk she had given them, the others let her go, their voices rising behind her, and she did not know that Dame Johane had followed her until at the path's turn at the garden's far end the younger nun said behind her, uncertainly, "Dame Frevisse?"

Surprised, Frevisse stopped and turned around. Dame Johane stopped, too, still several yards away, as if unsure she should be there but so openly troubled that Frevisse said with an effort at kindliness, "Yes?"

Still uncertainly, Dame Johane came forward a few steps, stopped again, and said, "Please, may I talk to you?"

"Assuredly," Frevisse said.

"It's Cecely."

"There's little you can do for her now except pray she amends in her soul."

"I have been. Ever since she left. It's just . . ." Dame Johane dropped her voice to barely a hush. "It's just . . . is she a heretic?"

In her surprise, Frevisse said somewhat curtly, "No. A heretic is someone who's troubled to think about his faith. Has come to wrong conclusions but at least has thought about it. Sister Cecely—" She stopped short. What she had been about to say was maybe too unkind to say straight out to Sister Cecely's own cousin. Then she decided she did not care and finished bluntly, "I doubt Sister Cecely thinks much about anything at all. She just 'feels,' and lets what she feels serve her in place of thought."

"I feel, too," Dame Johane said in a half-whisper, with enough torment in her voice that Frevisse paused over answering her, before finally saying carefully, "We all feel. There's never a way not to feel. Nor should there be. We were given hearts for a reason. But when our judgment of what's good or bad comes down to what we 'feel' about it, with no thought behind it, then that's wrong and weak." She paused again, to be sure of her thought, then went on, "It's even, possibly, evil. If not in its beginnings, then in what grows from it. Because something grows from everything we do, and we were given minds as well as hearts, that we could judge what we do as well as merely feel it."

She was not aware of ever having thought that through before now. Her own surprise at it kept her silent when she had done, and Dame Johane was silent, too, before finally saying softly, "She's so changed. Cecely. She's older."

Despite that seemed to be away from what they had been saying, Frevisse knew it was not and answered, softly, too, "Her feelings have cost her dearly these past years."

Dame Johane gave a sudden, despairing sigh. "What troubles me is that I don't know how much better I am than she is. Even after my years here, I'm so very far from being holy, and now there's Cecely come back, and despite how very wrong she's been, she's making me look at how far from grace I am, too."

"No one is ever far from grace," Frevisse said quickly. Long years ago she had had very much this same talk with Domina Edith of blessed memory, except she had been the one tormented by her failures and Domina Edith offering answer to her—answer that had stayed a comfort to her in even the driest of spiritual times through all these years afterward. Now she offered it readily to Dame Johane, saying, "What we're too often far from is willingness to open our self to grace. From willingness to let grace come to us. We keep our minds between it and our hearts."

"But it's giving way to her heart that's ruined Cecely," Dame Johane protested.

"Was it her heart she gave way to, or her lusts?" Frevisse returned. "There *is* a difference."

Dame Johane stared past her with a gaze turned inward, looking at that thought.

Frevisse found herself going on, "As for our becoming holy—" and stopped, wishing she had not started; but Dame Johane's look had come back to her, expectant, and so she went on slowly, "I don't think we have to become 'holy' to succeed in our life here. I'm not even certain what 'holy' would be for us."

"Dame Thomasine."

"Yes," Frevisse granted, still slowly. "But it seems more a gift given to her than something she 'became.' I haven't been given it. I know that. My hope isn't for holiness, only that I grow enough—can set my roots of faith and belief and love deep enough—that like a deep-rooted plant growing taller than a shallow-rooted one, I finally come as near to God in my mind and soul and heart as I can, no matter how much in the world my body has to be."

She stopped. There should have been more to say than that. From the way Dame Johane went on looking at her there was surely need of more, but Frevisse did not know what it was and ducked her head as low as Dame Thomasine so often did, said rather desperately, "Benedicite," and feeling very insufficient, walked away.

Chapter 14

n the next morning's chapter meeting, Domina Elisabeth told them more fully of Sister Cecely's treachery and that they must endure with grace until this matter was ended. Then, for a mercy, she added a stricture against talk of Sister Cecely in the cloister.

"We'll say what needs to be said and nothing more. If you need to speak of her, the hour of recreation will suffice. Otherwise, let there be nothing said."

There was restless shifting by some of the nuns at that, thwarted of how they had meant to spend the day, but Frevisse was grateful. Her own hope was that with Sister Cecely now shut away, the days and Offices would take their right shape again, or as near to a right shape as might be, until whomever Abbot Gilbert sent took Sister Cecely away.

And, please God, he *would* take her away.

Unfortunately, although talk was curbed in the cloister, Frevisse had to go to the guesthall where there would be no escape from the matter of Sister Cecely, and admitting cowardice, she went first down to the kitchen, wanting to hear from Ela how things had been, before she dealt with anyone else.

"They're not giving trouble. That much I'll say for them," Ela told her. "Master Breredon and his folk keep to his chamber, except when his man comes out to fetch their food or empty the pot. The Rowcliffes leave it at that. For now anyway."

"What of Mistress Lawsell? Has she thought of going early? To have her and her daughter away from this?"

"Can't. She sent their horses home with a servant. He's not to be back until week's end. Odd, though," Ela said. "She's not carrying on like I thought she might. Not bothered at all by there being so many men about and only her and her daughter. Doesn't even keep the girl to their chamber."

"Ah," said Frevisse somewhat shortly. That would most certainly be strange in a mother who wanted her daughter to become a nun, but then, according to Elianor, a nun was not what Mistress Lawsell wanted her to be. In truth, it seemed she wanted it so little that she was willing to set Elianor deliberately among men, assuredly not with intent that anything happen here but probably in plain hope of stirring the girl's blood, that the body's lust might persuade where a parent had not.

It would be interesting, Frevisse thought, to see how that went with Elianor.

"Now," said Ela, "about what we're supposed to feed these folk."

All Frevisse could tell her was that when she had raised the matter of feeding their guests in chapter this morning, Domina Elisabeth had said she would send to learn if there was chance of lamb or mutton from the nunnery flocks and if anyone in the village might be willing to sell flour. Until something came of that, Ela would have to do with what was on hand, with green cheese and brown bread and stretching the oat-pottage to last as best she could.

That settled, Frevisse gave herself up to the next necessity, sighed heavily, and went up to the hall. The trestle table had been left standing after breakfast, and Rowcliffe and the man Symond were seated on the benches there, the nunnery's battered old chess set between them. By the captured pieces at his side of the board, Symond was rather thoroughly winning. Neither Jack nor either of the Lawsells was in sight, and the door to Breredon's room was shut. Other than the guesthall's Tom clearing ashes from the fireplace, with wood waiting for him to lay a fire ready for tonight's chill, she had Rowcliffe and Symond to herself and she went, however unwillingly, to stand beside Rowcliffe while he finished moving a bishop to a square that she saw would do him no good against the attack Symond had ready against him. Seemingly not seeing it, Rowcliffe said "There!" in a satisfied voice and followed Symond in rising to his feet to bow to her.

She gave them both a slight bend of her head in return, but before she could say anything, Rowcliffe demanded, "Have you heard from your abbot yet?"

With more outward mildness than she inwardly felt, Frevisse answered, "It's somewhat early in the day for that."

"I want to see Edward."

"I'll tell Domina Elisabeth your desire," Frevisse answered stiffly.

"This morning. I want to know he's as well as you say he is."

"Ease back, John. She's God's servant, not yours, for you to be ordering her to anything," Symond said half-laughingly, his gaze on Frevisse so that possibly he was reading a-right how near she was to snapping back at Rowcliffe.

Rowcliffe blew out his breath impatiently but seemingly at himself rather than anyone else for he next said, sounding abashed, "I ask your pardon, my lady. It's not you I'm angry at. It's Cecely and maybe Breredon. I want to be mourning my nephews, not having to waste time forestalling that woman's idiot-doings."

Frevisse accepted that apology with another slight bow of her head and said, "We're as willing as you to have this matter settled and be done with her."

Symond laughed outright at that.

Frevisse looked at him and said, "Please, sir, no one has said what your part in this is, or even your name."

He looked surprised. "My part? I'm cousin to all of them." He nodded at Rowcliffe. "My mother was older sister to John's father. I'm Symond Hewet, but count as a Rowcliffe in all of this."

So she had been right about that, Frevisse thought. They *were* all Rowcliffes and together "in all of this."

"It was to Symond that Guy told his secret," Rowcliffe said. He gave his cousin a hard stare while adding bitterly, "Then he kept it to himself until she disappeared with Edward."

"Guy swore me to secrecy before he told me," Symond said simply, not noticeably bothered by Rowcliffe's unspoken but very clear accusation. "He said someone should know the truth, on the chance something ever went to the bad. Then things did go to the bad, and so I told."

"Fool of a woman," Rowcliffe muttered.

"Wasn't there something you wanted to do when next you saw—" Symond paused, looking at Frevisse.

"Dame Frevisse," she obliged.

"When next you saw Dame Frevisse?" Symond finished.

"Ah. Yes." Frevisse could not tell whether Rowcliffe was relieved to be reminded or irked, but he reached with seeming willingness to the leather purse hung from his belt, brought out several silver coins, and held them out with, "A guest-gift. To help against the cost of all our being here."

While the Benedictine Rule required the receiving of guests without asking payment from them, even to the impoverishing of a house, it did not *require* the impoverishment, and Frevisse took the coins with true thanks, then said, as much to Symond Hewet as to Rowcliffe, "I promise you we're doing the most we can toward making an end to all this."

"Keeping close hold on Cecely the while, I hope," Symond said with a smile.

"Very close," Frevisse said grimly.

"Good," snapped Rowcliffe.

Frevisse suspected his dislike of his cousin's "wife" went back far further than her present treachery. Maybe it had even underlain Sister Cecely's choice to flee rather than deal with him. She could never have thought they would find her here, not knowing her flight would bring worse trouble on her by loosing Symond Hewet to tell her secret.

Leaving the Rowcliffes to their game, she went to knock at Breredon's shut door. His man opened it warily, then widely when he saw her there. As she entered, Breredon rose from where he had been sitting at the window and bowed to her. The manservant's wife likewise stood up, sewing in her hands, from where she had been sitting on a stool, to curtsy, and Frevisse asked her, "How are you?"

"Much bettered, my lady," the woman said softly, with downcast eyes. She was altogether a soft little woman but cleanly kept in a plain gown and apron and headkerchief, just as her husband looked the proper servant in his plain doublet.

He had stayed beside the door, and his wife edged away

to join him there as Frevisse went toward Breredon. Since yesterday it had crossed her mind to doubt the woman had been truly ill. At the same time she had doubted that Dame Claire would have been deceived, but as somewhere to begin, she said at Breredon, quietly, to keep their talk between themselves, "So, was your servant's wife truly ill? Or was that another lie to serve your ends here?"

Openly surprised by the attack, Breredon answered, "No. She was ill. She's better but not well yet, your infirmarian says." He dropped his voice even lower than Frevisse's to add, "She miscarried a child last autumn. It left a shadow on her mind. A melancholy. Then this spring she began to sicken. When I needed a woman with me, to keep an honest front to my dealings with Mistress Rowcliffe . . ."

"Sister Cecely," Frevisse said coldly.

Breredon acknowledged the correction with a slight bow of his head and continued, ". . . my man Coll and I thought to make a double purpose in bringing Ida, both for my need and to ask help for her." He smiled. "For Ida at least it's gone better than we hoped. Your infirmarian has given her something that seems be easing the melancholy. I think she said something about borage? Would that be it?"

"Very likely."

"Besides, it seems Ida is with child again. That was what had her ill these past three months. But Coll isn't going to tell her that until he has her safely home again. So," Breredon shrugged, still smiling, "however it goes with my business here, it's been to the good for them."

"About your 'business' here."

Breredon's smile left him. "Ah. That."

"That," Frevisse agreed.

"I do owe you—your priory and St. Frideswide—my apology."

"You do. Both for lying to us and for what you meant to do."

He admitted that with another slight bow of his head but said, "Still, I refused to steal her out of here on Easter day, which she first demanded of me. That should count something in my favor."

Frevisse immediately saw how Sister Cecely would have purposed that, thinking they would all be too deep into the day to keep close watch on her. She had not counted on Domina Elisabeth taking her in charge. Even had Breredon agreed, there would have been no chance of Cecely's escaping the prioress' keeping, but neither she nor Breredon had known that when he refused her, and Frevisse asked bluntly, "Why didn't you help her away then, as she wanted?"

"On Easter?" Breredon's surprise was open. "I'd not do such a thing on that holy of a day."

Frevisse held back from asking why he thought *any* day was acceptable for helping an apostate nun escape into sin again, because she thought she could guess his reason well enough—that if the only way to some worldly gain was through a spiritual wrong, he was willing to it. Or maybe he simply thought that Sister Cecely was so far gone into sin that he would be hardly adding to it by helping her away, and that whatever sin he did in doing it, he could be rid of later by some manner of payment to his priest or church.

As if a man's dealings between himself and God were a merchant's matter of debt and payment.

Was it so hard to remember whom Christ had driven from the temple, and why?

But all that was not to the present point, and she asked curtly, "To where were you to steal her away?"

"Simply out of here. When I had her well away, then I was to pay her a goodly sum of money and she would hand Neddie over to me with the deed to his manor and warrant to have him in ward and the right of his marriage, and that would be that. What she meant to do afterward she never said."

So much for Sister Cecely's desperate claim to care for her son above all things. If Breredon said true, she had meant to sell the child like merchandise for the sake of her own ends. But, "Did she ever say why she came back here, of all places she might have run to?" Frevisse asked. She meant to ask that of Sister Cecely, too, no more trusting her answer than she meant to trust Breredon's but hoping that, together, their answers might tell enough.

Not that Breredon's answer amounted to much. He made a vague gesture with hands and head and said, "We needed somewhere to meet that wasn't too near to Wymondham for any search to cross our path. Somewhere no search would think to come, some place well out of the way but somewhere we'd be sure of finding each other and at the same time somewhere she and Neddie would be safe until I came. She said the Rowcliffes would never know to look for her here." His voice took on a bitter edge. "Fool of a woman."

Frevisse did not trouble to tell him that, for all Sister Cecely had known, the Rowcliffes had never heard of St. Frideswide's, should not have been able to find her here. Instead she said flatly, "It was not chance you were in talk with Sister Cecely in the church the other day."

"It was not."

"How did you know when she would be there?"

He smiled friendliwise. "That would be telling."

Frevisse snapped, not friendly at all, "Yes. It would be. And you should."

She waited, but although his smile faded under her stare, he said nothing, and after a long moment Frevisse said curtly, "Very well," turned sharply away from him and left, ignoring the bow he started toward her.

Her thought, as she passed through the hall, was that he would not say who had served between him and Sister Cecely because he still held hope of winning to his end. Let him hope. There was no chance of Sister Cecely being trusted enough now for her to have chance of escape, no matter who had helped her. Nor was anyone outside the nunnery going to lay hand on Edward until matters were far more clear than they presently were.

But poor Edward.

Whatever he had been told or come to understand of the use his mother had meant to make of him and whatever he knew or did not know about everything happening around him, he was the one innocent in all of this and yet likely to be the one who would suffer the most from it. Frevisse could hope he would be kept from more hurt than he already had, but she ruefully admitted to herself that hoping was all she could do for him. Or hoping while trying to do something toward curbing all the wrongs intended around him.

And there, she thought as she came out onto the guesthall steps and saw across the yard Jack Rowcliffe in talk with Elianor Lawsell and her mother beside the well, was maybe another wrong in the making. Young Jack's heed was all too openly on Elianor rather than her mother, and all too openly Mistress Lawsell was not minding that, was even drifting back a step, as if about to make excuse to leave them alone together; and Frevisse called, going down the steps, "Mistress Lawsell, may I ask the use of your daughter for a few moments?" Adding to Jack as she went toward them, "Your father wants to see Edward. I'm going to ask our prioress about it." And to Mistress Lawsell as she reached them, "If your daughter comes with me, she can bring word back to the guesthall when I've done and thereby spare me that much more walking."

A shadow of displeasure passed over Mistress Lawsell's face but her hesitation was minute before she answered, courteously enough, balked of any reason to refuse, "Of course. Elianor, make yourself useful to the nun."

Elianor made a slight curtsy of obedience to her mother, kept her eyes downturned from Jack who was bowing to her, and wordlessly followed Frevisse away. Only when they were into the cloister passageway, with Frevisse closing the door between them and the yard, did she give way and say with with open delight, "I've been praying for chance to be in here! Thank you!"

Level-voiced, not acknowledging the girl's pleasure, Frevisse said, "We'll go to Domina Elisabeth first. Her permission is needed before anything else is done."

Elianor accepted that with an eager nod and followed Frevisse along the passageway until, as they came from it into the cloister walk, her steps slowed. Glancing back, Frevisse saw she was looking all around, eyes bright. Not letting her linger, Frevisse started up the stairs to the prioress' parlor. Elianor was forced to follow but paused to look out the narrow window that gave the stairway light and a view over the roof of the guesthall to the world beyond the nunnery's walls, then had to hurry to catch up as Frevisse scratched at the prioress' closed door. Beyond it, Domina Elisabeth called, "Benedicite," and Frevisse went in, Elianor now crowding on her heels.

Frevisse had thought to find Domina Elisabeth at work at her desk beside the window, and indeed she was sitting there but with no sign she had been working. Instead, she had one hand idle in her lap and the other stretched out to the nunnery cat presently curled and comfortable on the window seat beside her. She looked with surprise at Elianor sinking in a floor-deep curtsy and then at Frevisse. Frevisse had reported in chapter what had passed between her and Elianor in the church; Domina Elisabeth had to know what was coming, but if that was why her look at Frevisse was somewhat pleading, almost as if asking to be spared this just now, Frevisse saw no way to help her. Talk with the girl and then her mother would have to come sooner or later. Best to start now and have it done, she thought, and perhaps Domina Elisabeth did, too, because she said graciously enough as the girl straightened, "I've meant to speak with your mother and you, now that matters have eased a little with Easter's passing."

"I've hoped to speak with you, too, my lady," Elianor said eagerly.

First, though, there was the matter of Rowcliffe's demand about Edward, and Frevisse told it, then added her outward reason for bringing Elianor, saying at the end, "I thought, too, it would give her the needed chance to talk with you."

"Of course," said Domina Elisabeth steadily. "As for Master Rowcliffe's desire to see the child, I think it should be Edward's choice, not his mother's. Ask Edward his desire in this and use your own judgment on it thereafter."

"I think Edward should go no farther than the church," Frevisse said.

Domina Elisabeth nodded agreement to that. "It might be well to have Father Henry there, too, that the Rowcliffes understand we'll have no tolerance of trouble."

"Yes, my lady," Frevisse said, with the thought that Father Henry's broad shoulders together with the authority of his priesthood would probably be sufficient to keep Rowcliffe from attempting anything foolish, should Rowcliffe have anything foolish in mind.

Domina Elisabeth gestured for Elianor to sit on the window seat near her and said, "Let us talk now, since we have this chance."

Frevisse willingly took that for dismissal, made curtsy, and left.

To reach Mistress Petham's chamber, she had to go down to the cloister walk again. Passing along it, she passed Sister Thomasine sitting her turn at guard outside the guest parlor where, for the sake of better light and air, the door presently stood open, and Frevisse had glimpse of Sister Cecely pacing in the small room's shadows. Sister Cecely had been a restless, unhappy girl here. Now she was a restless, unhappy woman. Was she simply that way always, inside the nunnery and out, or only here in St. Frideswide's, Frevisse wondered as she went up the stairs to Mistress Petham's chamber. However it had been for Sister Cecely, much of it had come by way of her own choosing, but Edward had had no choice in anything, and Frevisse inwardly admitted she was interested in how he would take this offer of chance to see his near kin again.

In the moment before she knocked at the frame of the open door, she saw him sitting cross-legged on the end of Mistress Petham's bed, reading aloud with somewhat labored slowness from a book laid open on his lap while Mistress Petham lay against her pillows, watching him with a kindly smile. When Frevisse knocked, he broke off, and they both looked toward her, Mistress Petham's smile changing to welcome but Edward's ease gone to wariness even before Frevisse said why she had come; and when she had told him, he stayed unmoving and unanswering, staring at her, much like a small animal gone frozen-still in the hope a passing hawk will fail to see it, until Mistress Petham prompted, "Edward? Do you want to see your cousin?"

Edward flinched a look toward her, then back at Frevisse, and hardly above a whisper, asked, "What does my mother say?"

"She's not been asked," Frevisse said, carefully quiet. "This is for you to say. No one else."

Edward ducked his head over the book still open on his lap. "I don't want to see him."

Frevisse could not tell whether that was from fear of John Rowcliffe or because he knew his mother would not want it. Trying for more answer, she asked, "Is there someone you would rather see instead?"

This time Edward's answer was a whisper that neither she nor Mistress Petham heard, and Mistress Petham leaned forward and asked, "What, Edward? Who is it you'd rather see?"

Edward did not raise his head, only his voice a little. "My father."

That silenced both women for a long moment, until Frevisse said very gently, "You know your cousins Symond and Jack are here. Would you like to see either of them instead of Master Rowcliffe?"

They waited again, until finally Mistress Petham said, "Edward?" and he lifted his head a little to say to Frevisse, "Jack."

She smiled at him. "Then you shall. Jack and no one else."

Someone began to ring the cloister bell, calling to the morning's Office of Tierce, and she went instantly silent and bowed her head in farewell to Mistress Petham. Mistress Petham bowed her head in return while holding out her hand to Edward. "Come," she said. "Let's follow Dame Frevisse to the church."

Chapter 15

itting on the bench, her back against the wall, Cecely scuffled her bare feet in the loose rushes covering the guest parlor's floor and stared at the room's far wall. It wasn't even that far a wall. A few yards away, no more, and the other walls hardly farther off on either side. It was a small room, a hateful room. A prison room. Just as it always had been. She hated it now the same way she had hated it when she was a nun here and had feared it was as near as she would ever come to the outside world again. Even then, she had only been allowed in here when she had a visitor or visitors, and because those had almost always been kin of one sort or another, Johane had almost always been with her here because they shared so many kindred that a visitor to one of them had usually been a visitor to them both.

Johane had used to laugh that they came in hope some of the nunnery's piety would wear off on them. Now did Johane even *remember* how to laugh anymore? Or had that been worn out of her along with every other memory of what pleasure life could be?

In those whiles of visitors, there had been talk and something to eat and drink besides the nunnery's usual dull fare, so that for that little while it would hardly matter that the room was small and bare and miserable. But it *was* small and bare and miserable, and she had been in it since yesterday with nothing to do but pace its little space or sit and stare at the bare walls, the ugly rafters, the dry rushes, or else try to sleep and mostly fail to do so. At least they had brought down the miserable mattress and pillow from her bed in the dorter, even if they'd only put them on the floor in the corner, and the door still stood open, but probably only to give her light enough to read the breviary Domina Elisabeth had given to her.

"Use it," the prioress had said coldly yesterday. "Look into your heart and see the wrong you've done to God and yourself. At least begin the search to find your way back to God's love."

Cecely had nearly spat at her feet.

They made her want to scream, these women. They had found nothing better to do with their lives than shut themselves up in here to die before they were dead. What did they know of love or anything else? *She* had had love. *She* knew everything they did not, and one of the things she knew was how useless God's "love" was when she was lonely or frightened or in need of a man's warmth. God's "love" and God's "care" and God's "comfort." Where were they? What use were they? It hadn't been God there in her bed at night when she put out a hand, needing someone. It hadn't been God who had laughed with her and pleasured her and made life bright around her. It had been Guy.

And where had God been when Guy died? If God "loved" and "cared" and "comforted," where had he been then?

Oh, they all had answers. The priest at home had had answers, and if she asked these women here, they'd have answers. But their answers were only words. Words weren't Guy's arms around her, holding her warm and safe. Words weren't what she wanted. What she wanted was Guy holding her against the miseries of this awful place.

Except she wouldn't be here if God hadn't taken Guy from her. He had taken Guy, and what use was his "love" and "care" when she ached for someone to be holding her? God was no use for that. There was no one to hold her, no one to put their arms around her and make her feel safe. She was alone and no words about God's "love" and "care" were going to change *that*.

Angrily needing to destroy something, she twisted at the skirt of her hated black gown. She wanted the pleasure there would be in tearing the ugly thing into rags. That would show these women what she thought of them and their "penance." But the wool's strength defeated her, had been defeating her for hours. She couldn't tear it with her bare hands and there was nothing else to use here. Even the water she was given with her bread came in a wooden cup. If it had been pottery she would have broken it and used the edge to cut with. Without even that, she was left with nothing, and she pitched to her feet and started the pacing that was her only other occupation. The few yards forward that was all the room allowed, and then around the table and around the table and around the table.

Someone started to ring the cloister bell for whatever Office was next in the dreary day. The nun sitting guard on a stool just outside the parlor's open doorway stood up, and Cecely froze, tense and staring at the woman's back. Even knowing she had no hope of going far, stripped as she was of everything except the coarse black gown, she still had the urge to run. Just let them give her any chance at all and see how fast and far she'd go!

But the nun stayed where she was. Whichever nun she was. Cecely had been unable to tell. From behind they were simply black-clothed shapes of somewhat different heights. How did they bear it?

The long skirts and soft-soled shoes of other nuns hushed along the cloister walk's stone paving, going toward the church from whatever tasks they had been at, and finally the nun outside the door went, too, but only because a servant had replaced her, some aproned woman from the kitchen.

Not Alson. Still not Alson.

Cecely dropped heavily onto the bench again. She had prayed last night for Alson to be the servant left to sleep outside the closed door, but it had been some other woman, who had snored and grunted when she turned over and been as much at fault for keeping Cecely awake as the thin mattress and the hard floor under it had been.

So she had prayed for it to be Alson sometime today but still it was not. So much for prayers.

But sooner or later Alson would have her turn. There weren't that many servants in the cloister. Which Office was this anyway? Sext? Were they that far through the day yet? Maybe it was only Tierce. Along with everything else, the day was overcast, giving no shadows sliding along the cloister walk by which to tell the time. There were only the Offices to break the day's long tediousness into worthless pieces.

But she was not yet reduced to reading or even opening the breviary she had been given. Not by a long way was she come to that. In truth, she had long since shoved the book angrily off the table and kicked it away somewhere among the rushes. Did Domina Elisabeth truly think that, now she was spared sitting through the Offices in the choir, she was going to do them here and alone?

She stood up abruptly from the bench. Was she hearing

something happening in the guesthall yard? She grabbed up the joint stool, set it under the room's single, small window high in the outer wall, and stood on it, not in hope of seeing out—she already knew the window was too small and high for sight of more than the ridge of the guesthall roof and a bit of sky—but to hear better what was happening. It was beyond hope that the Rowcliffes would take their rotten selves away, but surely Master Breredon wouldn't desert her. They couldn't have forced him to leave, could they? He wanted that manor and Neddie too much.

Or was it someone arriving? As bad as Master Breredon leaving would be someone from the abbot arriving.

Hooking her fingers over the windowsill, she pulled herself higher on her toes, straining to see out despite she knew it was no use.

It was all supposed to have been simpler than this. How had John found her out? He wasn't supposed even to know she had ever been a nun. If he hadn't come, everything would have all been the way she had planned it to be. Master Breredon would have fetched her and Neddie away and given her the promised money for Neddie's wardship and marriage, and with Neddie safe, she would have been on her way to somewhere. London, she thought. No one could have found her there among so many people. Or maybe Bristol, clear away to the other side of the country, if she'd heard a-right. Somewhere, anyway, with no way for the Rowcliffes to pick up her trail and follow her. That was how it was all supposed to have gone. Now they had spoiled it all by finding her.

Whatever was happening in the yard, it was not much. She could hear a cart's wheels on the cobbles, so it was not anyone riding in or riding out and couldn't be Master Breredon or the Rowcliffes.

She stepped down from the stool, shoved it away with her foot so it fell over with a satisfying thud, and went back to the bench, glaring at the back of the servant sitting like a lump outside the door. Her prayer for Alson to be there was just another prayer unanswered. These fools of nuns lived believing that cold prayers mattered. Let them. *She* had had Guy, and if she could have any prayer at all answered, it would be to have him back and everything the way it had been. But that was another prayer that God would only answer with his great, unmerciful *No*.

Whatever the Office had been, it ended. Nuns went quiet-footed along the cloister walk again, some of them talking in low voices that paused as they passed her door. Did they think they would be defiled if she so much as heard their voices? They were talking about her, surely. Let them. She didn't care what they said. Let them say whatever they wanted to say about her.

She stood up and took the two steps from the bench to the doorway, keeping enough aside that she could hear without being readily seen, but the nuns were all past. No one had come to relieve the servant, though, and Cecely lingered because there might be others who would come talking.

Yes. Here came slow footsteps and a woman saying something.

Except it was not a nun who answered her but Neddie. Neddie's dear little voice. Someone was bringing him right past her door, and she could not help herself. She darted out and there he was, walking with that Mistress Petham holding his hand, and before the servant could even exclaim at her, she had snatched Neddie to herself, fallen to her knees, and clutched him close. For a startled moment he seemed almost to pull back from her. Then he flung his arms around her neck and clung to her in return, and she whispered in his ear, "Do you still have it all safe and hidden?"

His head moved against hers in the smallest of nods. She kissed him. Her dear, warm, clever little boy. She would have smothered him with more kisses except someone had her by one arm, was pulling her to her feet, while Mistress Petham laid a hand on Neddie's shoulder, drawing him back from her. Poor, brave little boy, he didn't even cry out or struggle. He just stared up at her one last moment with large, frightened eyes, and then Mistress Petham was hurrying him away along the walk, and Cecely was being turned around to face a very angry Domina Elisabeth saying at her, "You can't obey even the simple order to stay in that room. Have you no sense at all?"

Her hold on Cecely's arm was hard and hurting, and behind her was Father Henry, not doing anything to stop her, and Cecely wrenched free, took a step back, and flared out with matching anger at both of them, "He's my son! He's all that's left of everything I had!" Tears of rage and grief burned her eyes. "God took all my others and then their father and now you want to keep even Neddie from me!"

Domina Elisabeth did not try to take hold on her again, instead took a step back from her as Father Henry came forward, saying, "Mind yourself, sister, and thank God for his mercy instead of blaming him. It could have been you who died, still in your sin, instead of your children in their innocence. They were spared the sins of the world. You've been spared to make good your sin."

Cecely's breast heaved as she tried for air enough to answer that arrogance and ended by turning her fury on Domina Elisabeth again with, "Why was Neddie in the church at all? You're supposed to be protecting him, but you let him in the church where anyone could snatch him! John Rowcliffe could grab him from there and there'd be nothing you could do! Who'd stop him? Any of you?" She rounded on Father Henry in raging scorn. "You?"

Like everyone and everything else in this place, the priest had grown older in the years she had been gone. When she had tried, all those years ago, to tell him what she was suffering, he had only told her she must endure in patience and pray for God's grace. From anything he had said to her since her return, he was grown no wiser. He had even tried to tell her of his guilt at having failed her all those years ago. He said he had been bearing the burden of it ever since. Was she supposed to care? Now he was saying, "What if Domina Elisabeth agreed to give you leave to attend the Offices again, would . . ."

Together she and Domina Elisabeth said back at him, "No!"

And with Father Henry startled into silence, Domina Elisabeth said at her, "Get back into that room. If ever you step over its threshold again without my leave, I'll have you tied to keep you there, I swear it!"

Chapter 16

Frevisse wondered angrily why Mistress Petham had not gone—or at least sent Edward—the long way around the cloister walk to avoid just what his mother had done. But then who would think Sister Cecely was such a fool?

Impatiently, Frevisse answered that question for herself. Anyone who knew her—that was who would think Sister Cecely was such a fool!

At the same time, she knew what made her angrier was how frightened Edward had been. Whatever else he might have felt when his mother grabbed him, what had shown on his face was fear. Of what? His mother? Certainly he had not resisted being taken from her or looked back as Mistress Petham led him away. And anyway, even if he was not frightened *by* his mother, he was frightened *because* of her, and it was grievously unfair that, already in grief for his father, he had to be frightened, too, for whatever reason.

Abbot Gilberd's man could not come soon enough to take all of this out of here and away into Abbot Gilberd's hands.

But her own duties went on, and returning to the guesthall, she sent the servant Tom to tell Father Henry of what was toward and ask him to meet her shortly in the church. She took on herself the task of telling Rowcliffe that Edward would rather see Jack than him.

Rowcliffe accepted that better than she had thought he would, saying with a shrug, "If that's what he wants, so be it. All we want is to know for a certainty how he is. Jack can do that as well as I can."

So it was with Jack she crossed the yard toward the church, explaining as they went why Elianor had not brought word as intended. Tom overtook them on the way, to say Father Henry would be there shortly, and she left Jack to go by himself into the church by its west door while she went through the cloister door to fetch Edward.

He was waiting in Mistress Petham's chamber, standing beside her bed where she was lying down again. His hand was in hers, and he looked freshly face-washed, with hair newly combed and tunic carefully straightened. Frevisse held out her hand to him and said, "Your cousin Jack is waiting to see you."

Edward let go of Mistress Petham, took her hand instead, and left the chamber with at least outward willingness. For safety's sake, they went the long way around the cloister walk, Frevisse keeping hold on him until they were in the church, only letting him go when she turned back to close the door behind them.

When she turned around, he had left her, was running with a quick patter of feet past the rood screen and down the nave to where Jack Rowcliffe now stood with Father Henry. Jack stepped forward to meet him, arms held out, and Edward flung himself into his cousin's hold. Jack swung him up and around in a glad circle, and Edward laughed aloud. Nor did Jack put him down afterward but carried him aside and sat them both down on the stone bench along the wall, Edward on his knee, one of his arms around Edward and one of Edward's around him.

Father Henry stayed where he was, beaming at them. Frevisse felt obliged to go closer, to hear what was said between them, not wanting to find out later that Jack had used the chance to persuade Edward to leaving the cloister or some other foolish thing. They were only talking of home, though, with Jack telling Edward that his little mare was safely at Rowcliffe's stable. "She's right there with my old girl Damsel," Jack said. "I led her over myself. After all, I couldn't ride her." He stuck out his long legs and wiggled them. Edward laughed. Jack's voice leveled and went kind. "I have your father's chest, too. The dagger is there that's to be yours when you're older. And his red leather belt with the silver-gilt buckle and studs. And the prayer book with the pictures. You remember?"

"Of course I remember," Edward said indignantly. "I'm not a baby."

Frevisse guessed that, in truth, he remembered all too well. Tears had swollen into his eyes with the pain of his remembering, and Jack put both arms around him and held him close, tears suddenly in his own eyes, too, as he said, "Of course you remember. It's very hard to have him gone, isn't it?"

With his face now buried against Jack's shoulder to hide the falling tears, Edward nodded.

"But do you remember," Jack asked, his voice lightening, "the time when he went up on the roof to see how the thatchers were getting on? And what happened?"

Edward remembered. His shoulders shook but when he lifted his head, it was laughter on his face along with the tears. "He slid right off! He slid off into their pile of straw!"

Frevisse turned her back to them. She would go on listening but they did not need her watching them. Jack Rowcliffe meant Edward no harm. She was glad to see there was someone among his kin who seemed to like Edward for Edward's own sake and that somewhere beyond Edward's grief there was still a little boy who could be happy, the way he had been happy in the orchard with Dame Amicia and Sister Helen, the way he was happy here with a trusted cousin. Come to it, he seemed to be content with Mistress Petham, too.

Was it only his mother who brought that stiff silence on him?

Frevisse found that easy enough to believe. She also found it regrettable how readily she believed ill of Sister Cecely. Even if Sister Cecely was a fool, there had to be good somewhere in the woman, buried though it might be under the heavy layers of her betrayals and lies. Frevisse's prayers for her would be the better, would be more than merely rote, if she could just find even a glimmer of that good.

The trouble was that she did not much feel like looking for any glimmer, and that was a regrettable thing to admit.

She gave Edward and his cousin as much time together as she could before she turned back to them and said, "Sext will be soon. I must needs return Edward to Mistress Petham now."

Jack slid Edward to the floor, both of them standing up unwillingly. Jack freed his hand from Edward's tight hold, put both his hands on Edward's shoulders, and bent to kiss the top of the boy's head, then said, "This won't go on forever, Edward. We just have to be brave about it. This Mistress Petham, she's good to you?"

Edward nodded. "She's helping me with my reading," he said, back to his usual half-whisper.

"Oh-oh," said Jack. "You'll be better than me at it if you keep that up."

Edward looked up at him with a sudden return to laughter. "That won't be hard, the way you read."

Jack made a satisfactory sound of outrage and rumpled his hair. Frevisse held out her hand, and dropping his gaze to the floor, Edward took it. Over his bowed head, Frevisse said to Jack, "If you would be so good as to wait here, I'd speak to you after Edward is safely back to Mistress Petham."

"As you will, my lady," Jack said with a slight bow.

Frevisse walked Edward the long way around the cloister again and to the foot of the stairs to Mistress Petham's chamber, watched him go up them and safely beyond the door at the top, then wondered why "safely" had come to mind. But the answer to that was easy enough. There were too many people—beginning with his own mother—with interest not so much in Edward himself but in what profit he could bring them, including Jack's father, if not Jack. Edward should be safe enough here in the cloister, but Frevisse did not want to chance finding by the hard way she was wrong about that.

As she turned to circle the cloister walk again, Dame Perpetua joined her, going the same way, and said, nodding ahead, "This is become such a bother. I'm to take Alson's place guarding Cecely. As if I've no work of my own to do."

Frevisse looked ahead, was surprised to see Alson sitting on a stool beside the guest parlor, and said, "It was Malde before. And where's Dame Thomasine? Shouldn't she be there now?"

"Yes," Dame Perpetua said disgustedly. "But Dame Claire needed her help with some medicine she's brewing in the infirmary. An ointment and poultice for the man who was hurt yesterday, I think."

"But where's Dame Johane?"

"Taking her turn at duty in the kitchen, trying to better

her skill at making pastry. I didn't want to let her off it, so I shifted Alson so Dame Claire could have Dame Thomasine who has the next best skill with herbs. But now Alson is needed in the kitchen to cut vegetables, being better with a knife than I am anymore." Dame Perpetua held up her right hand, where the arthritics that had come on her in the past few years were bending two of her fingers awry. "So I'm taking Alson's place for the while." Dame Perpetua sighed. She was not enjoying being presently cellerar and in charge of the kitchen and meals and the necessary servants, and plainly Sister Cecely was making her work no easier.

Frevisse made sympathetic sounds while, ahead, Alson stood up as they came and bobbed a curtsy. Dame Perpetua made a nod at the doorway and asked, "How does she?"

"She's crying, poor lady. She's frighted what those men mean to do to her and to her boy," Alson answered, sounding worried.

"It's Abbot Gilberd she'd best be frightened of," said Frevisse.

"You can return to the kitchen now, Alson," Dame Perpetua directed. "I'll take your place for the while."

Alson ducked her head in another bobbed curtsy and hurried off as if glad to be away. Frevisse gave Dame Perpetua a nod of her own and went on her way to the church where she was not pleased to find Jack Rowcliffe in talk with Elianor Lawsell in the middle of the nave. The girl did not seem pleased either, was backing away from him toward the rood screen, and although he was not threateningly close to her, he was undeniably following her, intent on whatever he was saying to her. At sight of Frevisse, though, he stopped still, and Elianor swung around with what looked to Frevisse like relief. As Frevisse went toward them, Jack stayed where he was while Elianor hesitated until Frevisse said, "I've come to speak with him alone, by your leave." Elianor answered with a bright smile, gave Frevisse a hurried curtsy, and went on up the nave, leaving Jack to her.

He gave a bow as Frevisse reached him and said courteously, "You had something more to say to me, my lady?"

Letting go by the matter of Elianor, she answered, "You seem to have been a good friend of Edward's father. I want to ask you about him."

"About Guy? We were friends, yes," he said willingly. "He and George and I. They treated me as somewhat the younger brother neither of them had." Jack's face and voice tightened, controlling apparent grief as he added, "The world seems emptier without them."

"What of Guy's marriage? How did that seem to you?"

"His marriage that wasn't a marriage?" Jack said bitterly. "Guy could be a true idiot sometimes. He always was where Cecely came into it, that's sure. We used to jibe at him for it."

"He never gave any sign of the truth?"

"Never. Though I think that of late—"

He stopped.

"Of late?" Frevisse asked.

Jack sighed and said, as if resigned to the thought, "I think this past year or so he had begun to weary of her ways. She always wanted every bit of him, begrudged him any moment he wasn't with her. I think he went on this trading voyage with George just to be away from her for a time."

"Do you know why he told the truth about her to Symond Hewet?"

"Maybe because he wasn't able to keep it to himself any longer? Maybe because if anything happened to him, someone would know and be better able to deal with her? If Symond knows why, he hasn't said. You'll have to ask him." Jack shook his head as if to shake understanding of it all into his thoughts. "If he'd just said nothing, if he had just kept shut about it . . ."

". . . she could have gone on living in the lie she and Guy had made," Frevisse interrupted sharply.

Jack gave a wry twist of his mouth, acknowledging that, but then burst out, "But how could he have done it to Edward? It's Edward who's being most hurt by it!"

"Given the way Sister Cecely is," Frevisse returned, "it may be Edward who's most saved by it, too, if it frees him from his mother."

Jack looked startled at that thought. Leaving him to be startled, she thanked him and went back up the nave. She would have preferred to escape beyond the rood screen, to the cloister's somewhat-quiet, but there was no hope of pretending Elianor Lawsell was not there, turning around as Frevisse neared her.

Looking down the nave to where the west door was just thudding shut behind Jack, then back to Frevisse, she said somewhat desperately, "Domina Elisabeth sees no bar to my becoming a nun here. But she wouldn't say *when*."

"There's your family to be thought about," Frevisse offered. "It's best if they can be reconciled to it first. If you . . ."

"I doubt my mother will ever be reconciled to it! What then?"

"*If*," Frevisse repeated firmly, "you practice patience now, you'll have begun to learn one of a nun's first lessons."

Elianor opened her mouth to continue with plea or passion, but stopped, stared at Frevisse, then very carefully closed her mouth, bowed her head, and said meekly, "Yes, my lady."

Frevisse fought the smile trying at the corners of her mouth and kept it from her voice as she said mildly, "Jack Rowcliffe is showing inclination to you."

Despite her head was still humbly bowed, Elianor said scornfully, "That's because there's no one else here for him to incline to."

"He's a comely enough young man and of good family and well-mannered," Frevisse suggested.

Elianor raised her head sharply. "And that's supposed to be enough, isn't it?" she said hotly. "*He* surely thinks it's enough." She made an impatient gesture with both hands. "Why do they think we're such idiots? Why do they think we should give up everything just for the sake of lust? Because lust is what it mostly is, no matter how much anyone throws the word 'love' around!"

Sternly, Frevisse said, "There are more kinds of love than one. A nun chooses to love beyond the world and the body, but that doesn't gain her the right to despise all other loves there are." She might pity them, Frevisse added silently to herself, but for the sake of her own soul she should never despise them. But that was more lesson than Elianor needed just now, and Frevisse went on, "Rather than spending effort in scorn of others, you should be looking inward at yourself, searching your own love and learning needed patience while you wait to have your will."

"Why?" Elianor burst out. "Why should I be patient when what I want is so very right?"

"Because patience," Frevisse said, sternly meeting the girl's gaze, "can make the person you're being patient at very, very irked."

She watched as that thought took hold on the girl, first with the beginning of a frown, then with dawning delight and a spreading smile as Elianor began to understand the possibilities.

Having given her that to think on, Frevisse made a slight bow of the head to her and escaped into the choir.

No matter what she had said to Elianor, her true thought was that it would be good to have the girl for novice as soon as might be. She seemed to have the true longing that would readily take deep root if it were carefully tended. The fierceness would need quieting, of course. Not quenched, but quieted before it burned itself out with its very strength. Fierceness in itself was not ill, but there was need to contain and guide it, so that it burned away the dross of body and spirit to leave only the soul's shining.

Or as much shining as the soul could do while still held in the world by the body.

With surely very little time until the bell would ring for the next Office, she went to her choir stall and knelt there, her forehead resting on her clasped hands. She could remember how carefully, all those years ago, Domina Edith had guided *her* fierceness, so that instead of blazing up and burning out, it had become a banked fire deep inside her, burning onward, strong and mostly steady through the years. Out of that memory, she made a prayer that Elianor, if her calling was true, might be guided as she had been, into the deep, high, wide places of the soul where true love and true freedom were.

Chapter 17

hrough Easter Week—the beginning of Paschaltide—the nuns' ordinary tasks were kept as slight as might be, to give rest from the rigors of Holy Week and Easter and time for their own prayers outside the Offices, but thus far in the week Frevisse had not found much chance for either rest or her own prayers, aside from that brief while before Tierce this morning. So when a pause in her duties came early in the afternoon, she returned to the church, somewhat hurrying in hope she could reach the shelter of her stall in the choir before someone needed her for something.

She succeeded, was a little surprised but nothing more to find no one else there except Sister Helen, huddled down on her knees in front of her own seat. The first sharp stab of wariness only came as the girl looked up at her, face pale and strained, and pleaded, "Please, will you talk with me?"

Frevisse's first urge was to tell the girl it was to Domina Elisabeth she should talk, that it was the prioress' place to comfort and guide St. Frideswide's nuns, but despite an inward quailing, she found herself saying evenly, "Assuredly," and came to sit in the stall beside her while Sister Helen shifted backward from her knees onto the narrow wooden seat of her own stall.

There, she seemed to lose whatever she had wanted to say. She sat looking down at her hands twisting together in her lap, bit her lower lip for a moment, looked sideways to Frevisse, looked back to her hands, and only finally brought herself to whisper, "I'm frightened."

That was so far from anything Frevisse had thought to hear that she said blankly, "What?"

"It's Sister Cecely," Sister Helen said desperately.

It would be, thought Frevisse.

"What if . . ." Sister Helen faltered. "She took her final vows and yet she . . . What if I . . ."

"Become as faithless as she did?" Frevisse said bluntly. "That you've the good sense to fear it gives good hope you won't."

"But what if . . ." Sister Helen turned her head and looked full at Frevisse, despair naked on her face, and desperately and in a rush, she said, "It's not her. Not really. It's that I don't feel what I felt when I first came here. Not always. Sometimes I don't feel it at all. Sometimes there's no joy in anything. Sometimes I have to drag myself to Offices, they're such a drudge. Sometimes I can hardly pray at all. I have to force myself. That can't be right!"

"Right or not, it comes to all of us," Frevisse said.

Sister Helen's eyes widened. "Even to you? Even now?"

Frevisse did not understand the "even to you" and let it pass, answering instead, very firmly, "Even now. The only

difference between what you're suffering and what I sometimes suffer is that now I know that sooner or later I'll come
out the far side of it, into the joy again."

"You do? Will I?" Sister Helen asked with mingled hope
and hopelessness.

"You will if you have the courage to go on despite the
darkness and even despair that comes," Frevisse said steadily,
hoping to steady her. "They do come. The darkness and the
despair. And more than once, I promise you. But it's not
what you're feeling at the moment that will make the difference. The difference lies in your willingness to go on despite
of it."

"What if I can't go on?"

"The only thing that can stop you going on is your choice
to turn aside. Or else death. If it's Sister Cecely you're thinking of, she turned aside. That will be the great difference
between you. Or the great likeness," she added in all fairness.

Sister Helen stared at her. Frevisse stared back, not
knowing what else to say, until finally Sister Helen said,
"Thank you," looked away, slipped forward onto her knees
again, and bowed her head onto her clasped hands resting
on the breviary there.

Frevisse's own urge to pray was gone, but she rose and
went quietly to her place, sat, closed her eyes, bowed her
head over her hands resting together on her lap, and wondered whether she had done well. By rights she should have
sent the girl to Domina Elisabeth with her doubts and fears.
She knew that. Sister Helen had turned to her simply because she was there, and she had answered the girl's fear simply because she had an answer, that was all. But why hadn't
Sister Helen gone to Domina Elisabeth with her doubts?
Why hadn't Frevisse sent her there?

And yesterday there had been Dame Johane, equally
worried and questioning, again someone Frevisse should
maybe have sent to Domina Elisabeth.

This was Sister Cecely's doing, Frevisse thought bitterly. Had the woman ever been anything but troublesome? That's what she had been when trying to be a nun here, had made more trouble by running off, then had been a troubling—but fading—memory.

That had been Sister Cecely at her best—as a fading memory. Now, by returning, she was making trouble all over again, not least by this stirring of doubts and unease among the younger nuns. Not that unease and doubts need be bad. Frevisse had had her full share of both over the years and knew now that, fairly faced and fully dealt with, they had strengthened her in ways she would not have been without them. Her unease and doubts and the need to deal with them had deepened and widened her faith.

Unfortunately, knowing that did not necessarily make either unease or doubts any easier to bear when they came.

And not everyone came out the far side of them. However passing the trouble of Sister Cecely was—and it *would* pass—there was no knowing yet what would come of the unease, the doubts, the fears she had stirred up—unease, doubts, and fears that might have come at one time or another, but instead were all come at once. And at a time when Domina Elisabeth seemed least ready to take on their burden and steady her nuns.

Frevisse shied from that last thought, then made herself look at it straightly because it had to be faced. In some unclear way, Domina Elisabeth had become remote of late. Lent's necessities seemed to have worn beyond the usual on her, leaving her deeply weary. To burden her just now with troubles beyond those come with Sister Cecely seemed unnecessarily unkind. Yet she had to be told. She was as bound by her vows as any of her nuns. It was her place, not Frevisse's, to comfort and guide them, and sooner or later Frevisse would have to answer for the wrong of usurping her place if she went on doing so.

Better, then, not to go on doing it. Better that Domina Elisabeth be told now and be done with it, Frevisse thought, and she quietly left the choir, trying to disturb Sister Helen as little as might be.

She carried her decision as far as the foot of the stairs to Domina Elisabeth's rooms and would have carried it up the stairs except Luce from the guesthall came hurrying down them. Suddenly confronted with each other, they both came to sudden stops, Luce saying, "Oh!" then bursting out, "I was just sent to find you! My lady wants you! Peter is come back from Abbot Gilberd. He'll be here tomorrow. The abbot. The abbot himself! Domina Elisabeth wants to see you!"

With hidden dismay and sinking heart, Frevisse thanked her and went on up the stairs. Domina Elisabeth met her in the doorway at their head, fretted and unsettled, exclaiming, "Come in! Luce told you. I heard her. What are we going to do? How can we be ready?"

Frevisse could have matched her for unsettled. To have one of Abbot Gilberd's officers here would have been one thing. As the abbot's man, he would have needed to be shown something of the courtesy due his master and St. Frideswide's could have done that well enough. To have Abbot Gilberd himself here was a far more difficult thing, and if giving way to alarm as open as Domina Elisabeth's would have done any good, Frevisse would have joined her in it. Since it would not, she said with an outward assurance that she inwardly lacked, "Very little needs to be done to be ready, my lady. Master Breredon will have to move into one of the lesser chambers. He can be shifted as soon as I say." And *that* would serve him rightly, she thought. She would likewise put fresh wariness of Abbot Gilberd into both him and the Rowcliffes, and that would be to the good, too. "There'll be time enough this afternoon to have the room cleaned and readied for my lord abbot."

Her steadiness had somewhat steadied Domina Elisabeth but, "What of food? What are we going to feed him?"

Frevisse refrained from saying, Let him eat what we eat, why should he eat better? Neither Domina Elisabeth nor Abbot Gilberd would see it that way, so more usefully, she offered, "Someone in the village should still have at least one ham they'll be willing to sell." She knew for a certainty that there were villagers who lived better than the nuns did. "Master Naylor can be sent to buy what he may. There'll have to be a lamb from the flock, no matter what. We still have honey and sufficient dried fruits, I think. Dame Perpetua will be best able to tell you what's to hand and what can be done with it. I think we've still a little white flour left." Domina Elisabeth seemed about to protest something— probably that none of that sounded enough—but Frevisse added very firmly, "Beyond that, why should my lord abbot think we live more richly than we do?"

That stopped whatever Domina Elisabeth had been about to say. She did not look so much reassured as too distracted to carry it further and said rather desperately, "Yes. We can only do what we can do. I'll leave the guesthall to you. Have Dame Perpetua come to me, please. Dame Juliana, too. The church will have to be readied."

"My lady," Frevisse said, made a curtsy, and left.

At least, with Easter just past, little would need doing in the church, but she suspected that Domina Elisabeth would nonetheless have them all scurrying from task to task from now until Abbot Gilberd arrived. Yet more trouble to be laid to Sister Cecely's account.

In the cloister walk again, she found that Luce's news had already spread; she was hardly away from the stairfoot when Dame Juliana and Dame Amicia passed her on their way to Domina Elisabeth without need for summons, and in the cloister's kitchen she found Dame Perpetua in the midst of laying a firm hand upon the flutter the news had caused there. Frevisse shared her thoughts on what was to be done about feeding the abbot, and Dame Perpetua agreed with her but said, "He'd better bring his own wine with him, though. Do we know how many men he's bringing with him?"

"It seems not. I would guess at least ten."

"Blessed Saint Frideswide. He'd better bring some food with him, too, then. Will you talk with Master Naylor or should I?"

"I will," said Frevisse. "This is going to fall mostly on the guesthall, after all."

"But feeding the abbot is going to fall mostly on me," Dame Perpetua said grimly. "He'll be dining with Domina Elisabeth in her chamber probably. I'd better see to our napery, too, I suppose."

Leaving Dame Perpetua to her share of the trouble, Frevisse went to the guesthall. Here old Ela was waiting for her just inside the door but blessedly not in any kind of fret or flutter, saying without the bother of any greeting, "I've already warned Master Breredon you'll be asking him to shift. You'd best send someone to the village to see what food is to be had there, and I'm going to need more help here, what with the abbot's men added to the lot we already have."

"Master Naylor will see to what can be had from the village. Hire who you need for help. Thank you for warning Master Breredon," Frevisse said but with a smile that old Ela matched. They understood each other. Between them, they would make all go well here—or someone else had better have good reason why it did not.

Master Breredon made no trouble over having to shift into one of the smaller chambers, cramped though he would be there with his two servants. At Frevisse's direct demand at him and then at the Rowcliffes, they all swore they would keep their quarrel quiet, abiding the abbot's arrival. Mistress Lawsell in her own chamber said she was content for herself and her daughter, unworried at it all. For Elianor, standing behind her mother, Frevisse said, "There is always the church. You can spend time there if the hall here becomes too busy for you. That might be best for Elianor, given your hope she becomes a nun."

"Yes. Of course," Mistress Lawsell said without convincing force, while Frevisse pretended not to see Elianor's smile.

Admitting to herself her cowardly desire to avoid whatever upheaval was going on in the cloister, Frevisse stayed busy at the guesthall as long as she could, only leaving when the bell summoned her to Vespers. After that the needs of supper, recreation's hour, and Compline filled the time until welcome bed. It was only in the morning after Prime and breakfast, as the nuns were on their way back to the church for Mass, that Luce came at them in the cloister walk, pale with sleeplessness and fear, exclaiming at Dame Claire, "It's Master Breredon! He's been sick all the last half of the night! Heaving and purging! Ela says you have to come. Come quick!"

Chapter 18

e looks like to die," Luce cried. "I swear he does! He won't stop heaving up, but there's nothing left in him to heave. Or go the other way either. He's been doing it for hours. It's terrible!"

Breaking away toward the infirmary, Dame Claire demanded, "Why didn't you come for me before this?" Adding, "Sister Johane, come with me."

"Ela didn't think it would last so long. He'd be sick and then he'd be done. That's what she thought. But he isn't." Luce scuttled a few steps after Dame Claire, then back to Frevisse, wringing her hands. "Ela says you have to come!"

"Of course," Frevisse said with far more outward calm than she felt inwardly. If this was some contagion broken out in the guesthall . . .

She looked to Domina Elisabeth for permission to forego Mass and, "Yes," Domina Elisabeth said. "Go. Go, of course." She pressed both her hands distractedly to her forehead below the edge of her wimple. "Why now? Why must this happen now?"

Having no answer to that and supposing none was expected, Frevisse made barely a curtsy and went around the cloister walk the other way from Dame Claire's, toward the outer door, Luce following her.

Outside the cloister, the morning was cool and fresh, with dawn colors still soft in the clear sky, though there was suggestion in the light wind of rain maybe not too far away. Inside the guesthall there was neither cool nor calm. The hall was shadowed, its air close, with a whiff of stinking sickness to it that told Frevisse more than she wanted to know of how bad Breredon's night had been. As she headed toward the chamber he had been given yesterday, she ordered at the nearest man—one of Rowcliffe's, as it happened—"It's morning outside. Open the shutters," but kept going without seeing if he obeyed.

Even if she had not known which of the lesser rooms opening off the hall Breredon had been given, she would have guessed it from Ela shuffling unhappily from foot to foot in its doorway. The night had not been good to Ela. She was more than ever bent and huddled in on her old body, her head cricked hard to one side so she could look up to Frevisse instead of only at her feet. More than that, she was the sickly pale of someone underslept and over-worked, and guilt panged in Frevisse, because she had done this to Ela, had willingly let Ela take the guesthall in charge again because it was so familiar and easy to work with her. But Ela was old, and while her mind was willing to much, her body was not; Breredon's illness looked to have served her almost as badly as it served him, and Frevisse said quickly, "How is it with him? Tell me, and then do you go to bed."

Time was that Ela would have scorned the latter part of that order; but then time was that it would not have been needed. Here and now she only ducked her head in an accepting nod to it while answering, "It was about halfway from Matins to dawn it took him. Maybe somewhat before. His man Coll came for me, said his master was taken with cramps in the belly, was in a cold sweat and likely to vomit. So up I got and came, and that's what he's been doing ever since. Only he's not thrown up for a time. He's maybe past the worst, but it's left him poorly and weak."

To Frevisse's eye it had left Ela poorly and weak, too, and she said, "Dame Claire will see to him from now, and I'll see to everything else here. Luce." She turned to the hovering woman. "See Ela to her bed and tend on her. Food. Drink. Another blanket or pillow if she wants. See she stays there until Dame Claire or I say otherwise."

It was sign of Ela's weariness that she made no complaint at that nor protested at all when Luce stooped to put a hand under her elbow and an arm around her to help her away. Only belatedly Frevisse asked, "Where's Tom?"

"Here, my lady," he said from Breredon's doorway.

In his own way, by rumpled hair, untucked shirt, and eyes red-rimmed with sleeplessness and worry, he showed as plainly as Ela did what a bad night it had been, but he was young and upright and hearty enough that he would take no lasting harm from it. What worried Frevisse was what he and the rest of them might take from Breredon, because if this was not something simply in the man's own belly, if it was something that could spread, the priory was in for a worse time than they presently had.

And Abbot Gilberd, almost here, would have to be warned away.

She wanted to join Domina Elisabeth in clutching her head and moaning, Why now? But she settled for asking Tom as she went forward, "How does he?" Then could see for herself as soon as she was in the room, with no need for Tom saying, "Not good, I'd guess."

The room stank of sickness, and Breredon lay curled on his side on the very edge of the bed, probably to be in ready reach of the basin on the floor near his head should the need come on him again. Just now he was lying quietly, eyes closed, but with a tautness to his stillness that said he was neither asleep nor at ease. He was pale-faced, too, his hair lank with old sweat while new sweat was beaded on his fore-head. The only bold thing left of the confident and prosper-ing man of yesterday was the black stubble of his beard against his pale flesh, and from where she stood near the bed his servant Ida pleaded, "Are you going to do something for him, my lady?"

Frevisse said, going no nearer, "Our infirmarian will soon be here," knowing there was nothing she could do for Brere-don except help Dame Claire. "Where's Coll?"

"Gone to wash out the other basin," Ida said.

"I just brought this one back," Tom offered, pointing to the one on the floor, to show he was not idle.

"He's still being sick, then?" Frevisse asked Ida.

The woman looked the least marked by the night, was neither strained with exhaustion like Ela nor disheveled like Tom nor gone dithering like Luce. She was openly worried, her apron was stained, and she had foregone her veil, her head covered by a simple cap tied under her up-bound hair, but she answered steadily enough, "It's not so often now. He was again a few minutes ago, but there was nothing come up. Only bile. I've asked some water be warmed so he can rinse his mouth."

"Anything you think he needs, ask for," Frevisse said, grateful for the woman's steadiness and even more grateful to hear Dame Claire in the hall behind her asking where the sick man was. Leaving the room, though, she saw Dame

Claire had come alone, carrying the box of medicines kept ready for need outside the cloister but without Dame Johane.

Before Frevisse could ask, Dame Claire said, "I thought better of her coming. On the chance it's contagious."

Frevisse accepted that with a nod and a deliberately calm face and left Dame Claire to her work. She was not free to leave the guesthall though. Far from it. The Rowcliffe father and son and their cousin Symond were standing on the other side of the hall, plainly waiting for her and surely with questions about just how ill Breredon was and with what, but they had to go on waiting because Mistress Lawsell was nearer and demanding as she closed on Frevisse, "What is it? What does he have? Is it plague? I want to leave. Elianor and I are leaving today, even if we have to walk to do it!"

Firmly Frevisse answered, "It doesn't have the look of any kind of plague. It's more likely an ague." And even if that was not the truth, even if Dame Claire determined it was one sort of plague or another, she would do all she could to keep the Lawsells here rather than let them take whatever it was with them to infect others. But that grievous need was not yet to hand, and still firmly calm, she went on, "We've had no sickness here for him to have caught, and his servants are untouched by whatever it is." So far, she silently added, while in the back of her mind she wondered sharply whether Peter could have brought something back with him from Northampton. But when would he ever have been near Breredon? And how could Breredon have sickened from it so quickly and no one else? No. This had to be something other than plague, surely, and she said with forced confidence, "Whatever it is, I think we're all safe from it. What we need to do is pray for him."

Fortunately, Mistress Lawsell preferred to be comforted. Mollified, she unflustered enough to say, "Well, we'll keep well away from him. Elianor and I. Well away."

"That would probably be for the best," Frevisse agreed. For Breredon as well as the Lawsells, she added silently.

John Rowcliffe's theme was different from Mistress Lawsell's. When Frevisse went to him, he said bluntly, angrily, "Breredon's feigning it. He's made himself sick, thinking we'll lower our guard against him."

"I doubt that," Frevisse returned, words clipped short with impatience.

"What you can doubt is that we'll lower our guard. You can tell him that. When is your abbot going to be here?"

"Sometime today is all I know. Now if you'll pardon me," she said, not caring whether she had his pardon or not, and left him with the barest jerk of her head in a nod of parting toward his son and cousin.

Jack, she noted, looked correctly worried, but what might have been the corner of a wry smile pulled at one corner of Symond's mouth as they copied Rowcliffe in slightly bowing their heads to her in return. What he might be smiling at she did not know and did not think about.

Father Henry must have made short work of the Mass and his opening blessing on the chapter meeting today. As she left the guesthall, he was coming from the cloister, and as they met in the yard's middle, he asked, "Am I needed?"

Understanding he meant for the last rites for a dying man, Frevisse said, "I don't know. Dame Claire is with him now. She'll say better than I can. Certainly he needs your prayers."

"He has them," Father Henry said and they went their separate ways, he to the guesthall, she into the cloister to the chapter meeting.

Whatever had been happening there, Domina Elisabeth broke it off to demand as she came into the room, "What does he have? Do we send to turn Abbot Gilberd back?"

"I don't know what it is," Frevisse said quietly. "Dame Claire will surely say."

Domina Elisabeth momentarily looked ready to protest that but then, with an open effort, steadied and returned to the day's business.

Frevisse, taking her place among the other nuns, found her worry about Breredon matched by worry about Domina Elisabeth. It had never been her way to be so easily, so openly unsettled by anything. She surely could not be worried her brother would blame her for either Sister Cecely's return or Breredon's illness. Abbot Gilberd had never been unreasonable or unfair. Even making his sister prioress here had not been unreasonable, and his choice had proved to the priory's good in the years since then.

No, Frevisse thought: Domina Elisabeth's worry had to be for her brother, for everyone here, should Breredon's illness be more than it seemed. St. Frideswide's had been fortunate in going untouched by plague and rarely troubled by any disease of any consequence in Frevisse's time.

They could only pray that was not about to change.

Fortunately for everyone's peace of mind, Dame Claire came just at the end of the chapter meeting with the welcome news that, "I judge something he ate or drank disagreed with him. It's not a fever or anything like."

"Poison!" Dame Amicia exclaimed with the delight of someone ready to be horrified.

"*Not* poison, I think," Dame Claire said quellingly.

"No reason then to forestall Abbot Gilberd," said Domina Elisabeth, openly relieved.

"None," Dame Claire said.

"Very good." Plainly freed by her relief, Domina Elisabeth made short end to the meeting, freeing them to their morning duties with her closing blessing, then saying to Dame Claire, "You and Dame Frevisse will want to talk over what it could have been that sickened him. We must needs be sure no one else falls ill of it."

That matched what Frevisse had intended, and she and

Dame Claire lingered while everyone else left except for Dame Johane who paused to ask hopefully, "Will you need me to help with tending him?"

"His two servants will see to him between whiles I go to him. No, I think you'll not be needed," Dame Claire said.

"Oh," said Dame Johane, not troubling to hide her disappointment. "I'd hoped to escape sitting watch on Sister Cecely."

"It would come tomorrow if you escaped it today," Dame Claire pointed out. "I'll bring you the herbal to study. You can look for Master Breredon's symptoms in it."

Dame Johane went, not looking much brightened by that, and Frevisse asked Dame Claire, "You think, then, it was indeed something he ate?"

"It's something that badly disagreed with him, that's all. I'm nearly certain of it. He's past the worst of it, but the worst was very bad, as you surely saw."

"*Could* he have been poisoned?"

Dame Claire looked at her with surprise. "Well, whatever he ate or drank was certainly poisonous to him, yes, but I'd doubt it was done of a purpose. Despite of Dame Amicia. Besides, what would he have had to eat or drink that was different from what anyone else in the guesthall had?"

"That's what I shall have to learn," Frevisse said.

As it happened, she learned it easily after she returned to the guesthall. Breredon was able to make weak answer for himself that he had had nothing to eat or drink aside from what was offered him, and everyone else—his own servants and the guesthall's—who had had anything to do with his food and drink assured her that he had had only what every other guest had had.

"There was nothing different for him," Tom said, looking scared while she questioned him and Luce in the guesthall kitchen.

"He didn't even come out of his room," Luce added. "He

had his supper taken in to him. He didn't come out all the evening."

"And no one went in?" Frevisse asked.

"Just his own folk," Luce said. "At least so far as I know. Tom?"

"I wasn't up there," Tom said. "It's old Ela you'd have to ask."

But Ela was sleeping, making hardly a heap under her blanket on her pallet in a corner of the kitchen, and Frevisse, not minded to wake her, said, "That I'll do later. Luce, come with me. I need to see the chamber is ready for Abbot Gilberd."

It was, and Frevisse commended Luce for it, then faced the necessity of questioning the Rowcliffes, no matter how little she wanted to.

This time it was Jack and his father who were playing chess, with Symond leaning on the table, looking on. As Frevisse approached them, Symond was shaking his head and clicking his tongue at the move Rowcliffe was in the midst of making, and Rowcliffe snapped, "Will you stop doing that?" but there was laughter under his protest and Symond was grinning.

Only young Jack, protesting on his side, "Don't help him! I'm winning," sounded halfway to serious, and while he stood up with his father and cousin to give Frevisse a slight bow, he did it without taking his eyes from the chessboard and sat down again while Rowcliffe and Symond stayed standing and Rowcliffe said, "We saw your infirmarian leave, and your priest come and go. Breredon *was* feigning it, then?"

"He was not and is not," Frevisse said. "He was very ill, apparently with something he ate or drank. Did any of you go into his room last night?"

"We haven't bothered with him," said Rowcliffe, sounding surprised. "There's nothing more to say between us until your abbot comes, so we've kept away from him and he's kept away from us."

"I don't think it's what we might have *said* to him that she's wondering about," said Symond. "It's what we might have *done* she's asking about."

"What?" said Rowcliffe, not seeming to follow his cousin's thought.

"She's wondering," said Jack without looking up from the chessboard, his hand poised over a bishop, "if one of us poisoned him."

"What?" Rowcliffe repeated, now more indignantly than questioningly, then added with pure indignation, "Hai!" as his son slid the bishop along the board to take the knight that Rowcliffe had just moved.

"I warned you," Symond said.

"I had plans for that knight," Rowcliffe grumbled.

"What you failed to think of was that Jack might have plans of his own," Symond said. "He'll have your queen in three more moves."

This time both Jack and Rowcliffe protested, "Hai!" albeit for different reasons.

Rowcliffe glared at the board for a moment more, gave a shrug as if giving the whole business up, and looked back to Frevisse. "No," he said. "None of us poisoned Breredon. Right is on our side. We've no need to poison him or anyone. Except Cecely maybe. Have you done anything about getting those deeds back from her?"

"We're leaving everything until Abbot Gilberd arrives."

"She's still closely kept though, isn't she?"

"She's still closely kept and under guard," Frevisse assured him. "Now if you'll pardon me, I've other things to see to."

"Besides accusing us of poisoning people, you mean," Rowcliffe grumbled, low enough she chose to pretend she did not hear as she went away, while behind her Symond cheerfully pointed out, "She didn't accuse us. She only asked."

She had already decided against asking any questions of Mistress Lawsell, partly because there seemed little point—the Lawsells had nothing to do with Breredon, no reason to want him ill or dead—but also because she did not want to chance stirring up Mistress Lawsell to no purpose. With no other questions to ask of anyone in the guesthall and expecting the bell to Tierce at any moment, she returned to the cloister, a little unsatisfied that she knew no more about what had made Breredon ill than she had when she started her questions but satisfied his illness was by chance, not of someone's doing. Jack Rowcliffe had been right: she had kept a thought of poison to the side of her mind, but the only people with possibly an interest in harming Breredon were the Rowcliffes—counting Symond Hewet as one with his kin—and as Rowcliffe had said, right was on their side. Unless Sister Cecely escaped with Edward and their deeds, they had little to worry about, and there was no one else here with any quarrel at all against Breredon. So he had not been purposely poisoned, and Dame Claire was certain it was not disease, and therefore so long as no one else fell ill of whatever had sickened him, there was nothing more that needed to be asked or done.

There was relief in that certainty, and it was with lighter mind that she went to ask Dame Johane sitting beside the guest parlor door with the promised herbal open on her lap, "Have you found anything useful?"

Dame Johane looked up from a page that was half words, half a picture of some plant, its stem and leaves drawn in plain ink but the flower of it painted red. Frowning a little with thought, she said, "The trouble is there seem to be any number of things that will bring on such vomiting and purging. I'd want to ask what color was . . ."

Sister Cecely came out of the parlor's shadows, almost

into the doorway but not quite, surely remembering Domina Elisabeth's warning even while she pleaded at Frevisse, "It was the Rowcliffes. Can't you see that? They poisoned him. You have to make them leave here before they do more, before they do worse!"

Frevisse looked at Dame Johane and said dryly, "She's heard, then."

"She's heard," Dame Johane agreed grimly. "While we were in chapter."

"Listen to me!" Sister Cecely cried. "You have to send them away! You can't let the Rowcliffes stay here and poison the rest of us!"

Frevisse looked at her coldly and said in a voice to match, "Abbot Gilberd will be here soon. The matter will be his to determine."

"We could be dead by then, Neddie and I!"

From the far side of the cloister walk, Dame Amicia was going toward the bell in its pentice in the middle of the cloister garth. In the moment before the call to Tierce would enjoin silence on her, Frevisse returned, "I truly doubt that," and turned away toward the church.

Behind her, Sister Cecely gave a smothered cry that might have been of despair or fear but to Frevisse sounded only angry.

Chapter 19

ierce went its brief, quiet way. Mistress Petham was there with Edward. So were Elianor Lawsell and her mother, but none of the Rowcliffes nor any of the nunnery's servants, the latter being all too busy readying for Abbot Gilberd's arrival. That he would be here soon was surely first in Domina Elisabeth's thoughts, because at the Office's end she made short work of the final prayer and response and afterward hurried the nuns from the church to give them her benediction quickly at the door before she hurried toward the kitchen. Abbot Gilberd would be staying in the guesthall, but at least his first meal would be taken with her in her parlor, and Dame Amicia said wearily, to no one in particular, "She wants it all to be as fine as may be for him. I'm already looking forward to him leaving," before she gathered herself and hurried after her.

Frevisse, not so hurried, overtook Dame Claire just at the infirmary, in the outer room where her medicines and all the means by which she made them were kept. Bunches of dried herbs hung from a roof beam, waiting for use, and Dame Claire crossed toward a clay pot on a low tripod over a small fire in a brazier in the room's middle where something was warming, asking as she went, "What have you learned?"

"Nothing. He ate alone in his chamber, and he ate what everyone ate. Dame Johane says any number of things could have caused the vomiting and purging, but I've found no way Master Breredon could have had anything that no one else did, nor any way the Rowcliffes could have come at his food."

"Maybe he did it to himself," Dame Claire mused, taking up a narrow wooden spoon.

"You mean he made himself ill?"

Dame Claire began to stir whatever was in the pot. "He could have."

"To make trouble for the Rowcliffes," Frevisse said. "Yes, I can see he might. But why would he have something like that with him? He didn't expect to encounter them."

"For some other reason?" Dame Claire ventured.

"But to make himself that ill would be mad."

"He might have misjudged his dose. An amount that barely touches one person can make another very ill. Or kill them."

"Sister Cecely claims the Rowcliffes did it, and that she and Neddie will be next."

"Sister Cecely is an idiot," Dame Claire said without looking up from whatever she was delicately stirring.

The sweet smell wafted from the pot, and Frevisse drew a deep breath of pleasure, then asked, "What are you making?"

"An essence of costmary. For the water when Abbot Gilberd dines with Domina Elisabeth."

"To drink?"

"To wash his hands. As you well know. I've also made a cordial of borage and betony that I hope will ease her mind somewhat. Worry as much as anything else is wearing on her. It's making me worried for her."

"But she's otherwise well?" Frevisse asked quickly.

Instead of the instant reassurance Frevisse wanted, Dame Claire paused in slightly frowning thought before saying only slowly, "I don't know that she's ill."

Frevisse waited until sure Dame Claire was not going to say more, then asked, "But you don't know that she's not?"

Somewhere still in thought, Dame Claire nodded before saying, still slowly. "I've thought that it isn't that she's ill but that, like Mistress Petham, she's tired. That may be all it is."

"Lent seems longer some years than others," Frevisse offered.

But, "This began before Lent. Before Advent even. That's when I first saw sign of it anyway."

"That she was tired?"

" 'Worn' might be the better word. She's not young, you know."

Frevisse almost protested that Domina Elisabeth had to be much about Dame Claire's own age and not that many years older than herself; but the thought came to her that, after all, neither she nor Dame Claire was likely to be thought "young."

"She's borne the burden of being prioress for twelve years, after all," Dame Claire went on. "It's not been a light burden."

"And now this," said Frevisse, meaning Sister Cecely and Abbot Gilberd and all the rest.

"And now this," Dame Claire agreed. She stirred delicately at the costmary. "So I'm doing what I can to ease her. Sadly, there's very little."

The cloister bell gave a sudden single clang. Both women raised and turned their heads, as if they could see it from where they were and Frevisse said, "And I would guess that's sign you're out of time anyway."

Dame Claire sighed. "Yes." She moved the clay pot from the fire. "You go on. I'll be there shortly."

Frevisse went, joining the other nuns in the cloister walk in time to see Domina Elisabeth come from her stairs, going toward the outer door to greet her brother in the yard and welcome him in. Dame Perpetua and Dame Margrett, as the eldest and youngest of the nuns, went with her while the rest of them lined together along the cloister walk in readiness for their own greeting. Elbows jostled as they placed themselves, straightening veils and shaking out skirts, Dame Amicia giggling a little, before they tucked hands into opposite sleeves and went still, a place left for Dame Claire who hurried into it, twitched at her skirts and veil, and joined them in stillness.

The outer door had been left open. Whoever had been set to watch for Abbot Gilberd's arrival had given good forewarning: for a few moments all was as still in the guesthall yard as in the cloister now. Then came the clatter of hooves on cobbles that would be the abbot on his mule and his men on their horses riding through the gateway. When that stopped, Domina Elisabeth's voice and then a man's could be heard giving greeting to each other, although the words were lost along the passageway. Then it was not words but Abbot Gilberd and Domina Elisabeth themselves coming along the passageway and into the cloister walk, and at sight of Abbot Gilberd, the nuns all together and with bowed heads sank in low curtsy to him, holding there a short moment until he said, "Rise, my good women."

They all rose together, and he raised his right hand and said a blessing over them. He was a large man, both in height and width, and made larger by the amply pleated long gown and surcoat he wore. They were correctly Benedictine black but their wool was closely woven and richly sheened, with black velvet edging the lower hems and the hanging sleeves of the surcoat, while black budge—lambs' wool—circled his throat.

All of that added to the authority of his blessing that Domina Elisabeth, Dame Perpetua, Dame Margrett, and Father Henry had probably received in the yard, because they simply waited behind him until he had done, Domina Elisabeth only then coming forward to say, "If you would please to come this way, my lord," with a small beckon toward the stairs to her rooms.

"I would, my lady," he returned and swept up the stairs and out of sight, leaving her and Father Henry to follow him, Dame Margrett trailing in their wake.

In the cloister walk straight spines went slack, heads lifted, and there were sighs of relief heaved before—like birds startled apart—the nuns all scattered to their next tasks. Dame Claire said at Dame Amicia, "I have the costmary for the water," while Dame Amicia said to Dame Juliana, "Are the cakes ready to go up?"

"The cakes and the wine both," Dame Juliana replied. "We'll fetch them. Sister Helen, come."

Dame Perpetua and Dame Thomasine were starting away toward the church, to make certain one more time that everything would be perfect to Abbot Gilberd's eye when he attended the next Office. Frevisse asked, "How many men came with him?"

"Six," Dame Perpetua answered without pause in her going.

Six was not as bad as it might have been, Frevisse thought. In truth, it was quite moderate for an abbot. Had he taken some thought for this being just after Lent? Or perhaps Domina Elisabeth had been bold enough to say something in her message to him.

Frevisse paused in her going to say to Dame Johane, "Are you grateful now you only have to watch Sister Cecely, instead of scurry with the rest of us?"

Bent over to pull from the shadows the stool she had pushed out of sight into the guest parlor, Dame Johane replied, "Grateful until I have to see her up to face the abbot."

"I won't go!" Sister Cecely declared from beyond the doorway.

"Then you'll be dragged," said Frevisse coldly. "Abbot Gilberd brought men enough for that."

Leaving Sister Cecely to think on that, Frevisse went yet again to the guesthall, as uneasy as everyone else that all be well for the abbot and happy to find that Luce had everything well in hand. Ela was awake, Luce said, but content to stay in the kitchen if she was not needed otherwhere. Even better, Luce said that one of the abbot's men had told her that there was a cart coming, on Abbot Gilberd's orders, bringing supplies of both food and drink. "The fellow said it should be here this afternoon some time."

Frevisse breathed a prayer of thanks and relief and said, "Be certain to tell Ela. She'll rest the better knowing it."

Luce gave a wide smile. "Already did." She gave a twitch of her head toward the best chamber's door. "They've already shifted in whatever was on the pack mule that came with them. Making themselves quite to home, they are."

"Good. So long as they do the work themselves," Frevisse said, her tartness not entirely in jest; but when she went to see what was toward in the room, she spoke mildly enough to the servant overseeing his fellows' work. The pack mule must have been well-laden. A finely woven red and yellow carpet was on the floor beside the bed and another one was laid over the otherwise plain table where the nunnery's pewter pitcher and goblets, brought especially from the cloister, had been removed in favor of Abbot Gilberd's silver ones. Frevisse did not wait to see what else might come out of the two small chests sitting open on the floor. Having ascertained that the abbot's men were content at what they were doing, she crossed the hall to where Rowcliffe and his cousin Symond had drawn themselves well aside from the abbot-bustle.

They were too near to Breredon's door for her liking, but there was only so much space in the hall; she could hardly ask them to sit in the kitchen or on the roof, but she did ask them where the men were who had come with them, not having seen them today.

"Told them they could stay in the stable," Rowcliffe said. "You've enough going on here without them underfoot, too."

She thanked him for that, and he offered, "You can have the rest of us out of your way if your abbot will hand over Edward and the deeds. Let him do that and we'll be gone. Is he dealing with the . . ." He thought better of whatever he had been going to call Sister Cecely and changed to, "When can we talk with him?"

"That's for him to say, not me. He's with our prioress at present." And although perhaps she should not, she added, "Soon can't be too soon for me, as well as for you."

Rowcliffe gave an appreciative grunt at her bluntness, Symond openly chuckled, and she went on to see how Breredon did.

The best that could be said was that he was better, but given how bad he had been, "better" was not anywhere near to "well." At least he was lying on his back, stretched out the length of his bed, instead of huddled in sickness and pain, but because he looked to be sleeping and his man Coll *was* asleep on a pallet beyond the foot of the bed, Frevisse saw him only from the doorway while asking Ida very quietly how he did.

"Whatever it was, he's at last resting quietly," the woman said. "He's kept a little broth down, too."

Contented with that, Frevisse left her, going to see what Mistress Lawsell's present complaint might be and found the woman very mellow, watching her daughter and Jack Rowcliffe sitting on the bed playing chess on the hall's battered board. He and Elianor made to stand up when they saw Frevisse, but she put out a hand to stop them, saying, "If you jostle the board, she'll say you did it because you're losing."

"I'm not losing," Jack said with easy confidence.

"Yes, he is," said Elianor pleasantly.

"Now, Elianor," her mother chided in soft warning, but whether against boasting or against winning a game from a young man, Frevisse could not tell. She guessed the latter and guessed, too, that it would make no difference to Elianor.

Leaving them, she had just time to tell Luce to collect the pewter pitcher and goblets from the abbot's chamber and bring them back to the cloister at her first chance. Then the cloister bell summoned her to Sext. The Office was sparsely attended. Neither Domina Elisabeth nor Abbot Gilberd nor Dame Margrett came. The nuns in their stalls looked at each other, made uncertain by the lack of their prioress, until Dame Juliana drew a steadying breath and began the Office.

The day continued disjointed from there. No reason for Domina Elisabeth's absence came down from the parlor. Nor did Abbot Gilberd or Father Henry or Dame Margrett, and neither did any of them come to Nones either. Afterward, dinner's food and drink went up, but Malde and Alson coming down could only say, "They're sitting there. Been talking, I'd guess," which was no more than anyone could have guessed on their own and therefore no help to curiosity at all.

It was early in the afternoon that Dame Margrett came briefly down, to tell Dame Johane to take Sister Cecely up. Somehow every other nun was in the cloister walk just then and watched the three women go from the parlor and up the stairs, Sister Cecely quietly between the other two with no sign of her earlier protests. Frevisse, at her desk in one of the several stalls along the walk beside the church where the nuns worked who copied the books that made some of the priory's income, had been trying to pretend to herself that she was working, but when they had gone, she admitted her pretence and did nothing more than sharpen several quills and count how many pages of the Festial she had left to copy, aware while she wasted that time of the other nuns likewise finding reasons to linger here and there in the walk, or if they went away, soon coming back, so that all of them— and several servants for good measure—were there when Dame Margrett brought Sister Cecely down from the prioress' parlor

Whatever they were hoping for, Sister Cecely's head was bowed too low and she retreated too quickly deep into the shadows of what was become her cell for anyone to see if she had been crying as Dame Margrett said to them all, "I'm to take Edward to them now," and to Dame Perpetua who was nearest, "Will you—" She beckoned with her head toward the parlor.

For answer, Dame Perpetua came forward, pulled the parlor door shut, and put herself in front of it, making it plain that Sister Cecely was going to have no chance at her son. Dame Margrett gave a tight-lipped, agreeing nod and went to fetch the boy.

Mistress Petham had surely foreseen he would be wanted. Dame Margrett came promptly back with him, Edward holding tightly to her hand. He was scrubbed and combed and tidy, but as they went past her, coming the direct way along the cloister, not the long one, Frevisse saw him roll his eyes toward the door shut between him and his mother, much like a frightened horse wary of a possible trap. Poor child, she thought.

He was rather a longer while with Abbot Gilberd than Frevisse would have thought necessary. Once Sister Cecely rapped on the inside of the door and demanded loudly if she couldn't have the door open again and at least glimpse her little boy. When Dame Perpetua did not answer, Sister Cecely hit the door hard with a fist and afterward was silent again.

Edward did finally come down, tear-stained and in Father Henry's care this time. The priest swept him along the cloister walk with what looked to Frevisse like anger—and not at Edward, Frevisse thought.

Dame Margrett was close behind them, and where the nuns had stood back from Father Henry's way, they flurried to her, wanting to know what had been happening, but she shook her head at them, saying, "We've been strictly enjoined to silence about it. I can't tell you." She added to Frevisse, still at her desk, "You're to go up. Domina Elisabeth wants you to see Abbot Gilberd to the guesthall now."

Frevisse willingly took her own curiosity up the stairs to Domina Elisabeth's parlor, to be met by a heavy quiet that answered none of her silent questions, only told her things were not well. Dame Johane stood beside the door with head down and hands folded into her opposite sleeves, still as a statue. Domina Elisabeth and her brother stood at the window in a matching stillness until at Frevisse's scratch at the doorframe they both turned. With her own eyes now properly downcast, Frevisse could not read their faces, but Domina Elisabeth sounded both weary and taut as she ordered, "Please see my lord abbot to his chamber, dame."

"Yes, my lady," Frevisse said, making a curtsy of obedient willingness to both her and Abbot Gilberd. "My lord."

Holding out his hand to Domina Elisabeth, he said, "I

will see you tomorrow, when I've had chance to talk with these Rowcliffes."

Domina Elisabeth took his hand, went down in a low curtsy, kissed one of the large-gemmed rings he wore, and rose. She let go his hand, but he took hers back in both of his, patted it comfortingly, and said firmly, "We'll talk more. Don't worry on it," then swept away from her toward Frevisse, who quickly turned and led the way down the stairs, out of the cloister, and away to the guesthall, hurried along by him following close on her heels.

He said nothing the whole way and therefore neither could she. Nor did he trouble, as Frevisse curtsied to him outside the door to his chamber, to offer his ring to her to kiss, merely went past her and in without a word, and she was suddenly fiercely glad he had provided food and drink for himself. He clearly had the wealth for it, and St. Frideswide's very much did not, and just at that moment she did not feel charitable toward him.

Also, as she returned toward the cloister, she found that she was angry—not at his wealth or even his neglect of courtesy to her but at whatever he had done to reduce everyone who had come near him in Domina Elizabeth's parlor to one degree or another of rigid quiet or strangled anger.

Domina Elisabeth did come down to Vespers and sat at supper in the refectory with her nuns, but she barely raised her eyes from her breviary during the Office or from the table during supper, and afterward she disappeared to her rooms again. As thwartingly, during recreation's hour Dame Margrett and Dame Johane held to their own silence, neither of them looking happy but both of them refusing to say anything of what had happened in the prioress' parlor today, meaning that everyone, including Frevisse, went to bed that night dissatisfied.

She found herself still dissatisfied when she came awake for Matins, groped her feet into her shoes in the darkness, slipped on her over-gown against the middle-night chill, and went from her cell and down the dorter stairs by the light of the single small lamp beside them to the dark cloister walk and the church. Besides the light ever-burning above the altar, another lamp waited there for them to light their candles along the stalls, but before even one was lighted they were all startled by running footsteps up the nave and Luce was suddenly there out of the darkness, her day's gown loose about her and only a cap tied over her disheveled hair as she grabbed the edge of the rood screen's opening to stop her headlong coming and cried out, "Dame Claire! You have to come! He's sick as anything! The Rowcliffe man this time!"

Chapter 20

The "Rowcliffe man" was Symond Hewet, and he was ill in much the way Breredon had been but far worse, vomiting blood before it was done. The fight to save him went on past dawn, so that when Dame Claire and Frevisse came finally out of the guesthall, it was into the clear daylight of another cool and cloudless morning. They stopped together at the top of the steps to take deep, grateful breaths, clearing the sick-room stench from their lungs, Frevisse breathing the air and feeling the sunlight as only someone could who had been dealing with death through the darkest hours of a night. It was a lovely morning, and Frevisse knew that when she stopped being so tired she could hardly think, she would be very glad there was a man alive who had been very close to dying, but just now all she felt was need to lie down and sleep for a goodly long while.

Beside her, echoing her feeling, Dame Claire said, "I am growing too old for that manner of night."

"If I never have another such, I'll be content," Frevisse agreed as they started down the steps. "As infirmarian, can you rule that you and I should sleep before we do anything else today?"

"I can. I do. We break our fast, then we sleep, if only until Tierce."

✝ The other nuns were already gone to chapter meeting, so the two of them had the morning bread—with butter today, as a Paschal pleasure—and ale alone in the refectory, with Dame Claire telling Alson, who waited on them, to report to Domina Elisabeth that Dame Johane was sitting with the sick man and that she and Dame Frevisse were going to sleep now for a time. Then, because the dorter was forbidden to the nuns during the day without the prioress' leave, they went to the infirmary. The few beds there were of course bare, but that was the very least of anything Frevisse cared about just then. She lay down on one and was asleep as she pulled the uncovered pillow under her head.

She awoke aware she was not ready yet to be awake. She tried lying very still to see if she might go to sleep again, but her mind had had rest enough that now it was remembering how in the night, with two men ill of quite surely the same thing, the fear of contagion had been as thick as the stench around Symond Hewet's bed. But from there she remembered how at the night's end, when she and Dame Claire had been aside from everyone, washing their hands in a basin and about to leave Symond to Dame Johane's care, Dame Claire had said, too low for anyone but Frevisse to hear, "It's not sickness. It's poison. I've no doubt of it."

Poison. Just as Dame Amicia had exclaimed yesterday and Sister Cecely insisted on.

And probably not a chance poisoning from food gone bad. Something chancing to be wrong in the guesthall's food or drink might strike down Breredon and only Breredon. But for a full day to pass and then one—and only one—other man to fall ill the same way . . .

It could have been by chance. Chance was an odd thing.

Lying with her eyes still closed, Frevisse slightly smiled in mockery at herself. Chance was, by its very nature, of course odd. But that was not the point of her thought and her smile left her. She wanted it to be likely that Breredon and Symond Hewet had been felled by chance, but she had to look at the possibility they had been sickened by someone's deliberate hand, because if they had been, whoever had done it had to be found out before more harm was done. Breredon had been ill, Symond Hewet very ill. Dame Claire had said that if he had had a weaker heart, he would be dead by now.

If someone else sickened, would it be to the death? Was that what someone was trying for?

Frevisse opened her eyes and made her unwilling body sit up. Dame Claire was gone and the light through the single, small window was the gray of an overcast day, keeping her from judging the time. As she rose stiffly to her feet, she felt the ill humour that came with too little sleep fraying at the edge of her thoughts. She tried to smooth them as she shook out her habit's rumpled skirts, telling herself that her discomfort was the least of what was happening. Bracing her hands in the small of her back, she carefully stretched a little and tried to turn her thoughts toward what mattered more than her body's discomfort. She would leave the question of what had been used to sicken the men to Dame Claire and Dame Johane. It was a lesser question. What mattered more, to her mind, was who had poisoned them. And why.

So far as "why" went, she could—barely—accept Rowcliffe

might poison Breredon to have the bother of him out of the way, as Sister Cecely had wildly insisted. What she could not do was make it seem a *likely* thing for Rowcliffe to do. With him she could see a shouting match, a hard blow from the front, a rough scuffle, maybe a dagger drawn and even used. She could see all of that, but poison, like an ambush or a dagger from behind, did not suit with what she had seen of Rowcliffe.

But then again, how much had she seen of him, to know one way or another what he would do?

And even if he would poison Breredon, why would he poison his cousin?

To keep suspicion away from himself?

Or could it have been Symond himself who saw to poisoning Breredon, then poisoned himself to keep suspicion away? Except there had been no serious suspicion that Breredon was ill by anything other than mischance.

And would Symond have so badly misjudged the dose he gave himself, have made himself so much more terribly ill than Breredon had been?

Still, as Dame Claire had said, poisons worked different ways on different people, just as medicines did. What sufficed for Breredon might have been too strong for Symond without he intended it to be. He—or whoever had given it to him. Unless whoever had given it to Symond had intended him to die.

Still, poison did not seem either Rowcliffe's or Symond's way of doing things.

What of Breredon's servants then? Would one of them have poisoned Symond as revenge for Breredon's poisoning?

But no one had thought Breredon's illness *was* poisoning. And even if Coll or Ida *had* taken hold on some thought that it was and set out on misplaced revenge, where had they got something to so nearly match Breredon's illness?

Or could one or the other of them have poisoned Breredon for some hidden purpose of their own, then poisoned Symond to confuse matters?

But again, since no one else had been thinking of poison for Breredon's illness, no one had needed to confuse anything.

Maybe it had gone the other way. Maybe the poison had been meant for Symond all along, and Breredon's poisoning had been meant to mislead. Or been done by mistake.

But who had reason for poisoning Symond?

Frevisse could just see why a Rowcliffe might think poisoning Breredon would be to the good: he was an added problem to the trouble they already had with Sister Cecely. But surely he was not that great a problem—not so great a one to warrant murder—not with the Rowcliffes' presence here having forestalled anything he and Sister Cecely might have purposed. Why make trouble that did not need making?

So back to Symond. She knew even less about him than she did about Breredon. Someone might have reason to want him dead without she had any way of even guessing what it might be. But then that someone would have to be either his uncle or his cousin, wouldn't it?

She could not help making that a question, but who else was there? Breredon? Poisoning himself first to avert suspicion from himself? Then depending on one of his servants to see to Symond's poisoning? Because surely Breredon had not been fit to do anything like that for himself yesterday.

Still, if this was about the Rowcliffe properties and Edward, John Rowcliffe would seem the more likely prey. Had it been Symond by mistake? He did not figure at the center of the trouble at all, so why poison him? Had he simply been simpler than Rowcliffe to poison?

All that seemed an even further stretch of likelihood than Symond being poisoned to divert suspicion from himself or from someone else when there had been no suspicion that needed diverting.

If Breredon and Symond had been on the same side in the

matter of Sister Cecely, there might have been some sense to be made of it all—that someone wanted to be rid of them both. Or that one of them wanted to be rid of the other. But they weren't on the same side. Were they? Could there maybe be something someone knew that gave reason to want them both dead?

This was useless. She could think of too many possible "whys," too many "maybes." They were making a maze in her mind without giving her any way to tell a true "why" from the rest. She should maybe start with "how" it had been done. "How" might tell her "who," and "who" could then be brought to confess to "why."

She found that at some point she had sat down on the bed again, was staring at the far white-washed wall without seeing it, and still had her hands pressed to her back because she had forgotten to move them. With a small grimace at that new stiffness, she let go of her back and stood up again. It was against the Rule to be this idle and alone during the day. Besides, she had gone as far as she could in her own mind. She needed to ask questions of someone besides herself.

She was not sure what questions—or of whom—until, going into the infirmary's outer chamber, she found Dame Claire standing at the wooden worktable there, the infirmarian's book laid open in front of her. It was a battered volume, its parchment pages dog-eared and stained. From her turns at helping in the infirmary, Frevisse knew there were leaves of various plants pressed among its pages, and that here and there dried plant stalks and other things marked places used by the several generations of St. Frideswide's infirmarians for reasons long forgotten but left by their successors because, Dame Claire had once said, "They were put there for someone's reason sometime. It makes me feel I'm keeping company with them, those other women, all of us leaving something of ourselves for the ones who come after us."

Just now she looked up, frowning, from a page showing a thin-lined drawing of some plant with carefully written script below it and less carefully written notes in various inks around it and said, "Poison doesn't seem to have been of much interest to my predecessors. There's nothing here that helps."

"Are you certain it was poison both times? Is it possible Master Breredon was honestly ill, and someone then used something against Symond that copied his illness?"

"Anything is possible," Dame Claire said wearily and somewhat shortly. "It's 'likely' that limits matters. Even if that was the way of it, from where did this opportune poison come from, since they would hardly be likely to have it to hand?"

Almost as one, they both looked up and around at the array of dried herbs hanging from the ceiling beams and the shelves of pots and small boxes along one wall; and after a silent moment, Frevisse asked, "Can you tell if anything has been taken?"

"Probably not." But Dame Claire was already going to a small chest sitting at a far end of the shelves. She kept her stronger medicines there, Frevisse knew, to keep anyone from laying hands on them mistakenly. The chest had no lock, though. Dame Claire simply raised the lid and looked inside, shifted the variously colored and tagged cloth bags and small, stoppered bottles around a little, held a glass vial up to what light there was through the window, shook her head, returned it to the box, closed the lid, and said, "I can't tell. Everything is here, but I'm not certain of quantities. There's never been need to be that precise about them."

Frevisse nodded that she understood. Dame Claire came back to the table, stared down at the book again, then turned some pages but not as if she thought to find any needed answers in it. Frevisse asked, "But you're certain it was poison?"

"You keep asking me that," Dame Claire said somewhat impatiently. "I'm as certain as may be. That's all I can tell you. Maybe I'm wrong. I don't know."

"Have you told anyone that it's probably not disease that struck them?"

"I haven't even let anyone know I'm awake yet," Dame Claire said. She closed the book. "I'd best go see how the men do before Tierce." She paused, frowning again. "How long did we sleep? Surely it's time for Tierce by now."

When they went into the cloister walk, they found out that it was more than time for Tierce. Dame Margrett, presently sitting guard outside Sister Cecely's door, said at them, "You're awake. Best you tell Domina Elisabeth. She had us called silently to Tierce, to keep from waking you."

"I'll go to Domina Elisabeth," said Frevisse, then laid a hand on Dame Claire's arm and said, too low for Dame Margrett to hear, "I'll tell her what we think, but that we think it best to keep it to ourselves for now."

Dame Claire gave a small nod of agreement, and they went their separate ways, she to see how the sick men did and release Dame Johane from her duty if she were still there, Frevisse up the stairs to the prioress' parlor where she was not much surprised to find Abbot Gilberd.

He and Domina Elisabeth were not alone, of course. Dame Thomasine was standing just inside the door, and of those who might have been there, she was best, Frevisse thought, because Dame Thomasine hardly ever spoke about anything and never beyond what she had, of necessity, to say. Her silence on whatever was said here need hardly to be asked.

As Frevisse made her low curtsy, Domina Elisabeth echoed Dame Margrett with, "You're awake. Good. Dame Claire, too?"

"She's gone to see how her patients do," Frevisse said.

"Do we know yet what it is they have?" Abbot Gilberd asked. "Or ate?"

Frevisse paused, brought herself to look at him straightly, and answered, "We think they were poisoned. Purposely."

Both Abbot Gilberd and Domina Elisabeth stared at her as if what she had said did not make sense to them. Dame Thomasine crossed herself. A moment later both the abbot and Domina Elisabeth did, too, Domina Elisabeth saying, "God forbid," and Abbot Gilberd demanding, "By whom? With what?"

"We don't know yet."

"Then you will have to find out," he ordered. "You have a marked skill at doing such. Do it."

The sharpness of his order startled her into momentary silence. She did have a skill at finding things out, and Abbot Gilberd knew it. Besides, whether he had bade her do so or not, she would have tried, and so she lowered her head, her eyes, and her voice, and said most meekly, "Yes, my lord." Then said, without raising her head, eyes, or voice, "I would ask, though, that nothing be said of poison, that people may go on thinking it's disease."

That silenced Abbot Gilberd a moment in his turn, before he asked, "Why?"

"So that I may ask questions without the poisoner knows he is suspected. Also, if we claim contagion, we can insist no one leaves, to take it with them. If poison is thought of, then there will be those who will want to go, claiming they want to escape it happening to them."

"Or to escape detection, if they're the guilty one." Abbot Gilberd said. "Yes. We'll keep silence on it. You, too, Dame—"

He broke off. Domina Elisabeth supplied, "Thomasine."

"Dame Thomasine. You will say nothing of what you heard just now."

Dame Thomasine bowed her head a little lower in assent.

From the cloister the bell began to call to . . . Sext, Frevisse reminded herself. To have slept straight through Tierce meant she was disordered in the day, but she gratefully accepted the summons and the silence it enjoined on them all, made quick curtsy to Abbot Gilberd and Domina Elisabeth, and all but fled the room for the stairs. They would have to follow in more seemly wise and Dame Thomasine come after them, but Frevisse made full use of the excuse to be away and in the sanctuary of her choir stall lost herself gratefully in the prayers and psalms of the Office. She had missed not only Tierce, but Matins and Lauds and Prime today. There was no blame to her in that, except maybe for sleeping through Tierce, but being guiltless did not lessen her relief as she joined in the opening, *"Deus, in adjutorium."*—God, come to help.—And for the while of the Office she was able to keep her mind only there, in that *now* that was at the same time a freeing of the heart and mind to join the soul's reaching out into the Forever beyond the world's bounds.

It was very hard, at the Office's end, to come back into the day and its troubles, but by the time Frevisse left the church with the others and received Domina Elisabeth's benediction in the cloister walk, her thoughts were already slipped away from her momentary peace to questions again.

She would set aside for now the matter of what had been used against both men and from where had it come. It was sufficient that Dame Claire was certain something had been used. And since she had no way yet to know the *why* of the poisoning, asking *how* it had been done seemed presently the best way to go.

The plainest answer, of course, was by something put into the men's food or drink, and she instantly did not like that answer. Their food and drink had come from the guesthall's kitchen, been served by the guesthall's servants.

But that might not be entirely true, she told herself. Both Breredon and the Rowcliffes had servants with them. She would have to find out who served them and where. If Breredon had indeed been keeping entirely to his room,

that limited who could have come at his food or drink. She
hoped.

She found she was standing alone in the cloister walk,
looking at a soft fall of rain into the garth.

When had the day turned to rain? she wondered. She
wondered, too, how long she had been standing there, finding that after all she was not so willing as she had thought
she would be to do what came next—to return to the
guesthall and ask questions.

Not that her willingness or unwillingness mattered.
Bound as she was by her vow of obedience, her duty was to
obey, willing or unwilling. So long as a duty was neither a
sin nor dishonorable, once it was given it had to be done,
and the guesthall and its guests were presently her duty.
Even without Abbot Gilberd's order, she must go back and,
once there, would ask the questions that were gathering in
her mind. Never mind that what she *truly* wanted to do was
go to sleep again and awaken to find everything was answered, all troubles ended.

That being impossible, she went on her way along the
cloister walk, only to have Dame Margrett, sitting on guard
again, say with a nod toward the open doorway beside her,
"She wants to talk to you."

Chapter 21

Cecely now mostly sat on the bench, keeping what watch she could on the cloister through the narrow doorway. Twice she had caught glimpse of Neddie passing along the far side of the walk with that woman they had keeping him, but plainly they were not going to let him near her. Nor did anyone come near her who did not have to. All she had seen of even Abbot Gilberd today was when he paused in passing the doorway and looked in. She had immediately bowed her head and gone into the necessary low curtsy, expecting him to say something at her, but by the time she had straightened and looked up, he was gone, not a word spoken.

They were trying to drive her mad. That was it and she knew it. To keep from satisfying them, she had finally been

reduced to finding the breviary among the rushes, to try passing the hours with reading. If nothing else, the psalms prais-
ing God for the striking down of enemies were to the good.
Her Latin had never been much, but she could read it well
enough in the psalms, and curses in Latin did seem stronger,
as if using Christ's own language gave them greater weight.
"*Qui autem perdere quaerunt animam meam, introibunt in pro-
funda terrae. Tradentur in manus gladii, portio vulpium erunt.*"—
Whoever seeks to ruin my life, they'll go into the depths of
the earth. They'll be given to the sword, foxes will eat them!

Yes. That was how it ought to be.

Without Alson she would have known nothing that was
happening. As it was, all she knew was what little Alson
knew, and she only heard it when Alson had her turn at sitting guard, meaning she knew very little and not very often.
Still, Alson had had one of her turns during Sext just now,
and goaded by what Alson had told her, Cecely made bold
to ask the nun outside her door if she might speak to Dame
Frevisse—no matter that "asking" anything of these women
stuck in her throat, the more especially because she had to
sound "humble" while she did it.

"Humble" seemed to work, though. Far sooner than she
had hoped, the long-nosed, stiff-spined woman was standing in the doorway, looking as if Cecely was a bad smell; and
Cecely, forgetting to be either humble or courteous, demanded, "Is it true Symond Hewet is dying?"

"No," Dame Frevisse snapped back. "How did you hear
he was?"

Not about to betray Alson, Cecely said, "Women talk. In
the walk. I can hear them. The abbot is here. When is he going to see me again?" Not that she wanted to see him again,
but this waiting, with nothing going one way or other, was
wearing at her.

"I suppose he and Domina Elisabeth have other matters
to talk of beyond you."

What matters? Cecely wanted to demand. Because they kept busy with something besides her for long enough, her chance might come after all . . .

Doubting Dame Frevisse would tell her anything even if she knew it, she asked instead, "How ill is Master Breredon?"

"He's mending."

"It was John Rowcliffe did it, you know."

"Did what?"

"Poisoned him," Cecely snapped, impatient at having to say it again. How often would she have to say it before someone got it into their head? "He's dangerous! They all are, the Rowcliffes. I told you that. They want me dead. They want Neddie dead. Your abbot should make them go away!"

With no sign of being moved in the slightest, Dame Frevisse asked, "What of Symond Hewet?"

Cecely felt herself blink with surprise and wariness. "Symond?"

"Why was he poisoned?"

"Why was he poisoned?" Cecely echoed.

"Supposing John Rowcliffe poisoned Master Breredon, why would he then poison his cousin?"

"To throw suspicion away from himself. Or—" Cecely leaped to a better reason. "Or because Symond was going to finally tell the truth. Or threatened to tell the truth. Then Neddie would get the manors he's supposed to have and John would lose them, and so he wanted to stop Symond saying anything and he poisoned him!"

Her triumph at that cooled under Dame Frevisse's level stare in the long moment before Dame Frevisse asked, "What has Symond Hewet been lying about? How would John Rowcliffe lose these manors if Symond Hewet told the truth?"

Glad of the chance to tell someone, Cecely said eagerly, "He's the last living of three brothers. He . . ."

"John Rowcliffe?"

"Yes!" Cecely said impatiently. How slow-witted was the woman? "There were the three brothers. And a sister. She was oldest. She was Symond's mother. Then there was the oldest brother. He died a long time ago. George was his son. It was George that drowned with Guy. Then there was John, and then Neddie's grandfather, Guy's father. The father of all of them had been a merchant in Norwich. After he was rich, he bought manors and moved away from Norwich. You see? His lands weren't entailed. He could will them any way he wanted to. They didn't have to go to only the eldest son. They were supposed to be divided between his sons, but John took them all!"

"How?" Dame Frevisse's voice matched her stare—level and bare of any feeling.

"How?" Cecely echoed.

"How did John Rowcliffe take the manors without his brothers made protest against him?"

"They were dead!" How *could* this woman be so slow? "They were dead and Guy and George were too young. Neddie's age, maybe. John had their wardships. There wasn't anything they could do, and when they were old enough to do something, John had brought them to think there was nothing wrong."

"How did you find all this out?"

"I asked questions. He'd raised them to have no questions. They just believed him. But I found out the truth. Now they're both dead, and he wants to do the same thing to Neddie! To steal his manor like he stole the others! But Symond must have decided enough was enough, and he was going to tell the truth, and so John poisoned him!"

"You're growing too loud," Dame Frevisse said. "Lower your voice. Why would Symond have kept quiet all these years about the wrongs done his nephews?"

"Cousins," Cecely snapped but with her voice down. She

had not meant to share this with the whole nunnery. It was just that the injustice of it and that no one *cared* made her so angry! "None of it was skin off his nose, was it? He had what he had from his mother, so he wasn't out anything. John probably bribed him some way, too. I don't know! But since he's the only one who can give John the lie, that's why John wants to be rid of him!"

"Except you have the deeds to the manors you claim aren't his. Won't those deeds give John Rowcliffe the lie as well as anything Symond Hewet might say?"

"What? Yes! That's why he wants them so badly! That's what I tried to tell Abbot Gilberd. That if Neddie becomes a monk, the manors will go his abbey!"

Dame Frevisse went on staring at her. Cecely barely kept from stamping her foot with impatience. The woman was so *slow*! But at last, Dame Frevisse nodded, said, "Yes. That interests him against the Rowcliffes, surely," turned, and left the room.

Cecely took two angry steps after her, wanting more from her than that. Then common sense caught up to her and she sank down wearily on the bench again. Demanding anything from a woman like Dame Frevisse—a woman who had never *been* a woman—was useless. She was as narrow as the cloister she lived in.

Still, something of what Cecely had said seemed to have struck through to her. If nothing else, it might get the Rowcliffes sent away, or maybe John arrested. That would make everything easier. *Something* had to turn her way soon.

FREVISSE made effort, while crossing the yard to the guesthall, to subdue her angry impatience at Sister Cecely and somewhat succeeded. If not rid of it by the time she entered the hall, she at least had it controlled as she went to talk to Ela where she sat on a low stool in her usual morning place at the head of the stairs to the guesthall's kitchen, watching what went on.

With her head crooked sideways to look up past her shoulders' increasingly rounded stoop, Ela said, "Good morning, lady," and made a slight attempt to rise, knowing Frevisse would gesture for her to stay seated.

Frevisse did, brought another stool, and sat down close to Ela, to say quietly, just between the two of them, "I have questions for you."

The hall servants had finished with their morning cleaning of the hall. The Rowcliffes were at their now-usual place in a far corner, a few men who must be of the abbot's entourage with them. Frevisse and Ela had their end of the hall to themselves, and Ela said, "Ask. I daresay I can make a good guess at answers."

"The evening Master Breredon fell ill, he was served in his chamber on a tray his servant took to him, yes?"

"That's so, as best as I recall. Nobody wanted him and the Rowcliffes meeting up if we could help it. Him no more than the rest of us."

"Did he fear them, do you think?"

"My thought was just he's a man who'll step aside from trouble if he can, rather than run at it head on."

"Who set the tray? In the kitchen, who put the food and drink on it?"

Ela held silent a moment, shrewdly eyeing Frevisse while thinking, before answering with a question of her own, "You're thinking, aren't you—you and Dame Claire—that it was poison that took both Master Breredon and Master Hewet?"

There being no point in denial, Frevisse answered, "We are, yes, and I want to know how it came to them."

Ela made the small bobbing of her head that had to pass for a nod on her age-stiffened neck, then considered a while before saying, "Well, I'm feared I can't say for certain about

Master Breredon's tray. Likely it was Luce set the tray, but it might have been Tom. I know it wasn't me. Nor I don't remember as it was carried up to him directly, or if his man came down for it. It would be Tom or Luce or his man you'd have to ask. As for Master Hewet, he's been served at table with the others, his kinfolk, every time. That would have been Tom. When it's this many menfolk all together, I keep Luce to the kitchen when I can. Not that they've been anything but well-mannered, except toward Master Breredon. But less tempted, less trouble, as they say."

"What about Mistress Lawsell and her daughter?"

Ela softly chuckled. "There's a problem. Mistress Lawsell doesn't know whether to keep her and her girl to their chamber, so they won't take ill—" Ela broke off to ask, "You want everyone to go on thinking it's maybe a contagion, do you?"

"Dame Claire and I think that would be best."

"Good, then. Less trouble than if they think there's someone poisoning them," Ela agreed and returned to answering Frevisse's last question. "But since the young Rowcliffe started taking heed of her girl, Mistress Lawsell is torn between keeping her closed up and loosing her to him."

"What does Elianor do?"

"Comes out. Stays in. Whatever her mother says. Butter-not-melt-in-her-mouth-obedient to her mother, she is, but she doesn't encourage him that I can see."

Frevisse wondered if Elianor's mother was deceived into thinking she was winning against Elianor's desire for nunhood. Or was Elianor slipping away from it herself, despite all she had said and maybe not even knowing that she was? Without talking with Elianor, there was no way to know, and there was no time now to wonder much about it. Frevisse thanked Ela and crossed the hall to Rowcliffe and the abbot's men. They all stood up to bow to her. Young Jack had briefly disappeared into their chamber but was just coming out. He joined their bows and she bent her head to them all in return, then asked Jack, "How does he?" supposing he had been to see his cousin.

"Asleep," Jack said. "But it's a quiet sleep. He's likely past the worst."

"How do you feel?"

Jack traded startled looks with his father, before saying, "Well, thank you," and his father echoed him.

"That's good to hear." Then to Rowcliffe, "If I might speak with you aside, please."

He rose and left the table, going with her to the end of the hall where he said, before she said anything, "We're not leaving while he's so ill. Whatever it is, we'll see it out here, him and—God forbid—whoever else comes down with whatever it is."

"We do pray God forbids more of whatever it is, and I promise you there's no thought of asking you to leave. What I hope instead is that you'll tell me what the line of inheritance is in your family."

Rowcliffe looked somewhat a-back at that. "For what?" he demanded.

"It's about the manors Sister Cecely claims are Edward's."

"The lecherous-tailed, thieving bitch. They're no more his than the moon is. I'm going nowhere until I have my deeds back."

"What I wonder," Frevisse said coolly, "is why she thinks Edward has claim to these manors."

"Because she's a fool!"

Frevisse raised her eyebrows at him. She watched while he throttled his anger into his control until finally he was able to say civilly enough, "It goes this way, no matter what she says. My father, God keep his soul, married twice. By his first wife he had my sister, my brother Robert, and me. Then my mother died, and a while after that he married again, God knows why, and had another son. When my father died, he left her—his second wife—with her dower lands to live on and her son Edward with moiety in a manor and an apprenticeship with a Norwich merchant."

"That Edward being your half brother and our little Edward's grandfather."

"Aye, little Edward's grandfather and my half brother. He was a good man." Rowcliffe shuffled his feet as if suddenly uneasy about something and said, almost apologizing, "Heed. What I just said about my stepmother—that God knows why my father married her—that's my anger talking. She was a good woman, a good wife, and the only harsh words she ever gave us were ones we'd earned." Something very like a boy's mischief warmed half a smile of remembrance from him. "Edward was a good brother, too. We're a family that likes each other." The remembered mischief faded, replaced by the weight of the present, and he said heavily, "It's hard to have both my brothers gone. Robert and Edward both. And now there's Guy and George gone, too, sudden and together, and while we're still in the midst of grieving, this fool of a woman brings all this other trouble on us, where there didn't need to be trouble at all." He glanced toward the chamber where Symond Hewet lay. "Now there's this," he said and crossed himself. "God keep us all."

Frevisse copied the cross before saying, "So Guy had only claim to a portion of a manor, not a whole one, as Sister Cecely says. And Edward has nothing, not being legitimately his son."

"No, there's a whole manor that's young Edward's, just as the—" He stopped, started again. "Just as his mother says. Guy bought a manor and willed it to Edward. Come to Edward that way, there's no question it's his and no quarrel about it." This time his glance was an angry one at Breredon's chamber. "Except over what she means to do with it. No, the trouble is she's got it into her addled head that

Guy's father should have had an equal share with my brother Robert and me in all my father's manors, and that share should have come to Guy and then to young Edward, and that he's been cheated out of it."

"But your father hadn't divided them that way?" Frevisse asked.

"He couldn't. He was a merchant rich enough he married into the gentry, but the three manors were my mother's, her inheritance from her father. They were to go to her sons after she and our father were dead, and that's what happened. Robert got two. I got one. Our half brother Edward had a moiety—a life-share—in one of Robert's, and besides that, our father had bought him into a good apprenticeship with a mercer in Norwich. The moiety went back to Robert when Edward died, but Edward had done well enough that he left Guy as well off as the rest of us, just not in lands."

"Because the lands were all from your father's first wife and couldn't go to his second wife's son," Frevisse said, to be sure she had followed all of this.

"You have it. Sometime or other your Sister Cecely took hold on it otherwise. She made the last three years or so a hell for Guy, nagging him to do something about 'the wrong' done him and his father. It was to shut her up he bought a manor and willed it to Edward. Didn't shut her up, though, and once he was dead, she pulled this trick on us, despite she knows—she *has* to know—that Edward, being a bastard, has no rights to inherit anything not straightly willed to him. Not that we were supposed to know there was no marriage," Rowcliffe added bitterly.

"Nor would you have known it if Symond had not told you."

"If Guy hadn't told him and he hadn't told us, no, we'd not have known. Even then, Symond might not have told us, except she ran and took Edward and the deeds with her."

That raised a few questions about Symond, but more

immediate was Frevisse's wondering why Guy had told him at all. Was there more to it than what Symond had already told her? She was looking forward to when he would be well enough for her questions, but that would not be now, and she asked, "Yesterday at meals who served your food? A guesthall servant or one of your own?"

Rowcliffe had been braced for more questions about inheritance, it seemed, or else he had to think about it to remember. Either way, he took a moment before answering, "One of yours. I wouldn't have one of my hamfists do it for fear of more on me than anywhere else."

"Would Symond have had to drink and eat whatever the rest of you did?"

"Of course."

"All the same," she persisted. "Nothing different."

"Nothing different," Rowcliffe said.

"From the same pitcher, from the same platter," Frevisse said, thinking aloud.

But not the same bowl or cup, said the back of her mind.

Rowcliffe had sharpened to her questions now and demanded, "Why? Are you thinking poison instead of disease? You're thinking he was poisoned?"

"I think that sometimes food spoils without anyone knows it in time," Frevisse said. "If it's that rather than disease, I have to find it out."

That was not a denial of poison, but Rowcliffe took it that way, as she had meant him to. "Better if it's that," he agreed. "Couldn't be poison, anyway. How would she get it here?" His voice hardened. "She's locked up, isn't she? You've said she is."

"She's confined in a room, with guard kept at the door at all times. She goes nowhere, even to the church."

Rowcliffe gave a curt nod, satisfied by that. His next likely question would be about Abbot Gilberd and his dealing with Sister Cecely. Frevisse avoided it by thanking him for his answers and walking away. Unfortunately she took with her the one question to which she had not even a glimmer of answer yet: *who* had poisoned Breredon and Symond. She expected that *how* would answer the *who*, but in truth she was a little afraid of what that answer might be, because it was more and more shaping toward being not one of the outcomers but someone of the nunnery, and why someone of the nunnery should want to do this much harm—and even murder—was something she did not understand at all, and not understanding it made her afraid that what she might find out would be not only altogether apart from but even darker than the matter of Sister Cecely.

Chapter 22

hatever Frevisse's fears, they did not release her from her duty, and she went next to Breredon's chamber, to be met at the doorway by his man Coll, who bowed and said before she asked, "He's fit to talk, if that's what you want."

It was, but more than that, Frevisse was pleased to find Breredon somewhat sitting up, leaned back on a pillow against the head of the bed. Color and strength were still gone from his face, but there was more life in his eyes than there had been yesterday, and before she could speak, he said, "They tell me Symond Hewet has sickened, too. Has anyone else?"

"Only the two of you thus far."

"I pray to God there are no more. This has been dire. How does he?"

"Badly. Worse than you, but better than he was."

"God keep him. Coll says you don't know what it is we have."

"We don't." Which was true enough: Dame Claire did not yet know what poison had been used.

"Just so it goes no further. That's what I pray."

"So do we all. Master Breredon, there's something I would ask you."

"Ask." He made an effort at smiling. "If I fall to sleep in the middle of your question, I'll answer later."

"It's about the Rowcliffes, about this property that Sister Cecely claims should be her son's. Not his own manor from his father but some of the other Rowcliffe manors. Which side has the truth? Do you know?"

Breredon considered before answering. Or maybe he was gathering his strength before he finally said, "My family knew John Rowcliffe's mother's family before ever Rowcliffe's father married into it. As I've always heard, the Rowcliffe manors come by way of her. The manor I want is one that Guy bought and willed to the boy, nothing to do with John, except it sits so well with one of his own."

"And besides that, you have a daughter to marry to Edward."

"I do."

"But you say you want nothing to do with the other Rowcliffe lands."

"Blessed Mary, no. Whoever Mistress Rowcliffe—your Sister Cecely—might have befooled into taking those deeds would have been pouring gold into lawyers' laps for years to come, fighting over it with the Rowcliffes." Breredon sighed. His eyes closed again. "Fool of a woman," he said on a fading breath and was asleep with the ease of a man still far from well.

Ida, as if she would warn Frevisse away from disturbing him, rose from the stool where she had been sitting beyond the foot of the bed. Frevisse drew back a step to show she meant to leave him sleeping, gave the woman a slight nod to which Ida was returning a curtsy as Frevisse left.

So now she had not only the two sides of the quarrel over the deeds but a very certain thought on who was in the right, and it was not Sister Cecely.

There was no surprise for her in that.

She likewise believed Breredon's insistence that he had wanted nothing to do with any stolen deeds. John Rowcliffe, being no fool and probably knowing Breredon for no fool either, surely did not think Breredon was after them, which meant Rowcliffe had no reason to poison Breredon, let alone his own cousin.

So surely there was something else to be learned about Symond Hewet and Breredon. There might be reason to poison one man or the other, but why both of them, as much on different sides as they were?

Different sides of what?

Of Sister Cecely's lies and ambitions.

There was surely, somewhere, a straight answer through the tangle, but all that Frevisse could yet see was the tangle, and she suspected that her sight of even that was blurred by her having had too little sleep since yesterday.

She found that she had come to a stop outside the chamber, was standing there with her thoughts, and realized that Breredon's man Coll beside the doorway had stood up from where he had been sitting on his heels, back against the wall, and was waiting to see if she wanted anything. She turned to him. "Coll, two evenings ago, before Master Breredon fell ill, was it you or Ida or someone else who fetched his supper from the kitchen?"

Coll gave her a startled stare while he put his mind around the question, then said, "I did, my lady. No. I didn't. The nunnery's man did. He brought it up from the kitchen, and I took it from him and took it in to Master Breredon."

"Where did you take it from him?"

"Where? Um, here." He made a small gesture at where they were standing, just outside Breredon's door. "Or . . . I came out the door and saw him coming, and I went a few steps and took it from him. But here, near enough."

Her questions had openly confused him. "Thank you," she said. "Tell no one I asked."

That confused him more, but he said obediently, "Yes, my lady."

She walked away, going toward the stairs down to the kitchen, trying to guess how long she had before the cloister bell would call to Nones. Still somewhat muddled by lack of sleep, she found she had no good guess and hurried a little, not having much in the way of questions to ask and wanting to have them done before she had to turn away from them.

In the kitchen Tom and Luce were as confused as Coll at being questioned, but their replies were straight enough. Luce had readied Master Breredon's tray. Tom had taken it up the stairs and given it to Master Breredon's man.

"Just like that?" Frevisse asked, not wanting to ask outright if there had been chance of anyone else coming close to it. She did not need more thoughts of poison starting around.

"Just like that, aye," said Tom, and Luce nodded agreement. With the unease of a servant afraid he was going to be accused of something, Tom added earnestly, "We didn't do anything wrong with it."

"I don't think you did," Frevisse assured him firmly. Ela would take it much amiss if she upset either Tom or Luce too much to work well.

But somehow, some place, something had happened to whatever Breredon had eaten or drunk two days ago. Maybe she needed to ask more questions about whatever food or drink of his own he had, that supposedly only his servants would have handled but might have been reached by some-one else.

But that would not explain how Symond came to be poi-soned.

Or, come to it, why either man had been.

She left the guesthall, hardly noticing the rain still softly falling as she crossed the yard, not going directly back to the cloister but to the church, entering by its west door and going up the nave, reaching the choir just as the cloister bell began to ring, so that she was first in her place for Nones, al-ready kneeling, forehead resting on her folded hands when the others came in. She slid backward onto her seat only as Dame Juliana began the Office and saw then that everyone was present except Domina Elisabeth yet again. Frevisse supposed that meant either Abbot Gilberd had left the cloister, and Domina Elisabeth for reasons of her own had chosen not to come to the Office, or else that one of the ser-vants was with them. Whichever it was, it was Domina Elisabeth's concern, not hers, she thought and from there set herself to go as deeply into the Office as she was able, into the greater realms of soul and mind and heart there were beyond the shallow troubles mankind made for itself. Her voice joined with the others in these prayers and psalms and was joined with the voices of all the women who had ever prayed them, women she would never see and never know, uncounted other women not only now but all the ones who had prayed them through centuries before and all the ones who would pray them through centuries to come. "*Etsi moveatur terra cum omnibus incolis suis: ego firmavi columnas eius. . . . Hunc deprimit, et illum extollit. . . . Ego autem ex-sultabo in aeternum . . .*"—Even if the earth with all dwelling there shift, I have made firm its pillars. . . . This one he humbles, and that one he lifts up. . . . But I will exult into eternity.

At Nones' end, she only regretfully came back to the day

and its questions and the nuns' midday meal. Time had been when Nones had come well after midday, halfway to Vespers, but for the sake of giving the day just one longer while of uninterrupted work, the Office had slipped backward to vaguely the day's middle, with what had been the late-morning's meal now coming after it, leaving all the after-Nones of the day for work. It was in Frevisse's mind that today she might well spend some of that time at the copying work she had set aside through Holy Week, her hope being that if the work did not help to clear her mind, it would at least give her brief relief from her thoughts. But at dinner's end, when the final blessing had been said and the nuns were readying to go their separate ways until Vespers, Dame Claire slipped to her side and said, "Mistress Petham has asked to see you."

Despite herself, Frevisse took and let go a deep, impatient breath, but there was no help for it. She was hosteler. More than that, Mistress Petham was a better guest than most and did not deserve her impatience, let alone the neglect Frevisse had had toward her these past few days. So she made herself say mildly, "I'll go now," before asking, "Have you any better thought on what was used against Breredon and Symond Hewet?"

"I mean to have Dame Johane go through our stores this afternoon, to see if there's less of something than she thinks there should be."

That would have to do, being the best that could be done about it, and Frevisse nodded and went her way up to Mistress Petham's room. She knew that Dame Margrett would have been seeing to her mother's good care by the servants and that Dame Claire had not neglected her health, but Frevisse had her duty, too, had not been doing it as well as she might have, and had her apology ready as she knocked quietly at Mistress Petham's closed door.

There was a quick patter of soft footfalls, and Edward

opened the door enough to look out the gap and see her. His eyes grew large and frightened and he backed away. That surprised her. She could think of nothing she had done to make him afraid of her.

From across the room, Mistress Petham called, "Come in," and Frevisse did, to find her sitting on the floor near the hearth beside a scatter of small, bright-glazed clay boules. She was just flicking one with her thumb, setting it rolling along the hearth stone. It clicked against another one, and Mistress Petham laughed and said, "There, Edward! I've not forgotten the trick of it after all!" She looked up and laughed again, this time at Frevisse's open surprise, and said, making to stand up, "They're Edward's. We're finding out just how badly he can beat me at every game."

Edward, who had retreated to her side, took hold on her near elbow, helping her to her feet while mumbling something toward his own.

"Yes," Mistress Petham agreed. "I am getting better. If we go at this for six more months, I might actually win." She wiggled the fingers of her free hand at Frevisse. "Stiff with age and use, I fear me." Edward, now that she was standing safely up, was clinging to her other hand with both of his own, his head still bowed. She looked down at him, reached across herself with her free hand to stroke his hair, and said gently, "Edward, she's here now. We need to tell her why." Still stroking his hair, she said, to Frevisse now, "I asked to see Domina Elisabeth but she's in talk with Abbot Gilbert and not to be disturbed, Dame Margrett said. She said I should speak to you instead. Thank you for coming."

Frevisse bent her head, acknowledging the thanks, still ready to make her apology for not having come more often, but Mistress Petham was going on, freeing her hand from Edward so she could put both her hands on his shoulders and steer him from her toward her bed. "It's time, Edward," she said, still gently. "We have to show Dame Frevisse what you have."

Edward stayed where he was for a long moment, then suddenly broke away from her, ran forward to the bed, reached under a pillow, grabbed something, and turned around, clutching a folded paper or parchment to his chest. He looked confused and frightened as he raised his head to look at Frevisse again, and she went down on one knee, to stop towering over him, and said, matching Mistress Petham's gentleness, "What do you have, Edward?"

He went on staring at her. It was Mistress Petham who said quietly, "The stitching on the inside of his tunic's collar was coming loose. I made to mend it this morning. These were in it for stiffening, along with the buckram. Edward."

Biting his lower lip, his eyes still frightened with what might have been fear or confusion or guilt or all of them together, Edward came to Frevisse and held out the folded something to her. Still kneeling, she thanked him and took it from him, a little smiling to reassure him that it was all right, whatever it was. Apparently not reassured, he broke away from her and ran to hide his face against Mistress Petham's skirts as Frevisse stood up.

"I didn't look at them when I first found them," Mistress Petham said, patting his shoulder. "I gave them to him, saying they were his. He says that, no, they're not, and that he wants Symond Hewet to have them."

Frevisse was unfolding what were proving to be several pieces of parchment folded together into a narrow strip to fit inside a small boy's collar, but at Symond Hewet's name she raised her gaze sharply to Mistress Petham. "He's . . ." she started and broke off, not certain how much to say.

"Not dying, we hope," Mistress Petham said quickly. "We'd heard he was sick but . . ."

"No, not dying," Frevisse answered as quickly. "He was very sick, but he's bettering now." Then, gently, "Edward, what is this? Why do you have it?"

"He isn't sure what it is," Mistress Petham answered for him again. "His mother sewed it into his collar and told him to keep it secret. Edward, you have to tell Dame Frevisse what you told me. What did your mother tell you?"

Edward reluctantly drew back from her and slowly turned around, one hand still clutching to her skirts, the other fisted at his side. Frevisse had half expected him to be crying, but he was not, and now that he was brought to it, he said with surprising steadiness, no matter that his eyes were still large and frightened, "She said I was not to tell anyone I had them in my collar. That they're ours and nobody else's. But that's not true, and I don't want to go with Master Breredon, and my father told me that if ever I was in trouble or needed help I should go to Symond, but I can't, and now he's sick, and I wanted to ask Jack but I didn't, and . . ." He paused for his breath to catch up to him, then burst out, "And my father said people should be good, but I don't think it's good for me to have—" He pointed at the parchments in Frevisse's hands. "I shouldn't have them, should I?"

"No, I don't think you should," Frevisse agreed gently. "You've done right to give them to me. It was a good thing to do and it will maybe make things well for everyone. You are very brave and very good, Edward. Just as your father would want you to be."

Edward kept his eyes fixed on her, as if looking to see how much truth she was telling him, until beside him, Mistress Petham said quietly, "Why don't you set up another game of boules for us, Edward, while I see Dame Frevisse to the door?"

Probably glad to be released, Edward immediately turned away and went to his knees beside the scatter of bright-glazed boules, beginning to gather them together as Frevisse stood up and moved with Mistress Petham toward the door. There, with one hand on the handle to let Frevisse out, Mistress Petham said, too low for Edward to hear, "He kept pulling at his collar. I think he meant for the threads to give way, so someone would find what was there." She hesitated, then added, "I looked at them. I think you—or Domina Elisabeth or my lord abbot—should read them before they're given to anyone else."

Frevisse nodded silent agreement to that and left, slipping the folded parchments into her undergown's close-fitted sleeve, having them against her wrist and out of sight by the time she reached the stairfoot. There she paused to decide what she would do next.

Surely best would be to go to Domina Elisabeth with what she had.

But that did not seem best when Frevisse thought on it. Domina Elisabeth was presently so removed from everything, so deep in dealing about Sister Cecely and only with Abbot Gilberd, that to take anything else to her felt nigh to impossible.

And then there was the blunt fact that Frevisse wanted to know for herself what was on these carefully secreted parchments, and she turned not toward the stairs to Domina Elisabeth's rooms but the other way, to the infirmary that was close at hand and almost a private place.

Thinking that, she was discomfited to find Dame Johane in the outer room, frowning in either thought or displeasure while putting small linen bags back into the chest of medicines sitting on the table. Not to waste the chance, Frevisse paused to ask, "Have you found anything missing?"

Dame Johane, still frowning as she took up one of the small bottles, made no other answer than a shake of her head. Frevisse took advantage of her silence to say nothing else, left her to her plainly heavy thoughts and went past her into the next room. Standing where the best light fell through the window, she unfolded the parchments.

There were three of them, each wider than it was long. Because there was no point in wasting parchment, a document was often cut off below the names signed at its end if there were any, as there were here, so that the unused portion could be used for something else. Of the three parchment pieces she held, one was far shorter than the others, hardly an inch and a half of parchment used. The other two were longer but short enough that they had been easily twice-folded, the shorter one inside them, to the width of a child's collar, making it simple to lay them along the stiffening already there, to be then stitched out of sight. There were signs that wax seals had been hung from the two longer ones, but the seals were gone, cut away probably because thick as such seals were, they could not have been hidden.

The longer writings were, as Frevisse expected, two deeds to carefully described properties. She judged that with a little forging of other documents and names, they could very well be used to make as much trouble for the Rowcliffes as both Rowcliffe and Breredon had claimed. She took up the third parchment piece and read it.

It was not a deed.

She lifted her head and stood staring at the near wall.

Not a deed. Instead, a bill of obligation between Guy Rowcliffe, Symond Hewet, and young Jack Rowcliffe, acknowledging that Jack had been loaned a large sum of money by his two cousins, with promise that he would pay them back in full before . . . Frevisse took up the parchment and read the date on it again. Before this coming first of May. Three weeks away.

Why had Jack bargained for money from his cousins rather than asking it from his father? Because he needed money for something he would rather his father knew nothing about. That was the most likely answer.

With Guy dead, Symond was his only debtor. Had Jack found he was not going to be able to repay the debt—or did not choose to—and been desperate enough to want Symond dead?

If that was the way of it, then Breredon's sickening could have been done to confuse the attempt on Symond when Jack made it.

She had already thought of that as a possibility, without having any name or reason to put to it. This bill of obligation maybe gave her someone with a reason. Or, come to it, if Jack feared Breredon was lying about what he wanted from Cecely, feared Breredon wanted these deeds after all, and knew the bill of obligation was with them, could he have been willing to kill him to block him having it?

And finding that whatever poison he gave Breredon was insufficient, had he given Symond a larger dose of it, whatever it was, when attempting his death?

But how had Jack known Sister Cecely had the bill?

Well, it could well have been among Guy Rowcliffe's papers. Symond would have known it was there, and if he and Jack had looked for it after Sister Cecely fled and not found it, they could well suppose she had it.

For the first time Frevisse wondered how Sister Cecely had come by the deeds. *Those* had assuredly not been in Guy Rowcliffe's keeping.

Never mind that for now.

She refolded the parchments and slipped them into her undergown's sleeve again, stood up, and tucked her hands into the opposite, fuller sleeves of her overgown in the ordinary way. With her hands folded in front of her that way, there was no way to tell she carried anything hidden, and that was surely safest, since it might be that two men had come near death because of these deeds and bill. Sister Cecely could not have known it would come to that danger, or she would not have used her son for hiding the things. Nor had Edward been thinking of his own safety when he gave the secret away. He simply had wanted to do right instead of wrong, had wanted truth instead of lying.

Frevisse thought, with a touch of bitterness, that if people simply told the truth, the way Edward had, and were good and brave to one another, there would be far less sadness and hurt in the world. Far less.

Among other things, there would not be two men in the guesthall who had come near to dying because someone was lying and hoping to hide it.

As Frevisse passed through the infirmary's outer room, leaving, Dame Johane was frowning at small glass vials and Frevisse did not trouble her with any question. Once in the cloister walk, though, she stopped, pausing while trying to choose between the several things she could do next. She was yet again considering going to Domina Elisabeth when Alson came from the stairs to the prioress' rooms and along the walk, head down, carrying a pottery pitcher and hurrying, passing Dame Margrett sitting outside Sister Cecely's door without a word, probably returning to the kitchen, not seeing Frevisse at the corner of the walk until Frevisse said her name.

Alson stopped, her head jerking up. She made a short, bobbed curtsy, saying, "My lady," and looking unsettled, even frightened.

"What is it?" Frevisse asked, with a glance past her, back toward the prioress' stairs. "How is it with Domina Elisabeth? Is she still in talk with Abbot Gilberd?"

At just above a whisper, Alson said, sounding as frightened as she looked, "She's crying."

"Crying? Domina Elisabeth?" Of any of the things Frevisse had thought to hear, that was not one of them. "Is the abbot angry at her and she's crying for it?"

"No," Alson whispered, almost as if giving away a secret. "It's more like he's trying to comfort her."

That explained nothing, but it decided Frevisse on what to do next. She nodded at the pitcher and asked, "Is that for the kitchen?"

"Aye, and I'm to say they won't be wanting more before Vespers. It's a good thing the abbot brought wine or we'd be near to out now."

"I'll take the pitcher and your message," Frevisse said, reaching for it. "I want you to go to the guesthall and tell Mistress Lawsell's daughter I'd to speak to her in the church. Just the daughter, not the mother. Make that plain."

"Yes, my lady." Alson gave over the pitcher, bobbed another curtsy, and hurried back the way she had come.

Frevisse went on to the kitchen, delivered the pitcher and the message, then went on around the cloister walk and into the church. The rain had sometime stopped but the sky was still low and gray, and the church, too, was gray with shadows. Even the light above the altar seemed dull and small as Frevisse curtsied toward it before passing through the rood screen, to wait for Elianor in the nave. While she waited, she slipped the parchments from her sleeve again, separated the bill of obligation from the deeds, slid the deeds back into her undergown's sleeve but kept the bill in her hand, hidden in her overgown's looser sleeve.

The girl came soon, alone and eagerly, saying as she rose from her curtsy to Frevisse, "You wanted to see me?"

"In truth," Frevisse said, "I want to see Jack Rowcliff without his father, and by you seemed the best way to do it."

While Elianor was still looking surprised at that, the west door, that she had shut behind her, opened again and Jack came in. Seeing Frevisse and Elianor together, he hesitated, but at Frevisse's sharp beckon, he shut the door and came toward them. While he did, Frevisse said to Elianor, "If you would like to go beyond the rood screen and kneel in prayer at the altar, you have my leave to do it."

Delight bloomed in Elianor's face. She made a short curtsy and swiftly, happily, left Frevisse as Jack neared them. While he looked, confused, back and forth between Frevisse and Elianor's departing back, Frevisse held up the bill of obligation in front of him. Pulling his heed away from Elianor, and thrusting his head close to the bill, he was probably just able to read it in the gray light, so that it was a moment before he realized what he was seeing. His eyes widened. He straightened sharply and asked in open surprise, "How did you come by that?"

Frevisse saw no alarm, no sudden wariness, no quick calculation going on across his face or behind his eyes, only the surprise. Not until she said, "Sister Cecely had it," did his face tighten with alarm and anger.

"Hell's fires," he said. "We feared as much." Sudden alarm took over from the anger. "Who else knows about it, knows it's here?"

"Not your father," Frevisse said dryly and watched him ease a little. So she had guessed rightly there. She slid the bill into her sleeve again. "Nor your cousin Symond yet, if that's who you meant with saying 'we.' I mean to ask him about it, though."

"But not my father!" That was clearly first in the youth's concern.

"Symond first, and maybe not your father after that. It will depend on what Symond has to say."

"He's still too ill to talk."

"I'll wait until morning. He should be better by then. In the meanwhile, we shall hope no one else falls ill." She very deliberately added, heavy with meaning, "And that Symond does not worsen."

Jack frowned at her, seeming perplexed. Then he startled into understanding and burst out in confused protest, "You think he's been . . . You don't think I . . . You don't mean you . . ." He could not seem to get the words out.

"Don't I?" she challenged.

"That I . . . that Symond was . . . that I . . ." He still could not find the words and finally settled for, "No!"

"There's good chance *someone* sickened him of a purpose, yes," Frevisse said steadily. "And Master Breredon before him."

"No!"

Believing him more with every protest he made, she relented enough to point out, "Better than that there be disease spreading among you all."

"Yes," he said uncertainly. "Maybe."

"But better yet that no one knows the truth while we're still trying to learn who did it."

"Yes," he agreed again, still doubtful.

"So you won't say anything about it, even to your father," she ordered. "Not before I've talked with Symond."

Jack nodded slow agreement to that, too, before asking, "But if it's tried again?"

"After two failures? I think they'll be careful for a time."

She prayed so, anyway—there being nothing else she could do about it for now.

Jack looked past her, toward Elianor, she supposed. Firmly gentle, she said, "She means to become a nun."

Jack's gaze snapped back to her. "Oh. But . . . her mother . . ."

"Is on the hunt for a husband for her. To her mother, you are no more than prey."

That way of looking at it had plainly never crossed his mind before. At the change in his face as the thought took hold on him, Frevisse had to hold back a smile while ordering quietly, "Go back to the guesthall now."

He bowed and went. She waited until he would have reached there and been there for a few minutes before she went herself for her end-of-day visit, to be sure all was as well there as it might be.

Thankfully, it was. At Mistress Lawsell's inquiry after Elianor, she murmured that she had left her in prayer in the church; and when Mistress Lawsell showed sign of alarm and intent to go there to fetch her out, Frevisse said that the church was chill and damp and Elianor surely uncomfortable by now and she meant to go herself to send Elianor back to the guesthall.

That Elianor would be uncomfortable in the church satisfied Mistress Lawsell into leaving her daughter to Frevisse, and finished in the guesthall, Frevisse did return to the church, into the choir to Elianor kneeling at the foot of the two steps up to the altar. The girl's hands were clasped, her eyes lifted to the cross, and she did not stir until Frevisse laid a hand on her shoulder and said, "Best you go now."

Elianor looked up at her, blinking somewhat dazedly. Frevisse knew the feeling of coming back from some far place. It came from being deep into prayer, well beyond the bonds and boundaries of the world, and she waited patiently while the girl gathered herself back to here, to now, and stood up shakily, to make a deep curtsy to the altar and a lesser one to Frevisse before going slowly, silently away.

Frevisse herself went to her seat in the choir and sat gratefully down, there being small point in going elsewhere; the bell would surely soon ring for Vespers. She thought briefly of how Elianor's deep quiet after prayer was a better sign toward nunhood than her high excitement had been. Then she let go of that thought and all others, not even trying to pray but simply sitting in stillness, giving both her mind and body respite from the need to think and the need to do, if only for this little, little while.

Chapter 23

omina Elisabeth came to Vespers but kept her head deeply bowed through the Office, and since the fading light of the overcast day was not yet thickened enough for the expense of candles, Frevisse had no chance to see if she bore the marks of tears until the Office was done. Only while Domina Elisabeth gave them her blessing at the end did Frevisse see that, yes, her eyes had the red rims of much crying and her face the tired sag of someone lately gone through a hard and wearying time.

What had been passing between her and her brother? Surely he had not spent the time scolding her over Sister Cecely? The time for that had been when Sister Cecely first fled. If anyone was to be scolded now, surely it was Sister Cecely.

Domina Elisabeth left them again after Vespers, returning to her rooms for supper to be taken up to her on a tray.
This was no more her usual way than the rest of the day
had been, and midway through her own supper the terrible thought came to Frevisse that perhaps Abbot Gilberd
wanted to leave Sister Cecely here, for them to see to her
punishment, and that Domina Elisabeth had been pleading
against it, had gone even to the point of quarreling with
him and, having lost, could not yet face her nuns with the
ill news. The possibility of a quarrel between their prioress
and their abbot was less frightening than the chance that
Sister Cecely might become part of their life here again, and
as supper finished, Frevisse tried to put the thought of it
from her.

Although the rain was stopped, the evening was not an
appealing one for spending the hour of recreation in the garden. Most of the nuns left the refectory for the warming
room, but Frevisse did not join them. Her day had been
very long, and last night very short of sleep. She would happily have said Compline right then and gone straight to her
bed, yet she could not bring herself to quiet sitting in the
warming room, instead chose to pace the square of the
roofed cloister walk. She had spent many an hour of recreation walking there, often in easy talk with Dame Claire, often simply by herself. Its familiarity and quiet could be a
balm on troubled thoughts or to a trying day's weariness.
This evening, though, it was a cheerless place, with twilight
heavy under the cloud-thick sky, and the closed door to
what was become Sister Cecely's cell a too constant re-
minder of what Frevisse wanted not to think about for a
time. Nor did Dame Claire join her. Instead it was Dame
Thomasine likewise slowly pacing around the cloister walk,
her head bowed as usual, her hands folded into her opposite
sleeves just as Frevisse's hands were into her own sleeves.
But whereas Dame Thomasine was probably so far into

prayers as barely to know anyone else was there, Frevisse was all too aware of the folded parchments still in her undergown's left sleeve.

She did not know how much Mistress Petham had weighted her words toward making Edward give up the deeds and bill. When she told him he could keep his secret, she had maybe been even-worded, but equally she might have made it plain, under the words, what she thought he *ought* to do and thereby forced him to it. Still, he had given his own reason for doing it, Frevisse remembered. He had said his father had told him people should be good, and he had understood he should not have the parchments. So even if Mistress Petham had brought him to give them up, he had known why he should and, in the end, had done it willingly, Frevisse thought. Willingly and bravely.

Why did it have to take so much courage to do what was right?

Why was it that the ill-doers and liars seemed able to do wrong so much more easily, while those who did well and right seemed so often to have to fight themselves to do it? It was the ill-doers who should need the greater courage, going so far aside as they did from what was right. Yet they mostly seemed to do it with such ease.

It had been fruit from the tree of the knowledge of good and evil that Eve and Adam had eaten. Before then there had been no choice between right and wrong. There had been simply being. Frevisse found it difficult to imagine what life would be if it were simply being, living sure in the love of God without need of all the choices that knowledge had brought on mankind.

Maybe it was laziness that let people do wrong rather than right. Ignorance was easier than knowledge, and so they did not trouble themselves with knowledge of right and wrong, of good and ill, but simply settled for doing whatever came easiest to them in the moment, while despising anyone who tried to live for more than easy greed and shallow pride and momentary pleasures.

She had noted before now how often those who did ill despised those to whom they did it, being too cowardly to face the truth of their own actions.

If more people were willing to be as good and brave as small Edward had been today—were as willing to the truth as he had been—there would be far less hurt in the world, she thought sadly.

Of course he had hurt at doing what he did, but it was the brief hurt of pulling out a thorn, against the long hurt of leaving it in the flesh to rot.

It came to her then that in her thought-slowed pacing she had just passed Dame Thomasine for the second time, that Dame Thomasine was no longer walking, was simply standing at the low wall around the garth, looking across to Sister Cecely's shut door. The door was almost gone from sight in the growing dusk, and even if there had been light, there was nothing to see there, not even someone sitting guard. For now the door was simply tied shut, because all the nuns were at the end of their day's work, and all the cloister servants were at their end-of-day tasks. Whosoever's turn it was among the servants would come in a while with her bedding and settle across the door for the night, the door staying tied until morning, Sister Cecely alone behind it, no other company than her own thoughts through all the night hours. So from here in the walk there was nothing in particular to see, and Frevisse turned back to Dame Thomasine, stopped beside her, and asked quietly, "Dame, is aught amiss?"

The younger woman went on looking at the door, the smallest of frowns between her brows, and only after a long moment did she finally say, very low, still staring across at the door, "I've never wanted to be what she's been. I've never had urge to give up everything to the desires of the flesh. I never have. Nor I don't now. But I'm so . . ." She looked up at Frevisse with pleading eyes, as if confessing to a thing of shame. "I'm so tired."

All unexpectedly Frevisse was reminded of a small child too worn out to know that what it needed was simply bed, and she took Dame Thomasine by the arm, turned her around, sat her down on the low wall there, sat beside her, and said gently, much the way she had spoken to Edward this afternoon, "Then rest a little."

Dame Thomasine gave a small sigh, folded her hands in her lap, bowed her head, and seemed to shrink in on herself as she settled, huddling round-shouldered as if the weight of her habit were too much on her thin body.

After a moment of nothing else, only the cloister's quiet, Frevisse said gently, finding the words as she went, "That you're tired is no unlikely thing. You've burned with the fire of loving God for a good many years now. Have lived more fully in that love than anyone I've ever known. It would be no surprise if you've burned yourself away to nearly nothing inside your poor body."

She did not know from where that thought had come. Dame Thomasine's holiness was so much a part of St. Frideswide's life that for a long time there had been small reason to think about it. It simply *was*, the way their whole pattern of life here *was*, without deep need to wonder about it. In truth, that someone as holy as Dame Thomasine lived there among them was even, perhaps, a small, secret source of pride to some. What that holiness might be doing to Dame Thomasine had never been a matter for thought. Except once, a long time ago, Domina Edith had said something about it, hadn't she? But Frevisse did not remember what. Whatever comfort she could give Dame Thomasine had to come from what she could think herself, and she said, "You haven't been kind to your body, you know."

Dame Thomasine made a small shake of her head, refusing that.

"No," said Frevisse, refusing in her turn. "Consider our poor bodies. They go through our lives burdened with all the necessities and longings of flesh, and then at the end, when our souls go free, the poor body goes into the ground to rot away."

"Resurrection comes," Dame Thomasine murmured, meaning the rising of all bodies from their graves when time's end came.

"Yes," Frevisse agreed. "But however that wonder is worked when Judgment Day comes, in the meantime our bodies rot. Whether they have served us well or ill in life, no matter if they've been indulged"—she gave a glance at Sister Cecely's door—"or been denied, the soul goes free and they decay. And yet our bodies are God's gift to us. Shouldn't we treat them with at least a little pity, with a little kindness, in what little time they have to be alive? Not drive them early to the grave where, when all is said and done, they may be for a very long time?"

Dame Thomasine lifted her head, turned her face toward Frevisse, slightly frowning. That told that she had at least heard what Frevisse was saying, was even considering it, and very gently Frevisse went on, "You're tired. Not in your soul, surely, but in your body. Have pity on it. Kind care for it isn't sin or weakness. Be a little kind to yours."

Dame Thomasine began another small, denying shake of her head, and with a sudden sternness that surprised herself, Frevisse said, "Our flesh is the vessel that carries the fire of God's love. You have no right to break your body, either on purpose or through plain carelessness." She softened her voice again. "Think on that, Dame Thomasine."

The warming room's door opened, letting out a momentary yellow lamplight with the shapes of nuns briefly black against it as they came from the room, before someone put out the lamp and there was only soft blue twilight in the cloister. Much of the year Compline was said simply in the warming room, but during Holy and Easter Weeks, in honor of the especially holy time, the nuns returned to the church for it each evening, and Dame Thomasine and Frevisse rose together from the wall to join the others going there, Frevisse both glad for reason to end her talk at Dame Thomasine and wondering if she had done any good at all.

She was surprised by how easily and well she slept, even with the folded pieces of parchment tucked between the mattress and the wooden edge of the bed. She left them there when she rose in the night for Matins and Lauds, but put them again into her sleeve when she rose for Prime, beginning the new day. They would soon become her guilty secret, she thought, if she did not give them to Domina Elisabeth at the first reasonable chance this morning.

It seemed, though, that she was going to be denied a reasonable chance. Domina Elisabeth had come to Matins and Lauds and she came to Prime, but after Prime she went again to her rooms, so that her nuns breakfasted without her, nor did she come to Mass, and when time came for the morning's chapter meeting, she sent word by a servant that Dame Claire should take her place.

The nuns, already gathered in the warming room, all looked at one another, confused and uncertain. She was not ill, or she would have asked for Dame Claire to come to her, not given chapter over to her, and Dame Perpetua said aloud the question showing on the faces of most of them. "What's amiss with her? This can't all be Sister Cecely." She looked directly at Dame Margrett who had been in the parlor so much yesterday. "What else is amiss?"

Looking miserable, Dame Margrett shook her head, refusing any other answer at all, which told she had been ordered to silence about whatever she had heard. "Dame Johane?" Dame Perpetua demanded, but Dame Johane shook her head against answering, too, leaving everyone unsatisfied, and chapter that morning was a shambling thing. Father Henry gave the blessing on it as usual, but quickly and not as if his mind was altogether there for it. As he left, Dame Amicia whispered that he had come from his time with Abbot Gilberd and Domina Elisabeth yesterday afternoon looking troubled. "Just as troubled as he still looks. Whatever it is, it's not getting better," she said.

Dame Claire uneasily took up the reading of today's chapter of the Rule, but afterward no one had much heart for reporting on their duties or confessing any faults, nor did Dame Claire show much desire to hear them. Chapter meetings were a kind of anchor in each day. As the Offices were the nuns' link to heaven, chapter meetings were their link to the world. The one with the other kept a balance between the two sides of their lives. Now that balance was wavering, and so were they, and so did Frevisse's certainty that she must give the deeds and bill to Domina Elisabeth.

She came from the warming room with the others at chapter's end to find Alson waiting in the walk to say that Dame Perpetua was to take Sister Cecely up to the prioress' parlor now, that Abbot Gilberd would be there shortly. Since today was Dame Perpetua's turn with Sister Cecely, this bidding could hardly be a surprise to Dame Perpetua, but she nonetheless cast a pleading look around, as if in hope of a rescue no one could give her. The most she got was an encouraging hand laid briefly on her shoulder by Dame Claire and, "At least now you'll hear what is happening."

Dame Perpetua looked only a little encouraged by that, but since she would surely be as enjoined to silence as Dame Margrett had been, none of the rest of them would be any the wiser, and Frevisse went away to the guesthall, feeling yet again forestalled from giving the deeds and bill to Domina Elisabeth.

Forestalled—or plain unwilling.

She faced it might well be the latter, then tried to tell herself again that burdening Domina Elisabeth with more just now seemed unfair. But if that was it, why not give them to Abbot Gilberd?

Because they were not his business.

That thought had come far too easily. She looked at it more closely. It stayed the same. Abbot Gilberd was here to determine what should be done with Sister Cecely. These other matters—the poisonings, the stolen deeds and bill, even Edward now he was under St. Frideswide's protection—were arguably the priory's to deal with.

Or—to be closer to the truth, Frevisse thought—they were *hers* to deal with, because she found she was indeed increasingly hesitant to give anything over to Domina Elisabeth just now. The way the prioress was presently slacking and forsaking all her duties, she might simply give any and all priory problems over to Abbot Gilberd, and that would not be to the priory's good in the long run of things. Giving over power to someone was always easier than getting it back, and Frevisse was not minded to let Abbot Gilberd have more of a hand in St. Frideswide's business than could be helped. If he took it into his mind that his hand was necessary here, getting his hand out again later might prove difficult.

So when, at the foot of the stairs up to the guesthall, she met Abbot Gilberd coming down, followed by one of his clerks with an ink bottle in one hand and a clutch of paper in the other, she made no effort to speak to him, merely stepped aside and sank in a low curtsy. He sketched a cross in blessing above her as he passed without pause, and she let him go his way to the cloister while she went up the steps and into the guesthall.

Ela was there, keeping an eye on matters. By this time on any usual day, the hall would have been fairly or altogether empty except for servants, with such travelers as had been there overnight gone on their way at first daylight, and Tom and Luce clearing and cleaning around such rare, few guests as were staying longer. But this past week and more had not been usual, and still was not. The hall was cluttered and loud with the abbot's men, and Ela cocked her head to look up at Frevisse and asked, rather than waiting for Frevisse's every-morning question of how things were, "What's toward? Father Henry was closeted with Abbot Gilberd a long while yester-evening and looked none so happy when he came out. Nor he looks no happier today, and not Abbot Gilberd either."

"Abbot Gilberd is going to speak with Sister Cecely this morning," Frevisse said, keeping aside from a straight answer. "I suppose Father Henry will be there, too."

"More patience to them both," Ela said back, letting Frevisse know she knew an aside-answer when she heard it but letting it go. "The Lawsells purpose to leave this morning. Their man came in with their horses about Compline."

Frevisse nodded. She would try to be present when they left, she thought, to bid Elianor farewell and encourage her mother to think of the girl's return.

"They're quarreling over it though," Ela said. "They were loud about it a while ago. It's why they're not gone yet, I think."

"Quarreling?" Frevisse asked. "The Lawsells?"

"Them. You should talk to them, maybe." Meaning she thought Frevisse had *better* talk to them.

Frevisse held back from a sigh, because Ela was right, and went toward their chamber at the hall's side, hearing as she neared their door Elianor's young voice saying, low but angrily stubborn, "Once you have me back there, you won't let me out again until I agree to marry someone. I know that's what you mean to do. Don't tell me it isn't."

"You know no such thing," her mother answered with the edged patience of someone determined not to show how angry she was. "What I am saying is we need to go home and talk about it more. I am saying . . ."

"You don't mean 'talk about it.' You mean 'talk me into changing my mind.'"

Frevisse knocked firmly at the door and opened it. Mistress Lawsell turned toward her, and Elianor, who had been sitting on the edge of the bed with her arms folded across herself—to show she did not intend to move, Frevisse supposed—stood up. Before either of them could say or do anything more, Frevisse said, "I wish to speak alone with your mother. Please leave us, Elianor."

Elianor, surprised, looked back and forth between her mother and Frevisse, then dropped a short curtsy more or less at both of them, and went out of the chamber. Frevisse turned back to Mistress Lawsell and said, "You do wrong to keep her from where her heart wants to go."

"You *would* say that," Mistress Lawsell snapped back. "Being a nun and in need of more nuns here."

"And *you* would say otherwise," Frevisse said evenly, "having come here in a lie."

That direct attack caught Mistress Lawsell off her guard. "What?"

"You didn't come here in the hope of turning your daughter toward becoming a nun. You hoped to turn her *from* it. What you want for her is a wealthy marriage, not the good of her soul."

"Marriage isn't damnation!"

"It can be, if someone's heart is altogether elsewhere. Force someone into a pathway against their nature, and the chance of damnation is very great." As Sister Cecely had been forced, Frevisse suddenly thought. She and Dame Johane had both come here by their family's choice, not theirs, and Sister Cecely must have gone through with taking her final vows because it was expected of her, not from any true desire. Dame Johane, however it had been with her at the beginning, had found a place here, had found work she cared about and become happy. Sister Cecely had failed, had made her life instead on lust and lies and broken vows. And Frevisse said, with a sad sense that she was pleading as no one had pleaded for Sister Cecely, however opposite that pleading was, "Think on it, I pray you, Mistress Lawsell. Which will be better? A daughter forced to go a way she does not want to go and angry at you for it, or a daughter gladly become a nun and praying for your soul's salvation all her days. Which will be better—for your daughter and for you?"

Mistress Lawsell's jaw had set stubbornly while Frevisse spoke. There was no surprise in her answering, "We're going home today. The matter can be discussed as well there as here."

Frevisse guessed that Elianor had the right of it. Having failed of her purpose to put her daughter off thought of being a nun, Mistress Lawsell would put her under duress of one kind or another once she had her home, to force her to do as she was bid. There was nothing Frevisse could do about that. The girl was her mother's. And somewhat more shortly than might be charitable, she said at Mistress Lawsell, "Very well. May God and St. Frideswide be with you both," and left the room, leaving Mistress Lawsell to remember—or not—what St. Frideswide had done to those who had tried to come between her and her desires.

In her quick look around the hall, Frevisse did not see Elianor. Or Jack Rowcliffe. Elianor was very likely gone to the church again. Had Jack followed her despite Frevisse's hinted warning yesterday?

But now that she thought about it, she had noted neither him nor his father when she first came into the hall. Maybe they were with Symond, or else had gone out somewhere— to see how their horses did or simply to stretch their legs. She was not so much concerned about where they were as with her desire not to have Jack to hand when she questioned Symond Hewet about the bill of obligation between them.

Breredon's chamber was nearer than where Symond lay, though, and for duty's sake, she went first to see how Breredon did, pleased to find him up and walking carefully back and forth in his room. To her inquiry he answered, "My guts still ache from the beating they took, but food and drink stay down me now. I'll be ready to talk with your abbot or whoever else about having Edward out of here and away home with me in no more than a day or so, surely."

He did not look nearly that near to being able to sit a horse, nor did Frevisse know if he was going to have his way about Edward when all was said and done, but not wanting to discourage him while he mended, she merely answered, "My lord abbot is seeing Sister Cecely even now," and went on her way.

Fortune was with her. No one was with Symond except a man who must be his own servant among the men who had come with him and the Rowcliffes, and by the look of Symond, she judged it was surely a good thing he was not being left alone. He lay with his head barely raised on his pillow, his arms and hands slack along his body on the blanket over him, his skin the color and look of dough gone bad; and even though his eyes were open and he turned his head a little when she came in, she asked the servant instead of him if he was fit to talk a little.

"I am," Symond answered for himself. His voice, though weak, was the strongest thing about him. "Does your infirmarian know what this is yet? Has anyone else fallen ill?"

"No one else is ill yet, no," Frevisse answered. "Dame Claire is still trying to learn what it is. Or was. We hope it's done." All of which was true, without being all the truth, and she went straight on, to leave it behind her, "There's something I must needs ask you, and you might want that I ask it to you alone."

"Geffe is to be trusted to keep quiet if I say so," Symond said. "What is it?"

For the seemliness of not being alone with a man—with two men—Frevisse had been standing in the doorway. Now, although no one was near enough to hear her if she kept her voice down, she took a single step into the chamber before saying, "It's about the bill of obligation between you and Jack Rowcliffe."

Symond made what passed, in his weakened state, as an effort to sit up. Geffe jerked forward to stop him, but there was no need. Symond's weakness sank him flat again, even as he demanded with what strength he had, "How do you know of that?"

"I have it," Frevisse answered evenly. "And the deeds that Sister Cecely stole."

Symond closed his eyes and breathed, "Thank God and all the saints." He opened his eyes. "Does John know?"

"I haven't seen him yet, to tell him."

"The bill. Don't tell him of that. That's between Jack and me."

Geffe made a humph sound that Frevisse took for his comment on that.

Symond ignored him, and Frevisse said, "If the bill is only between you and Jack, then there's no need his father know of it. But I would know what it's about."

"It was between him and me and Guy. It matters to no one else but us."

Frevisse hesitated, then decided nothing would serve but the outright truth and said, very careful that her voice not carry out the doorway, "Dame Claire thinks neither you nor Master Breredon were honestly ill. She thinks that indeed someone gave you both some manner of poison."

Symond stared at her, frowning, openly not understanding what that had to do with what he had said. Then understanding came. He startled with it, started to say,

"Jack . . ." choked and began to cough dryly, so that Geffe came hurriedly forward, lifted him a little with an arm behind his shoulders, took up a cup from the small table by the bed, and held it for him to drink. When he was quiet, Geffe eased him down again, only then sending a reproachful look at Frevisse. She made a small shrug, silently saying that it was not her fault.

Eyes closed, Symond said, still somewhat breathlessly, "Not Jack. If anyone poisoned us, it was Cecely. Not Jack."

"Why not Jack?" Frevisse said.

"No reason he should." He looked at her to be certain she was listening. "He's already paid back half the money, and neither Guy nor I would ride him hard to have the rest. He knows that. If he took fifty years, I wouldn't ride him about it."

"What was it for?"

"A woman, of course."

Symond must have felt the weight of her disapproval bearing down on him because he gave a single short-breathed laugh and said, "Not that way, no. A widow in the village. A young and pretty widow in the village. He'd had some sport with her. Then she started to threaten him that she was going to claim he had promised her marriage. You know the tangles that can get into, if it comes before the church courts. Not adding on what his father would do to him for being so much a fool."

"*Had* he promised her?"

"He swore to us he hadn't and, knowing the widow, I'd take his word over hers. I don't doubt he would have won clear of her in the end, but in the long run it would have cost him in more than money. So he begged Guy and me for help, to keep it all secret from his father. We helped him, and last she was heard of, the widow had used our money for a dowry, got a little shopkeeper to husband her, and is happy in Norwich."

Needing to rest after all that, Symond closed his eyes but lifted the fingers of his nearer hand to tell Frevisse he wanted her to stay. After a few moments, without opening his eyes, he murmured, "It's been to the good. Between the widow with him and Cecely with Guy, he's learned the cost of sport with women."

"And maybe that true dealing will cost him less in the end," Frevisse said dryly.

Symond gave a single, silent laugh. He lay quietly a moment longer, then opened his eyes and said, frowning upward at the rafters. "Guy talked me into helping him. I wonder if that's why Guy was so willing to help him—that Guy had learned his lesson but the hard way and was having to live it out, whether he would or no, and wanted to save Jack from the same." He looked at Frevisse. "Poison?"

"Poison."

"That would be Cecely." He closed his eyes again. "Why she'd poison Breredon, I don't know. But me . . . yes, she'd like me dead."

Frevisse judged he was fading, would soon be to sleep, but she asked anyway, quietly, "Why?"

"Because I wouldn't let her use Jack's bill to extort money from me, maybe. She found it among Guy's papers. Before he was dead or after, I don't know. But after he was dead, she told me if I'd give her money, she wouldn't tell John about it. Bitch."

"But you didn't pay her."

Symond's slack mouth twitched toward a smile. "I told her if she did anything of the kind"—His words had begun to slide apart as he slipped toward sleep—"I'd make trouble for her . . . like she'd never seen before."

Frevisse took another step forward, trying to reach him for just a little longer. "You told her you knew she was a nun."

But his breathing had evened into sleep. Geffe moved as

if to warn Frevisse against waking him, but Frevisse knew better than to do that. She shook her head at Geffe to let him know his master was safe from questions for a while and started to leave, then turned back and, with no one but Geffe to see what she did, slipped the deeds and bill from her sleeve, took the bill, and held it out to him. He took it with a questioning look. Frevisse whispered with a small beckon of her head at the sleeping man, "For him. Tell no one else."

Understanding sharpened in Geffe's face. He was bowing in ready agreement as Frevisse left him.

Chapter 24

Knowing there could be scant time before she would have to go to Tierce, Frevisse stayed in the guesthall kitchen only long enough to know that, despite what food and drink Abbot Gilberd had brought, there would soon be no avoiding sending someone maybe as far as Banbury to buy more because only so much could be had from the village. Domina Elisabeth would not welcome hearing that, but then, Frevisse did not welcome the thought of having to tell her, so they were even, she supposed, as she came up the outer stairs from the kitchen and saw John Rowcliffe and his son walking through the gateway from the outer yard, back from wherever they had been.

Frevisse was immediately glad she no longer had Jack's bill of obligation as she turned to meet father and son in the middle of the guesthall yard. They both bowed to her, and she said, with a bend of her head back to them, "I thought you would care to know that Abbot Gilberd is questioning Sister Cecely again this morning. I have a question for you in turn. These deeds that she stole from you, how did she come by them?"

Rowcliffe made an irritated growl in his throat. "She told me a mouse had got at some of Guy's papers, that part of the deed to Guy's manor—that one that's Edward's now—was chewed and she wanted to see if there was a copy of it among my deeds and all. That was likely. We do that—keep copies of one thing and another in each other's strongboxes, so if one is lost—fire or storm or mice or whatever—all isn't lost. So I didn't think that much on it. She came asking it one morning just as I was leaving with my wife to go to market day in Wymondham. On purpose, that was, I'll wager. I just gave her the key to the box and told her to be sure to lock it when she was done and give my steward the key."

"When did you know they were gone?"

Rowcliffe grimaced. "When she disappeared, and Edward with her. Right frighted we were that something had happened to them, until Symond gave up her secret. He knew more about the thieving wench than we'd ever guessed and said that if she was gone, she wasn't gone empty-handed. That's when I found the two deeds were gone with her."

"And they're why you came after her."

"For Edward, too. I don't want to leave the little mite to her. No telling who she'd sell him to. Well, James Breredon, plainly, but that's no help to me. Better he be with family."

"How does he?" Jack asked. "When I talked with him, he said he was well enough, but is he?"

"He and Mistress Petham seem happy in each other's company," Frevisse said.

"You're keeping him away from that mother of his?" Rowcliffe demanded. "She's poison, she is."

Frevisse hid her thought that there it was again—poison and Sister Cecely together in the same breath—and said, "We're presently keeping Sister Cecely away from everyone, except now she's with Abbot Gilberd and Domina Elisabeth."

"Just so they remember to find out what she's done with my deeds," Rowcliffe grumbled.

"She hid them with Edward," Frevisse said and slipped them from her sleeve. "I don't know that he knew for certain what they were, but he knew they aren't his mother's, and he gave them to me." She held them out. "Here they are."

Rowcliffe gaped at her, while something like smothered fear started up in Jack Rowcliffe's face and did not fade until his father had gathered his wits, took the deeds from Frevisse, and opened them. Jack could see then they were only the deeds, no damning bill of obligation with them, and he exclaimed, "That's them! We've got them back!"

"We do, indeed," John Rowcliffe said, his eyes fixed on the parchment and satisfaction rich in his voice. "There's a world of trouble saved." More than satisfaction: naked relief. Glowing with it, he looked at Frevisse. "I owe you much for this. Is there aught I can do for your priory in return?"

Frevisse had been going to prompt him to that thought. To have him come to it himself was even better, and she said, "We're nearly out of food. I know you can't leave yet, because your cousin is far from strong enough, but we're almost out of anything to feed so many people, even with what Abbot Gilberd brought for his own use. If you could help with that, it would be repayment in plenty."

Rowcliffe gave a sharp nod. "That I can do. I'll send two of my men off to—where's nearest? Banbury? To there, to get—What would serve best?

"Old Ela in the guesthall will be able to tell you," Frevisse said. "Our thanks to you. It will take a great worry off us."

"As you've taken a great worry off me," Rowcliffe returned, and they parted, pleased on both sides.

The bell began to ring to Tierce as she closed the cloister door behind her, and she went gratefully to the church, glad for the coming respite of the Office. So she was not best pleased to find Dame Perpetua and Dame Amicia standing in the middle of the choir, not taking their places but staring at someone kneeling on the step below the altar. Someone not a nun. Not in that green dress. A green dress that Frevisse knew with a sinking heart, even before Elianor Lawsell turned her head to look back over her right shoulder at them. Despite the silence that should hold once the bell had rung to an Office, Dame Amicia started, "Who's she? What's she . . ."

Frevisse made a sharp gesture, silencing Dame Amicia, and pointed to the choir seats. Dame Perpetua understood, started toward her own, then came back to take Dame Amicia firmly by one elbow and steer her toward her place while Frevisse went to her own. The other nuns, coming in, each had their turn at stopping and staring at Elianor, but with the example set by Dame Perpetua, Dame Amicia, and Frevisse, no one said anything, just silently took their seats. Only Dame Thomasine seemed not to note the girl.

There was an uncertain pause then, when they were all in their places, but before Dame Juliana could decide to start the Office, Domina Elisabeth all unexpectedly came. She, too, paused at sight of Elianor, now facing the altar again with deeply bowed head and hands clasped in front of her. Frevisse, her own head bowed, could see only the lower half of Domina Elisabeth's skirts but was able to tell by that how long—longer than anyone else—she stood there before finally stepping up into her place. More than that, when she began the Office it was unevenly, with a tremor in her voice, and it was soon clear that her mind was barely there. The nuns, depending on her for their lead, got almost none. Their first antiphonal "Alleluia" came raggedly, and raggedly the Office went from there, until Frevisse could only be glad when the closing "Amen" came.

But with Tierce's end, when Domina Elisabeth should have risen from her place and led the nuns from the church, she stood abruptly up and stalked toward the altar, demanding as she went, "What are you doing here? What do you mean, being here this way?"

Along with everyone else, Elianor stood up, too. She turned around but stayed where she was and said, her voice only shaking a little, "I claim sanctuary. I want to be here. I claim sanctuary."

From beyond the rood screen where she must have been waiting for the Office's end, Mistress Lawsell ordered, anger bursting from every word, "You come out of there, Elianor! You stop this foolishness and come here! We're going home!"

Elianor returned as fiercely, "I won't! I'm going to be a nun!" And to Domina Elisabeth, no less fiercely, "She can't force me to leave. I claim sanctuary. You have to let me stay!"

Domina Elisabeth's uncertainty, as she looked from one of them to the other was painful to see. She had never shown uncertainty about anything. But neither had she ever been absent or inattentive to the Offices before now. Only finally, sharply, did she draw herself up straight and order forcefully against the affront to her church and self, "Both of you be silent!"

Mistress Lawsell's mouth, opened toward another demand or protest, snapped shut.

Still sharply, Domina Elisabeth said, "This is hardly something that will be settled by shouting. Not here or anywhere else, but most especially not here. Elianor, you've decided then that after all you want to be a nun? As your mother *told us she hoped for you?*"

That was less a question at Elianor than a cold challenge at Mistress Lawsell, but it was Elianor who answered, saying scornfully, "She never hoped for me to be a nun. She *lied* to you about why we were here!"

"Is that true?" Domina Elisabeth asked at Mistress Lawsell.

Not seeming the least abashed, Mistress Lawsell said back at her, "Yes. Now tell her to come out of there. This can all be talked out at home."

Elianor started, "I won't go! Once you have me back there you'll . . ."

Not raising her voice but with the full weight of her will on the words, Domina Elisabeth ordered, "Enough. Both of you." And when the Lawsells' mutual silence assured her that she was obeyed, she said at Elianor, "You may stay where you are for the time being." And at Mistress Lawsell, over the beginning of a protest from her, "*You* will content yourself with waiting in either the guesthall or here in the church, with thought that prayer for forgiveness for lying to us would not come amiss." Mistress Lawsell made again to say something, but Domina Elisabeth raised a hand to stop her, going on with unrelenting sternness, "This will have to content you for now. We presently have weightier matters on us than you and your daughter's quarrel. When we have time, then we shall turn to your lies and misleadings. Now leave us. Or else kneel to your prayers."

Mistress Lawsell opened her mouth toward some manner of furious reply, then seemed to think better of it. Or maybe she was suddenly aware of the several servants there and staring. Either way, she drew herself up straight, jerked her head in very false respect at Domina Elisabeth, and stalked away, down the nave and out the west door. It was a heavy door, not easily dragged shut into a slam, but she accomplished it.

When the thunder of that ended and she was gone, everyone's gaze swung back to Elianor, who was still standing at the altar, glowing with triumph. She made as if to turn around and kneel again, but Domina Elisabeth ordered, "Come away from there. Come here to me."

Elianor startled, faced her, hesitated, then obeyed, with carefully bowed head and hands quietly folded in front of her in good nunly seeming.

As unrelenting as she had been to Mistress Lawsell, Domina Elisabeth said, "You have been disobedient to your mother and possibly disrespectful to us. Dame Juliana will take you from here to the warming room. There you will wait in patience until we have time to consider this matter further. Dame Juliana."

Dame Juliana rose from her place and stood waiting. Elianor cast what might have been a frightened look into Domina Elisabeth's stern face, dropped her gaze again, and followed Dame Juliana away. The onlookers beyond the rood screen were leaving, too, but the nuns stayed where they were, unable to go until Domina Elisabeth gave them leave.

She should have dismissed them then. There was nothing to keep them there longer. Instead, she groped out a hand for the tall edge of her choir stall, took hold on it almost blindly, drew herself to it, bowed her head to the wood, and stayed there, bent over, clinging with both hands, silent and unmoving. Her nuns stayed equally silent, heads turning side to side as they looked at one another, no one knowing what to do until finally Dame Claire rose carefully from her own place and went to her, put an arm around her, drew her upright, and led her away, out of the church.

Only when they were gone did the rest of the nuns, in silence and carefully, leave, too. In the cloister walk they were in time to see Dame Claire starting with Domina Elisabeth up the stairs to her rooms. Still no one said anything, simply went their separate ways in deep silence to whatever were their present tasks.

Frevisse, needed nowhere else just then, slipped away to her desk in the cloister walk for some place to be. From habit, she opened the box that sheltered the paper, pens, and ink of her work but took nothing out and after a moment shut the lid again and simply sat.

What was happening with Domina Elisabeth?

For that while in the church just now, confronting Mistress Lawsell, dealing with Elianor, she had been herself, but the very difference of that to how she had been these past few days and how she had collapsed afterward only made more plain that something was very wrong, either bodily or mindfully. So far as Frevisse knew, Dame Claire had not been treating her for anything of the body. Was her trouble of the mind then?

Whichever it was, the lack of her strong hand over them was starting to be felt in the cloister. From there it would soon spread through the whole priory if something was not done. So maybe it was just as well Abbot Gilberd was here. No matter how little anyone among the nuns wanted his meddling in their lives, best to have it quickly if it was needed, Frevisse thought.

She also thought she would put off attempting to confess to Domina Elisabeth that Elianor's presence in the church was her fault, that when she asked to speak to her mother alone this morning, somewhere in her mind—where she deliberately had not looked too closely—she had thought Elianor might very well take the chance to escape into the church. And Elianor had. Now the trouble of that—and Frevisse's fault in it—had to be dealt with.

Still, among the other present troubles, that one could wait. The why and who of Breredon's and Symond's poisonings mattered more, and she looked across the cloister to where Dame Perpetua now sat again outside Sister Cecely's cell and knew that—whatever the how and whatever the why—Sister Cecely was surely the center of all.

Cecely had given up pacing, could no longer sit on the hard bench, would not read their damnable breviary anymore, was tired of lying down on the thin pallet, was tired of everything and all of it. All she wanted was to grab Neddie and get as far and as fast from this place as possible.

Except neither grabbing Neddie nor fleeing here were possible. Not while she was trapped in this room. Trapped here, all she could do was sit on the pallet with her back against the wall, her legs drawn up, and her arms around her knees, staring at the room's nothingness.

Both of her times with the abbot had gone badly. There was no disguising that from herself. He had had no interest in anything she had to say except admittance of her guilt and had been angry when she would not give it to him straight out and in so many words. Before she was brought before him, she had promised herself she would be humble to him, but when it came to it, she could not, *could not*. He had demanded of her where she had been and what she had done since she fled St. Frideswide's, and she had refused him even a straight answer to that until she found he already knew all the answers, that he had already talked to John Rowcliffe and knew everything he wanted to know.

The unfairness of that still overwhelmed her—that he was so openly ready to believe John Rowcliffe before he believed her.

Nor had he cared at all about her grief for Guy. "Your paramour," he had said coldly.

"My husband!" she had said sharply back at him, no matter she had meant to gain time by seeming what they wanted her to be. Gain time until . . .

And then what he had said about her dead babies. He ought to be damned to hell for that alone, let be all the rest!

The doorway darkened with a nun coming in.

Cecely did not bother to rise, simply raised her head, was not pleased to see Dame Frevisse, and stubbornly said nothing. Neither, at first, did Dame Frevisse. Instead, they stared at each other across the room's small width until finally Dame Frevisse said, "Did it go well with Abbot Gilberd?"

Cecely nearly spat into the rushes with disgust. "*Him,*" she said angrily. "Do you know what he said of my dead babies? He said that was God's mercy, taking them in their innocence but sparing me, that I"—she deepened her voice in mockery of the man—"might have time to repent my sins here on earth, rather than pay for them in Hell after my death." She went back to her own voice. "Hateful man! God's mercy," she mocked. "What God is is cruel."

Dame Frevisse snapped, "What God is—" but stopped.

Pleased at having stung her into even that much, Cecely jibed, "What? What are you going to tell me God is? That he's a loving god? That because Guy and I loved one another, my babies died because God *loves* me?" She grabbed up a handful of rushes and threw them down. "I can do without that kind of love!"

"What God is," Dame Frevisse began again, coldly now, "is a victim of our foolishness. Loving us, he's hurt by the hurts we bring on ourselves. The way you would hurt with any hurt Edward might have. The way . . ."

"Neddie!" Cecely cried. "How does he? Is he well?"

"He's well," Dame Frevisse said stiffly.

"When can I see him again? It isn't right to keep a mother from her child."

"Given the wrongs you've done," Dame Frevisse said, still coldly, "you'd do well not to invoke 'right and wrong' for anything you want."

Cecely made an impatient noise at the woman. There was no way through these women's thick skulls to their shriveled brains, and going a different way, she demanded, "How does Master Breredon?"

"Much better. He's far along to being altogether well again." She paused as if waiting for something else from Cecely.

What Cecely wanted was to know when he would be fit enough to find a way to carry through what she wanted of him. Hardly able to ask that, she said sullenly, "It was the Rowcliffes did it to him. I told you that. They should have been sent away after they did it. But no one listens."

"If you're so certain the Rowcliffes did it," Dame Frevisse said, "you'll have to find why Symond Hewet is ill, too. Or you might want to ask how he does. He is, after all, something like kin to you and certainly to Edward."

Rage flowered like fire in Cecely, welcome for its heat and brightness against all the cold fears gathering around her. "Symond!" she hissed. "That treacherous, miserable *cur*! If it wasn't for him, none of this would be happening! Isn't he dead yet? I thought he was dying."

"He was near to dying, yes." An edge came into Dame Frevisse's voice that sounded to Cecely like mockery. "But no, he isn't dead. He even looks likely to live."

Cecely trembled with doubled rage. "All of this is his fault! All of it! I didn't do anything against him. It's all his doing! Guy was hardly cold in his grave and I was mad with grief and . . ."

"I thought Guy drowned at sea."

"The bodies washed up on the shore, didn't they? That's how the wreck was known!" How stupid could this woman be? Vicious with her rightful anger and the scraped-raw edge of her grief, Cecely said sharply, "I didn't know which way to turn. All I had left was Neddie, and Symond came to me, saying he wanted Neddie. He said he and Guy had talked of it and that Guy had wanted him to have Neddie. I called him the liar he is and said he'd best leave me alone or I'd tell John about Jack's debt. That stopped him. He said he'd let me think on it, and we'd talk about it later. The way he said that, it frightened me. He meant to hurt me! I know it! And Neddie! That's why I wanted us away from him!"

Dame Frevisse regarded her in unfriendly silence a moment, then said, "But you were willing to sell your son's wardship to Master Breredon."

"That was different. I needed . . . They were against me, always. All Guy's family, not just Symond. They were going to turn on me now Guy was gone. They were going to take Neddie from me, and I'd rather anyone had him but them! Anyone but Symond most of all!"

Grief and anger at all the wrongs done against her rose up, choking her. She had always deeply delighted in knowing that she and Guy lived together inside a secret that only the two of them knew. Their secret had made a world where there were only the two of them and no one else, a place where *Guy* was all her own and no one else's. That he had told someone else—that he had broken their secret, broken their world—that was a betrayal as great as his death had been, and giving way to the boil and pain of her anger, she burst out, "How *could* he have told Symond our secret! Why did he tell him? *Why?*"

She was demanding that, yet again, at God rather than at Dame Frevisse, but it was Dame Frevisse who answered coldly back, "He likely did it to protect his son from whatever foolish things you might do. Any such foolish things as what you *have* done."

Cecely gasped at the unfairness and cruelty of that and cried out on the higher-mounting wave of her anger at God and Guy and this hateful nun, "Neddie didn't need protecting from anything! He had me! He *has* me! Except you've taken him away from me!"

Dame Frevisse, untouched by any answering anger—cold bitch of a woman—said, "But you're willing to sell him to Master Breredon when no one else in his family wants that."

"Only because they made me! If they had just left us alone . . ."

"Did you threaten to tell Master Rowcliffe about his son's bill of obligation?"

"Only because Symond made me! He . . ." Cecely broke off on a gasp, strangled on a new fear. "How do you know about the bill?" she demanded, then answered that herself, saying bitterly, "Symond told you."

"Symond did not."

"Then—" Cecely sprang to her feet. "Then you stole it from Neddie! The deeds and the bill! You stole them from him!"

"He gave them to me. Of his own choice. Because he thought it was wrong that he have them."

"You stole them from him! From a little boy! You stole them! They're mine!" She started toward the nun. "Where are they?"

"They are not yours," Dame Frevisse said, still not raising her cold voice. "They were never yours, and they are back in the hands of the men to whom they belong. The bill to Symond Hewet, the deeds to Master Rowcliffe."

Cecely took a step back in mingled horror and disbelief. Her heel caught against the edge of the pallet and she stumbled a little and was forced to turn sideways and brace a hand against the wall to keep from falling but all the time not taking her horrified stare off the nun. The woman meant it! She had given everything away! Nothing was left! Guy was gone, and her hopes were gone, and there was only Neddie and what she could get from Breredon for him. But she didn't know how she was going to get her hands on Neddie and away from here. And even if she did, what Breredon could give her wouldn't be enough now. But there had to be some way. There had to be!

But she did not see it. All she could see was Dame Frevisse watching her. A cold, unbending woman who was, at best, uncaring about her pain or, more likely, was enjoying it.

Nothing was the way it was supposed to be! Guy had betrayed her. Neddie had lost what she'd trusted to him. Symond hadn't died. Everything was lost and gone wrong, and with a cry she put her hands over her face and crumpled down into a huddled heap on the pallet, trying to hide not just from the nun but from everything, everything, *everything*.

Chapter 25

haken, Frevisse stared down at the huddle of Sister Cecely. The grief and anger that had torn her voice, the outright terror on her face before she collapsed, had been of a woman in vast, staggering pain.

And yet Frevisse found herself turning away from her with no word said.

Found herself leaving the room.

Found Abbot Gilberd standing in the cloister walk just outside the door.

Dame Perpetua, surely having risen to her feet when the abbot approached, was standing, too, her head deeply bowed as she probably did her best to be invisible. She would have heard everything, but how much Abbot Gilberd had heard, Frevisse had no way of knowing. She started a deep curtsy that he stopped with a flick of his hand, then made a sharp gesture for her to follow him. With folded hands and her head as bowed as Dame Perpetua's, Frevisse did, hearing behind her the whisper of Dame Perpetua's skirts as she sank rapidly down onto the stool, probably in relief that it was not to her the abbot wished to speak.

On her own part and judging by her startled glimpse of his stern stare at her before she had started to curtsy, Frevisse very much doubted she was going to like the next few minutes and tried to brace herself as he led her along and around the cloister walk to the corner near the foot of the dorter stairs. There, most away from where they might be overheard by anyone while still in sight of anyone who cared to look, Abbot Gilberd turned to her and said, "You gave that woman no comfort."

Even without Abbot Gilberd's stern saying of it, Frevisse was unsteadied by that failure, now it was done past undoing. Whatever else Sister Cecely was, she was a woman in breaking-hearted torment and yet Frevisse had walked away from her with no offer of comfort at all. From where had that cruelty come? Frevisse did not know until slowly, staring at the paving stones between the hems of her black gown and Abbot Gilberd's black robe, she found her way to an answer and, still slowly, feeling her way through the words, finally said, "Sister Cecely has lived comfortably in her lies for years. She's lived in them happily and never cared what was the truth. Now all her lies are breaking down and taking her comfort with them. But to have the lies broken and all her comfort gone may be the only way she'll ever be able to grow into facing the truth."

And Frevisse prayed silently that it had been an innate knowing of that—even if not understood until now—that had kept her from giving any kindness to Sister Cecely just now. An innate knowing, not a cold heart.

Whichever way it had been, Abbot Gilberd said nothing

for an uncomfortably long moment. Then he sketched a cross in the air above her, said, "Benedicite, dame," and walked away along the cloister walk.

Keeping her head bowed, Frevisse said, "Thank you, my lord," at his departing heels and stayed where she was. Only when he was well away, probably going to see Domina Elisabeth again, or perhaps Sister Cecely, did she move, going swiftly along the walk behind him as far as the door into the church. There she lifted the heavy latch and went in, closed the door with care for silence, and went—nearly fleeing in her need—to her place in the choir, sank to her knees in her stall, clasped her hands on the reading ledge, pressed her forehead to her hands, tightly closed her eyes, and began to whisper, *"Omnipotens deus, misereatur mei et dimissis peccatis meis. Omnipotens deus, misereatur nostri et dimissis peccatis nostris."* Almighty god, have pity on me and dismiss my sins. Almighty god, have pity on us and dismiss our sins.

Repeating and repeating it until the upheaval of her feelings steadied and her mind cleared a little.

Then, falling silent, she lifted her head and eased carefully backward onto the seat behind her.

One thought at last came cold and calm to her.

There were still lies in this matter.

Cecely said Symond Hewet had asked for Edward's wardship. She said that she had forestalled him with threat of telling Jack Rowcliffe's father about the bill of obligation, that then she had become frightened and decided to flee.

On the other side, Symond Hewet claimed that she had tried to extort money from him with the bill, that he had warned her off with promise of trouble for her if she made trouble for him.

The stories were close enough to one another. Cecely had notably left out mention of stealing the deeds. Symond had said nothing about asking for Edward's wardship. Both agreed that Cecely had tried to use Jack's bill, whatever the reason. So, if nothing else, that was likely true, however little way it went to answering anything.

Maybe it was not necessary to know precisely what had passed between them. It was maybe enough to know that—whatever the truth behind her choice—Cecely had fled from the Rowcliffes, taking her son and the stolen deeds, not knowing that Symond knew her deepest secret and that, knowing it, he would have somewhere to look for her.

Even Cecely was not such a fool as to come here if she had known—even suspected—anyone knew her past.

Of course returning here at all had been a fool thing to do, whatever her reason, but Cecely had never been as well-witted as she plainly thought she was—well-witted while everyone else were fools; that was how she seemed to see the world.

Frevisse thought wryly that an almost greater question than who had poisoned Breredon and Symond was why no one had yet tried to do away with Cecely. Cecely was the root cause of everyone's troubles, and yet it was at Breredon someone had struck first.

Another thought eased into Frevisse's mind, drawn by that one. When Breredon had fallen ill, Cecely had immediately said the Rowcliffes had done it and should be sent away. She had said it again just now in bitter insistence.

Frevisse could see why Cecely wanted the Rowcliffes gone. If Cecely were fool enough to think she still had chance of escaping here, her hope of it had to hang on Breredon, and so long as the Rowcliffes were here, the thing would be impossible, even to Cecely's poor thinking. Hence her insistence that they were guilty of Breredon's sickness.

But she had been insisting on their guilt from the first, before anyone else had thought of poison at all. Because of her open anger at the Rowcliffes no heed had been given to her, but what if . . .

Frevisse felt her way carefully into her next thought.

What if Breredon had been poisoned not to kill him or even to make him very ill but only ill enough that the Rowcliffes might be accused of poisoning him? Doses were hard to judge. He may have fallen more ill than was intended by . . . whoever had done it.

But then had come Symond Hewet's sickness. He had been far nearer to death than Breredon had been. Had that been meant? Or had both men been meant to die, and Breredon's sickness been less and Symond's greater only by chance? By ill chance for Symond.

But the first question was still—Why had they been poisoned at all?

Frevisse gave way and finally looked straight at the thought she had been circling—that somehow Cecely had seen to Breredon being ill so that the Rowcliffes would be accused and sent away.

So far as she had been able to learn, no one had reason to go to the trouble of having Breredon dead, not even the Rowcliffes now he was forestalled of getting Edward. But his *sickness* could have served Cecely if she could have made anyone believe her accusations against the Rowcliffes.

How she might have seen to Breredon being ill was something Frevisse would consider in a while. A question that came first was why, if Cecely had wanted Breredon ill as a way to having the Rowcliffes sent away, it would have made sense for her to then have Symond sicken, too. If what she wanted was for the Rowcliffes to go away, Symond's illness only served to keep them here.

Unless . . .

Cecely made no secret of her angry bitterness against him, both for knowing her secret and for "betraying" it to the Rowcliffes, and just now she had been openly, resentfully disappointed he was not dead.

What if whatever had been given to Breredon had been

meant to sicken him, but what had been given to Symond been meant to kill?

Certainly Cecely's angry bitterness against him seemed almost sufficient to that.

Or fully sufficient?

Murder was a sadly short-witted answer to anger, Frevisse thought. Or to anything, come to that.

That being given, who was the most short-witted person in this business?

Cecely.

And given the anger she had just shown at her paramour's betrayal of their secret to Symond and at Symond for leading the hunt to her here, with the added edge that Symond was in reach while her paramour was not—yes, Frevisse was afraid she could see all too readily how Cecely, short-witted, might give way to wanting Symond dead.

Might want it enough to try somehow to kill him.

It was the "somehow" on which it all fell down.

Cecely had had no chance to do anything to anyone in the guesthall, and between the guesthall and the cloister the only link was Frevisse herself, if Dame Claire and Dame Johane were discounted, and Frevisse thought with a grim humour that they could be.

Oh, other folk went back and forth between the cloister and guesthall. Not nuns, of course, except by the prioress' leave, and none of them would have helped Cecely at anything like this anyway. But servants did, when there was need to take or fetch something from one place to another, as was happened lately with the guesthall's needs drawing heavily on the cloister's stores of food. But how would a servant, briefly in the guesthall kitchen, have had chance at only Breredon's or Symond Hewet's food or drink? To have poisoned either one, let alone both, someone from the cloister would have had to be in the guesthall kitchen at just the right time, knowing just which food or drink was meant for either man, with just the right chance to poison either the food or drink.

Unless these attacks were not, after all, aimed at anyone in particular.

Frevisse stopped short on that thought and looked at it again.

What if the poisonings were without particular purpose, just happening to happen to Breredon and Symond?

That, in its way, was worse than imagining Cecely was behind them, because if the poisonings were, one way or another, Cecely's doing, then there should be some way to find the trail between her and them. But if the poisonings were by someone run mad and taken to happenstance killing . . .

No. Better to hold to the thought that these were, somehow, Cecely's doing, Frevisse thought. If, after following that trail as far as it went, she found that it went nowhere, then she would look at that other possibility.

She stood up. There might be time left before Sext to ask Dame Claire or Dame Johane about the medicines. If they could give a firm answer about them, she would be that little further ahead.

It was only while she was passing along the cloister walk toward the infirmary, past Dame Perpetua still sitting guard on Sister Cecely, that she suddenly wondered why Abbot Gilbert had not asked why she had taken it on herself to give up the missing deeds and bill. He had surely heard at least that much of what had passed between her and Sister Cecely. He might very reasonably have demanded an explanation of her. Instead, he had said nothing about it at all. Why not?

A twinge that was not quite worry, but might be if she had time to dwell on it, passed through her thoughts that were otherwise mostly on poison. She let it go, pleased, as she came to the infirmary, to find both Dame Claire and

Dame Johane there, heads bent together over the infirmary's book laid open on the worktable. They both looked up, their foreheads tightened with almost identical small frowns, and Dame Claire said, "If you've come for an answer about the herbs and all, the best we can tell you is that we don't know."

"Don't know if you're missing any, or don't know what was used?" Frevisse returned.

"Either," Dame Claire said.

"I think there may be some missing from several things," Dame Johane said. "As if someone took a little from each instead of much from one."

"What would they do, mixed together?" Frevisse asked.

"We don't know," Dame Claire said. "What may—and only may—be missing are herbs and drugs we've never mixed together. There was no purpose to doing so."

"Unless to make someone very ill," Frevisse said. "Or kill them."

Dame Claire's face settled into hard lines. "Or kill them," she agreed. "Yes."

"But you can't be certain anything was taken at all," Frevisse said.

"We can't," Dame Claire said. "Oh, I'm certain enough none of the truly potent things were taken. The dwale. The monkshood. Those are untouched. But among the herbs that could do what was done—" She shook her head. "We can't tell for a certainty."

"But I *think* there's less than there should be," Dame Johane put in earnestly.

Dame Johane, who was Cecely's cousin and might have more loyalty to her than she had outwardly shown.

Frevisse shook off that thought. Surely, if Dame Johane had had her own guilt to cover, she would have been more firm that nothing was missing.

The bell rang to Sext, blessedly ending talk, but as she

left the infirmary with Dame Claire and Dame Johane, Frevisse saw clearly how that brief squirm of suspicion was fresh warning of how deeply Cecely's return was corrupting the nunnery's peace.

Frevisse had learned early that a nunnery was not a peaceful place by either nature or chance. However much—or little—a nun might desire to give herself to God, she remained herself, and selves tended all too easily to grate, one against another, the more especially when cloistered, with no choice about being together. It was the cloister's peace that gave best chance for deepest prayer and the growing away from the world and self that were the reasons for coming into a nunnery, but there was constant need for great, kind, firm care by a prioress ever-watchful against the very many things that could undermine and overset her nunnery's peace. As Cecely was oversetting St. Frideswide's peace, both by her grating self and by the outward-spreading circles of trouble around her.

And just when a prioress' firm hand was most needed, Domina Elisabeth was all but vanished from among them.

Still, she came to the Office this time, belatedly again as she had to Tierce, but that was better than not at all, like yesterday. Judging by the flatness of her voice as she started the Office, her mind was not much there, but Frevisse had to admit that neither was her own when she found herself saying, *"Quam dilecta habitation tua, Domine exercituum! Desiderat, languens concupiscit anima mea atria Domini . . ."*— How delightful is your dwelling, Lord of the host! Fainting, my soul desires and longs for the halls of the Lord . . . — while thinking, What if Cecely had simply brought poison with her?

Why she might have done so could be set aside for now. Just let the question be, What if she had?

But everything had been taken away from her after she came here.

But not from Edward.

And there had been her demands to see him. Could she have given him the poison to keep, the way she had given him the deeds?

Possibly. Possibly.

There were too many possibles about all of this. Frevisse felt an impatient need to move past possibles to something *certain*. She looked for and found Mistress Petham and Edward in the nave, and after the Office she overtook them in the cloister walk and in as plain a voice as she could, free of undertones or over-meanings, she asked Edward whether his mother had given him anything else to keep secret.

Edward looked worriedly from her to Mistress Petham, then at his toes, then finally said, "Yes."

"Do you still have it?" Frevisse asked gently. "Where is it?"

For answer, Edward freed his hand from Mistress Petham's, unclasped the small leather pouch hanging from his belt, took from it a little leather bag closed by a drawstring, and said, "It's in here."

Frevisse held out her hand. Slowly he set the bag into it. By the feel of it, it held the little glazed clay boules with which he and Mistress Petham had been playing the other day. She loosened the drawstring and felt inside but found only boules.

Watching her, Edward said softly, "It's in the bottom."

She had been looking for a vial or box or something else that could hold poison. Instead what she felt, now she was feeling for it, was a folded paper, or maybe it was parchment. She tried to draw it out but it seemed stuck.

"It's stitched," Edward said. "So it won't come out."

He answered her questioning look by pointing at the bag's bottom. Frevisse lifted the bag high enough for her to see the bottom, and indeed in the middle of the bag's bottom curve was a single stitch, where no one was likely to note it or think about it if they did, enough to hold in place something folded and put inside the bag. Frevisse lowered the bag and looked at Edward. "What is it?" Because whatever it was, it was not a packet of poison, attached so firmly it could not be taken out of hiding.

"My manor," Edward said, still softly.

"The deed to your manor?" she asked, carefully gentle. "The one your father left you?"

Edward nodded.

"Your mother took out your boules, turned the bag inside out, folded the deed very small, stitched it in place, turned the bag right side out, and put your boules back in. Was that the way of it?"

Edward nodded.

And who would trouble a small boy about his bag of boules?

Still, without much trying, Frevisse could think of several ways things could go wrong with that as a hiding place; but by now she knew all too well that Cecely was not long on either thought or imagination. Cecely saw what she wanted to see, and when the world failed her vision of what it should be, she was angry and resentful of everyone and everything except herself.

Mistress Petham stroked the back of Edward's head, telling him, "You are a very brave boy. You didn't give the secret away, you know. Dame Frevisse found it out."

He nodded without seeming much comforted. Whether it was his fault or not, he had lost yet another secret he had been supposed to keep.

Frevisse could only hope that when he was older, he would accept that there were secrets with which he should never have been burdened, that the guilt of them was not his.

That he had carried the weight of worry and might carry the guilt for who knew how long was yet another thing to be set in the scale against Sister Cecely.

But the deed was not what Frevisse had been seeking or had even thought about—making her wonder what else had she failed to think about in all of this—and she asked, very gently, as she gave him back his bag, "Edward, did your mother give you anything else to keep?"

Softly, cradling the bag, his eyes downcast, he said, "No."

Frevisse did not insult him by asking if he was sure. From wherever it had come—not from his parents, surely—there was a strong strain of truth in the child, and she quietly thanked him for his help. Eyes downcast, he nodded silently. Then he looked up with silent pleading at Mistress Petham. She gave him a small nod, seeming to know his question, and asked Frevisse, "Is all well with what Edward gave you yesterday?"

Frevisse looked down at Edward and answered, "They're back with the men to whom they belong. Your cousins are all very grateful. All's well about it."

Edward bit his lip, looked at his feet, looked up at her, and whispered, "Does my mother know?"

Frevisse answered his worry quietly. "She does. It's made her unhappy, but she's unhappy about a great many things just now. What she meant to do was wrong, and what you did was right. Your father would be glad of it and proud of you." Or if not, he should have been, she added silently and somewhat savagely.

Edward nodded and let Mistress Petham take his hand again and lead him away. He was not fully reassured, Frevisse feared, watching them go, and she had to wonder whether his mother would turn against him now his truth had lost her everything she had meant to use in her stolen life. Very possibly Edward wondered the same. How much did he understand about what his mother had been doing? Children might be innocent and they might be ignorant; neither was the same as being stupid. Edward maybe understood full well his mother had meant to sell him to Breredon as his last piece of usefulness to her, and that understanding might ease his guilt at what his truthfulness had cost. He might even understand that, even if he had lost his mother by his truthfulness, she had been intent on losing him for her own selfish ends.

Frevisse could only hope that in time to come he would take what comfort he could in knowing that by doing right he had kept greater wrongs from being done.

But that was much to ask presently of a small boy.

Frevisse went back along the walk to her desk in its stall and sat down. Beyond the thin boards between her desk and the next, the sound of a pen scratching said Dame Johane was as honestly at work as Frevisse should have been, but she left pen and ink and paper where they were and simply sat, brooding on poison, the poisoned, and the poisoner.

If nothing had been taken from the infirmary and if Cecely herself had brought nothing, then . . .

What if Breredon poisoned himself with something he had brought with him, as cover for then poisoning Symond? Or maybe John Rowcliffe himself had been meant, and Symond been struck by accident.

But that would mean Breredon had known he would encounter the Rowcliffes here and had had reason to plan to kill one of them.

Or maybe it was not a Rowcliffe he had had in mind to kill when he brought the poison with him. Maybe it had been meant for Cecely, for some reason other than anything of which Frevisse yet knew or had even clue.

Or then again, perhaps one of the Rowcliffes was the poisoner.

Or then again . . .

No.

Frevisse firmly stopped that wide ranging of her thoughts. If she disproved the most straightforward likelihood—that

Cecely was guilty—then she could go roaming to other possibilities.

But was she looking at Cecely as guilty for any better reason than how much she disliked her? Did she have more reason than that to suspect her before anyone else?

Frevisse rested her elbows on the desk, clasped her hands together, and bowed her head onto them, closing her eyes not in prayer but in thought, trying to look at it all from the beginning.

Cecely had come here in flight from the Rowcliffes, needing a "safe" place to wait for Breredon, to deal with him behind the Rowcliffes' backs. She . . .

Frevisse stood up, eyes wide.

Among all her twisting around of possibilities, all her trying to suppose everything that might have happened or could have happened or maybe had happened, there was one thing she had failed to wonder.

Chapter 26

ymond Hewet was sleeping when Frevisse came to his chamber. His cousin Jack was sitting on a stool beside the bed and stood up at sight of her, bowed his head courteously, and whispered in answer to her inquiring look, "He's been sleeping more easily. I think he's better."

Symond's breathing did seem more even and there was perhaps somewhat more color in his face. It was surely a pity to wake him, and Frevisse hesitated; but she needed two answers, one of them as soon as might be, and she reached down and touched his shoulder. Jack made a small sound but no other protest and she ignored him. Symond awoke slowly. Still too weak to be surprised, he peered up at her and asked vaguely, "What?"

Frevisse stooped to put herself closer to him, so he need make less effort in answering her, and said, "Sister Cecely claims that you meant to have Edward's wardship. That you threatened to take Edward from her. Did you?"

"Threatened?" Symond sounded puzzled. "His wardship, yes. Not threatened. No . . . I told her we'd agreed on it. That we meant . . . all of us . . . not to leave him . . . to her."

He made a small lift of one hand's fingers toward Jack as if bidding him to take over, and Jack said, "After Guy died, when we all talked together—my father and mother, Symond and his wife, and me—we all found that, one time and another we had all had Guy say to us he didn't think Cecely should have the raising of Edward if anything happened to him. He hadn't done anything about it before he died. There was a lot he didn't do before he died. But none of us thinks she's fit to raise a cat, let alone Edward, and we think Guy had come to know it, too."

"Didn't . . ." Symond started, paused to take several shallow breaths, then finished, ". . . I tell you that?"

"You didn't," Frevisse said. "You simply said she threatened to tell about Jack's bill of obligation."

Symond made an effort toward a smile. "Thank you for that, by the way. And for the deeds."

"I told him," said Jack.

"It means though . . . Cecely will hate you . . . as much as she hates us."

That brought a sudden, startling new thought to Frevisse. She set it aside for later and said to Symond, holding steadily to the present point, "So it was decided among Guy's kin that you were to have Edward."

Symond made a small grunting sound of agreement, and Jack said, "Yes."

"What happened was that you told Cecely you wanted Edward's wardship, and she then countered with the threat of Jack's debt."

Symond made the barest nod, agreeing to that.

"One question more," Frevisse said. "Then I'll leave you to sleep again. Did you say anything to Cecely about knowing she was a nun? Or anything by which she might have guessed you knew it?"

"Nothing. To her or anyone," Symond whispered. "Not until she had gone. Guy had me swear . . . it was only if there was . . . trouble. Otherwise . . . secret always. I swore . . . that to him."

Frevisse straightened. "Thank you. I'll leave you to your rest now."

Only when she was out of the room did she find how greatly angry she was all over again. At this time yesterday Symond Hewet had been a hale man, fine in both wits and body. Today he was so ill and damaged that dying could come to him almost more easily than living, and if she was right about why this had been done to him, she was going to be even angrier than she already was.

There was momentary relief in seeing neither John Rowcliffe nor Mistress Lawsell as she passed through the hall. Just as when she had been going to Symond, only a few of the abbot's men were sitting about, taking no interest in her. Meeting Rowcliffe would probably have been no great matter, but she was certain that encountering Mistress Lawsell would be anything but pleasant. At any other time, the trouble between the mother and daughter would have been the center of everyone's heed. Now it was an aggravating distraction that Frevisse wished Abbot Gilberd would see to, rather than spending his time in long talks with his sister and far too little time, so far as Frevisse could tell, on the problem of Cecely. Unless—again that terrible thought—they were talking over at such length what was to be done with Cecely because Abbot Gilberd wanted to leave her here and Domina Elisabeth was resisting it.

If that was it, Frevisse prayed Domina Elisabeth held her ground at whatever cost.

That being a worry about which she could do nothing, Frevisse pushed it away from her. There were an irksome number of things in the world about which she could do nothing. Let her keep her heed on those that she maybe could. Even though that meant she had to talk to Cecely again and never mind that was least among things she wanted to do. With the question that had taken her to Symond Hewet still stark before her, she went grimly to do it.

Dame Perpetua looked up from the book she was reading to say as Frevisse neared her, "Whatever you did to her last time, don't do it again, if you please. She has been pacing and angry ever since. If she kicks that stool across the floor one more time, I may hit her with it."

"Has she said anything?"

"Said anything? Other than damning all of us and everyone else she can name to Hell? Only that man's name—her paramour's—over and over, angrily some of the time, crying the rest of it." Dame Perpetua did not seem moved to pity by that.

From the shadows beyond the doorway, Cecely said bitterly, "I can hear you talking of me!"

"Then know I've been hearing you, too," Dame Perpetua snapped back at her, "and not liking you any the better for it!"

Frevisse went in. Standing against the far wall, Cecely said, "Go away. I don't have to talk to you. I don't *want* to talk to you."

As bluntly back, Frevisse asked, "How did you know it was Symond who told the rest of the Rowcliffes you were a nun and might be here?"

"What? Because . . . because he's the one Guy told."

"How did you know that? That Guy had told him?"

With the anger that seemed so often to serve her in place of thought, Cecely flung back, "Because Guy told me! How else would I know?"

Frevisse stared at her a long moment, then swung around and left her.

Dame Perpetua asked, "What was that between you?" but Frevisse only shook her head against answering and went away along the walk. She paused at the foot of the stairs to the prioress' rooms but could not find it in herself to turn to Domina Elisabeth or Abbot Gilberd for help in this just yet, and she went on, out of the cloister and back to the guesthall, to the kitchen this time.

With a great many people to be fed at midday, Luce and Tom were bustling while Ela sat hunched on her stool well out of the way, ready to give orders if need be. There was pause when Frevisse came in, with Luce bobbing a quick curtsy from where she was slicing some pale vegetable at the worktable, and Tom giving a kind of bow without stopping stirring a large pot of something on the fire. Ela did not try to rise with her stiff knees but gave a respectful nod of her head while Frevisse came fully to a stop, taking a deep breath of the good smell with surprised pleasure before crossing to kneel down beside Ela and say, "Whatever is cooking, its smell is a delight."

"Pease pottage with ham, and in a while there'll be a bit of onion in it, too," Ela said. "Master Rowcliffe talked with me, thank you much for that. He's already sent a man off to Banbury, so we don't need to eye everything we put into the pot with a question as to whether there'll be anything left for tomorrow and who knows how many days. Besides that, Father Henry brought in two conies, and Luce is going to make a cony pie for tomorrow."

All of that made for one less trouble off Frevisse's mind, leaving only the greater ones, and she asked first, "How does Mistress Lawsell?"

"Last heard, she was demanding that Abbot Gilberd talk to her. He's promised he'll do so after Vespers. That didn't make her happy. Doubt he's looking forward to it. What's toward with Domina Elisabeth? Is she so taken up with the whore's trouble, she's no heed to give to the Lawsells and be done with them? She's ill, is she?"

Frevisse found answer to that came more slowly than she liked. Only after a pause did she say, "She's not had Dame Claire to see her. That's all I know of it."

"Hm," said Ela.

Before Ela could ask more, Frevisse went quickly to the question that had brought her here, saying, "I need you to tell me who from the cloister has been in here since Easter."

"Here? In the kitchen? Malde has come twice or so to help since the abbot came with all his folk."

"I mean in the hall itself, too. Anyone anywhere around here."

Ela gave her a narrow look but did not ask any of the questions probably crossing her mind, just answered after a moment's thought, "You. Dame Claire. Dame Johane." Ela paused in more thought. "That's all." Then she added, "Tom's sister. Not in the hall. Here. Didn't come in, though. Was just there at the door." Ela nodded toward the kitchen's door to the yard.

"Tom's sister?" Frevisse echoed blankly.

"From the cloister. Rabbity. Might find herself cooked into a pie one of these days, she's so rabbity."

"Alson," said Frevisse.

"That's her name. Tom's sister."

"But she didn't come in."

"Nay. Some evenings, when work's done, they go out for a time together. Then there's been those that came with Master Breredon and the Rowcliffes and the abbot, too. They've, one and another, been in and out of here to fetch this and that."

"Thank you," Frevisse said. She could see Ela readying to ask her own questions now but gave her no time for them, simply stood up and left, taking unhappy thoughts with her.

Returning to the cloister, she went again to the church for somewhere to think. Dame Thomasine was kneeling in front of the altar, undisturbed by Frevisse's coming, nor did her presence trouble Frevisse as she settled into her choir stall and to her thoughts.

It was nine years since Cecely had fled from St. Frideswide's. There had been the alarm of her disappearance and the search for her, then the report to the abbot and the following descent on the nunnery of officers from Abbot Gilberd and the bishop asking questions of the nuns and everyone else, and prying into every part of the nunnery's life for sign of other trouble either present or possibly to come. Even after all of that was over, the nuns were left with penances and an enforced heart-searching among themselves for what had or had not been done to keep Sister Cecely safe. The problems brought on by her flight had seemed as if they would go on forever, but they had finally ended, were long past and gone.

The memories of them were not.

Neglected until brought back by Cecely's return, but not gone.

Alson.

Alson then. Alson now.

Poor, foolish Alson.

Nine years ago she had admitted, with frightened weeping, her part in Cecely's flight, had admitted she took Cecely's place in the kitchen so Cecely could meet a man but sworn, still weeping, that she had not known Cecely meant to run away. She had wept and denied and sworn, and been believed. She had been told she was a fool but been forgiven and, out of pity, not been dismissed when well she might have been.

Surely, with that behind her, she was not fool enough to have been drawn into some new trouble at Cecely's asking.

Surely she was not.

But—Alson then and Alson now.

Alson a link between the guesthall kitchen and the cloister, with a brother who could come at food and drink with no one thinking twice about it.

Frevisse was thankful when the bell rang for Nones.

Domina Elisabeth came again, which was surely a good sign; but Mistress Lawsell did, too, and stood close beyond the rood screen, glaring, impossible to ignore. The sooner the problem of her and her daughter was settled, the better, Frevisse thought, then tried to turn her mind away to the Office, only to find, as she had feared, no respite in it, and at its end she finally, fully faced that time for thinking was ended.

Given what she suspected, time was come for something to be done.

After all, if she suspected correctly, she might herself be the next one poisoned.

Chapter 27

The day that in the morning had been half clouds, half fair, was now, in the late afternoon, gone all to clouds. A glooming gray twilight filled the church, deepening to thick shadows in the far corners of nave and choir. Only the altar existed in light, haloed by a dozen bright-burning candles on tall stands behind and beside it, with four candles in their gleaming brass-gold holders standing on the altar itself, sheening the gold and scarlet of the letter filling half the page of the missal standing open there and flickering gold from Abbot Gilberd's long-cuffed, gold-embroidered glove as he moved his free hand in benediction over the nuns gathered before him in this hour before Vespers. In his other hand he held his abbatial crozier, the foot of the staff set firm against the stone step of the altar, the carved, curved top rising above his head.

All of the nuns but not their prioress were there, a cluster to either side of him, hands folded into their opposite sleeves, heads bowed, seeming in their black gowns a deepening of the church's shadows save for the white of their faces and wimples.

Abbot Gilberd ended his deep intoning of the Latin words and lowered his hand. The nuns did not stir, but now Domina Elisabeth and Father Henry, equally dressed in black, came forward from the far end of the choir stalls into the light, a frightened-eyed Alson between them.

She had been given chance to take off her kitchen-apron and wash her hands and face, but that was all. Nor, if Domina Elisabeth and Father Henry had done as Frevisse suggested, had she been told why she had been taken from the kitchen and brought here. She had to know she was in some manner of trouble. How much she guessed was impossible to tell, but by the way she sank to her knees when Domina Elisabeth and Father Henry stopped in front of Abbot Gilberd at the foot of the altar steps and let her go, her legs must have only barely been holding her up until then; and when Abbot Gilberd said grimly, "Alson Pye," she made a soft moan and crouched lower on the stone step.

"Alson Pye, look at me."

Alson whimpered and lifted her head, her shoulders still huddled, her fear naked on her face.

Standing with the other nuns, Frevisse felt pity for her and, unreasonably, regret for having brought her to this. Or maybe it was simply regret that the whole miserable matter was come to this—to terrifying a poor woman who had not had sense enough to keep out of it.

But this had seemed the most direct way to an end of it all.

Cecely had not known Symond Hewet knew her secret

when she came back here. If she had, she would never have come, no matter what she lied about it now. So she had learned it after she came here. How? Not from Abbot Gilberd. To be certain of that, Frevisse had asked Domina Elisabeth, who had said the matter had not come up in his questioning of her.

Then it had to have come from someone else, and the only time that Frevisse knew for a certainty Symond's part in it all had been said aloud for anyone to hear had been in the guesthall after the Rowcliffes came. And when she set to remembering who had been there to hear it besides the Rowcliffes and herself, there had been Tom Pye. Tom who talked sometimes with his sister Alson. Alson who sometimes sat for guard outside Cecely's door with no one to know what was said between them then. Alson who had had part in Cecely's flight nine years ago.

Frevisse had been stopped by the gap between those pieces and how Cecely could have persuaded Alson to set Tom on to poisoning two men. She had already settled in her own mind why Cecely would want them poisoned. Master Breredon was so the Rowcliffes would be accused and, at the least, be sent away. Symond Hewet was for plain revenge. What had slowed her in untangling it all was that she had kept looking for the sense behind it all, when there was no sense. Or not sufficient sense. And that was Cecely, who seemed to have so little common sense behind almost everything she did. How else could she have come to the thought that poisoning two men was a reasonable thing to do?

Yet poisoning them had made sense enough to Alson and her brother, too, because it had to have been Alson who took something from the infirmary, and Tom who put whatever it was into the two men's food or drink. Frevisse could see no other way of it.

Why Alson and Tom should be such fools still escaped her. That could only be found out by bringing them to confess.

The trouble there was that, when accused, they would both, surely, deny it all, and there was no proof to hold up in front of them, to force them to the truth.

Besides that, nine years ago Alson had convinced them all, with her weeping and denials, that she was innocent of knowing Cecely meant to escape. Frevisse now very much doubted her innocence, and if Alson had lied so well then, she might lie equally well now. And so there was this gathering in the church, and Abbot Gilberd in Father Henry's white and gold Paschal cope standing on the altar step, towering over Alson as he demanded at her, deep-voiced with authority, "Alson Pye, do you believe in the salvation of your soul?"

Alson's head trembled in a desperate nod.

"Alson Pye, do you believe in the damnation of your soul?"

Alson froze, then trembled another nod.

"Then rise, Alson Pye," Abbot Gilberd ordered. "Come forward, up these steps, and lay your hand on God's consecrated altar."

When Alson did not immediately rise—maybe gone too weak with fear to do it—Father Henry took her by one arm and gently raised her to her feet, and when even then she stayed rooted where she was, he urged her forward, lifting as much as guiding her up the two steps to the altar. There she slid from Father Henry's hold onto her knees again and huddled forward, her head deeply bowed, her arms clutched against herself, her clenched hands pressed between her breasts.

"Woman," Abbot Gilberd ordered, "lay your hand on the altar."

Alson gave a shuddering sob and huddled lower.

"Father Henry," Abbot Gilberd ordered, and Father Henry bent over her, pried her right arm away from her, and stretched it out to the altar. Her arm was rigid and resisting, and her hand stayed clenched. Father Henry bent close and whispered something to her until, still unwilling but finally obedient, she opened her hand and laid it, trembling, against the front of the altar cloth, another sob shuddering through her.

Above her Abbot Gilberd said, "Now I will ask you certain questions, woman, and as you hope for your soul's salvation rather than the flames of eternal Hell, you will answer me truly. Do you understand?"

With a whimpering sob, Alson nodded that she did.

"First, have you, in these last few days past, talked with the woman called Sister Cecely?"

Alson managed, faintly, "Yes."

"Has she asked you to do things, and have you done those things she asked of you?"

Alson began to whimper.

"Have you?" Abbot Gilbert demanded.

Alson whispered, "Yes."

"What were those things she asked of you, that you then did?"

Alson's whimpers turned to outright sobs. Through them, she cried, "To take medicines from Dame Claire!" The last of her will crumbled. Still sobbing, she wailed, "She wanted me to steal one of the strong potions. But they're in little bottles and little boxes. Dame Claire would *know* if I took any of those. So I took other things, bits of this and that. Just a little, little bit of some of the herbs she keeps on the highest shelf. Strong ones but not the worst ones. Not the worst ones like she wanted me to! I'm *sorry!*" Overwhelmed by her sobs, she grabbed her hand away from the altar and covered her face with both.

With no sign of pity, Abbot Gilbert ordered at Father Henry, "Her hand."

Father Henry took Alson's right hand again, dragged it back, and pressed it to the altar again, and held it there.

Sternly, Abbot Gilberd demanded down at her, "What did you do with what you took?"

"Nothing!" But even Alson knew the foolishness of saying that, and before Abbot Gilberd could challenge her, she gulped and gasped, "I put some in that man's . . . those men's food. I did that."

"We know for a truth you were never near those men's food," Abbot Gilberd said. "This is your soul we're trying to save, woman. Who helped you?"

Alson broke into full sobs again and tried to twist her hand free of Father Henry. Abbot Gilberd bent, placed his own right hand over both of theirs, and pushed them hard against the altar. Very near her ear now, he demanded again, "Who, woman?"

Alson froze, staring fixedly at the back of the abbot's glove, its gold embroidery glinting in the candlelight.

"Who, Alson?" Father Henry said gently. "You have to tell. For his sake as well as yours."

Alson moaned, then gasped out, "Tom. My brother. I talked him into doing it. God forgive me. God forgive us."

Abbot Gilberd freed her and straightened. "We pray he may."

Father Henry freed her, too, and she covered her face again and huddled completely down into a bow-backed heap on the altar step, brokenly sobbing.

Frevisse looked at Domina Elisabeth. Now was time for the question to which Frevisse had prompted her. If she did not ask it, then Frevisse would, because it had to be asked; but Domina Elisabeth took a step toward the altar and said in a voice that matched the abbot's in stern demand, "Alson, nine years ago, after Sister Cecely fled, you told us that she asked you to take her turn at kitchen duty that day without she told you anything else. You said you knew nothing of what she planned. Was that the truth?"

Alson shook her head.

"Speak out, woman," Abbot Gilberd said. "Are you saying you lied then, too?"

Alson straightened and swung around, still on her knees and fumbling for balance on the altar steps, trying to answer him and tell Domina Elisabeth at the same time, suddenly fierce the way a cornered animal was fierce when all hope was gone. "She said she was going to meet this man of hers in the orchard. She said he was leaving and this would be their only, last chance to be together. Just a little while, she said. Just a little while and nobody would know. That's what she told me! Only then she never came back. And I thought how happy she was going to be and how much trouble I'd be in if I told I knew about the man. So I said I didn't, and everyone was angry at me anyway, but not like you would have been if you'd known! Then she came back, and she said if I didn't do what she asked of me, she'd tell how I'd known everything about her leaving, even though I didn't. I swear I didn't! Then you'd throw me out. So I did what she said to do. Only everything's gone wrong!" she wailed with a freshened flow of tears.

No one showed sign of being moved by her misery. Abbot Gilberd gestured toward one of his men waiting at the far end of the darkened nave. A moment later the west door opened, and a few moments after that two more of his men brought in Tom Pye.

Alson, seeing her brother, gave a gulping sob, crouched lower on the altar step, and went very still, as if that might make her invisible. Tom, brought there under guard, had to know he was in some kind of trouble, and by his defiantly lifted chin and stiff face Frevisse guessed he had been maybe ready to out-face whatever it was; but when his guards brought him to a stop at the rood screen and he found himself confronted by abbot, priest, nuns, the candle-lighted altar, and—his eyes fell on her last—his sister kneeling there in abject, open misery, Frevisse saw all the defiance go out of him.

"Oh, Alson," he said.

Briefly, sparing nothing, Abbot Gilberd told him everything to which his sister had confessed. Visibly wilting between his guards, Tom did not try to bold it out. Instead, he pointed at Alson and cried, "It was her doing! She said it would be a good thing. She said that if I didn't do it, that woman would tell how Alson helped her run off. She said she'd lie about it, and then Alson would be in trouble again. I only did it because she told me to!"

Adam, disgraced in the Garden of Eden, had made the same defense, Frevisse thought.

It was not an excuse that had improved with age.

Abbot Gilberd's men took Alson and Tom away. Father Henry went with them while at Domina Elisabeth's bidding the nuns moved to take their seats in the choir.

Frevisse, for one, was more than willing to sit there in silent thought for the while until Vespers. What they had just done—what she had done—to Alson had left her shaken. Needed though it had been to have the truth, to have so deliberately torn a woman open, to have ruined her life and her brother's . . .

Domina Elisabeth, instead of stepping up into her own stall at the choir's end, was stopped beside it, her head bowed, her brother beside her, his tall abbatial crozier still in one gloved hand, his other hand resting on her shoulder. One by one, all her nuns, not yet all into their places, stopped where they were, staring, until Abbot Gilberd said, "Be seated, dames."

They finished taking their places but went on staring at their prioress and abbot. Frevisse wondered if the others felt the same sick worry and wondering what came next that she suddenly did, but giving them little time to wonder, Abbot Gilberd said, "A parting of the ways has come, my ladies. After long talk and much prayer together these past days, I have granted your prioress' request to relieve her of her office and allow her to return to the nunnery from whence she came."

Domina Elisabeth did not stir, but while Frevisse, Dame Claire, and Dame Thomasine stayed silent, there were exclaims among the others and heads turning and accusing looks at Dame Perpetua and Dame Margrett because they must have heard something of this while keeping their prioress company in her parlor.

"They were under my order to say nothing, hint at nothing," Abbot Gilberd said, bringing instant quiet and all the nuns' attention back to him. "As for your prioress, she came to you in your need twelve years ago. She has made well what was ill. She has made strong what was weak. The good to you has been great. The cost to her has been heavy. She is weary and has asked for rest. That I have granted her. In two days' time you will hold election for your new prioress. I bid you pray well between now and then, that your choice be acceptable in the eyes of God."

Or, more to the immediate point, acceptable in the eyes of Abbot Gilberd, thought Frevisse. His was the final word on who became prioress in a nunnery under his care, unless things went so badly that the bishop himself had to settle matters, God forbid. It had been the disasters brought on St. Frideswide's by a very ill-chosen prioress that had forced the abbot to use his authority and bring his sister from a London nunnery to be their prioress, trusting none of them to the place. Now he was saying he trusted them again to make their own choice. What he did not need to say was: And woe to them if they chose ill again.

Mercifully, the bell rang for Vespers, silencing them all. Abbot Gilberd took his hand from his sister's shoulder.

Head still bowed, she went to an empty stall at the bottom
of the choir, slipped into it and to her knees. Abbot Gilberd
signed the cross toward her bowed head and then at them
all. Then he left, disappearing into the shadows of the nave,
and after an uncertain moment Dame Juliana unsteadily
began the Office. The other nuns unevenly followed her.

The familiarity soon steadied them, but they went forward at an almost gabbled haste, so that Frevisse, who would
have preferred to make the Office last as long as might be,
found no peace in the prayers and psalms and all too soon
was leaving the church with the others. Supper was next,
with no chance to talk then either, only for long looks and
wondering head-shakes at the head of the table where Domina Elisabeth was not, having stayed in the church when
they left.

Frevisse was not looking forward to recreation's hour,
when talk would burst out freely. The talk about Cecely and
Alson and all of that was going to be bad enough, but now
it would be mixed with exclaims over Domina Elisabeth.
Frevisse was not ready to face all that, and by the time the
nuns rose from their places along the refectory table and
rapidly said final grace, her set intent was to escape directly
from the refectory to the church.

She was forestalled as she reached the refectory door by
Malde coming to her and saying in an almost frightened,
too loud voice that she was wanted in Domina Elisabeth's
chamber. The others all turned to stare at her. She walked
away from them quickly and walked faster as the gabbling
started up behind her, aware that she would now be among
the things they exclaimed over.

Her way took her past the closed door of Cecely's cell,
now guarded by one of Abbot Gilberd's men. It was unset-
tling to see a man simply sitting there in the cloister, neither coming nor going. He stood up respectfully as she
approached. She gave him a nod as she passed, but her

thought was on Cecily in that lightless room beyond the shut door. Under the clouded sky, night was coming fast; even what little light let in through the slit of a window would soon be gone and then she would be alone in unrelieved darkness with nothing but her thoughts and maybe prayers, although Frevisse had doubt about the prayers of someone who had tried to kill a man because of her hurt feelings. Without prayer, all that Cecily had were her memories—now mostly of losses—and her anger. And even anger must be a cold comfort in that room.

Frevisse slowed as she reached the prioress' stairs and unwillingly went up them to scratch at the door and enter at Domina Elisabeth's bidding. Domina Elisabeth was standing near the small fire burning on the hearth; Abbot Gilberd was seated in the tall chair that was usually hers. The shutters had been closed across the window against the on-coming night, but several lighted candles showed the remains of their supper on the table, and Luce from the guesthall standing in the shadows beside the door. The abbot must have brought her with him from the guesthall, that Domina Elisabeth not be alone with him, but he said now, "You may go, woman," and Luce dropped a curtsy and slipped behind Frevisse and out the door with a quickness that said she was grateful to leave.

"Come forward, dame," Abbot Gilberd said. "Join us."

Retreating into her nunhood, tucking her hands into her opposite sleeves and bowing her head, Frevisse obeyed, going forward to stand beside Domina Elisabeth.

"In our haste to bring an end to these poisonings," Abbot Gilberd said, "there are some questions that have gone unanswered. Master Rowcliffe has ceased to go on at me about his stolen deeds. Do you know why that is?"

Toward the floor but firmly, Frevisse said, "Because they've been returned to him, my lord."

"By your doing?"

"Yes, my lord." As he had surely known before he asked the question because he *must* have overheard her in talk with Cecely.

"Your explanation for doing so without asking my leave or word for it?"

Not trying to judge either his displeasure or anything else, she answered straightly, "Sister Cecely had hidden the deeds with her son. He gave them up to me because he understood that neither he nor she had any right to them. Because they are Master Rowcliffe's, I returned them to him. To make an end of at least one of the troubles."

"You did not see fit to consult with either your prioress or myself about it. You simply did it."

Her gaze still on the floor, Frevisse said, "Yes, my lord."

As Abbot Gilberd's silence drew out, she wished she had tried for humble rather than firm in her answer. She also wished she had not bowed her head quite so deeply; she could not see either his face or Domina Elisabeth's, to read between them what they might be thinking. All she could do was wait, and only finally and slowly did Abbot Gilberd say, "That was, probably, well done. With his deeds returned, he should be satisfied to leave Sister Cecely to us. It might have been better to keep them, until we were sure he'll make no trouble over our claim on the boy, but what's done is done."

Frevisse forgot humble and looked at him. "The boy? Our claim on him?"

"I believe there is property that comes with him, and that his mother intends to give him to the Church," Abbot Gilberd said.

"I believe she intends no such thing," Frevisse said, just barely keeping sharpness from her voice. "That was simply another of her lies, and now that she's been thwarted in everything she intended here, she will surely never consent to such a thing."

"Her consent has no part in this. By all her vows, she is the Church's. That makes whatever she has gained likewise the Church's."

Did that include her shame and the burden of her sin? Frevisse wondered sharply, and with her gaze unlowered, she said back at him, "I think it likely that, insofar as Edward is concerned, there are lawyers enough to contest that as would drag the matter through the courts for years. His little manor is not worth *that* much."

She was guessing. She did not know that much about either Edward's manor or the church's law in such a matter, but she was offended by thought of Edward being wrenched even more hither and thither for no better reason than whatever use people could make of him. So she looked at Abbot Gilberd as if she knew whereof she spoke and waited to see if he knew better.

If he did, he did not say so, only looked back at her through a long moment's silence and finally said, "Something must be done with him. He cannot be left with her, the more especially where she is going."

Frevisse flashed a look at Domina Elisabeth who had been standing with statue-stillness through all this exchange, but it was Abbot Gilberd who answered her unspoken question with, "My sister has persuaded me, yes, that to leave Sister Cecely here would be too great a burden on St. Frideswide's. She will be removed elsewhere. But neither do I think you wish to have the boy left on your hands."

"Let him go back to his family. That is where he belongs. Enough of 'the sins of the father' have been visited on him," Frevisse said. "Let him be done with the sins of the mother, too."

Abbot Gilberd regarded her in silence through another long moment, then nodded slowly. "Yes. Sometimes the simplest way is the best way."

Frevisse held back from saying that *usually* the simplest

way was the best way. And in this matter, anyway, the simplest way was also the kindest. It was unkindness and the tangles that people made in their lives that led to misery, and with thought of misery, she asked, "What of Alson and Tom Pye?"

Abbot Gilberd looked to Domina Elisabeth. "We have been considering them," he said, in a way that suggested they had been disagreeing, too.

Speaking for the first time since Frevisse had come in, Domina Elisabeth said, her voice tautly controlled but threatening to break, "I don't want the trouble of law brought on them and all that will come from that. I just want this all to be over and done with."

Beyond the words Frevisse heard the weary strain that must have been behind much of what Domina Elisabeth had said and done these past months. When she had sent her plea for help with Cecely to her brother, she must have likewise sent word of her own plight. That had been why Abbot Gilberd had come himself—in answer to his sister's plea for herself, rather than for the small, sad matter of an apostate nun.

But the small, sad matter had grown into something large and ugly with the poisonings of two men, and for all that she must have been holding herself together by plain force of her will for who knew how long, her will was beginning to break apart under the threat of yet more trouble when all she wanted was an end to it all, and Abbot Gilberd did not help by saying, "I doubt that Symond Hewet or Master Breredon will be willing to simply let the matter end. Not with what they've suffered."

Domina Elisabeth looked as if she were about to burst out that she did not care what they had suffered, but before she could, Frevisse said, "You might ask it of them, my lord. It could be pointed out to them that Master Breredon came here falsely, ready to do grave wrong in helping Sister Cecely away. And Symond Hewet, too, did no little wrong in keeping his cousin's secret."

"That they were poisoned could very likely be counted to outweigh both those matters," Abbot Gilberd said.

"Then you could point out to them," Frevisse returned, "that any prosecution of the Pyes would require both Master Breredon and Symond Hewet, as well as the Rowcliffes as their witnesses, to return here or to wherever else the trials were held for who knows how many times or when. Upon thought, they may well find that the inconvenience of that and the open telling of their own guilts that would come with any trial outweigh their need for justice against the Pyes. Since, if there is no trial, the Church is willing to forego its rights against them in the matters."

"*Is* the Church willing to forego its rights?" Abbot Gilberd challenged.

"That would be the simplest way to have this done and over with, my lord."

Abbot Gilberd regarded her with narrowed eyes and the fingers of one hand drumming on the wooden arm of the chair for a discomfortable length of time before he finally said, "Yes. Again, the simplest way may very well be the best."

Determined to return to humility, Frevisse bowed her head and murmured, "Yes, my lord."

Her hope was that he would now dismiss her. Her fear was that he would not. Nor did he but after another pause asked, "Why, dame?"

Keeping her eyes down and truly not understanding his question, she said, " 'Why,' my lord?"

"Why do you care what happens to this Tom Pye and his sister?"

She paused over her answer before saying carefully, "Because what they did was done more from foolishness than evil."

"What they did was evil. If either man had died, it would have been more evil," Abbot Gilberd said.

"But it was evil from foolishness, not evil from the heart. Alson is small-witted. For all she says now that she was forced to it by threats, she may have truly thought she was doing Sister Cecely good service in making Master Breredon ill, to have the threatening Rowcliffes sent away so Sister Cecely might have chance at flight again. Having done that, she probably thought herself trapped into doing more. Nor does her brother being persuaded to it, too, surprise me. He doesn't see things further than what he's told."

"He did the poisonings skillfully enough," Abbot Gilberd said sharply.

"I never said he was a fool." Just barely Frevisse kept sharpness from her own voice. "The poisonings—those were done with what he has—low cunning."

That was the trouble with all this tangle, she thought bitterly. There had been low cunning in plenty but a grievous lack of good sense.

She remembered to add, "My lord," and lowered her head again.

That meant she did not know where Abbot Gilberd was looking through the long silence that followed, but it ended with him saying, apparently to Domina Elisabeth, "This will suffice? That I see to everything, save you deal with the Pyes as you see fit, if I persuade the Rowcliffes to forego the law?"

"Yes," Domina Elisabeth said wearily. "I'll deal with them if you see to all the rest. And to Mistress Lawsell."

"Ah. Mistress Lawsell." Abbot Gilberd sounded no happier at thought of her than Frevisse felt, but it seemed he accepted her along with the rest of the burden Domina Elisabeth was setting down, because he next said, "Yes. Her, too." He rose from the chair. "Now I shall leave you to your rest, dear sister. Dear sisters," he added, including Frevisse.

He murmured a benediction over them both while making the sign of the cross in the air, then left, and Domina Elisabeth moved toward the chair where he had been, the prioress' chair, where every prioress of St. Frideswide's through the years had sat in her turn; but her step was so unsteady—as if merely moving was almost too much to ask of her body—that Frevisse put a hand under her arm and helped her the few steps until she could sink gratefully onto the chair's cushion.

She gestured toward the room's only other chair for Frevisse to sit, too, and Frevisse did, wishing Domina Elisabeth had dismissed her instead, but Domina Elisabeth, with her head leaned against the tall back of the chair and eyes closed, said, "What am I to do with the Pyes? Even if the Rowcliffes don't demand the law on them, I'll have to send them away. Alson stole from us and suborned her brother. He poisoned two men. How could they be such fools? They can't stay here, and I can't give them a good word to take with them. What could I say?"

"That they've been good workers," Frevisse offered. "That much would be true about them."

"That they've been good workers but will follow any stupid plan that's offered them?" Domina Elisabeth shot back with a little anger-fueled sharpness.

"If all you write is that they've been good workers, whoever thinks to hire them will wonder, then, why you've let them go, but at least you've not turned them off with nothing for all the years they've served well here."

"And it will let them say they left by their own choice if they want to lie further and . . ." Domina Elisabeth broke off, made a frustrated gesture with both hands, and gave up, saying with all her weariness returned on her, "It just goes on and on. It never stops. One trouble after another. I am so tired of it all. So tired."

She was; but she was also being rescued by her brother

and would soon have her longed-for rest. Frevisse wondered whether, if it had been someone other than his sister who made the plea, Abbot Gilberd would have agreed to her resignation and all else she wanted.

But she was still prioress for now, still bound by duty, and Frevisse asked, "What of Elianor Lawsell? Where is she? Gone back to the guesthall for the night?"

"On the abbot's word, she's been given a bed in the infirmary." Domina Elisabeth shut her eyes. "One more trouble."

Frevisse looked at her tired face and how slackly her hands lay on the arms of the chair. There was no doubting how near to the end of her strength Domina Elisabeth was, and Frevisse brought herself to say, "I shall regret your going from us. You've served St. Frideswide's well."

The faintest of smiles curved Domina Elisabeth's mouth. "I've sometimes thought you did not approve of me, dame," she murmured.

Sometimes Frevisse had not, but she answered honestly, "That doesn't mean you've not done well. Only that I was wrong."

Her eyes still closed, Domina Elisabeth gave a single small laugh. In the silence then the fire whispered among its coals and there was the tat of rain at the window glass beyond the shutters. Frevisse was waiting to be dismissed or for Compline's summons, whichever would let her leave here, but into the quiet Domina Elisabeth said softly, "There is strong likelihood that you'll be elected prioress in my place. You know that, don't you?"

Frevisse strangled back her instant, urgent need to refuse even the thought, able only after a long moment of struggle to say evenly, "No. Nor do I wish it."

Domina Elisabeth held silent, letting the knowledge lie there between them that once a nun's vow of obedience was given, "wish" had nothing to do with "duty" except insofar as a nun should wish to do whatever duty was given her. Instead, finally and far too quietly, Domina Elisabeth asked, "On which of your sisters, then, would you rather lay the burden?"

The stroke of the bell calling to Compline saved Frevisse from answer.

Chapter 28

It took two days and a little more for everything to be sorted out.

Sister Cecely, to no one's surprise, made trouble over Edward. She cried out that he was hers and she would consent to nothing, nothing, *nothing* about him.

Frevisse, sent by Abbot Gilberd to deal with her, had told her coldly, "You may agree to this, or what is done with him will be done *without* your consent. And I will move Abbot Gilberd to change his mind and leave you here, to us, through the time of your punishment."

Those threats were blunt enough that even Cecely could not simple-wit herself away from understanding them, and being deep in hatred of St. Frideswide's and short on thought of what might be worse than here, she had signed the agreement that released Edward's wardship to the Row-cliffes.

Frevisse had asked her then if she felt guilt for what she had brought on Alson and Alson's brother, almost certain of the answer but wanting to hear it; and Cecely had given a harsh, short, angry laugh and said, "It's their fault they were found out. They didn't do as I said, did they? She didn't take what I told her she should, and he didn't give Symond enough."

"You truly wanted to kill Symond Hewet?

"Of course I did! Him and his lies."

"His lies?"

"Guy never betrayed our secret. He never would have done that to me. Symond is a liar. When Alson told me her brother had heard Symond saying that—"

Cecely had broken off, fury twisting her face, her hands clenching and unclenching in her lap, and Frevisse had left her, sad at the foolishness of it all, at the arrant, persevering stupidity of a life lived entirely by lies. Lies that Cecely had chosen to tell herself and was still choosing to tell, rather than have anything to do with the truth.

Later, at the end of that first day of trying to sort matters to sense, Frevisse had said something of her thoughts to Dame Claire during the hour before Compline when they were walking together around the cloister walk, and Dame Claire had shaken her head sadly and said, "So with all her lying about everything, she's been lying to herself as well as us."

But Frevisse had found herself hesitating rather than agreeing, then finally saying slowly, "I don't know that she did."

"You just said," Dame Claire said patiently, "that everything she's said has been a lie, from beginning to end."

Not her love for Guy, Frevisse thought. That had likely been true enough, as far as it went. Although that was probably not very far, there being too little of Sister Cecely for anything to go far and certainly for nothing ever to go very deep. But still slowly, Frevisse said, "I mean I don't think it's always deliberate lying with her. She brings herself to believe that what she wants to believe is true. Having brought herself to believe it's true, she believes it completely and so isn't lying when she says a thing. She believes it. The lying came earlier, when she lied herself into that belief."

And she and Dame Claire had looked across the cloister to the shut door of Cecely's cell, with Frevisse more aware than she had ever been of the pity of it all.

And Cecely in her darkness, companioned only by her anger.

By more than anger.

By rage.

Burning, helpless rage.

At everyone who had worked to ruin her.

At all of them for being alive when Guy was not.

At Guy for being dead.

At God for letting every one of her careful plans be broken.

Thought-blurring rage at all the unfairness of her life, but with nothing left that she could do except sit ripping, one by one, the pages from the breviary until it lay in a ruined pile on the floor around her feet.

With nothing left to do then but to sit and wait until they came for her.

Hating all of them for all the wrongs they'd done her.

Mistress Lawsell left, not graciously, on the morning of the second day. Abbot Gilberd had had her in long talk, and Elianor remained behind, soon to put on the plain black gown and white veil of a novice.

Master Breredon looked likely to be able to travel in a day or so.

The Rowcliffes would be staying longer because of Symond, only very slowly recovering.

At some time Frevisse did not know, Alson and Tom Pye were set free, taken to the priory's outer gateway, and told not to be seen here ever again.

So, with one thing and another, it was the late forenoon of the third day before Abbot Gilberd finally left. Cecely was given chance to say farewell to her son in the guesthall yard, with the abbot and all his retinue looking on. Warned by Abbot Gilberd to make it brief and keep a curb on her tongue, she said little, took Edward in a smothering embrace, stroked his hair once, then turned away and did not look back at him as she went to her horse.

Edward stood for a small, forlorn moment looking at her back, then turned and ran across the guesthall yard and up the steps and into the guesthall where the Rowcliffes were keeping quietly from sight.

A few minutes later Abbot Gilberd and all his men and Dame Elisabeth and Cecely rode in a clatter of hoofs out of the gateway and were gone, leaving St. Frideswide's in quiet at last.

And in that quiet Frevisse stood alone at the window in the prioress' chamber, looking out on the empty yard. Simply stood. In the room that was now hers.

The only vote against her in the election yesterday had been her own.

The ceremony that made her prioress had been this morning.

And here she was. Where she had never wanted to be.

Domina Frevisse, prioress of St. Frideswide's.

Author's Note

One problem in writing books set in medieval England is that people "know" what the Middle Ages were like, when all too often what they know are the Victorian clichés that were too often based more on nineteenth century narrow-minded arrogance than on facts. So readers find elements and attitudes they think are "modern" in these stories but are not. Take, for example, the idea of disease being contagious—a modern notion the primitives of medieval England could not have had? To the contrary, the words "contagion" and "contagious" date from at least the 1300s, according to the *Oxford English Dictionary*, and are probably older. Also "infect" and "infection." There was even speculation that disease was caused by some manner of animals so small they could not be seen, but their existence was deduced from the observed evidence. A theory of germs before they were ever seen under a microscope.

Likewise, the words "detect" and "investigate" were in use in medieval England, putting paid to the idea sometimes expressed that to have a detective at all in medieval times is inaccurate because nobody understood about detecting then. Admittedly, the word "detective" is centuries later, but there are books extent from at least the 1200s detailing how to go about investigating a crime.

They were not fools in the Middle Ages. They were as varied a people as we are now—some wiser, some more foolish; some more capable, some less; some skilled one way, some skilled another—all living a complex and multi-layered life, not sitting about in squalid ignorance waiting in dull-minded violence for the Renaissance to enlighten the world (which it did not; it merely threw a different light).

In more cheersome vein, there are young Edward's "boules," which could not be "marbles," although they so obviously are. Games with small balls made out of various materials go back into antiquity as well as forward to our own time, but only after machinery was developed in the 1600s that could readily shape stone into small balls did these small balls become known as "marbles."

The lack of politics in this story may have been noted. There was a major confrontation earlier in this year between the Duke of York and the King's party, but it did not come to battle, and so little more than rumor and slight report were likely to have reached northern Oxfordshire and then would be quickly lost under the more immediate interests of people's lives. An advantage, perhaps, to not having twenty-four-hours-a-day streaming news: Without it, people have chance to go more deeply into their own lives, rather than distracting themselves by skimming along the surface of myriad other people's.

Of course that very narrowness is what would drive someone like Sister Cecely out of a nunnery, while at the same time being what someone like Dame Frevisse values. Two different desires of how to live a life, and Sister Cecely's tragedy coming because she was forced into the wrong one for her and she could not bear it.